Moral Fibre:
A Bomber Pilot's Story

Helena P. Schrader

Cross Seas Press
91 Pleasant Street
Blue Hill, Maine 04614
www.crossseaspress.com

ISBN: 978-1735-3139-2-4 (paperback)
        978-1735-3139-9-3 (eBook)

Library of Congress Control Number: 2022906454

Foreword and Acknowledgements

Although this book is fictional, it is largely based on first-hand accounts both written and verbal from aircrew that served with RAF Bomber Command during the Second World War. For the coherence of the story, the dates and sequence of some of the more famous raids have been altered; for details of those changes see the Historical Note. The decision to include these more spectacular operations was based on the wider availability of source material about these sorties, enhancing the accuracy of my descriptions, and the desire to draw attention to some the more significant contributions of the strategic bombing offensive to victory in Europe.

This novel continues the story of Pilot Officer Christopher "Kit" Moran, the principal character in my novella *Lack of Moral Fibre*. In the earlier novella, flight engineer Moran had just been posted off his squadron for refusal to fly on a raid to Berlin. He had been sent to a so-called DYDN Centre, where a psychiatrist had to determine whether he required psychiatric treatment or disciplinary action for "Lack of Moral Fibre" (LMF) — i.e. cowardice. (Because of the importance to this novel of the RAF concept and procedures associated with LMF, I have added a note on the subject at the end of the novel.) The earlier novella largely looks backwards at the factors that led to Moran's refusal to fly in late November 1943. This book takes his story forward, following what happens to Moran after he agrees to return to operations. To set the stage, the Prologue of this novel overlaps with the final chapter of *Lack of Moral Fibre*. Chapter One is the actual beginning of this novel *Moral Fibre*.

For readers unfamiliar with the RAF in WWII, the following information will make the novel more comprehensible. First, the RAF has its own, unique system of ranks. (A list of RAF ranks and their USAAF equivalent is provided in the appendices.) Because the RAF initially expected all commissioned officers in the new air force (formed in 1918) would be qualified pilots, the rank designations suggested flying duties, e.g. Pilot Officer, Flying Officer, Wing Commander and the like. However, it rapidly proved impractical to insist on all officers being qualified pilots. Many officers with duties in such areas as intelligence, engineering, medical and financial support etc. did not need to be able to fly. Thus, the commissioned ranks of Pilot Officer etc. did not automatically imply an ability to fly. Instead, a man's qualification as a pilot was indicated by a pair of silver cloth wings worn above the left breast pocket of the uniform.

Second, all members of aircrew held the rank of Sergeant or above, regardless of whether they had qualified as pilots or as navigators, flight engineers, bomb aimers, wireless operators, or air gunners. The other members of a crew wore a "brevet" or badge similar to the pilot's wings which identified them as air crew. These cloth brevets, worn in the same place as pilots' wings, consisted of a single wing attached to a circle which contained a letter designating the specific trade, e.g. "N" for "Navigator," "AG" for "Air Gunner" etc.. Like pilot's wings, brevets were worn by all qualified in these trades regardless of rank, i.e. by Sergeants, Warrant Officers, Pilot Officers and so on.

Third, RAF commissions in WWII were not connected to specific jobs. The RAF (like the Luftwaffe) had non-commissioned pilots as well as commissioned pilots. The same was true of every other aircrew trade, i.e. navigators, flight engineers, bomb aimers, wireless operators, and air gunners. Any of these positions could be filled by men with — or without —a commission, i.e. they might hold the rank of Pilot Officer, Flying Officer and so on. The separation of job from rank led to the anomaly (at least in American eyes) of bombers sometimes being flown and commanded in the air by a Sergeant (pilot) although other members of the crew outranked him and enjoyed greater status and privileges on the ground.

I wish to take this opportunity to thank David Imrie my editor for encouraging me to undertake some major revisions to the original draft, expanding on the story and making it much stronger as a result. I also wish to thank my test readers for their diverse input. All have contributed in their own way to the authenticity and strength of this book.

The cover uses historical photos now in the public domain. The upper image on the front cover is taken from the Imperial War Museum documentary film "Night Bombers." The selected slide shows a Lancaster crew preparing for take-off on an operational flight over Germany. I am indebted to Anna Dahlberg for her wonderful cover which features this and the other historical photos of RAF Bomber Command aircraft and crew.

Helena P. Schrader
Blue Hill, Maine 2022

There's one debt you'll forever owe

(Lie in the Dark and Listen)

A Poem by Noel Coward

Lie in the dark and listen
It's clear tonight so they're flying high
Hundreds of them, thousands perhaps
Riding the icy, moonlit sky
Men, machinery, bombs and maps
Altimeters and guns and charts
Coffee, sandwiches, fleece-lined boots
Bones and muscles and minds and hearts
English saplings with English roots
Deep in the earth they've left below
Lie in the dark and let them go
Lie in the dark and listen.

...

Lie in the dark and listen
City magnates and steel contractors
Factory workers and politicians
Soft hysterical little actors
Ballet dancers, reserved musicians
Safe in your warm civilian beds
Count your profits and count your sheep
Life is passing over your heads
Just turn over and try to sleep
Lie in the dark and let them go
There's one debt you'll forever owe
Lie in the dark and listen.

Table of Contents

Prologue: A Second Chance
1943

Part I: Preparing
1944

Part II: Performing
1945

Epilogue:
Those Who He Loves Less
October 1945

Prologue
A Second Chance

RAF Psychiatric Diagnostic Center, Torquay, 15 December 1943

Wing Commander Dr Grace opened the therapy session pleasantly as he usually did. "Pilot Officer Moran, you've been with us almost three weeks now, isn't that right?"

"Yes, sir."

Grace nodded, drew a deep breath and then parted his elegant hands in a gesture of vague helplessness. "We have a bit of a problem. You see, I can't find the slightest evidence of mental illness. In fact, I would venture to say that you are one of the sanest young men I've talked to in a long time."

"Well, sir, you are working at a mental institution, so you may not be seeing a representative sample of the population," Moran pointed out.

Dr Grace laughed shortly but sobered rapidly. "The point, I'm afraid, is that in the absence of a clear mental disorder, you cannot be admitted to a psychiatric hospital."

"That's just as well," Moran nodding his understanding. "I'd probably go mad there."

Dr Grace leaned back in his chair with an amused smile playing tentatively upon his features. "I have to admit I'm somewhat surprised — but glad — to see you can face the future with this degree of levity."

"I think it's called 'gallows humour', sir."

"Hm." Dr Grace thought a moment and then admitted, "Moran, I can't make a recommendation about your case unless you are more candid with me about why you refused to fly on November 23. I know you don't want to talk about it, but unfortunately I must insist on you telling me what happened."

Moran drew a deep breath and sat up straighter. He'd come to respect and trust Dr Grace and decided that, despite his earlier reticence, it wasn't that hard to explain after all. "There's not that much to it." He ignored Dr

Grace's suddenly raised eyebrows. "On an operational sortie to Berlin on November 22, the bomb aimer was injured by flak and three other crew members, including the pilot, were severely wounded in a night fighter attack. We made an emergency landing at Hawkinge, pancaking at roughly 2:30 am on the morning of November 23. While still on the tarmac, I was informed that the skipper — my best friend — Flight Lieutenant Selkirk was dead. Apparently, he had died immediately after landing. By flying the Lancaster back to England and making a perfect landing he had saved the lives of the rest of us on board.

"The three of us who were not injured were told to take trains back to our operational station at RAF Elsham Wolds in Lincolnshire. We spent the rest of the night and most of the next morning in railway stations, sleeping as best we could on platform benches in our flying gear, or standing up in overcrowded trains. Apparently, no one in this country thinks bombing Berlin is important enough to give up their seats to tired aircrew returning from an op there!"

Dr Grace grimaced and shook his head in sympathy.

Moran continued bleakly, "We reached Elsham Wolds roughly twelve hours after we'd landed. I had only been in bed about two hours, when I was told I was slated to fly as engineer with a sprog crew that same evening. I was not amused, but I didn't balk until they opened the curtains at the briefing and it was yet another run to Berlin."

Dr Grace did not have to urge him to explain himself. Moran suddenly wanted someone to understand. "It was as if bloody Butcher Harris was punishing us for not hitting the target in a tight pattern the night before — as if we were to blame for the 100 mph winds, for Met getting the forecast wrong, for being scattered and ravaged by the Luftwaffe's wild boars! We're not people to Harris — just tools to prove that bombing alone can force Germany into surrender.

"He could have given us a night off to recover. Or he could have sent us against a different target — something closer and less hotly defended like Bielefeld or Muenster or Brest. Sending us back to Berlin the very next night was too bloody much to ask!"

Dr Grace didn't answer for several minutes, during which time Kit started to become uncomfortable. All the rumours about what happened to men like him who "lacked moral fibre" crowded his brain — court martial, demotion to aircraftman, assignment to humiliating duties such as cleaning latrines or working in the morgue, or a dishonorable discharge and industrial conscription to the coal mines or a munitions factory. Whatever they did to him, the blot on his record would be forever.

Finally, Dr Grace drew a deep breath. "It is probably immaterial that I agree with you. I make no pretence of understanding the strategy behind our bombing campaign. As for asking you to fly the very next night, my understanding is that many squadron and station commanders feel that airmen who have undergone a traumatic experience need to be sent out again as soon as possible in order to prevent the trauma from taking root. It's the same principle by which a rider who is thrown from a horse is told to get back on immediately. It's well known that if they don't, the fear of riding can become overpowering. Likewise, many pilots who have crashed need to overcome a fear of flying again. That fear increases the longer a man stays on the ground. In short, there would appear to be some justification for the actions of your CO. Would you agree with that?"

Moran nodded reluctantly. He wasn't entirely sure this made sense. If you went out again immediately and had another terrible sortie, didn't that just reinforce the trauma? Increase the fear?

Dr Grace was speaking again. "Now, let me ask you this — a purely hypothetical question, you understand. Could you imagine any circumstances under which you would be willing to fly operations again?"

"Of course. With a skipper I know and trust, I'd be happy to fly tomorrow."

Dr Grace nodded but remarked with a mildly reproving smile. "That may just be a touch over-zealous, Pilot Officer Moran."

"You did say the question was hypothetical," Moran reminded him with the hint of a smile.

Dr Grace smiled back in acknowledgement, but then turned serious again. He leaned forward, his elbows on the desk and his hands clasped. "RAF Psychiatrists such as myself have been looking at the evidence, and we have come to the conclusion that the tours of duty are too long and the breaks between tours too short. The men who volunteer for aircrew are, with very few exceptions, men of superior dedication and character. Nevertheless, as a colleague of mine put it, courage is like money in the bank. If you use it up more rapidly than you can replenish it, you will eventually have nothing left."

That sounded to Moran as if the wing commander was implying there was nothing fundamentally wrong with him. Indeed, he seemed to suggest that Moran had nothing whatever to be ashamed of. The psychiatrist appeared to be saying that what had happened was perfectly normal and almost inevitable. "I'm not sure I understand what you're saying, sir," Moran admitted.

"Nothing very complicated, Pilot Officer Moran. I'm simply positing that on the afternoon of November 23, 1943 your personal reserves of courage had been wiped out by a severe blow — the loss of your close friend and skipper on an operational sortie the previous night. You needed time to recover your confidence, your equilibrium, and indeed your physical health. You also needed time to grieve. You were a wreck when you arrived here — in case you didn't notice."

"Are you saying, sir, that you don't think I'm lacking in moral fibre?"

"That is a ridiculous term with no medical basis whatsoever," the psychiatrist retorted with an irritated gesture. "The entire notion of LMF was nothing but an administrative solution to an unexpected problem: the refusal of some volunteers to continue volunteering. Such men had, temporarily at least, lost the confidence of their commanding officers and needed to be removed from active duty, yet they could hardly be charged with desertion or insubordination. Volunteering is, after all, voluntary."

"That doesn't entirely answer my question, sir. I understand that for you the term LMF isn't scientific or medical or however-you-want-to-word it, but it does describe aircrew who have failed to do their job, doesn't it?"

"Failed? Do you feel you have failed, and if so, in what way?"

Bombarded by emotions and confused by his own thoughts, Moran couldn't answer.

Dr Grace gently resumed talking. "Isn't it true that the only way in which you have failed is in not living up to your own expectations? Is it not your high standards — as a member of an elite military force — that trap you into thinking that you have failed?" Grace paused and then continued, "Objectively, you have already done a great deal more to win this war than ninety-nine percent of the British population. Many would say you have indeed 'done your bit.'"

"What 'many' say isn't really the issue, is it?" Moran shot back. "The question is what does the RAF say? What do you say? It seems to me that my future is very much in your hands, Wing Commander." Moran realized he was tired of being in limbo. Tired of waiting for the axe to fall. He wanted to know what they were going to do to him.

Dr Grace shook his head. "Not really. You future is more in your own hands than mine."

Moran frowned. He didn't see how he had any control of the sitation whatsoever. After a moment he asked, "How so, sir?"

"As I noted earlier, you are clearly not mentally ill, so transfer to a psychiatric hospital is not an option. On the other hand, almost anything else is possible. You are a trained fitter. If you choose, I can recommend that you again be re-mustered as a fitter. You would lose your commission

and aircrew status, but you would also never have to fly operations again."
Dr Grace paused, watching for a response. Moran shook his head only
once but decisively. He'd been a fitter for two years and he was good at it,
but he'd volunteered for aircrew because he had been dissatisfied with his
situation. He couldn't just turn the clock back and pretend he hadn't flown
thirty-six ops, been commissioned, and decorated — and then funked.

"At the other extreme," Grace continued, "you could agree to return
to operations and resume your second tour as flight engineer where you
left off, simply with a new crew on a new squadron."

Moran thought about that, but shook his head, slowly this time.
What Grace was suggesting was that he be reassigned to the pool of
flight engineers. What that meant was that he'd be an "odd bod"
dropped into the first crew that needed a replacement flight engineer. As
such, he'd be an alien outsider in close-knit team — and he'd be flying
with a skipper he didn't know and trust. After flying thirty-six operations
with Selkirk as his skipper, he just couldn't picture himself flying with a
complete stranger as pilot. "Is there anything in between those two
options?" Moran asked cautiously.

"Yes, you could request to remuster as another kind of aircrew. You
would retain your rank but would undergo training as, say, a navigator
or bomb aimer. Once qualified in your new trade, you would be posted to
an operational training unit where you would crew up before joining an
operational squadron. I would like to draw your attention to two aspects
of this option. Firstly, none of your new comrades would ever need to
know that you had been posted away from your old squadron for LMF —
unless you chose to tell them. Secondly, during training, you'd have time
to rebuild your reserves of self-confidence, and come to terms with your
losses."

The suggestion immediately attracted Moran. It appeared to be an
honourable option that enabled him to salvage something of his self-
respect. It would even justify Georgina's Redding's faith in him. Georgina
had been Selkirk's fiance, and despite her intense grief, she had vehemently
rejected Moran's assertion that he should have died in Selkirk's place. She
had been adamant about his life not being "worthless." If he learned a new
trade and returned to ops, it would vindicate her faith in him. "Do you
have any particular recommendation in mind?" he asked cautiously.

"Yes. I'd suggest flying training."

That took Moran completely by surprise. "Pilot training? Is that
possible?"

"Why not? Isn't that what you wanted when you first joined the RAF?

Before that recruiting sergeant talked you into mustering for ground crew instead?"

"Yes, but that was a long time ago. What makes you think they'd accept me in flight training now?" Moran's tone reflected his scepticism.

"Well, let's start with the fact that you've already flown a Lancaster, haven't you?"

"What makes you say that, sir?" Alarm sounded in Moran's voice.

"It's only hearsay, I suppose, but I've been told that many Lancaster pilots turn the controls over to their flight engineer now and again. That way, they say, another crew member can spell them on long flights or when they want to go back to the Elsan. It also increases the probability that someone can land the aircraft safely should the pilot be unable to do so. Didn't Flight Lieutenant Selkirk let you fly now and again?"

Moran smiled sheepishly as he admitted, "Well, yes. He even made me land back at base once. It was a bit of a prang and we got an awful ticking off for it."

"Hm." Grace commented. After a pregnant pause, the doctor came out with. "Contrary to your own account, Moran, the medics at Hawkinge are convinced that you landed the Lancaster on your last flight. They claim Selkirk was long dead." He paused, waiting for a response, but Kit said nothing. He knew the scientifically-trained psychiatrist would never believe what had happened. Nobody did — except Georgina, and she was a vicar's daughter.

Grace took a deep breath and continued. "In my humble opinion, Moran, you'd make a first-rate skipper. You demonstrated the necessary qualities on the flight you earned the DFM and again on Selkirk's last sortie. Furthermore, flight training is the lengthiest and so it would give you the greatest amount of recovery time. Another consideration is that most pilots receive elementary and advanced training overseas via the Empire Training Scheme. South Africa is one of the regions handling a large number of aspiring pilots."

Moran caught his breath and looked over sharply. His father was in the Colonial Service, and Moran had been born and raised in Africa. Indeed, his Zulu grandmother and her Scottish husband were buried near the latter's mission in the Transvaal. Furthermore, his parents were currently serving in Nigeria, and he hadn't seen them in six years. If he were posted to a flying school in South Africa, he knew they'd find some way to visit him. He risked looking at Dr Grace with something bordering on hope. "I'd like the chance to spend a little time in Africa."

"I thought you might. And flying?"

Moran smiled self-consciously. "You're right. Deep down, I have always wanted to fly."

"Then I may recommend that you be accepted for Flying Training immediately?"

Moran had made up his mind. He nodded vigorously. "Yes, sir."

Dr Grace broke into a broad smile, the first Moran had seen the psychiatrist wear since they had become acquainted. He brought his hands together almost triumphantly as he declared, "Excellent. I am delighted with your attitude, Moran."

"When will I know if I've been accepted?" Moran asked cautiously.

"If I recommend it, acceptance is a formality." Dr Grace assured him, before going on to explain, "Your familiarity with engines and operations makes you a safer bet than green youths of unproven character, so you'll be able to jump the quene for training and should get a slot almost right away."

But Moran wasn't listening anymore. He had been prepared for degradation and humiliation. The one thing he hadn't expected was a second chance.

Part I

Preparing

1944

Chapter 1
Out of Africa

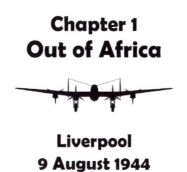

Liverpool
9 August 1944

Panic didn't set in until the train pulled out of the station. After fighting what seemed like half the merchant navy on the platform, Kit had, thanks to his RAF railway warrant, secured a seat in a First-Class compartment. Squeezed between a RN first lieutenant and a self-important civilian, he suddenly felt trapped. Why on earth was he travelling half-way across the country to spend a week in a village he'd never seen with people he didn't know?

Christopher "Kit" Moran had just spent six months in South Africa under the Empire Training Scheme. The former flight engineer now wore the distinctive silver wings on his RAF tunic that proclaimed him a pilot, while his sleeve bore the single wide stripe of a Flying Officer. He had seven days of "disembarkation leave" before he reported for operational training. His family, however, lived in Nigeria, and since he had no relatives in England, he had accepted Georgina Reddings' invitation to spend the week with her parents in Yorkshire.

Georgina had been engaged to Kit's former skipper, Donald Selkirk, who had been killed in action in November of the previous year. Georgina's intense grief at his death and open display of emotion had embarrassed her fellow students at the teacher training college, shocked family friends, and convinced her doctor that she needed psychiatric help. Kit, on the other hand, hadn't minded listening to her talk incessantly about Don. He felt it the least he could do for his dead friend. In the last four weeks before he left for South Africa, Georgina and Kit had shared their memories of Don. They had seen a lot of each other in this time but had not become romantically involved.

To Kit's surprise Georgina had written to him while he was in South Africa — fifty-eight times. At first, her letters had been all about Don and her feelings for him, but she politely ended her letters by asking Kit about himself. He answered cautiously, saying nothing about his feelings, only what he was doing, the people he met, the places he went. Gradually, she enquired further, apparently finding vicarious joy in his sense of accomplishment as he mastered flying or his pleasure at seeing his parents again when they came all the way from Nigeria for a short visit. Gradually, her letters became more about the present than the past, about the two of them rather than Don.

Cautiously yet with studied casualness, Kit had risked mentioning that he would have a week's leave on arrival and didn't know what to do with it. He'd hoped Georgina would suggest meeting up and spending time together. Instead, she suggested he spend the week with her parents. Kit wasn't quite sure what he should make of that.

As the train got up steam, Kit studied his fellow passengers in the six-seater compartment. The RN lieutenant was sleeping with his cap pulled low to shield his face. The civilian was making corrections to some paperwork and handing it page by page to his personal secretary, who sat opposite him. The other two passengers, middle-aged women in WVS and VAD uniforms respectively, were lost in knitting and reading. The wheels clacked, the carriage rattled, the dusty curtains swayed to the rhythm of the rails.

Kit undid the left breast button of his tunic to remove Georgina's last letter. Holding it up in the dim blue overhead light, he read it for the hundredth time. "*Why don't you spend your leave with my parents in Foster Clough?*" She asked in her lovely, elegant script, evoking her melodic voice in his mind. "*It's a beautiful part of the country that you really ought to get to know, and there's excellent shooting too. No big game such as you have on your safaris, of course,*" he could hear her tinkling laugh in those written words, "*but lots of pheasant, partridge, grouse and hare. It's wonderful country for riding, too, and my two hunters could use the exercise. But if it rains (as it does a lot), you'll love the books in my father's library.*" All very nice and inviting, but not a word about wanting her parents to meet him. It was, he decided, pointedly impersonal, despite being tailored to his known interests of hunting, riding and reading.

To make things worse, the letter continued, "*I'll try to join you if you're there over a weekend, but my apprentice teaching starts this autumn, and the college has a rigorous summer program of preparation and orientation. Given how difficult travel is these days, I doubt I'll be able to get home for more than a day.*" That was all understandable, but it didn't exactly sound like a young woman willing to move heaven and earth in order to spend time with the young man she was keen on, either.

Kit's eyes lingered over the sentences one more time, and then with an inward sigh he folded the letter and slipped it back into his pocket. No matter how he read it, it did not sound like a love letter.

So, why was he doing this to himself? Wasn't he facing enough challenges returning to England and to operations? In roughly five months he was going to have to get into a bomber and fly it through God-knew-what-awful weather, flak and enemy fighters with six other men depending on him to get them there and back. He believed he could do it. He was determined that he *would* do it. But why complicate his life with unrequited love?

Because, of course, he hoped that Georgina would come to love him — if only they could see a little more of one another.

Foster Clough, West Riding, Yorkshire
9 August 1944

The Reverend Edwin Reddings looked nervously out of the front window of his library for the umpteenth time this afternoon. He could not concentrate on the sermon he was writing. He had selected the theme "Among the Dark Satanic Mills," a phrase which, as a man from West Yorkshire, had always conjured up vivid images to which he knew his parishioners could relate. Yet he wanted them to think beyond their own back yard to the Continent, where, under Nazi rule, all of Europe had become dark and satanic. Not only had whole cities burned, but the very moral fibre of society had been crushed by the Nazi jackboot and undermined by the craven and cynical self-interest of collaborators. Even after a military victory, Edwin believed that moral recovery would be extremely difficult. Which was precisely why it was vital to start thinking about building something positive — yes, a new Jerusalem — amidst the ruins. It was a topic Reddings felt passionate about. The words should have flown from his pen, but his mind was strangely blank.

Frustrated, he pushed his writing materials aside and reached for Dietrich Bonhoeffer's The Cost of Discipleship, hoping for inspiration. The closer the end of the war came, the more Reddings found himself drawn to the German theologian. Bonhoeffer had warned against racism based on his experiences in America long before the Nazis came to power. He condemned National Socialism at a time when many British still found it admirable. Just last year, Bonhoeffer demonstrated the depth of his commitment to Christ by risking his own life and freedom to assist Jews — and been arrested by the Gestapo. Reddings was convinced that men like Bonhoeffer, good Germans, were vital to the re-construction of Europe and to the establishment of an ethical post-war international order.

Yet, he had hardly opened Bonhoeffer's book before he set it aside again. He simply could not concentrate. He put a bookmark in his place and cleaned the lenses of his wire-framed glasses with his handkerchief before standing and going to look out of the front window.

It had started to drizzle. He looked at his watch and with a sigh noted that it was nearly 6 pm. Georgina had rung through to say that Flying Officer Christopher Moran was on the 5 pm train and would take a taxi to the vicarage. He might arrive at any minute. Then again, trains rarely ran on schedule these days. With another sigh, Edwin returned to stand looking at his unfinished sermon.

The door opened and his wife Amanda swept in with a vase of fresh cut roses from their garden. Moisture from the misting rain clung to the petals. "Edwin!" she exclaimed, sensing his unsettled state. "What's the matter?"

"I'm having misgivings about this whole thing. I don't think we should have agreed to host Flying Officer Moran. There's not a cinema or a dance hall for twenty miles. He'll be completely isolated and bored to tears. It was a silly idea to invite him here in the first place."

"Very likely, but if he's unhappy he is free to leave. We can't change our minds now that he's on his way. Furthermore, Georgina just rang to say she'll skip some sessions on Friday so she can catch an earlier train and be here for dinner."

"I don't like the sound of that either! She's barely holding on by her toenails as it is! She came within a hair's breadth of failing last term. She can't afford to miss anything."

"Edwin, that's not fair. Georgina is conscientious and dedicated to getting her qualifications. She's not going to do anything that might seriously endanger her status. She said all she would miss was some administrative thing; apparently, they're still sorting out the school assignments and lodgings and suchlike. She only did so poorly last term because of her distress over Don."

"Yes, exactly, and what do you think this visit is all about?" Edwin countered, gesturing vaguely. "She's going to spend the whole weekend here with Don's best friend and what are they going to talk about? Don. It is only going to reopen all the old wounds that were just starting to heal. It will most probably trigger a new wave of anguish. We should not have allowed ourselves to be sucked into abetting this orgy of grief."

"Don't jump to wild conclusions about what might or might not happen, Edwin. In any case, it's too late. That's a car in the drive now."

Edwin looked towards the window and saw a battered taxi draw up. With a sigh of resignation, he put his glasses back on his nose, and went to greet their guest. By the time he reached the front porch, the RAF officer had already climbed out and the taxi driver had opened the boot to remove his luggage. Edwin wasn't sure what he'd been expecting, but not this slender, sharp-faced young man with dark hair. Unlike the Royal Navy uniform, the RAF uniform was not flattering to everyone who wore it, but Moran was lean enough and tall enough to look good in it. His face was too narrow to be conventionally handsome, though it was by no means unpleasant. His smile was tentative — not the easy, self-confident grin one associated with the adulated "fly boys." His eyes also showed a wariness which matched Reddings' own. Well, that suggested intelligence and awareness, Edwin told himself; at least he had the sense to be unsure of himself!

Edwin stepped down from the front porch to offer first his hand and then help with the luggage, taking one of the bags. Amanda was waiting in the hall, and Edwin introduced his wife. She held out her hand with a smile. "How do you do, Flying Officer Moran. I hope the trip wasn't too dreadful?"

"Better than expected. The first-class travel warrant is a genuine godsend." He offered a fleeting smile before adding more seriously, "It's extremely kind of you to take a complete stranger into your house, Mrs Reddings. I would never have thought to impose if Georgina hadn't—"

Amanda waved him silent. "That's just the way Georgina is! She's always inviting friends to come and stay with us. We're quite used to it, and we have plenty of room. I'm more worried that you'll be bored to death in this isolated village. But for now, you must be tired. Come along. I'll show you up to your room, while my husband gets the fire going in the library. It's turned decidedly chilly with the rain. I'm sure you'd like a drink before dinner, too."

As Amanda took the guest upstairs, Edwin dutifully followed his wife's instructions to stoke up the fire in the library. When he finished, he found himself staring at the photo taken shortly after Georgina and Don became engaged. It was a formal, posed, studio photo with them sitting side-by-side. Georgina's hand had been laid carefully on Don's sleeve, beside his Flight Lieutenant's rings, to show off both the engagement ring and Don's rank. Don looked steadily at the camera, proud and pleased but serious despite his smile; Georgina, in contrast, had turned to look up at him, her face expressing boundless adoration. Edwin shook his head sadly and felt a shiver of unease as he sensed the return of his visitor.

Moran's polished shoes were silent on the thick carpet, and he moved with the caution of a big cat, Edwin thought as he pulled on a smile. "So, what would you like to drink?"

"What are you having, sir?"

The young man was clearly on his best behaviour, Edwin registered, trying to be as agreeable as possible. "Would whisky and soda suit you? Or if you're feeling chilly in this gloomy English weather after six months in the African sun, I could put together a rum toddy."

"A toddy sounds very tempting, sir."

"Excellent. I'll just go and tell Amanda to put the kettle on before I mix the other ingredients."

When Edwin returned, he found Moran standing before one of the bookcases his head tilted to the side the better to read the titles. The young man immediately stepped back embarrassed as Edwin entered.

"You're welcome to read anything you like," Edwin tried to put him at ease, although he felt compelled by his honest nature to admit, "There's not much else to do here, I'm afraid."

"It would be wonderful to read something other than technical manuals for an RAF exam," Moran countered with a smile so fleeting it was gone almost before Edwin noticed it. "A novel would be divine."

"Oh, we have a large selection of those over here." As he spoke, Edwin crossed to the other side of the window and indicated a ceiling to floor bookcase. "Most are quite old, I'm afraid, largely cast-offs from the local library." Leaving Moran to peruse the novels, Edwin crossed to his drinks cabinet to mix rum, Grand Marnier, and lime juice.

Just like the sermon he hadn't been able write, Edwin found himself struggling to find something to talk about with his visitor — mostly because he had so many questions that he dare not ask. Evidently plagued by the same problem, Moran shuffled his feet a bit and cleared his throat before cautiously asking, "Would you be able to bring me up to date on the latest war news, sir? It was difficult to follow the developments while at sea."

Edwin welcomed the neutral topic. "We must listen to the BBC at nine, but it seems that two days ago the Americans achieved some sort of breakthrough, only for reports of a German counter-offensive to be announced yesterday. The situation appears very fluid, not to say precarious. Reading between the lines, I'd say casualties have been severe. And as if that weren't bad enough, I read just the other day that these 'flying bombs' have killed over five thousand people already. The paper said they are making twenty thousand homes uninhabitable every single day. That's worse than at the height of the Blitz back in '40-'41! Absolutely devastating!"

"I had no idea," Kit admitted, clearly shocked. "Isn't there anything we can do to stop them?"

"According to the official news, half *are* being shot down by our fighters, but even then they still explode. As for striking the launching sites, I gather Bomber Command has targeted them on several occasions, but with only limited success. All in all, as you must know better than I, the RAF has never been more overstretched than now, what with providing tactical support for our ground forces, defending England from these flying bombs and still pursuing strategic objectives in Germany." Edwin looked over at his guest, almost turning his statement into a question

"They were certainly in a hurry to train pilots and get us back to England," Moran admitted. "The course was condensed to the absolute minimum, making it extremely intense."

"Do you go on operations at the end of your week's leave?" Edwin tried to sound casual but failed utterly.

"No. There's — I don't know if you want the details — quite a bit of operational training I have to complete first. Altogether, it could be another five months before I'm back on operations."

"But that's what you want?" The question just popped out, and no sooner did it hang in the air than Edwin regretted it. Asking it implied doubt about the moral character of a young officer who was practically a stranger. What right did he have to question this man's patriotism or dedication to duty?

"Yes. That's what I want." Moran replied slowly and deliberately, but Edwin noted that he had gone stiff. His expression had become wary and defensive.

"It's just..." Edwin didn't want Moran to think he was judgemental or disapproving. "You see, Georgina told us, ah, that you had refused to fly after the last flight with Don."

Moran seemed almost to have stopped breathing, so Edwin hastened to explain himself. "I don't think less of you for that. On the contrary, I wish more people would show such depth of feeling in these times." He was not just saying this to put his guest at ease. It was like the need he saw to rebuild society ethically as well as physically; he perceived a new, widespread emotional numbness, and it disturbed him deeply. People, he thought, were becoming increasingly superficial. He tried to put his thoughts into words. "Sometimes it seems to me that we've all become callous; indifferent to death, loss and destruction."

Moran slowly let out his breath and said calmly but pointedly. "Thank you for your understanding, sir. Georgina was a tremendous help. I'm grateful to her for not cutting me off or making any recriminations when I was officially posted 'Lacking in Moral Fibre.'" He spat out the last four words resentfully.

"Georgina has a great heart," Edwin replied and paused. He supposed he ought to leave it at that, but he couldn't. It was something that had been bothering him ever since Georgina had asked them to open their house to Moran. If he didn't find out what had happened, it would be a barrier between them that he had to dance around the whole time. So, taking a deep breath he continued: "I'd heard that aircrew posted LMF were subjected to harsh disciplinary measures. I was surprised to learn you were instead in flying training and would return to operations."

"I was given the choice. I could have been reassigned to ground duties, but I chose aircrew." Moran's tone was definitive, almost belligerent, and then he added with emphasis, "I wanted a second chance."

To their mutual relief, Amanda burst in with the kettle, exclaiming, "Edwin! You haven't forgotten about the beasts, have you? They're making quite a racket out there."

"Good heavens! I *had* forgotten about them!" To Moran, Edwin explained with an embarrassed smile, "It's the horses. Believe it or not, we have three of them out the back, and it's past time for them to be fed."

"You go and feed them," Amanda told her husband. "I'll put the kettle back for now, and you can make the hot toddies when you're finished."

"You'll have to forgive me, Flying Officer Moran," Edwin explained apologetically.

"May I help?" Moran offered.

"Well, yes, if you don't mind?" Edwin liked that attitude. Then noting that his guest was in his best blues, he suggested, "Might want to change your good shoes for Wellingtons first, though. You should be able to wear our son Gerald's things. Come with me."

Amanda put the potatoes in the oven and checked her watch for the timing. She'd add the apples in another fifteen minutes, and the main course would be ready twenty minutes after that. They should sit down for the appetisers right after the apples went in, which left her just enough time for a sherry. What on earth was keeping the gentlemen?

She peered out of her kitchen window toward the stables. The rain had let up, leaving the cobbles wet and glistening. She was about to turn away when her husband and their guest emerged from the stables laughing. And laughing heartily! That was rare under any circumstances, but it was almost unheard of for Edwin to be at ease with a stranger so quickly. She couldn't remember him ever laughing like this with Don.

As she put the kettle back on the burner, Amanda reflected that although Edwin had liked Don very much — even calling him the "best son-in-law imaginable" — he had never been totally at ease with him. Somehow Don always seemed too diffident and Edwin too fatherly. Amanda, on the other hand, had been a little in love with Don, totally enchanted by his shy charm. He'd been a perfect gentleman, and his treatment of Georgina had been impeccable. He seemed to read her every wish from her eyes and had done all he could to make her happy in every way. He had been protective of her interests, too. Indeed, he had left a considerable amount of money to Edwin in his will with instructions that it was to be used for Georgina's education. In his testament he had asked that she not be informed about the source of the money. "Now that I am dead, I don't want her feeling indebted to me in any way. I want her to go on living."

Amanda felt a wave of grief for the young man who had almost been her son-in-law and was jarred by the sound of laughter and animated voices in the hall. Her husband and Flying Officer Moran had come through the back door and were removing their wellingtons and oilskins. She opened the kitchen door and poked her head into the hallway to remark, slightly admonishingly, "You two seem to be in good spirits. *Do* share the joke."

"That rascal Hannibal got out of his stall again and raided the feed room—"

"Hadn't you put the padlock on?" Amanda asked in exasperation. Hannibal was her horse, and his ability to open his stall door was nothing new.

"Of course not!" Edwin snapped irritably, knowing he was in the wrong. "We'd only just given them their grain and had gone to the loft to get the hay. It didn't take more than five minutes!" he added defensively.

Before Amanda could reply, Moran elegantly intervened with the remark: "I was just telling your husband, Mrs Reddings, that in Kenya we had a horse that could escape his stall no matter what we did. I admit, we didn't try padlocks, but we used to tie the latch down with twine and later wire. It didn't matter what knots we used, Ras would not only free himself, but open the stall doors of all his friends too. We'd come home and find them trampling my mother's flowers and helping themselves to whatever they fancied in the kitchen garden. My mother was in despair and wanted to sell him, but I admit I loved him for his cleverness."

As Amanda felt the same way about Hannibal, Flying Officer Moran instantly went up in her estimation. "That's quite the way I see it too," she declared smiling. "Did you say this horse was in Kenya?"

"Yes, that's where I spent most of my childhood."

"For some reason I thought your family was in Nigeria," Amanda admitted.

"That's where my parents live now. My father is in the Colonial Service. My parents met in Pretoria, where I was born, then moved to Nairobi, and from there to Moyale on the Ethiopian border, then Kisumu on Lake Victoria. It wasn't until 1935, that my father was sent to Calabar in Nigeria as District Officer."

"So, you've spent your whole life in Africa?"

"Until I came to England on an apprenticeship at sixteen, two years before the war."

"But where did you go to school?" Amanda asked, surprised. She'd thought the children of most colonial officials came to England for their secondary education at the least. Both Georgina and she had had friends at school whose parents were in India.

"I attended St. Andrew's College in Cape Town. It's an old C of E school with a good reputation."

The school meant nothing to Amanda but based on Moran's accent and manners it couldn't have been terrible. "And your parents? Didn't they miss England and want to come home for visits?" Amanda had lived her entire life in Yorkshire. She couldn't imagine being away for long.

"My father was born in India, where his father rose to Brigadier in the army. He went to Winchester and Oxford, but he hasn't been back since. My mother was born in South Africa, the daughter of an Anglican missionary to the Zulus, and she's never been to England."

"How extraordinary!" Edwin exclaimed. "A long time ago I read a wonderful book written by a missionary to the Zulus. It was recommended to me when I was in seminary. I must still have it in my library, so we'll have to go and look for it. It was not at all the kind of tripe one expects from missionaries; you know, just anecdotes about primitive natives and wild animals. Nor was it self-congratulatory. It was much more about the wisdom he *gained,* rather than the wisdom he sought to impart. It had a very catchy title too —"

The kettle started screaming in the kitchen. "There's the water for your hot toddies," Amanda told the gentlemen. She went to turn off the heat and returned to the hall to hand the kettle over to her husband. "Go and make the toddies, and I'll join you shortly."

While the men continued to the library, Amanda checked the potatoes in the oven, and put the apples in. Satisfied, she removed her apron, and went to join the gentlemen in the library. As she walked in, she found Edwin and Moran with their heads together over a book on Edwin's desk.

"You must see this, Amanda!" Edwin greeted her enthusiastically. "I found the book I was talking about. It's called *Finding Gold in the Dark* and it's by Flying Officer Moran's grandfather! Isn't that an amazing coincidence?"

Amanda cast her husband a raised eyebrow. She had learned that in her husband's vocabulary "coincidence" was a code word for "Divine Providence." Edwin believed that every coincidence demonstrated the active presence of the Hand of God in the daily lives of mortals. Although Amanda did not share his conviction on this matter, her curiosity was piqued and she went to see what they had.

Open on Edwin's desk was a slender book with fragile, yellowing paper. A faint, over-exposed photograph of a man and woman, both wearing stiff, white, "tropical" kit gazed out at them. The couple stood upright and unsmiling before a little wooden church. About a dozen black children sat cross-legged on the ground in front of them. Instantly intrigued, Amanda exclaimed, "Are those your grandparents?"

Moran seemed to flinch slightly before answering, "My grandfather, yes, but the woman is his first wife, his Scottish wife. My grandmother was South African. He married her several years after he was made a widower." He flipped to copyright page. "Yes. This was published in 1892. His first wife must have passed away shortly after this was released. He did not remarry until 1896 and my mother, his only child, wasn't born until 1899."

Moran returned to the page with the photograph, and Amanda looked more closely at the picture. She thought the couple looked as though they were in their mid-thirties, so Moran's grandfather would have been in his early forties when he married a second time. Her eyes sought the caption and she read out loud: "Rev Dr Christopher Hinkley and his wife Victoria, nee Ramsey."

"He was a Doctor of Theology?" Edwin asked, impressed.

"No, education. I was named after him," Moran admitted, adding with one of his timid smiles, "Although when I was growing up, I believed I'd been named after Christopher Robin of Winnie the Pooh fame."

They laughed together.

"I've always liked the name Christopher," Amanda admitted. "It sounds so distinguished."

"Yes," Moran nodded, before adding with a sidelong, impish smile,

"Maybe that's why everyone calls me Kit." They all burst into laughter again.

Turning serious, Kit asked Edwin if he could borrow the book, "I never knew my grandfather had written one. I'd like to read what he has to say."

"But of course!" Edwin looked as though he was about to launch into a new flood of observations, so Amanda interrupted with the gentle prod, "Edwin, it's almost time for our meatless dinner." In an aside to Moran she explained, "I'm afraid, we didn't have enough warning of your visit to save up meat coupons for a roast or the like, so you'll have to make do with a vegetarian meal."

"That's quite all right, Mrs Reddings," Moran assured her.

Turning back to her husband, Amanda continued, "Would you be so kind as to pour me a quick sherry before we sit down, Edwin? We can continue the discussion at the table, after all."

"Certainly, darling." her husband sprang to comply, while Amanda sat down and gestured for Moran to take a seat opposite her. "Now, as I was saying when you arrived, there isn't much to do here in Foster Clough; I hope you are prepared for that?"

"Georgina suggested I might enjoy riding her horses. I grew up with horses, but I admit I've had no opportunity since the start of the war."

"You won't want to tackle Teros then. He's the big bay with a white blaze. He's a bundle of mischief and nerves, and Georgina is practically the only one I've met who can get him to behave. You'll be happier with either my gelding Hannibal or Georgina's old mare Hester, whom she couldn't bear to part with when she bought Teros. Both are sensible and pleasant horses for a cross-country hack."

"Georgina also mentioned that there was good shooting in these parts. I was rather hoping to get a little in."

"Definitely," Edwin answered as he returned and handed Amanda her sherry. He remained standing behind the sofa. "You can take any of my guns and go off on your own, or if I can I'll come with you. If it rains, there are many more treasures in this library," Edwin gestured to the bookcases around them. "I'd particularly recommend Dietrich Bonhoeffer. He's a German theologian—"

"Edwin! Flying Officer Moran is an RAF officer not a seminary student! Let's all migrate to the dining room and start on the appetisers."

The conversation flowed easily after that and together they listened to the nine o'clock news, after which they discussed the war at some length. Just after 10:30 pm, Moran excused himself to go to bed.

The Reddings' wished him a good night and followed his progress with their ears until they heard the bedroom door click closed. Amanda leaned back in her chair and propped her feet on a footrest, asking Edwin to pour her a glass of port before announcing, "I quite like him. Don't you?"

Edwin smiled faintly as he brought her her drink. "I like him very much, unfortunately."

"Why 'unfortunately'?" Amanda asked, startled.

"Because he's going back to operational flying in a few months."

Amanda started. She hadn't given a thought to that all evening. Despite knowing him for so short a time, she did not like to think he might be killed as Don had been, before he really lived. She protested lamely, "Well, we are winning the war. Germany may well have surrendered by the end of the year."

"We can pray for that, but I doubt Germany is going to collapse that quickly. The Germans may withdraw steadily from occupied territory, but they will dig in and defend their fatherland like the devil. If you want my opinion, as a former infantry officer, this war is going to last at least another year. What that means, my dear, is that Flying Officer Moran is almost certain to face operations again. He told me flat out that he'd volunteered for aircrew because he wanted a second chance."

"That's understandable."

"Yes. But a second chance for what?"

"Presumably to prove he's not a coward."

"Surely a man with a Distinguished Flying Medal doesn't need to prove that?"

"But he refused to fly—"

"I know. I know. But — well — never mind. Maybe I'm just imagining things." Edwin waved at the air as if to chase away an unwanted thought.

"Edwin." Amanda addressed him ominously as she brought her feet off the footrest and planted them firmly on the floor again. She fixed her gaze on her husband and insisted in a deadly serious tone. "Finish what you were going to say."

Her husband removed his glasses and closed his eyes as he pinched the bridge of his nose. "It was just a thought," he muttered.

"No, it wasn't." Amanda countered. They had been married more than twenty years, and she knew exactly what this was. "It was one of your intuitions, wasn't it?"

"I don't know. It was just that when he said he wanted a second chance, I thought —"

31

"Yes?"

"I had this horrible feeling that he believes he should have been killed instead of Don, and that he's giving himself a second chance to die."

Chapter 2
The Vicar's Daughter

Lincoln Diocesan Teachers Training College
11 August 1944

Georgina hastily brushed her shoulder-length brown hair into a ponytail and pulled a hand-knitted cardigan over the dress she'd made for herself out of an old linen tablecloth. She was just looking around for her hat and handbag when her roommate Fiona came through the door. Like Georgina, Fiona was twenty-one and in her final year of teacher's training. She was shorter, with a fuller figure, and bobbed, dark hair. She was dressed in one of this year's "utility dresses" that was neat and tailored but used a minimum of fabric.

The girls had shared a room for three years and knew each other well. At the sight of Fiona's worried face, Georgina feared bad news and burst out, "Please don't say you can't take notes today. The later trains are so impossibly overcrowded."

"It's not that, Georgina. I'm happy to take notes. It's just ..." Fiona drew a deep breath as if to give herself courage and announced: "It's that I don't think you should be doing this."

"Doing what?" Georgina asked confused. "Skipping class?"

Although clearly uncomfortable with what she was about to say, Fiona continued resolutely: "No. I don't think you should be spending the weekend with Kit Moran."

"But he's staying with my parents. I can't very well leave him there alone the whole time." Georgina countered, as she pulled a small, fitted, felt hat over her head. She knew it was not particularly flattering combined with her combed-back hair, and it made her look like a schoolgirl of sixteen or so, but she didn't care.

"He's only staying at your parents' because you invited him," Fiona pointed out.

"I invite people home all the time," Georgina answered glibly. "You must remember the Swedish exchange student, and that girl who was preparing for her National Horse Association instructor's exam."

"That's not the same!" Fiona countered, irritated by Georgina's evasiveness. "Nice girls don't invite boys home. Not unless they're serious about them; and for the last eight months you've been telling me that you aren't serious about Kit Moran."

"I'm not! How could I be? I'm not ready to get emotionally involved with anyone. I'm still raw and wounded inside. It's because Kit knows how I feel that I'm willing to see him at all. You know I've been avoiding men ever since Don was killed, but Kit's different; he was Don's best friend. And he knows exactly how devastated I was, if for no other reason than because I've written scores of letters to him that laid out my feelings in gruesome detail."

"Georgina, you're not listening to me! It's precisely because you aren't interested in Kit that inviting him home to your parents is misleading." Fiona stood her ground. "You are being very unfair to him."

Defensively, Georgina snapped back, "That's priceless coming from you! You were the one who ditched him when he needed you most."

"That's not true! You know as well as I do that I only went out with him because you were infatuated with Don but afraid to go out with him alone. So, we did all that double-dating in the beginning, and yes, I did become fond of Kit in a way, but I was never in love with him. Never," Fiona stressed unrepentant. "Ending the relationship was the only honest thing to do. Maybe it hurt him at first, but it was fairer than dragging things out and keeping his hopes for an engagement alive."

"I'm not blaming you for breaking up with him," Georgina countered. "Just for the timing of it. Why did you have to announce your rejection of him while he was officially LMF? It was like trampling on someone who was lying wounded at your feet. You could have stood by him as long as he was under a cloud, then, when he was back on his feet again, gently suggested you weren't suited to one another."

"You don't understand men, Georgina. If I'd stood by him then, he would only have become more dependent on me. That would have made it harder to break up later. We were never going to be happy together. The sooner we faced that fact the better."

"Don't you see that rejecting him while he was LMF was like saying you agreed with the Station CO? It was like calling him as a coward?"

"Nonsense. I respected him more for refusing to fly than for volunteering for a second tour, much less returning to ops again now. I'll never understand why men think they have to prove their virility by killing other men."

"That's not what this is about!" Georgina replied flabbergasted.

"What is it then? Why should Kit return to operations after having the sense to refuse last November? What has changed?"

"Kit feels he owes it to Don."

"Owes what to Don?"

"Completing the tour, contributing to the defeat of Hitler, putting an end to this horrible war."

"You are so naïve, Georgina. If that's what Kit's told you, it's pure malarkey. He's just trying to make you admire him — which shows he is interested in you, and you shouldn't be leading him on."

"I don't think you know Kit better than I do, and I certainly don't think you have the right to tell me how to treat him. So, let's say no more on the subject. Are you going to take notes for me or not?"

"Of course, I'll take notes," Fiona responded with a shrug, but her face showed resentment.

"Thank you," Georgina said in a clipped, frosty tone. "I'll be going then." She grabbed her small, wicker suitcase and pushed past her roommate and through the door.

Foster Clough, Yorkshire

Fiona's words rankled. Throughout the irksome, six-hour journey, Georgina kept mulling over what Fiona had said. Was she being unfair to Kit? Might he misunderstand her intentions? She certainly didn't want to lead him on, much less hurt him. She liked Kit. She always had, even when he was nothing more than Don's best friend. Yet he had secured a special place in her heart when, in the darkest days of her grief, he had helped her more than anyone. Furthermore, their correspondence over the last eight months had distracted and cheered her, making her value Kit more and more.

Yet she could not risk getting involved with him — or any man — again so soon. Certainly not a man in the RAF. She just wouldn't be able to take it if something happened. She couldn't survive another bout of the grief she'd felt after Don died. For her own protection, she had to avoid falling in love again — at least until the war was over.

Instead, she wanted to concentrate on her future as a teacher. It was a wonderful vocation, one she'd wanted to follow ever since she was in school herself. Don had encouraged her to continue teacher training too, saying he wanted her to have professional qualifications. Since his death, however, the notion of becoming a teacher took on a new significance. It became an alternative to the future she had planned with Don, the future that died with him. Without him, teaching moved from the periphery to the centre of her stage. Georgina admitted that a man might one day come along who would lay claim to her heart, but she didn't want to contemplate that yet.

By the time the train pulled into Mytholmroyd station, Georgina had regained her equilibrium. Fiona had been talking out of turn. She was sure that Kit understood how she felt. Everything would be fine.

With a loud hiss from the engine and the clunking of carriages banging against one another, the train came to a halt. The metallic voice of the announcer squawked unintelligibly from the station loud-speakers. Around her the other passengers stood and jostled one another to get their luggage down from the overhead rack. Georgina pulled her wicker suitcase down and followed the others onto the crowded platform.

The day was partly sunny and a brisk wind chased broken cloud across the sky. When the sun shone it was almost hot, but the moment a cloud blotted it out the air took on an ominous chill. Georgina was glad she was wearing her cardigan and felt hat as she hurried through the underpass, hoping the bus that passed through Foster Clough hadn't left yet. As she emerged from the tunnel, she was astonished to see her parents and Kit waiting for her across the street. Her father had an ancient car — and as a rural vicar was entitled to petrol rations — but it broke down so often that she'd never expected to be picked up.

She felt a little stab in her heart at the sight of an RAF officer. Kit was roughly the same height as Don and had the same slim figure and dark hair. From a distance they resembled one another. As she got closer, she was more disoriented to notice that Kit looked absolutely marvellous. She hadn't realised that he was handsome before. He'd always been overshadowed by Don, even after Don was dead. Yet, there was no denying the charm of the smile he flashed her.

Spontaneously she greeted him with "Kit! You look wonderful!" Without thinking, she went on tiptoe to deliver a kiss on each cheek. Then hearing Fiona's accusatory voice in her head, she pulled back, warning herself she mustn't give him the wrong impression.

"Just the African sun," Kit joked, but he seemed to bask in her greeting. "You aren't looking so bad yourself."

Georgina was suddenly self-consciously aware that she had not put on makeup or lipstick. Indeed, she'd gone to no effort to look *good* at all, just neat and respectable. Embarrassed, she countered, "Well, I could hardly look much worse than the last time we saw one another." Turning to her alertly observing parents, she delivered hugs to each in turn, ending by asking her father, "However did you get the car repaired?"

Edwin bowed his head and indicated Kit. "Flying Officer Moran deserves full credit for getting the wretched thing working again."

"It would be a sad commentary on RAF training if a flight engineer couldn't mend a simple car engine." Kit started to explain, "The only thing wrong with it—"

"Please spare us the details!" Amanda intervened. Georgina was briefly taken aback by her mother's apparent rudeness, but then realised that she and Kit had apparently already developed a rapport. Meanwhile, her mother continued, "Gerald used to insist on telling us exactly what was wrong with it and how to repair it; I assure you, it just goes in one ear and out the other. Come along, let's get back to the house. I still have lots to do for dinner, and the horses need to be brought in."

From Georgina's perspective, everything went very well after that. Kit and her parents evidently got along swimmingly, and the conversation flowed easily. They spoke of the horses, Georgina's studies, the latest parish gossip, but nothing too personal. Nor, with her parents always present, was any hint of romantic inclinations possible. While Georgina helped her mother with dinner, the gentlemen looked after the horses as if they had been doing this together all their lives. It was almost like having a second brother, Georgina decided. After all, she reasoned, if her brother Gerald had been home when Don was killed — instead of somewhere in the Far East aboard *HMS Illustrious* — surely, he would have comforted her as Kit had done.

They had just settled into the sitting room after dinner, however, when Kit briefly disappeared only to return with three wrapped packages. Georgina tensed.

"I thought this might be the right moment to give you my thank you gifts," Kit announced with an embarrassed smile that revealed how awkward he felt.

"Oh, you didn't need to bring us anything!" Amanda exclaimed at once.

"If my mother found out I accepted hospitality without bringing a house gift, she would roast the soles of my feet! The problem was, without

37

knowing either of you," he addressed Georgina's parents, "I hardly knew what to bring. I'm afraid your gift, Mrs Reddings, is a trifle generic as a result." With these words he delivered a box of South African chocolates.

Since chocolate rationing was strict and her mother loved chocolate, so Georgina knew her mother was not just being polite when she expressed her delight and thanks.

Next Kit handed a box to her father, explaining: "When we lived in Moyale on the Ethiopian border, my father became interested in Ethiopian crosses, and he started collecting them. We happened to have two of these, the Lalibela Cross. Knowing that you were a clergyman, I thought you might like it."

"Oh, good gracious!" Edwin lifted the elaborate, small bronze cross out of the box and examined it in fascination. "This is lovely! Absolutely lovely. Though I'm not sure I would have recognised it as a cross," he admitted, a little puzzled, prompting Kit to go over to explain it to him.

By the time Kit turned to hand Georgina a small box, her stomach was tied in knots. Fiona had been right! Her invitation had misled him. Yet, surely, he wouldn't give her a ring *in front of her parents*? Would he?

He seemed to read her thoughts and reassured her, "There's nothing to be afraid of, Georgina. Just something I thought you'd like." The words were casual, but his smile was a little twisted and his eyes were sad. Her obvious apprehension at his gift had already sent the necessary message.

Still terrified of what might be inside, Georgina undid the ribbon and opened the box. Inside she found a pair of thumbnail-sized ebony earrings. They were delicately carved elephants with tiny ivory tusks. How ambiguous, she thought. Not a ring or a pin, the acceptance of which signalled a girl's commitment to a young man, but hardly consumables either. They were something she was expected to wear and remember him by. Was there anything wrong with that? She couldn't make up her mind. Conscious of her parents' as well as Kit's gazes, she removed one from the box to look more closely. "They're sweet! So delicate!" she exclaimed. Did her voice sound as forced and silly to the others as it did to her?

"You wrote in one of your letters that you hoped I hadn't shot any elephants on my safari because you thought they were wonderful animals."

"That's true!" She agreed more naturally. "I've always loved the elephants at the zoo because they look so intelligent." As she spoke, she held an earring up to her earlobe so her parents could see. They both made appreciative noises, but she could sense that they were watching her and Kit like hawks. They clearly liked Kit, but she suspected they shared her reservations about her giving her heart again too soon.

"They really are lovely," Georgina insisted, putting the earring back in the box. "Thank you so very much."

"Speaking of safaris and Africa, I was wondering if you had any photos of your family that you could show us?" her father said, smoothly ending the awkward scene.

"Oh, yes," Her mother joined in, an enthusiastic accomplice. "I would so love to see pictures of your home in Africa. I must admit, I can't imagine it at all."

"I'm sorry," Kit replied, turning to face her parents with a sorrow that had nothing to do with his lack of pictures. It hurt Georgina just to see how much she'd disappointed him, but it was better now than later, she told herself. Meanwhile, Kit was saying, "I only have a few photos of my family, and none of our house. Mostly I've snapshots from the wings parade and our safari together."

"Oh, I'd love to see those!" Her mother insisted. "Wouldn't you, Georgina?"

"Very much!"

"Me too!" Edwin joined in. "Why don't you get them, and I'll pour us all a drink." With that the issue of the gifts was closed and buried under a cheerful session sharing photos until the evening news.

The next day Kit and Georgina packed a picnic lunch and went for a long ride. It was a glorious, warm, sunny day. Georgina rode her high-strung gelding Teros, and Kit rode Amanda's sixteen-year-old hunter Hannibal. Both were eager, and the breeze, sunshine and splendid views put them in a cheerful mood; the awkwardness of the evening before appeared forgotten. Georgina convinced herself that her reaction to his gift had given Kit the message. He understood now that they were and could remain good friends, but no more than that.

With that settled, being with Kit seemed perfectly natural, and Georgina found herself feeling wonderfully alive for the first time in ages. Furthermore, because Kit didn't know this part of the country, Georgina could play tour guide, pointing out and explaining all the landmarks. She had planned the ride so that around midday they reached a particularly pretty spot with long views across the surrounding countryside. Here, Georgina set out the picnic things, while Kit loosened the girths and hobbled the two horses.

Lunch consisted of sandwiches, tea in a thermos and ended with pears from the tree in the churchyard. As they finished the first course, Georgina tossed Kit an pear and settled herself more comfortably. The sun shining from a near cloudless sky made her drowsy. She lay back and closed her eyes to soak in the unusual warmth. After a moment, she opened her eyes and turned her head in Kit's direction to tease, "It's so hot, I almost feel like I'm on safari."

Kit laughed and took a bite from his pear. He was sitting beside her, his elbows on his knees, gazing into the distance. Dressed in her brother's breeches and boots, he looked much more like the young man in the safari pictures she'd seen last night than the RAF officer Georgina had known up to now. The photos had revealed a different Kit, Georgina reflected, someone more youthful and more easy-going, almost jaunty. His father was a taller, older version of Kit, always in immaculate tropical kit with wiry, muscular arms and hands, and skin dark with tan. The affinity between father and son had been obvious in the photos: in the identical way they held their guns, their casual yet comparable poses around the fire, the way they sat shoulder to shoulder on an old log, or worked side-by-side pushing their vehicle out of a muddy gully.

Yet it had been the photos of Kit's mother that most surprised and fascinated Georgina. Mrs Moran was much shorter than her two men, and her tan even deeper than Kit's father's. It had made her broad, white smile stand out, and her pride in Kit shone from every picture. Georgina had been particularly attracted by a picture of Mrs Moran surrounded by an excited crowd of little black children. They clustered around her, their faces alight with curiosity, some pushing and squeezing to get nearer. Mrs Moran was showing them something not obvious in the picture, bending over and utterly at ease with the children.

"I wish I could meet your mother." Georgina announced as Kit chewed silently on his pear. "She looks like just the kind of teacher I'd like to be one day."

Kit looked over astonished, as though he couldn't believe his ears. "What makes you say that?"

"The photos last night." Georgina thought about that and added, "And what you wrote in your letters. I particularly loved that picture of her with the children."

"Oh, that." Kit looked down and brushed an insect off one of his borrowed riding boots. "That's not formal education. She just tries to make people interested in the world around them, to inspire them to *want* to learn." He bit into his pear again.

"But that's exactly what I feel is important!" Georgina replied, sitting up. "Here in England, schooling seems to be so much more about getting ahead, wearing the right 'school tie,' building an 'old boys' network. Most people don't care if they actually *learn* anything at all. Even at university, everyone seems more impressed by sports than scholarship."

"There's some truth in that, I suppose," Kit ventured cautiously, "but England still offers some of the best education in the world."

"Only for those who come from the right class and can afford it, or the few who can win a scholarship. Most children in this country still leave school at fourteen. So much potential is being wasted!" Georgina spoke passionately, adding, "That's why I've volunteered to do my apprenticeship in a council school."

Kit looked over frowning slightly, although he didn't comment. He just asked, "Do you know where you'll be?"

"Not yet, but I hope to remain in Lincoln," Georgina admitted.

"Because of Don?"

Georgina shrugged in embarrassment. "Yes. For the memories, I suppose. So many places in Lincoln have an association with him. I'm afraid that if I move away, I'll start to forget Don."

There was silence, almost like a moment of mourning, and then Kit said, softly but surely, "No, you won't."

"Or maybe I'm just afraid of the unfamiliar." Georgina suggested self-critically, tossing away the core of her pear and clutching her knees as she gazed across the Yorkshire countryside. "I think I should try to be more like your mother."

"In what way?" he asked back warily.

"Well, you said that whenever your father was transferred to a new post, she had to pack everything and move. Every time she had to start her whole life all over again."

"We all did," Kit noted dryly.

"Yes, of course, but I think it must have been particularly hard for your mother. Children are adaptable and your father always had his job, but your mother had to hold everything together. She had to make new friends, hire new staff, find medical care, schools, church — everything. She must have been very flexible, open-minded and inventive."

"She didn't have much choice," Kit retorted sharply.

Georgina couldn't fathom why Kit sounded so curt, almost hostile. She supposed he just didn't understand how difficult it could be for a woman to move around. "She could have closed her mind and heart and simply created an 'English' bubble around her," Georgina pointed out. "I've known so many women like that: totally inflexible and close-minded. They think there is only one 'right' way to do everything. Indeed, most *teachers* are like that. All they do is repeat what they learnt decades ago and make their pupils repeat it back to them parrot-fashion. It's that attitude that makes so many children uninterested in learning. A teacher should set a good example by being curious and eager to learn. Surely you agree with that?"

"I don't know. I haven't ever thought about it." Kit hesitated and then he turned his head to look straight at Georgina and something in his gaze and his tone warned her that he was about to say something that was both serious and unwelcome. "My mother could never be like those Englishwomen you described, creating a 'bubble' of Englishness around her, because she's not English — despite her passport. You see, my mother isn't white. She's what the South Africans call 'coloured.' Her father was English, but her mother was a South African native, a *black*."

Georgina was startled. Nothing about Kit's looks suggested he had African blood. He was fair skinned, tall and bony with silky, straight, dark hair. Yet, now that she thought about it, his mother *had* looked more exotic — darker, and curly-haired. She frowned slightly as she grasped the significance of what he'd said. Yet, this revelation only made Kit's mother more interesting, even inspiring to her. What a young woman she must have been to capture the heart of a colonial officer! How courageous to face the bigotry of the other colonial officials' wives.

"She must be amazing!" Georgina declared. "One day you must tell me how your parents met and fell in love — and how *her* parents did too. You can't seriously think that knowing she isn't white would make *me* think less of her? Surely her heritage doesn't matter to you?" Georgina asked him.

"Yes. It does matter." Kit countered caustically. "It affects her entire life — our lives. My parents flew all the way down from Nigeria to attend the wings' parade, only to have the staff at the station make her feel unwelcome. There I was, wearing my new wings, recently promoted to Flying Officer, and they treated my mother as though she was one of the cleaning staff! They literally asked my father and me what we wanted to drink while refusing to acknowledge that she was standing between us."

"That's outrageous!" Georgina gasped.

"I'm slow to anger," Kit told her, "But I came so close to causing a scene that my father felt he had to hold me back physically. Then the Chief Flying Instructor, who was British, swept over and introduced himself to my mother and starting blathering nonsense about how exceptional I was. He insisted that my mother join him at the head table, seated directly beside him where he personally ensured she was properly served. My British colleagues also made a point of coming over and being friendly, but it was too late. My mother was so distressed that she refused to stay for the rest of the day's programme."

"I can understand," Georgina murmured. She would have felt the same way.

"We left immediately after the meal, and I vowed to myself that I'd never return to South Africa. Not for any reason. Certainly not after the war."

Georgina could sense how angry and bitter he felt about the incident. Her natural instinct was to reach out to him in a gesture of solidarity and support, but Fiona's voice in her head made her hand drop. After a moment to broke the silence to ask gently, "What *do* you want to do after the war?"

"I'd like to get an engineering degree. I want to build things, create rather than destroy."

"What a lovely thought."

"But I try not to think about it," Kit added, tossing his pear core away with a strong overhand fling that revealed lingering anger.

"Why ever not?"

"I can't afford to have too much to look forward to. It might make it harder to fly."

Had he said "fly" or "die"? Georgina felt a chill run down her spine and her insides became taut with disquiet. "What are you talking about, Kit? You make it sound as if you expect to be killed."

"No," he kept his gaze on the horizon rather than looking at Georgina, "but my goal is to be as good a skipper as Don was. Don must have told you that in an emergency it's the pilot's job to fly the aircraft straight and level long enough for the rest of the crew to bail out. If the fuel tanks catch fire, the crew has less than 30 seconds before the aircraft either explodes or the wings fall off and the fuselage plunges into an uncontrollable dive. I don't want to fail at that critical moment."

"You won't," she told him firmly, "but you have to *want* to live, too. If you don't, you might give up on your own life too soon. Surely you see that?"

"Let's not talk about it. The horses are restless." He stood and walked toward Hannibal without looking back. Georgina was left to collect and pack away the picnic things.

Kit drove Georgina to the station early the next morning. It was Sunday and her father had to read the service, while her mother always helped out with Sunday school and tea and buns afterwards. Collecting her things, saying goodbye, giving Kit directions and so on distracted them at first, but once they were on the main road, silence descended.

Georgina was acutely conscious of being sorry that their time together was already over. Despite the few awkward moments, the predominant feeling had been one of happy compatibility. Whether alone with Kit or the both of them together with her parents, she had been comfortable. They had talked about countless topics, yet barely scratched the surface of all the things still to discuss and learn about one another. Nor could she remember laughing so much in a very long time. Yesterday evening, for example, the four of them had played roll-a-word together, and Kit had matched her father for obscure words. Fortunately, neither of the men could spell very well, giving grounds for much hilarity, and the victory to the ladies.

When had she last had so much carefree fun? She supposed it might have been that weekend at the Selkirk estate after she and Don had announced their engagement. They had played charades, ladies against gentlemen, and Georgina remembered being blissfully happy. Yet, when she thought about it, Don had been too shy to be good at the game; Kit had been the one who had them all laughing. Yes, it felt good being with Kit, and she was sad to part.

Which was exactly the problem! She was *already* far too fond of him. It was ridiculous to pretend he was like a brother to her. She could sense that if she saw more of him, she would lose her heart to him.

They had reached the grim outskirts of Mytholmroyd, and the grimy factories reminded her of her father's words. She shared her thoughts out loud, "My father always claimed that it was towns like this that William Blake had in mind when he talked about the 'dark Satanic Mills.'"

"In which case, they are where the new Jerusalem will be built," Kit retorted, glancing sidelong at her, almost smiling.

"That's exactly what my father claims!" Georgina exclaimed exasperated. Kit was so like her father sometimes that it unsettled her. Stubbornly she declared, "I'm going to tell you something I wouldn't dare tell him: I don't believe it is possible to build a new Jerusalem — certainly not here." She gestured at the dilapidated, smoke-stained terraced houses.

Kit followed her gesture, considered the ugly, working-class dwellings made even more depressing by five years of war which had starved them of any kind of maintenance, and admitted. "For now, I'd be content just for the war to end."

"Yes. Me too." Georgina agreed, thinking that even that seemed like an impossible dream.

They fell silent again. The war seemed endless to Georgina. It had devoured her youth and left her a widow before she had become a bride. Then she had another thought: if the war was over, there would be less risk to falling in love again. If Kit were not flying ops, what would be the harm of letting him into her heart?

Kit turned into the next road and the railway station loomed ahead of them. Their time was almost up. Sudden panic swept over her as she realised that they had only a few moments more and she didn't even know where he was going. "Do you have an address where I can write to you?" Georgina asked.

"No. I'll have to send it to you." He paused and then glanced over with a tentative smile. "But I hope, now that we aren't separated by half the world, we can do better than just write. I'm entitled to leave every six weeks. If you like, we could meet up in London..."

She started shaking her head vigorously before he had even finished speaking. She couldn't deal with that. The war wasn't over yet, and Kit *would* be flying ops. She had to break this off before she completely lost her heart to him. Assuming a cheery voice, she exclaimed as lightly as possible, "Oh, I don't think I'll have time for that. I'll start my apprentice teaching in a couple of weeks. We'll stay in touch by letter instead."

"I see." By the way he said it, she knew he understood. After a moment, he added a little bitterly, "That's fine."

They left it at that.

Chapter 3
Crewing Up

RAF Moreton-in-Marsh (21 OTU)
15 August 1944

Georgina's lack of interest in meeting in London hit Kit hard. He'd thought they'd been getting along exceptionally well and getting closer. Her reaction both baffled and upset him — enough so that he hadn't wanted to remain at her parents' home. Using the uncertainties of wartime travel as an excuse, he'd departed for his Operational Training Unit a day ahead of schedule.

For most of the journey, he reflected on what had just transpired with Georgina. One thing was certain: his affection for her had grown in their short time together. Being with her, watching her with her parents, the horses, and with him brightened his entire life. Her presence lessened his apprehensions, increased his self-confidence, and made him more optimistic about his future. Her spontaneous admiration for his mother touched him deeply. Discovering her stuffed animal collection, which included an entire "African menagerie" with a sleepy hippo, a wise elephant, a grim lion and a sweet mother and baby zebra, endeared her to him. He could see reflected in her the influence of both her idealistic father and her practical mother. He now knew that Georgina was more complex and profound than she'd first seemed. In her old riding and casual clothes, she looked less glamorous than other girls he'd gone out with, yet he found her more appealing. The gentle hues of her hair and skin no longer struck him as wishy-washy; instead, they seemed subtle and nuanced, more genuine than bright blond or dark brown. He found her green eyes particularly alluring. He could no longer understand why he'd initially thought she looked unexciting and pale, nor how he could have been attracted to the more flamboyant Fiona instead.

Georgina was the woman he wanted in his life — now and in the future. Yet each time he had tried to indicate this, Georgina had reacted with alarm. She clearly didn't want their relationship to move beyond "just friends."

Pacing up and down the railway platform while waiting for his train connection at Birmingham, Kit briefly considered writing a letter laying out his feelings and asking her to tell him bluntly if she thought she might ever change her mind about them. He quickly discarded the idea because he feared she might say "no."

Yet despite her discouraging response to his suggestion about London, Kit wasn't ready to give up all hope either — at least not just yet. He decided instead to send Georgina a short note with the address of the OTU and wait to see what sentiments her letters conveyed. He would calibrate his response to her tone, even if that meant curbing his own emotions a little longer. If he didn't rush her, maybe she would come around. Then again, maybe he was just torturing himself?

On the last leg of the journey, he wrote a heartfelt thank-you letter to the Rev and Mrs Reddings. Writing on his lap as the train swayed its way south, he stressed how welcome they had made him feel. Kit liked them both. Although he was careful to make no mention of it, he also thought they would make wonderful in-laws.

By the time he reached RAF Moreton-in-Marsh, he was ready to be reabsorbed into "the mob." It would be a relief to stop agonising about his feelings and immerse himself instead in the routines, habits, jargon and jokes that made up the smothering blanket of service life. Here he could surrender his individual identity almost entirely and blend in seamlessly with the others. If he wanted, he could become just another uniform performing a job.

This wartime station looked like most others — three intersecting runways, giant hangars, a two-storey brick Watch Office, semi-circular corrugated Nissen huts in long rows, and bicycles everywhere. Utilitarian in the extreme, it offered none of the grace or comfort of the South African Air Force station where Kit had recently done his training. There the officer's mess stood amidst sun-soaked gardens and met the standards of a grand hotel with servants to keep everything immaculate. Here, in contrast, everything was cloaked in grey-green camouflage paint. The buildings and vehicles alike were battered and rundown, and the air smelt of aviation fuel, coal smoke, and boiled cabbage. Yet a shared sense of purpose emanated from it all.

The adjutant welcomed him to "Course 73," and directed him to the cluster of Nissen huts that made up the Officers' Quarters. Kit was disappointed if unsurprised to discover that on this wartime station four junior officers shared a room, two rooms to a hut, each flanking a common sitting room with a coal-fired stove in the middle. He chose a bed against the back wall, which adjoined the heated central room because he remembered how bitterly cold these huts could be in winter. It might be warm now, but training would last until mid-November.

He put his kitbag on the bed and unpacked his clothes into the lone cupboard. There was a single shelf over the bed for personal items, but Kit had little to place there. He laid his grandfather's book on the shelf, a parting gift from Edwin Reddings. Beside it he propped up a picture of his parents, in which his mother beamed radiantly while his father stood with his arm protectively around her. Only an alert observer might detect the troubled look in the elder Moran's eyes.

Kit had talked a great deal with his father during their days together, and they'd become closer. His father feared for him and hated to see him return to England and to war, but he was equally disturbed by the undertow of growing tension across Africa. "Don't plan on building a future here, Kit," his father warned. "When the Colonies go up in flames, you don't want to be anywhere on this continent."

His mother's treatment at the wings' parade had already decided Kit against returning, yet he found it hard to picture a life in England. What sort of future could he have? He held only a short-service commission in the RAF and would be demobilised at the end of the war — if he lived that long. He had no university degree, only two years as an apprentice with a civil engineering firm. Worse still, he'd lost his interest in civil engineering. His years as a fitter and flight engineer had sparked an enthusiasm for aircraft engines and aerodynamics, but he didn't want just to service and repair aeroplanes. He wanted to design them or the engines that powered them. To become involved in that kind of work would require an engineering degree. Kit didn't know if he could pass admission to a British university, but that was almost a moot point: for him the bar was set higher, at winning a scholarship. Without one, the cost of studying would be prohibitive.

The Nissen hut started trembling as aircraft engines sprang to life nearby, and Kit realised he was worrying about something that might well never be an issue. First, he had to survive the war, and his chances of doing that were less than fifty-fifty.

The door crashed open and a large, red-haired man with a broad, stub-nosed face and carrying an oversized kitbag squeezed in. "G'day, Mate. Mind if I bunk down here?"

Kit opened his hands to indicate the three spare beds.

The newcomer looked around, chose one, and threw his things down. "Name's Forrester. Guthrie. But I prefer Red." He held out a big, fleshy hand. Kit took it, giving his own name. Forrester's accent, darker blue uniform and distinctive wings declared him to be Royal Australian Air Force, as clearly as the "Australia" on the top of his sleeve.

"Have you been over here long?" Kit asked him, not wanting to assume, boorishly, that the Australian was new to England if he wasn't.

"About ten days. Bloody cold, and they call it summer."

"To make up for it, we serve the beer warm," Kit quipped back with a smile.

Forrester laughed appreciatively, before replying, "Found that out the day I arrived. Where do you hail from?"

"Calabar."

"Where on earth is that?" Forrester asked pausing in his unpacking to stare at him.

"Nigeria," Kit answered as if there was nothing surprising about it.

Forrester gave him a second look and then shrugged. "Whatever you say, mate. What are we flying here, do you know?"

"Wellingtons. Or Wimpys as they're affectionately called."

"Bugger! I was hoping for Mossies." From this remark, Kit gathered that Forrester had his sights set on the Pathfinders, the elite squadrons that marked the target with flares to make it easier for the following main force to bomb accurately. More and more Pathfinder squadrons were being equipped with the light and versatile twin-engine De Havilland Mosquito.

The Pathfinders were considered an elite and Kit doubted whether he could qualify for Pathfinders, but even if he could have, he wouldn't have wanted that posting anyway. Mossie's carried a crew of just two, and he wanted the camaraderie and teamwork of the Lancaster's crew of seven. "As far as I know, they don't use the Mossies for bomber training," Kit explained to the Australian.

"Is the Wellington a good kite?"

"Yes."

"Have you flown them, then?"

"No, but in them," Kit admitted.

"What do you say we go and see if we can talk ourselves into a cockpit?"

Kit readily agreed. Getting back into flying was the best way to end all this pointless brooding about Georgina and his possibly non-existent future.

Together, Forrester and Kit left their quarters and made their way to the airfield. They counted five Wellingtons spread out around the field with ground crews working on them. A couple of the hard-standings were empty, however, suggesting that several aircraft were in the air, presumably on flight tests. "Been assigned to a Flight yet?" Forrester asked.

"B Flight."

"Me too. Let's find B Flight dispersal."

They asked an aircraftman for directions and he pointed the way. Here, they had the good fortune to run into a flying instructor, Flight Lieutenant Vaux. He was in the office of the tiny hut with his tunic removed doing paperwork. At the arrival of the two trainees, he remarked, "You're here early. Most of the trainees won't arrive until tomorrow."

"We're eager beavers," Forrester explained.

"Meaning you want to go up for a flip?" Vaux interpreted the remark correctly.

"Could we?" Kit chimed in hopefully.

"You've both flown twins, I presume?" he asked looking from one to the other.

"Airspeed Oxfords," they answered in unison.

"In that case, since you're so keen and I'm so nice, yes, I suppose it could be arranged. You chaps would be a sight more comfortable in flying gear, however."

Forrester frowned as if annoyed, but Kit immediately offered. "Give us ten minutes?"

"Aim for five."

When they returned to the dispersal, Vaux was already wearing a flight jacket. He had also organised an aircraft and led them over to MM-E for Easy. As they climbed up into the narrow fuselage, the familiar and unique smell of oil, dirt, and cordite enveloped them. It triggered memories that made Kit inwardly tense, but none of his inner turmoil showed as he moved with apparent ease and evident familiarity towards the cockpit. He might not have flown a Wellington, but he'd trained as a flight engineer in them. Vaux glanced over at him but said nothing. Instead, the instructor commenced providing familiarisation with the aircraft in a cheery tone, pointing out the wireless operator, navigator and bomb aimer seats to them. "Do get acquainted with the positions — just in case you wash out and get re-mustered," he jested meaningfully.

This Wellington was still configured for two pilots. Vaux sank into the left-hand seat, and Forrester didn't wait to be invited. He secured the second pilot's position at once. Moran sank onto his heels behind them, trying to see between the two while Vaux went over the controls and the cockpit drill. Next, he called Flying Control and explained his intentions. Having received permission to start his engines, he signalled to the ground crew, and then turned to Forrester. "Tell me what to do."

Forrester was good. He made only a few minor mistakes. Vaux taxied them out to the runway but paused before turning onto it. He looked over at Forrester and explained, "The Wimpy is fairly easy to fly. Where she'll kill you is on take-off and landing. You need about 15 degrees of flap for take-off and need to retract your wheels at about 105 mph or roughly 400 feet of altitude. You want to ease — ease — your flaps up at 120 mph or some 300 feet higher because she'll sink when the flaps come up. If you're still at only 400 feet, you'll go straight in. The problem is the levers for flaps and undercarriage are identical in feel and located right next to each other here." He pointed out the levers. "Just last week, one of the trainees confused them and now he and his entire crew are six feet under." He paused only long enough for this to sink in and then continued cheerfully, "I'll explain the landing challenges later, but rest assured you won't be taking-off or landing a Wimpy for several weeks to come." He then turned on the runway and made a perfect take-off.

Kit felt an unexpected thrill to be flying over England again. Roads, streams, woods and hedges broke the green and hilly Gloucestershire countryside into mosaic pieces. It was so different from the dry, open spaces of South Africa. There the towns sprawled dusty and transient; here the neat and tidy villages and churches sat rooted to their surroundings by gardens, walls and graveyards. Even the sky was different, littered with broken cloud all the way up to 10,000 feet. Kit might have learned to fly in South Africa, but he'd been a flight engineer in England for more than a year before that. Being back in an English sky over that country's clouded hills and pleasant pastures made South Africa seem very far away — and Don much closer.

Forrester's loud voice shook Kit from his memories. "First time I've seen real sunshine since I got to this ruddy island," he growled as they rose above the last of the clouds.

Kit laughed along with the instructor briefly, but then Vaux took his hands off the control column and announced. "She's all yours, Forrester. Put her into a 20-degree port turn." After that, the instructions came fast and sharp. Routine manoeuvres were followed by increasingly demanding flying. It was almost as bad as a wings exam, Kit thought, as memories of flight training obliterated his good feelings about English skies. The South African instructors had always made him feel as though he were on the brink of calamity. He felt himself tensing up.

Forrester, in contrast, seemed utterly at ease. Kit admired the Australian's casual tone as he responded to the instructor's orders and occasional interventions and corrections. "Port again? Didn't we do that twice already?" The Australian complained.

"I wasn't counting, but I thought you might not be able to master starboard. Everything turns clockwise down where you come from, doesn't it?"

"Except me."

"In that case, make it starboard, if you like."

Forrester appeared to be a confident and aggressive pilot whereas, Kit's skills had been officially assessed as "average", and only grudgingly at that. Being an average pilot might be good enough to earn his wings, Kit reflected, but was it good enough to get him through an operational tour?

Satisfied with Forrester's performance, Vaux ordered the Australian to turn over the controls to Kit. As he climbed out of the right-hand seat, Forrester clapped Kit on the shoulder and remarked, "You were right, mate. Good kite!"

Kit took his place already nervous, and he concentrated hard in an effort not to make mistakes as Vaux called for various manoeuvres. Several minutes passed before Kit noticed that Vaux wasn't teasing and niggling him the way he had Forrester. He wasn't making any snide comments either. Was that good or bad? Kit glanced at the instructor.

Vaux nodded to him and gave him a thumbs up before adding casually, "Now, give me a slow roll, would you?"

Kit looked over at him uncertainly. Twin-engine aircraft did not particularly like rolling, and not once had Don rolled the Lancaster during operational flying.

"Go on!" Vaux urged, "Nothing to it. Just try not to get stuck upside down." Over his shoulder he ordered, "Forrester, strap yourself into the navigator's seat."

Kit really did not want to roll the Wellington, at least not yet. He'd been flying this aircraft for no more than twenty minutes, and barely knew it. By way of subtle protest, he pointed out, "I'm never going to need to roll a bomber on operations,"

"How can you know that?" Forrester interjected from behind him.

Vaux turned and looked straight at Kit before saying in a deliberate tone, "Aerobatics increase a pilot's confidence in himself and his aircraft. Now do it. Anticlockwise."

Kit drew a deep breath and slowly lifted the starboard wing. Overcoming his own discomfort, he kept rolling the aircraft until dust, scraps of paper, rusty screws, and other bits of rubbish rained down on them from the various nooks and crannies of the old aircraft's floor.

"Keep the nose up and keep going," Vaux ordered before throwing over his shoulder at Forrester, "Get that green look off your face, Forrester! Being from down under you ought to be used to hanging upside down!"

The starboard wing fell below the horizontal and kept swinging. For a second, the wings were vertical again, but then the aircraft gracefully continued through the last quarter of the roll until they returned to the upright. Vaux was grinning. "That wasn't so bad, was it?"

Kit shot Vaux a sidelong grin and admitted, "No, sir."

"Good. Then show me some corkscrewing."

"Corkscrewing?" Forrester asked from behind them. "What the hell's that?"

"Now I *am* shocked, Forrester! I have never before met an Aussie without a profound familiarity with corkscrews."

Kit meanwhile was trying to work out what to do. Don had corkscrewed many times to avoid searchlights and night fighters. He knew exactly what it *felt* like, but he had only a vague idea what a pilot did with the controls to produce that unique motion that disrupted the aim of both flak and night fighters. They didn't teach corkscrewing in flight school.

Vaux's attention had returned to Kit, and he ordered: "Commence corkscrewing."

Kit took a deep breath and pushed the nose down, lifted the left wing and turned hard to the right. Then as the Wellington gained speed, he pulled back on the column and lifted the right wing as he turned left. Vaux's assessment was a cool, "Not bad for a first try, but you need to make everything more violent and erratic. Avoid anything predictable."

"How many tours did you do, sir?" Moran asked, as he felt himself start to relax a bit.

"Completed two. Bostons and then Hallibags. I'm mostly here to show you sprogs survival is possible. What was your former position?"

"Flight engineer."

"You'll be fine, Moran." Vaux spoke with the kind of emphasis that told Kit he had seen through to his nervousness. Then switching his tone of voice, Vaux called more jocularly, "Forrester? Asleep back there or are you ready to come here and learn something useful?"

On the ground, Forrester grumbled about Kit not mentioning his earlier tour, and they went together to the mess for dinner and to get better acquainted. They retired at a reasonable hour, but loud singing and shouting yanked them from their sleep. Forrester went out to find out what was going on and returned grinning with the intelligence that a half-dozen Royal Canadian Air Force (RCAF) aircrew had got themselves into a brawl with English aircrew from RAF Honeybourne, another OTU. "Would have done Australia proud," Forrester commented approvingly, and then flopped down and went instantly to sleep.

The next day the rest of the trainees arrived in waves as RAF buses met the trains and brought them to the OTU. Two more pilot officers, a taciturn Welshman and a talkative Londoner, settled into Moran and Forrester's room.

In the late afternoon the Station Commander made welcoming remarks and the following day the orientation lectures started, followed by introductory ground training organised by trade. Meteorology, mostly reading the clouds, dominated the training for Moran and the other pilots, interspersed with lectures on how to deal with various emergencies. They were told what to do if the engines or wings iced up, the hydraulic system broke down, the undercarriage refused to lower, or the tires were shot away. The suggested measures sounded logical, but Moran suspected implementation of most might prove challenging. On the other hand, learning the theory beat having no idea whatsoever of what to do in a crisis.

The ground instruction for navigators and wireless operators focused on their various instruments and navigational aids such as Gee, Oboe and H2S, as well as how to drop "window," a simple but effective method of overwhelming German radar by dumping bundled strips of aluminium glued to paper out of the flare-chute. Bomb aimers, on the other hand, were expected to become familiar not only with their bomb sights, but to learn about reading flares and target indicators. In addition, they received lectures on the various types of bombs and mines used by the RAF and their impact on the target. Aircraft identification constituted the core of air gunner training along with practice dismantling the guns, clearing ammunition blockages and conducting other repairs in the confined space of the turrets.

Moran and Forrester soon realised how lucky they had been to get an introductory flight in the Wellington. The standard course did not allow them to take the controls until they had undergone extensive cockpit drills, including being asked to find each instrument while wearing blacked-out goggles that completely blinded them.

After what seemed an eternity of theory (but was really only about ten days), each trainee was told to sign up for a flight a day by writing his name on the roster beside an aircraft in the space for his respective position. This process ensured that most men had flown with several other trainees from each trade before the actual "crewing up" began at the end of the first fortnight.

Kit had been through the crewing up process before, when he'd been recruited for Don Selkirk's crew. Then, as now, he'd found the exercise absurdly informal and haphazard. The members of the course collected in a large, empty hall and were told, literally, to "sort themselves out." They were expected to organise themselves into crews of five with one pilot, one navigator, one bomb aimer, one radio operator and an air gunner. Two additional members of the crew, the mid-upper gunner and the flight engineer, would not join until they went to a Heavy Conversion Unit (HCU) several months from now. The five men who teamed up here, however, formed the core and largely determined the character of each crew. As a flight engineer, Kit had been accepted into Don's crew at the HCU after it had already become a close-knit and well-functioning team. It felt as if he'd been adopted by them. As a pilot, in contrast, he had the responsibility to create a crew nucleus from scratch by selecting airmen who were both competent in their respective jobs and would work together well. The best crews melded into a well-functioning team. Those that didn't were often the first to "go for a Burton."

Kit remembered the bomb aimer on Don's crew complaining that they had less time to choose a crew than a wife. Yet, as he put it, "choose the wrong wife and you may be miserable; choose the wrong skipper and its curtains." Don had retorted that the wrong navigator, radio operator or air gunners would be just as deadly. "All seven of us have a vital job to do, and all of our lives depend on each of us doing his well."

Kit surveyed the chaos in front of him and wondered how he could possibly identify the right men from this horde of virtual strangers. Forrester, on the other hand, approached the process with a methodical and nearly scientific singlemindedness. For two weeks, he had been bluntly asking men about their assessments and exam scores, marking down their answers in a small, notebook. As soon as the Station Commander told them to get started, Forrester made a beeline for the Canadians. Forrester had told Kit the troublemakers were "feisty" and "aggressive," qualities he wanted in his crew, especially for the air gunners.

Kit didn't agree, but the bigger problem was his reluctance to choose anyone at all. Kit didn't *plan* to die, but he couldn't escape the feeling that his chances of survival were poor. Statistically, more than half the men in this room would be dead before they completed their first tour. Kit's unease, however, extended beyond the statistics.

For one thing, Don had been the best skipper imaginable, yet he'd bought it. Clearly a pilot judged "average" had an even lower chance of making it. The odds meant Kit would need good luck, and a profound sense of having already used up more than his fair share of that unsettled him. He'd made it through thirty-six ops without a scratch. On the night Don was killed, the bomb aimer, navigator and radio operator had also been injured, the navigator and radio operator critically. Yet while shrapnel had torn slices through his flight jacket and burned holes in his boots, Kit remained completely unscathed. Kit didn't think he *deserved* to escape injury and death more than the others. If anyone had *not* deserved to die, it was Don. His mother might credit his survival to a 'guardian angel,' but Kit thought rather he had been dicing with the devil — and the devil didn't like to lose, not in the long run.

Of course, there was no reason to assume he would take his whole crew with him when he got the chop, but the RAF had done away with "second pilots" long ago. That meant that if he bought it his crew stood little chance of returning safely. The best they could hope for was to bail-out.

Standing in that echoing hall filled with eager young men chatting, laughing, gesturing and shaking hands, Kit felt like bad luck. Tapping someone on the shoulder would be like the grim reaper pointing a finger at them. On the other hand, if he approached no-one he would be left with the dregs, the men no one else wanted. The result would be a crew of misfits, further diminishing his — and their — chances of survival.

Then an odd thing happened. Pilot Officer Peal walked over to him. As one of the few commissioned navigators, he and Kit had run into one another regularly at the officers' mess. Tall, blond, slender, and elegant, Peal was a film-maker's image of an RAF officer. Forrester alleged that Peal's father was a famous and successful barrister, while his mother was supposedly the daughter of a fabulously wealthy American "railway baron". Kit mistrusted rumours of that sort, but there was no question that Peal had a ready smile and an easy-going nature combined with the manners of a perfect gentleman.

"Moran?" He smiled as he approached. "Any objections to me as your navigator?"

Objections? Moran already liked the modest and soft-spoken Englishman. Furthermore, he and Peal had shared a couple of pints just a few days ago, during which they had discovered a common interest in buildings, Moran as would-be civil engineer and Peal as a man with a degree in architecture. What mattered most, however, was that Moran had flown with Peal, and he'd been absolutely first-rate. Peal had been precisely atop of every check point dead on time. If anyone was *not* a misfit or 'the dregs' it was Peal. If further proof were needed, Forrester had targeted Peal as the man he wanted for his crew. Moran glanced towards the Australian and, sure enough, Forrester was making his way back across the large chamber in evident haste.

Still reeling from the unexpectedness of the offer, Kit stammered uncertainly, "No, of course I have no objections. I'd be pleased to fly with you, Peal—"

Peal didn't give Kit a chance to express any reservations. He broke into a smile and held out his hand. "Shall we go by first names? I'm Adrian, in case you forgot."

"Right. Kit." They shook hands just as Forrester arrived.

"Don't tell me that you've already signed on with Moran, mate? Without even giving me a chance to chat you up?"

Before Kit could answer, Adrian spoke up with a vaguely apologetic smile, "Oh, I'm so sorry, Forrester, but we did indeed just shake on it. A gentleman's word and all..."

Forrester took it well, congratulated Kit with a "Well done, mate," and excused himself to go in pursuit of another man he wanted.

"You seem very sure about this," Kit observed to Adrian as Forrester's back retreated across the room. He couldn't imagine why Adrian had chosen him. Several other pilots on the course seemed more Adrian's type — the right school tie and all that.

"Although you don't talk about it, everyone knows that you've completed one tour already, and you can't hide that DFM either," Adrian noted, with a nod towards the ribbon below Kit's wings which indicated he'd earned the Distinguished Flying Medal. Although not explicit, Adrian's look said: "that kind of over-modest line-shoot won't wash with me."

Kit was glad to be distracted by the arrival of a young sergeant with an air gunner badge. "Sir!" He addressed Kit with a smart salute, forcing Kit to answer in kind. Then he opened in a pugnacious voice, "Have you already selected a rear gunner, sir?"

"No," Kit admitted.

"In that case, sir, I'd like to fly with you. My gunnery assessment was above average, and you flew with me on the first day."

Kit was amused by his brashness and couldn't resist reminding him, "Didn't you get air sick when I was corkscrewing?"

"That was just because I wasn't expecting it, sir. I can cope — even if I have to skip the pre-flight meal. Went without dinner often enough as boy," he added with an engaging grin.

The boy, because he was still that, was very slight and thin, ideal for the cramped rear turret, but he looked too young to be in RAF uniform. Kit found himself asking, "Just how old are you, Sergeant?"

"You mean to the RAF or how old I am really?"

"Is there a difference?"

"Lied to get in, sir," the boy admitted candidly. "I was only 15, almost 16, but I'm 18 now."

"What's your name, Sergeant?"

"Osgood, sir. Nigel Osgood. I'd really like to fly with you, sir. I've got good night vision."

Osgood's eagerness discomfited Kit. The boy was treating him as though he were some sort of wizard skipper, like Don had been, and he wasn't. He tried to curb the youngster's enthusiasm. "I've got no doubts about your vision, Osgood, but..." But what? "Tell me more about your background." Since Osgood was a sergeant, Kit had had no opportunity to interact with him outside of training as he had with Peal.

"Not much to tell, sir. Wasn't good at school so I left at 14. It bored me a bit," he admitted with a grin.

"Your parents didn't object to that — or you lying about your age to sign up?"

"Why should they? Me mam takes in laundry. By the docks. Liverpool docks, that is." With his accent, that had never been any doubt. "Not good money, and she had me and me two brothers to feed. Me dad wasn't around much."

"A sailor?"

"When he wasn't too sozzled to get a berth." Contempt ladened his tone, but then he seemed to realise that this fact might not recommend him, so he hastened to add, "I don't take after him, sir. Don't need to worry about that. Besides, me mam threw him out five or six years ago."

Kit liked the boy, which was exactly why he was reluctant to take him on, but he couldn't find a legitimate reason to say no. He looked over at Adrian. "We're in this together now, Adrian. What do you think?"

"Sergeant Osgood looks like a fine gunner to me."

Kit turned back and offered his hand. "Welcome aboard, Osgood. Off duty, I'm Kit."

Osgood broke out in a relieved grin. "Thank you, sir — Kit." He grinned wider at that.

"My name's Wright, sir." Another sergeant who had been hovering beside them held out his hand at once. "I'm the best bomb aimer on the course, and I'd like to join your crew, Flying Officer Moran."

Wright's accent was public school, and Kit had been around long enough to know what that meant. The RAF still assumed anyone with a public school background was officer material and automatically gave them an acting commission along with the opportunity to go to flight training if they wanted, which almost everyone did. Nearly all bomb aimers had started out in flight school but washed out at some point. When they did, they also lost the rank of "Acting Pilot Officer" and were reclassified as Sergeants. There was nothing wrong with that as far as Kit was concerned, but calling himself "the best bomb aimer on the course" seemed a bit of a line-shoot. Kit had heard nothing to confirm that self-assessment, but he had noticed that during briefings and collective training, Wright liked to draw attention to himself. Kit viewed his behaviour a sign of immaturity, and his instincts said that they would not get along.

Out loud Kit responded, "I'm flattered, Sergeant, but I don't think we've flown together. I'd like to do that before we make a formal decision about crewing up." Since he'd flown with both Peal and Osgood, Wright could not claim Kit was being unfair.

"I don't mind, sir, but Forrester is only one of the other pilots interested in having me join their crew. I don't expect I'll be available tomorrow."

"Well, then, best of luck," Kit told him with a smile. He didn't like being pressured.

Wright looked stunned. He glanced at Peal as if expecting the navigator to come to his defence, but Peal simply smiled and shrugged apologetically. Wright turned on his heel and made a beeline for Forrester.

Shortly afterwards the session ended, as arbitrarily and haphazardly as it had begun. Noting the time, the Station Commander announced that that would be all for now and informed them they had another couple of days to complete the process of crewing up. Henceforth, however, those that had teamed up should do all flying together.

The *Green Man* was crowded, and RAF blue predominated. Crewing up was still in full swing around the pub, and conversations were particularly lively where newly formed crews clustered together. Kit, Adrian and Nigel had hardly sat down before a Sergeant approached their table and addressed himself to Kit. "Flying Officer Moran, sir? I'm Stuart Babcock. I'd like to be your bomb aimer."

Kit looked up at a pleasant-looking young man with light brown hair and an open, friendly face. It wasn't one he remembered, and Kit didn't think they'd flown together. From his accent, Babcock came from a good background, but he wasn't brash as Wright had been. Kit gestured for him to sit down noting, "No need to have this conversation at a shout, Babcock. Have a seat."

Babcock happily pulled out a chair and settled himself at the table, where he sat straight with his hands folded together, evidently conscious that he was not yet "in." He looked like a schoolboy sitting for his oral exams, Kit thought.

Nigel pushed back from the table and lit a cigarette. He seemed to assume he had no say over whether his skipper took Babcock into the crew or not. Adrian, on the other hand, leaned in, asking Babcock where he'd gone to school.

Babcock's answer meant nothing to Moran, but Adrian nodded knowingly and commented positively, "Decent rugby team, as I recall. Did you play?"

"No, I was a cricket man myself."

"Good show! Cigarette?" Adrian offered Babcock one from his silver holder.

"Don't mind if I do," Babcock answered self-consciously yet smoothly.

As Babcock lit up and inhaled, Adrian asked to Kit's amusement, "What business is your father in?" He'd taken over interviewing duties, but that was fine with Kit because it left him free to observe.

"He's a printer and has a photography studio too."

"Sounds interesting," Adrian replied nodding, and Kit could see that the two men were connecting. Yet Babcock struck Kit as too unformed and immature for what he was about to encounter. Kit would have preferred someone more like Don's bomb aimer, a cheeky, tough youth from the slums who had fought his way up — someone more like Nigel, actually. He glanced over at the gunner. Nigel was smoking nervously and looking at the ceiling. On the other hand, Kit didn't expect to have endless options. He leaned forward to ask, "Did you do any flying training, Babcock?"

"Ah, only 20 hours, sir," Babcock admitted, uncertainty returning to his voice and posture as he faced the pilot.

"Washed out in *ab initio*?" Kit concluded with a smile to show it was no disgrace.

"Yes, sir, but I'm a good bomb aimer — well, not the worst."

Kit laughed at that, preferring his honesty to Wright's bragging. He glanced around the room conscious that the number of "odd bods" still floating between tables looking for a berth were fewer than before. His options were narrowing even as they spoke, and he certainly didn't feel

Babcock would make a bad choice. He turned to Nigel. "What do you think, Nigel? Do you want to trust Babcock with our bombs?"

Nigel was so startled to be asked his opinion he inhaled the wrong way on his cigarette and started coughing. Even so, he nodded vigorously. "Whatever you think best, sir."

"Adrian?"

"Babcock looks like a good choice to me."

"Right then, Babcock, you're with us. What's your first name?"

"Stuart, sir—"

Kit waved the 'sir' aside.

"Stuart. Go by 'Stu'."

"Welcome aboard. I'll go and buy the first round." Kit stood and pushed his way to the bar.

Forrester was already there, and he caught Kit's eye. "A word with you, mate." The Australian pulled Kit over to one side. "Just want to warn you about that bloke," he gestured with his head to a rather ugly sergeant with thick glasses who was now hovering around Kit's table. "He's going to try to talk you into signing him on as your wireless operator. The Canadians told me all about him. He's practically blind, cheated on his eye exam to get in, and he's completely wet. Spends all his time in his hut reading. A loser, I tell you."

"Thanks for the tip," Kit answered, and placed his order while Forrester shouldered his way out of the crowd around the bar carrying five pints in his big hands. Clearly his crew was already complete.

Sure enough, as Kit waited for his order to be filled, the short-sighted wireless operator approached him. He swallowed visibly before asking nervously, "May I have a word with you, Flying Officer Moran, sir?"

Kit nodded, noting that the sergeant was skinny though not short. His face was crooked, with a mouth full of too many teeth jumbled together and a long nose that bent in the middle, presumably from a break that had not been properly set. Everything about him screamed poverty, the nose hinting at scraps and brawls. Yet the dark framed glasses gave him an aura of vulnerability. Intuitively, Kit knew this was not the kid who picked fights; he was the kid the others ganged up on.

The sergeant drew a deep breath, "Your crew said you were still short a wireless operator, sir."

"That's correct. Are you interested in the job?"

"Yes sir. If you give me a chance you won't regret it, sir. It's true I can't see particularly well, but I don't need to for my job." It all spilled out at once as if he'd been practicing the phrases in his mind. "It's because I'm half-blind that I've trained my ears, sir, and I'm very good with Morse, sir. Twenty-eight words a minute, thirty on a good day." He stopped, apparently expecting this fact to impress.

It did. After all, Moran had never managed better than eight or nine words a minute. Forrester's warning rang in his ears though. Completely wet, the Australian had said. Nor was this sergeant the type of bloke Adrian and Stu would warm to. Still, Kit was reluctant to brush him off. "What's your name, Sergeant?"

"Tibble, sir. Terence Tibble. Been called 'Terry' as long as I can remember."

There was still no sign of the pints he'd ordered, so Kit asked Terry to tell him about his background.

He echoed Nigel with, "Not much to tell, sir." Then elaborated, "Never had a dad. Mum died when I was ten. My mum's sister looked after us for a while, but then couldn't cope and sent us to an orphanage. I got work as a delivery boy at fourteen, and at sixteen took a job in a paper mill."

"When did you join up?"

"Soon as I turned seventeen, sir."

"When was that?"

"Thirteen months ago."

Another boy, Kit registered mentally, with a sense of growing panic. If he took him on, he'd been responsible for him, too. Then again, he needed a wireless operator, and they were nearly all so young, he reminded himself. He made himself focus on Tibble. "I hear you read a lot."

The youth looked embarrassed. "I don't like going to the pub all the time. Can't afford the high life. Reading's not so expensive because I read library books. Been sort of educating myself, sir, though not systematic."

Damn it! Kit thought. Terry reminded him of all the orphans his mother had 'adopted' over the years — the abandoned children left to fend for themselves with one kind of handicap or another, but a hunger to learn. Kit liked a man who liked books, and if he didn't take Terry into his crew, he might wind up with a worse pilot and an even poorer chance at survival. His problem was that he questioned whether Terry would he get on with the others. Adrian and Stu were too posh, while Nigel was too cheeky.

"Please give me a chance, sir." Terry begged.

Kit couldn't turn down such a direct plea. He decided to make this call regardless of the others' opinions. His first command decision. Just then the barman shoved four brimming pints in Kit's direction and demanded two bob in payment.

"Here. And I'll need a fifth pint please." Kit slid the coins over the bar and turned back to Terry with a faint smile. "Done. You're on my crew."

Terry's grin of relief was almost painful and he started thanking him effusively.

Kit waved him silent. "Come meet the others!" As the barman shoved the last pint in his direction, he reached for them but realized he was never going to get all five glasses to table unspilt. Without a word, Terry hastened to take two of them and they grinned at one another.

As expected, Kit saw surprise and wariness in Adrian and Stu's eyes as he introduced Terry, although they were both polite. Nigel, on the other hand, seemed positively relieved to have Terry join them, and he grinned as they shook hands.

Kit turned away to hunt for another chair, and Forrester came up behind him. "You didn't really take that loser, did you?"

Kit looked over his shoulder. "Loser? What makes him a loser? I have no reason to assume Sergeant Tibble won't make a first-rate wireless operator."

Forrester shook his head pityingly, "You're out of your mind, mate."

"Actually, I have a clinical diagnosis of 'not insane.'"

"I'm not following you."

"Never mind. We've both got a crew. Let's see how they work out."

As the words hung in the air, Kit felt a great burden settle on him. It was a heavy, almost smothering weight. He'd always known he'd have responsibility for "a crew," but up to now, that had been only an abstract concept. Now they were names and faces. If he failed them, it would be manslaughter.

Chapter 4
Crowing Up

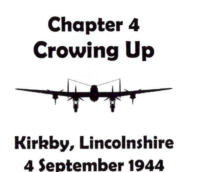

Kirkby, Lincolnshire
4 September 1944

Kirkby Grange School was not what Georgina had expected when she requested a co-educational school. It was not a council school nor even an urban school. It was a boarding school situated in the middle of nowhere. The grounds were generous, albeit now over-grown and ill-tended, and the school itself was housed in a complex of Victorian buildings in neo-Gothic style. There were cracked tennis courts and empty stables too, remnants of better days when this had been a proper boarding school for the upper middle class. Now, however, it was home to nearly six hundred children from a London school. Georgina was excited at the prospect of relevant and challenging work in this surprising setting.

The elderly porter led Georgina through an echoing entry hall and up a flight of shallow steps past rather poor portraits of famous figures. In a wood-panelled waiting room lit by tall windows, half a dozen nervous children awaited judgement from the headmistress. The porter disappeared through the inner door, leaving her with the children. They stared at her, and she smiled back. The two girls and one of the boys muttered something resembling "Afternoon, Miss." Two of the other boys simply looked down or away, but one smiled at her. Not knowing what their various misdemeanours might be, Georgina automatically — and quite unfairly — took the side of the children. She winked at the boy who had smiled at her, and he giggled in delight.

The porter re-emerged and gestured towards the door behind him. "Miss Townsend will see you now, Miss Reddings."

Uplifted by the boy's giggle, Georgina felt full of enthusiasm and confidence. She wanted to be the best trainee teacher the school had ever seen. As she entered the headmistress' office, her smile froze. Before her was a sour faced woman with her hair pulled severely back from her face. Wary apprehension replaced Georgina's short-lived self-confidence.

"Miss Reddings, is it? From the Lincoln Diocesan Teachers' Training College?"

"Yes, Ma'am." Georgina fell back into the role of dutiful vicar's daughter.

"Please. Sit down." Miss Townsend indicated a chair before her massive oak desk. "So, Miss Reddings, you are to be our trainee teacher for the whole of the autumn term. Is that correct?"

"Yes, Ma'am."

"I see from your records that you went to Holy Trinity in Ripon?"

"Yes, Ma'am."

"A very good C of E school. As I recall, they have extremely exacting standards of admission and are far from cheap."

"Yes, I was very lucky. My father is a vicar and so I had a scholarship."

"Yes, well." Miss Townsend clearly wasn't happy about something. She folded her hands together on her desk. "I'm going to be brutally honest with you, Miss Reddings. I fear that you may not be the best candidate for the position here. This school may once have been a decent school — maybe not Holy Trinity, but we had a very good reputation, nevertheless. However, times have changed. Nowadays we are making a contribution to the war effort by providing refuge to the Old Palace School, which was evacuated from Bromley by Bow at the very start of the war. Their entire staff came here with all the children whose parents didn't refuse the evacuation scheme. Those children make up the vast majority of the pupils now in residence here."

"Oh—" Georgina wanted to explain that she understood this, but the look Miss Townsend gave her for daring to interrupt silenced her at once. She resumed her dutiful pose, her feet side-by-side and her hands together on her lap.

"Back in the last century," Miss Townsend reminisced, looking at the oil painting that hung over the fireplace opposite her desk. "Kirkby Grange was built on the model of the old double monasteries, with a girls' school and a boys' school side-by-side and sharing selected facilities such as the church, the assembly hall, the sports fields and stables, but strictly separated by stout walls and strong discipline." She added the last remark with a conviction that entertained no contradiction on Georgina's part.

"It was built," Miss Townsend continued, "for 400 boys and 200 girls, and it was a sought-after and prestigious school. Unfortunately, the post-war era saw a drastic decline in the enrolment of children and in 1931 we were forced to close the boys' school altogether. The facilities in the boys' wing were locked up. Meanwhile the girls' school roll gradually fell to half its previous number. It was, I suppose, inevitable that when the government developed plans to evacuate schools from urban areas subject to bombing to 'safe' regions, Kirkby Grange would come to their attention." She sighed deeply.

Then, pulling herself together, she declared firmly, "Please don't misunderstand me, Miss Reddings. Providing refuge to children subject to aerial bombing is not only a patriotic but also a Christian duty. Nevertheless, I cannot describe to you the state in which some of these children arrived. Nor the manners some of these city urchins still lack! Fully fifteen percent arrived with lice. Lice! As for the teachers, most of them are Bolshies — outright revolutionaries with no respect for the Church, much less the crown. I hope you can appreciate that although we still have eighty-seven of our own girls here, whom we keep separated from the evacuees, we have more than enough staff for them. Your position, I'm afraid, is as an assistant to the teachers from the Old Palace school, teaching both girls *and* boys. It is not something I would willingly ask of a well-bred young woman."

Georgina was at last given a chance to get a word in edgeways. "I honestly don't mind that, Miss Townsend," Georgina assured the headmistress. "I requested this assignment because I wanted the opportunity to teach in a co-educational environment. That's where I hope to spend the rest of my teaching career."

Miss Townsend raised her eyebrows in apparent astonishment, then shook her head in disapproval. Georgina knew she had said the wrong thing. She clearly wasn't supposed to be enthusiastic about teaching boys, much less city urchins.

"I question whether a girl with your background and education has the slightest idea of what she is talking about," Miss Townsend commented acidly. "And I most certainly doubt whether you are capable of handling the pupils from the Old Palace. Most of you young things struggle to handle even children from a proper home environment. These slum brats require a far firmer hand, I can assure you."

"Yes, ma'am. I understand. I promise I will do my best," Georgina tried to salvage something of the interview, despite thinking that Miss Townsend was the epitome of everything she hated about British schools: class-conscious, opinionated, and smug.

As if washing her hands of Georgina altogether, Miss Townsend announced in a brisk, almost indifferent tone, "You were told, I assume, that there's absolutely no housing for you here."

Georgina nodded. "Yes, ma'am. I was given to understand, that I would be able to find lodgings in the village of Kirkby. That's why I brought along my bicycle to make sure I can get there and back easily."

"Well, at least that was prescient of you," Miss Townsend conceded. "Let me see. I had a list of billets here somewhere." She searched about her desk, lifting one stack of papers and then another until she found what she was looking for. "Yes, here they are." She pulled the list towards her and copied some onto a page of her notebook. This she tore out and handed to Georgina. "Start with these three addresses, and I suggest straight away. I will expect you back here at 8:30 tomorrow morning for the weekly staff meeting. You'll be teaching First Form under Miss Evans from Old Palace."

"Yes, Ma'am."

Miss Townsend stood, and they shook hands briefly. Georgina found herself outside again, wincing slightly as Miss Townsend bellowed "Carter!" behind her. One of the waiting boys rose and shuffled reluctantly towards the door to the lion's den wearing a fearful face.

The first address on the list of billets was a shock. Georgina found herself backing out faster than she had gone in. The house was filthy, the kitchen full of unwashed dishes and laundry, and the landlady slovenly. She couldn't help wondering if Miss Townsend knew what this house was like, and if so, whether she'd put it first on the list to upset her?

The second address, on the other hand, brought her to a large, Victorian house with a garden that had gone to seed, two collies and three cats. The landlady, Mrs Radford, was dressed in what looked like a man's modified tweeds and trousers — something quickly explained by the fact that she was the local vet. "My husband and I had a joint practice until the army recalled him three years ago. He's been in Burma for almost two years now, which leaves me looking after the cattle and sheep rather than the adorable little kittens and puppies who used to be my bread-and-butter. Don't mind me! I don't always ramble on like this. Come in and I'll show you the room."

The "room" turned out to be the entire attic, with four lovely dormers and a separate fireplace and sink. The wallpaper was stained and peeling in places as one would expect after five years of war, but Georgina loved it nevertheless.

"I'm afraid there is one little problem," Mrs Radford warned.

"Oh, dear," Georgina exclaimed deflated; she'd been so pleased.

"The billeting people rated this as two-person, and I already have a lodger."

Georgina had subconsciously noted that the room looked lived in, so she was not put off. Reasonably, she pointed out. "That's not a problem, Mrs Radford. There are two beds and plenty of wardrobes and dressers.

I'm quite happy to share the room."

"Well, yes, but *I shall* be much happier if my present lodger, Miss Wycliffe, agrees to have you. Two lodgers who can't get along is not something I want in my house."

Georgina could understand that.

"Miss Wycliffe should be here by 6 o'clock. Would you mind coming back then?"

Georgina could hardly object. As that was still an hour away, however, she biked to the third address on her list. She discovered this billet lay a mile from the village in a rural cottage with outside facilities. As she approached, she heard a woman shouting rudely, and a moment latter a doddering old man in soiled trousers shuffled his way to the outhouse. Georgina lost her nerve before she even knocked on the door. She turned the bike around and returned to the village, praying all would work out with Mrs Radford's other lodger.

Mrs Radford kindly invited her in. "Miss Reddings I was so annoyed with myself after you left because, regardless of what Miss Wycliffe thinks about long-term arrangements, we can't have you wandering around the village in the dark with no place to lay your head. So, plan on spending tonight here regardless. I'll have Mrs Kennedy, my housekeeper, make up the second bed in the attic and lay the table for three for supper as well."

"That's so kind of you, Mrs Radford," Georgina replied in relief. Dusk was gathering outside, and she'd been starting to wonder where she could go.

Just then they heard another bicycle arrive and a pleasant, female voice called, "I'm back, Mrs Radford!"

Mrs Radford excused herself, and Georgina listened tensely to the voices in the kitchen as Mrs Radford explained the situation. A moment later a WAAF officer walked into the parlour, pulling off her cap and hair net in a single motion. She shook her head to let her long dark hair fall lose, and Georgina found herself confronted by a strikingly beautiful young woman with a full but graceful figure and straight dark eyebrows over large, dark eyes. Her lipstick was perfect, and her nail polish red. Georgina thought she'd heard that WAAF weren't supposed to wear either, but as her prospective roommate came across the room with her hand extended, Georgina sensed she was the kind of woman used to privileges. "Hello! Mrs Radford says you're a trainee teacher over at Kirkby Grange and in need a room. I'm Philippa Wycliffe." Her accent was perfect BBC.

"Georgina Reddings," she answered as they shook hands, "and, yes, I am looking for lodgings for the autumn term. I know it would be an inconvenience to share —"

"Good heavens, I'm used to that after five years in the WAAF! The only problem is that I do shift work, which means I come and go at all hours of the day and night. You might find it a touch annoying." She raised her eyebrows making it a question.

"Oh no, I don't mind at all," Georgina hastened to assure her. Having seen the alternatives, Georgina thought a little disturbance in the night was nothing.

"Well then, I don't see why we shouldn't get along, so that's settled."

"Thank you so much!"

Georgina's tone expressed so much relief that Philippa laughed. "The other places were that bad, were they?"

"Well," Georgina hesitated embarrassed, but admitted, with a conspiratorial titter, "Yes, they were."

Philippa shared the giggle, and Mrs Radford put her head into the sitting room to ask, "Did I hear laughter? Is everything settled?"

"It is indeed," Philippa told her. "I'm sure Georgina and I will get along swimmingly."

"I'm so glad! Why don't you take Miss Reddings up and help her settle in while Mrs Kennedy and I get supper?"

In Philippa's wake, Georgina climbed the central stairs to the attic again. Philippa pointed out the unused bed, cupboards and dressers, and Georgina put her suitcase on the bed to unpack while Philippa bushed out her hair and pinned it on the back of her head in an elegant swirl.

"Have you been with the WAAF long?" Georgina asked.

"Practically since war was declared. I mustered in November 1939 and was very lucky to be trained on RDF, so I received a commission earlier than most WAAF."

In the suitcase before Georgina, a silver-framed photo of Don lay where she had packed it carefully between her layers of clothing. She lifted it and stood it on the bedside table.

"Your fiancé?" Philippa asked, moving closer to get a better look. "Very handsome! And already a Flight Lieutenant. Is he stationed near by?"

"No." Georgina paused, looking at the beloved face that gazed calmly out from the photo. "No. He's dead."

Philippa looked over sharply, but there was no shock, just understanding in her gaze. When she said, "I'm sorry," Georgina could tell she meant it. "Was it very long ago?" Philippa asked gently.

"November of last year. It was his 36th sortie."

"I'm sorry," Philippa said again, looking more closely at the photo as if trying to remember if she'd seen him somewhere. "He looks lovely."

"He was," Georgina gasped out, suddenly overwhelmed by a sense of grief more intense than she had felt in weeks. She found herself fighting back tears as she stammered out, "He was absolutely wonderful, and ..." The tears escaped and ran down her face.

Wordlessly, Philippa put an arm around Georgina and held her firmly. It was strange, Georgina thought; they had only just met and yet she felt understood and comforted in a way she had never felt with Fiona. After a short, indulgent moment she took a deep breath and drew back mumbling, "I'm sorry."

"Nothing to apologise for, dear. I've been there."

They said no more about it. Georgina finished unpacking and they went back downstairs.

When they sat down to eat, however, Georgina was surprised to find it impossible to have a pleasant chat. The dogs and cats wanted feeding, the housekeeper was complaining to Mrs Radford about something to do with the rationing, and farmers kept ringing for Mrs Radford's advice.

"Let's go over to the pub," Philippa suggested. "It should be quiet tonight."

Georgina was slightly startled. She'd never before gone to a pub with just one other woman. Once or twice the girls from the college had gone as a group to one across from the college, but that was in a nice part of Lincoln and they'd had each other for protection. The idea of going with just Philippa seemed rather daring, yet also fitting for the start of her life as a quasi-independent woman. Besides, Philippa looked like she knew what she was doing. Georgina agreed, trying not to betray her inner awkwardness.

Outside the air had turned very damp and the clouds hung low, blocking out the stars. The air was decidedly chilly, making Georgina want to dart into the *Pig and Whistle* as they drew near it, but Philippa walked past.

"Is there something wrong with that pub?" Georgina asked looking wistfully at the nearby pub.

"No, it's just where the erks go."

"The erks?"

"Sorry, you may have to correct me more than once. I've been in the service so long that I no longer speak proper English." She announced this while enunciating her words as perfectly as The Queen. "'Erks' is RAF slang for aircraftmen."

"And as an officer you're not allowed to mingle?"

"It's not that. You just don't want to walk in there looking the way you do."

Georgina looked down at her neat skirt and blouse, both carefully chosen for her interview with the headmistress. "Aren't I properly dressed?" she asked baffled.

"It's not what you're *wearing*, Georgina. Trust me, they can see through that."

Georgina blushed at the thought. She was torn between feeling indignant for being patronised and grateful for avoiding unpleasantness. The latter feeling won out. Much as she wanted to think of herself as a grown woman, she recognised that she didn't have much experience — at least not with pubs.

They walked instead across the green to the *King's Head*, a nice-looking building with a steeply pitched roof over white-washed brick. Black shutters closed over windows with round glass panes. Inside, it was warm and cosy, with low ceiling beams, horse-brasses and hunting paintings. The pub was nearly empty, and Philippa led Georgina to a small booth at the back. "Hopefully, none of the locals will notice us here. Now, what are you drinking?"

"I don't suppose a country pub like this would have wine, would it?" Georgina asked wistfully. She didn't really like beer and didn't drink hard liquor but had been brought up on fine wines by a father who had learned to love them while in France. Indeed, Edwin Reddings' wine cellar had been so generously stocked with pre-war acquisitions that it was not yet exhausted.

"Normally not," Philippa agreed, "But there's a South African squadron at East Kirkby, and ever since they arrived the landlord has an astonishing quantity of very drinkable South African wines. I'm not sure how *legal* it all is, mind you, but as customers we can't be called to account for merely drinking the stuff. Do you want red or white?"

"I prefer white."

"Excellent. So do I. I'll get us a bottle. My treat." Philippa was gone before Georgina could protest.

Georgina heard cars pull up outside and male voices, but she didn't think anything of it until the door swung open and what seemed like two dozen RAF officers poured into the pub. All wore aircrew badges on their left breast pockets. Georgina stiffened. Seeing Kit in uniform with pilot's wings had scratched at the scab on her heart, but he was still Kit, Don's friend. This was different. She felt as if Don might be over there, in that crowd. Shy as he was, he'd hang at the back, trying not to draw attention to himself. But if she looked hard enough, she imagined she might find him, that tentative smile of his on his lean face, waiting and hoping that she'd look over at him.

The RAF officers were in high spirits, and they swarmed around Philippa who was at the bar trying to order. Georgina watched in astonishment and amazement as Philippa light-heartedly brushed off their compliments and invitations. "I'm here with a friend," Georgina heard her say.

They all seemed to look over toward the booth.

"Hiding her from us, are you? I thought you had a kinder heart than that Pippa!"

"She's too nice for you Billy."

"I can be nice," he protested.

"Really?"

They laughed.

"Come on Pippa. Bring her over and introduce her to us."

"When hell freezes over!"

"That should be in about," one of them looked at his watch as if preparing to synchronise it, "fifteen minutes from now."

"Not likely."

"Where's she from? Is she staying around here?"

"We're roommates."

"Oh dear. You mean we have to get past you?"

"Precisely. Now let me through."

One of the officers held out his arm to stop her but she ducked under it, carrying two wine glasses and the bottle. Fortunately, none of them followed her over to the booth.

"I'm sorry about this," Philippa announced immediately. "I wouldn't have even *suggested* coming if I'd thought they'd be here. They were on tonight. When I left the Station, start engines was scheduled for just about now." She looked at her watch to confirm her statement. "The met forecast must have changed for the worse, and they scrubbed the op. I am sorry, Georgina, I really didn't think they would be here tonight. You don't want them to join us, do you?"

Georgina shook her head vigorously. "No, not at all. I'm not ready to — well—"

Philippa put her hand on Georgina's. "I understand. If they try anything I'll shoo them away."

Already more RAF had arrived, and three officers wandered over to the booth. "May we join you?"

"No," Philippa answered looking up at the intruders with a dazzling smile.

"Why not?" They leaned over the back of the booth and Georgina instinctively moved deeper into the corner. She felt overwhelmed and intimidated. Don had avoided taking her to the RAF watering holes.

"Because we're having a private conversation," Philippa explained.

"Can't it wait? Let us buy you a round."

"We haven't finished what we have. Be nice and leave us alone, will you?"

This crowd moved on only to be replaced by another pair. "Pippa, what's making you so antisocial this evening?"

"I'm not antisocial, I'm just trying to have a quiet conversation with a friend."

A bomb aimer smiled directly at Georgina and reached over his hand. "Julian Trent. Don't you want us to join you?" Georgina felt trapped and near panic. She felt as if she was close to tears again.

"No, we don't," Philippa answered firmly for Georgina. Then raising her voice slightly, she called to someone standing a few feet behind Trent with his back to them and a pint in his hand. "Excuse me, sir?"

The officer who turned around was notably older than the others, and he had braid on his cap. Georgina knew enough to know that this man must be a very senior officer. "Flight Officer Wycliffe?" He asked.

"Would you please call your dogs off, sir? My friend and I really don't want to be disturbed at the moment."

He raised his voice enough to be heard throughout the room, "Chaps, leave the ladies alone — for once."

They *were* left alone after that, but Georgina did not feel comfortable all the same.

"I'm sorry," Philippa said again. "We'll just finish our wine and go home. I would never have suggested coming if I'd known the op had been scrubbed."

"Who was the senior officer?"

"That's Group Captain Seymore, the station commander at East Kirkby."

"How far away is the station?"

"Three miles."

"So they are often here?"

"If they're not flying or making a nuisance of themselves somewhere else."

"You seem quite indifferent to them," Georgina observed. As long as they were on the other side of the room, they looked splendid. Half the teachers at college dreamed of having RAF boyfriends.

"As I said earlier, I've been in since the start of the war," Philippa answered. "I've broken my heart too often already. They're a good lot to work with but when it comes to romance, give me a civilian any day."

Shortly afterwards, they finished the bottle, and slipped out to a chorus of cheerful "Good nights!" and "Maybe another time!"

Outside, a deep fog smothered the whole village. They could hardly see across the village green. As they moved cautiously forward, Georgina felt a terrible chill run down her spine. From the pub came the dampened sound of male voices all talking at once, and in her mind's eye she could see them still, clustered around the bar, chatting, gesturing and laughing. So much life and energy and concentrated masculinity living on borrowed time. It was almost unbearable.

Chapter 5
Sorting Things Out

RAF Moreton-in-Marsh (OTU)
September 1944

"Missed the target again, Moran!" Forrester noted as they crowded around the board displaying the photos of each aircraft's drop on the training target. "You should have snapped Wright up before I had a chance to grab him."

Wright stood grinning beside his skipper, with his top button undone and a silk scarf twisted inside his open collar instead of a tie — as if he were a fighter ace. Silly sod, Moran thought to himself. Wright's smug expression only reinforced his sense of 'no regrets' about rejecting him. Yet there was no getting around the fact that his own bombing results were, again, miserable. Moran nodded to Wright and muttered "well done" before turning away. Babcock and he had to do better, or they were in trouble.

The results of every exercise were posted so that everyone on the course and on the staff could see how well each crew performed. Some crews nearly always landed near the bottom of the list. A few were there because they viewed the exercises as "tedious" or "superfluous," others because by nature they were more interested in drinking, carousing and having fun than performing well. Forrester's crew, in contrast, consistently took one of the top three places. They were proud of it, and loudly made sure everyone knew where they stood.

Moran didn't particularly care how well he and his crew did in comparison to the other crews, but he knew that once they were on a squadron the bomb photos would be examined by both intelligence and his commanders. Crews with poor bombing results got a bad reputation. It was assumed that they rushed the run, released too soon, or took evasive action while bombing — all because they had the wind up. In short, bad bombing was associated with bad nerves, and Moran didn't want his crew tarred with that kind of reputation. Besides, it could too easily lead to someone looking more closely into his personnel files and discovering he'd been LMF. He didn't know what might happen after that, and he didn't want to find out.

"I'm sorry, Skipper," Babcock spoke into his thoughts. "I don't know what I'm doing wrong. I aced all the exams." He sounded genuinely miserable, but there was also a slight whine in his voice that got on Moran's nerves. He told himself he mustn't let it. Don must have been upset with all of them from time to time, but he never let it show. Moran took a deep breath intending to say something blandly reassuring and had a sudden realisation. "How many flying hours did you say you'd had, Stu?"

"Twenty. Why?"

"On what; a Tiger Moth?" That was the open-cockpit biplane in which all aspiring RAF pilots received their initial flying instruction.

"Yes. Why?"

"Just a thought. Let's go and get a drink." Moran clapped Babcock on his shoulder and appeared to have forgotten about the bombing results.

The next day, however, as soon as they reached their cruising altitude on their way to the bomb range, Moran called Babcock up to the cockpit. As Babcock emerged out of the nose, Moran switched on the autopilot, undid his straps and climbed out of the pilot's seat. "Sit down!" he gestured for Babcock to take his place.

Babcock's eyes widened. "Skipper! I've never flown anything with two engines on it!"

"I know, and I think that's the problem. You obviously understand the theoretical side of bombing and you can do the maths. It's the hands-on aspect of it you haven't mastered. I that is because you don't understand how a heavy aircraft responds to the controls. So, sit down and take the controls."

With obvious reluctance Babcock eased himself into the pilot's seat and gingerly put his gloved hands onto the control column.

"Good. Now: Left!"

"What?" Babcock looked up startled.

"Pretend you're the pilot and I'm the bomb aimer giving you instructions — but switch the autopilot off first."

Babcock only gazed at him more bewildered than ever.

Moran leaned forward and disengaged the autopilot himself. Before he could say anything more, the intercom clicked. "Is this safe, Skipper?" Osgood asked from the tail. "Or should I go and put my parachute on?"

"This is perfectly safe. I'm right here beside Babcock. Just sit tight."

"Yes, sir," Osgood sounded less than happy.

Meanwhile, Peal and Tibble had left their cubicles to peer into the cockpit.

Moran frowned at them. Tibble took the hint and returned to his little desk, but Peal remained where he was.

"Left! Left!" Moran ordered Babcock.

Babcock kicked the rudder and the aircraft yawed so violently that Osgood, Tibble and Peal erupted into loud protests.

"Steady," Moran tried to sooth Babcock with his voice. When Babcock had the aircraft straight and level again. Moran said: "Let's try that again."

"But Skipper..." Babcock pleaded.

"Just try to get a feel for it. Ready?" Babcock nodded miserably. "Right!"

Babcock kicked less violently this time, but he also banked. This time Moran leaned forward to take hold of the control column and level the aircraft. Then he reminded Babcock, "How are the bombs going to clear the bomb bay if we're rolling? Now let's try it again and keep her straight and level."

"I can't do this, Skip!" Babcock babbled in alarm.

"Left!" Moran ordered in reply

After another ten minutes, Babcock was drenched in sweat and his hands were starting to tremble, but he had almost mastered the technique of easing the aircraft from one side to the other without banking or yawing perceptibly. Moran decided it was enough. He signalled for Babcock to unstrap himself and told him to return to the nose. "Just think about me up here at the controls when you give your instructions on the bomb run," Moran cautioned.

From that day forward the accuracy of their bombing started to increase measurably, until they were neck-and-neck with Forrester for the best results.

The fighter affiliation exercises, presented a different problem. The trainee bomber crews were intercepted by RAF fighters flown by pilots at night fighter OTUs. The fighters were not armed, but their gun cameras were activated. When they engaged the gun button, photos rather than bullets were shot. After the fighter pilots had a chance to see how successful they had been at "shooting" a bomber, the photos were forwarded to the appropriate bomber OTU where the bomber trainees could judge how well they had evaded the fighter and/or shot back. The latter was measured by the same method as for the fighters: the firing of their rear guns triggered cameras.

In these exercises bombers were rarely judged to have been "shot down." The trainee fighter pilots never normally got close enough to deliver damaging fire, but most managed to nibble here or there at a wing or tail. Nevertheless, Moran was pleased to see that he had perfected his corkscrewing to the point where not one photo showed a "hit" on his Wellington. It was good, but nothing compared to Forrester and his Canadian gunner Levesque being credited with "hitting" one of the attacking Mossies, an achievement they were full of themselves for. That would have been bad enough, but the gunnery practice against towed targets also showed Forrester and Levesque scoring consistently better than Moran and Osgood. While Moran could live with that, Osgood became increasingly upset.

Four weeks into the course things came to a head. As they increasingly did, Kit and Adrian had settled in for a quiet evening at the officers' mess together. They were deep in a discussion of aqueducts when a mess orderly interrupted Kit with an urgent call.

Kit jumped up hoping, irrationally, that it might be Georgina. Then he remembered, she didn't have his telephone number. Distracted by the reminder that she had not written to him once since his arrival, he answered the phone with a glum, "Moran."

"Skipper! You've got to come down to the *Green Man*. The Canadians are clobbering Nigel!" Stu gasped into the phone. The sound of breaking furniture and shattering glass accompanied his words.

"What?" Kit exclaimed.

"Levesque said something to Nigel at the bar and he swung at him. Levesque hit back and then all the other Canadians piled in. Now, everyone in the pub is trying to beat each other's brains out!" Before Kit could answer, a particularly loud crash rattled down the wires and the phone went dead.

Kit hurried back to where Adrian was sitting. "Nigel's got into a fight with Levesque at the *Green Man* and Stu wants me to intervene."

"Good heavens! By the time we get there, it'll all be over. And if not, what can you do? You'd be better off informing the police instead."

It wasn't necessary, the publican had already called them. All involved in the brawl were put on charges and confined to the station for three days. Tibble, fortunately, was not in the pub at the time, and Babcock had managed to hide under a table and avoid both injury and arrest. Osgood, however, identified as the instigator, was given extra duties as well.

"I'm beginning to wonder about Nigel," Adrian remarked offhandedly to Kit as they left the officer's mess the following evening. Another night fighter affiliation exercise was laid on for tonight.

"What do you mean 'wonder'?" Kit asked back, without looking at him as he pulled on his silk gloves.

"I mean, I'm beginning to wonder if he was such a good choice for our rear gunner. A bit rough, don't you think?"

"He's not a troublemaker. I'm sure he was goaded into the brawl. Levesque has a way with words that rubs me up the wrong way too."

"True enough, but the real problem is that Levesque has the rights of it, doesn't he?" Kit's look of disbelief forced Adrian to be more explicit, "I mean about being a better gunner than Nigel."

"Maybe, but Nigel's still better than most," Kit reminded Adrian. "Levesque is the only other gunner who consistently scores higher."

"You may be right on the towed targets, Kit, but Nigel's score against fighters is terrible so far."

"I don't care about shooting down fighters, Adrian," Kit replied steadily. "I only care about escaping them."

They entered the crew room where all aircrew had a locker with their flying kit. Kit scanned the room looking for Nigel and found the gunner slumped on the wooden bench in front of his locker pulling on his thick, wool socks. His nose was swollen into a pig's snout, and the right side of his jaw looked badly bruised as well.

Kit went over to him and asked cautiously. "Are you fit to fly, Nigel? It doesn't look to me as though you could breathe through that nose."

"I have a mouth, don't I?" The gunner snapped back in a voice slurred by his injuries. He evaded Kit's eyes.

"You're sure you can wear an oxygen mask?"

"Yes, sir."

The words were correct, but Nigel's tone was so furious that Kit felt compelled to point out: "I'm not the one who hit you, Nigel."

"I may look puny, but I could have handled that twit Levesque!" Nigel burst out furiously. "'Cept his whole ruddy crew, *including his skipper*, piled in on his side. And where were my crewmates?" He glared at Kit. "Most weren't even there, and the one who *was* dived under the nearest table!" He threw the last words in Stu's direction provocatively.

Kit, who had stopped fist-fighting at the age of eleven or so, could hardly fault Stu for not being drawn into the brawl. Nevertheless, he sympathised with Nigel's sense of being left in the lurch. Before he could think of an appropriate response, however, Nigel continued, "If a couple of the other gunners hadn't come to my aid, I'd have been creamed — and I wasn't even the one who started the fight! It was that flaming arse Levesque, who thinks he has the right to insult me. I'm not going to put up with it, Skipper!"

Kit scanned the locker room and spotted the Canadian. He had a black-eye and a broken lip, but he was joking happily with his crewmates. Feeling Kit's gaze, Levesque glanced over, grinned, and then put his fingers to his lips to give a piercing, attention-getting whistle. "Two shillings to one I score better than you do, Goodie!" Goodie was apparently the Canadian's corruption of Osgood's name.

Nigel jumped to his feet as though he was going to attack. Kit physically held him back while, with some good-natured shoulder punches, Forrester herded Levesque and the rest of his crew out of the door.

The Canadian gunner still managed to shout over his shoulder, "Toodaloo, Goodie! See you at the debrief!"

Forrester poked his head back into the crew room to up the ante. "I'll make that five quid to one, Moran. Are we on?"

"I don't gamble," Kit answered steadily.

"Not when you're sure to lose, eh?" Forrester laughed and continued on his way.

"The only reason that effing arse Levesque scores better than me on the fighters is because you corkscrew too bloody well!" Nigel burst out, his hands still balled into fists.

Kit laughed, but Nigel glared at him. "I'm bloody serious, Skip! Couldn't you pause in the middle of the corkscrew so I can get in a good shot?"

"Don't be ridiculous! I'm not suicidal," Kit dismissed the request.

"This isn't my idea, Skipper. One of the instructors at gunnery school, a veteran of more than fifty ops, told me about this trick."

"Only you?" Kit asked sceptically, certain that if this was a legitimate tactic, he would have heard of it before now.

"He was a bit of a mean old sod," Nigel admitted, wiping at his battered nose with the back of his hand before adding, "and he was pissed off with most of the trainees because they didn't pander to him the way he wanted, but I played along, and we got pie-eyed together one night. That's when he told me this trick. I'm sure it works, Skip. He said that if the pilot first takes evasive action and then suddenly throttles back and goes still for a couple of seconds, it upsets the enemy's aim. Not the gunner's though; if he knows it's coming, he can get in a perfect shot."

By now the other crews had left the changing room. Only Adrian, Stu and Terry were left. Fully kitted up, they'd drifted over to Kit and Nigel.

"If it works that well, why doesn't everyone do it?" Kit challenged Nigel with a glance at the others.

"Because, as this bloke warned me, most flaming skippers are too effing arrogant to listen to their gunners, that's why!" Nigel underlined his point by turning his back on Kit and slamming his locker shut.

"That's going too far, Osgood!" Kit called him up short. "I welcome ideas and discussion, because we're all in this together, but I won't tolerate disrespect and rude language. As for your proposal, much as I sympathise with your anger at Levesque, it's more important that we don't get shot down than that you score."

"Just *try* it once, Skipper." Nigel pleaded, turning back to face him. "The gunner who told me this was an *ace*, and didn't Vaux say the key to success against night fighters was doing what they didn't expect? What could surprise them more than a bomber that stops jinking and throttles back under attack?"

Kit glanced round at the other members of his crew.

"Why don't we try it, Skipper?" Terry supported Nigel, earning a nod of thanks from the gunner. "The cameras will show if it works or not. If it doesn't work, we don't have to do it ever again — certainly not on ops."

Adrian, a thoughtful, lawyerly expression on his face, mused, "I can't see any objective reason not to try the manoeuvre while we're still here in training."

"I agree," Stu chimed in; he agreed with almost everything Adrian said.

"I'm sure I can do this, Skipper." Nigel insisted. "Let me show you!"

Kit knew that the cameras would only tell them how inexperienced RAF pilots reacted. He didn't think they were comparable to the Luftwaffe's best. Still, it might be better for them to all see the photo results. Otherwise, they might harbour illusions about something that wouldn't work. If he didn't prove them wrong now, they were likely to urge him to do this when a Junkers 88 was on their tail. "All right. We'll try it tonight, but if the results aren't decisive, we won't do it again."

"Thanks Skipper!" Nigel brightened visibly.

Outside the crew bus hooted a warning, and Kit sent the others down while he finished kitting up.

The RAF night fighters were guided by controllers to within 1,000 yards of the bombers and then left on their own to find and approach their targets. The Wellingtons, meanwhile, were given the rough coordinates of where the fighters would intercept them. Moran was acutely aware that on ops things were considerably more difficult because one had to be alert for much longer periods of time and the danger of daydreaming or getting distracted was greater.

Tonight, however, Osgood was very keyed up and he spotted the first night fighter, a Mossie, when it was still a long way out. "Rear gunner to pilot: Fighter on our starboard beam. High. Range 800 or 900 yards. Corkscrew right!"

Moran immediately put the Wellington into a violent right-hand corkscrew. The Mossie appeared not to see them at all, or at least made no attempt to follow.

"Bugger!" Osgood exclaimed eloquently.

Moran straightened out the Wellington and resumed comparatively straight and level flight, weaving only gently to enable Osgood to scan the sky around them more comprehensively.

"Rear gunner to pilot: Fighter to port. Low, 600 yards! Corkscrew left!" Moran did as ordered. "He's following!" Osgood reported excitedly. Moran reversed the corkscrew and lifted the nose, but the fighter stayed with them. "Four hundred yards. Let me try for him! Pause the corkscrew in three...two...one...now!"

Moran drew a deep breath and throttled back, reminding himself that the Mossie had no ammunition. From the tail of the Wellington, Osgood fired his empty guns. Although they still caused the aircraft to shudder, they made a clacking sound very different from when they were loaded. The noise reminded Moran of the chattering monkey. Moran counted to three and then upended the Wellington on its starboard wingtip and dived for the earth. The Mossie, which had only just adjusted to the paused corkscrew, was taken completely by surprise and overshot into the darkness.

Hmm, Moran thought. He conceded that the pause might indeed serve to disorient night fighters, but it was extremely risky all the same.

"Rear gunner to pilot: Fighter starboard beam. High. 800 yards. Coming down. 700 yards and turning. Dead astern. 600 yards." Osgood's voice contained a subtle, new note of confidence.

Moran yanked the Wellington it a sharp turn to the right and then started to dive away.

"Following! Five hundred yards. Four hundred. Three... two... one. Hold it, Skipper. Throttle back now!"

Against his better judgement, Moran again did what his gunner asked. The Wellington seemed to hang in the hair. The guns chattered toothlessly. Again, Moran counted to three and then threw the Wellington into a left-hand, upward corkscrew so violent that the Wimpy shuddered and creaked. Just before it stalled, he let the left wing fall and pushed the nose into a power dive.

"Bloody hell, Skipper! You've shaken him off entirely!" Osgood complained in disgust.

"That's his job, Nigel," Peal reminded the rear gunner with an audible laugh.

The following morning, they were told to report to the briefing room to see the photo results of the affiliation exercise. On the way over, Adrian excused himself to drop by the station post office and see if he had any mail. Kit had stopped going. He didn't get any mail. It had been five weeks and Georgina had not written to him once. No need to "calibrate" his response, he thought bitterly. Or rather, calibration meant that he didn't write either. He certainly wasn't going to beg her to pay attention to him.

Adrian emerged from the post office smiling and waving something. "Two letters for you Kit!"

"What?" Kit lit up. Apparently, Georgina's letters had simply been held up. That was not unusual. Sometimes in Africa he'd get three or four all at once, although Georgina had written them as much as a week apart.

"Postmarked in London," Adrian noted as he handed them over.

"London?" Why would Georgina post her letters from London? Then his heart sank. The letters weren't from Georgina. Rather, his father's clean handwriting was boldly scrawled across one letter and his mother's gentler penmanship graced the other. Kit understood: they had been enclosed in an official communication to the Colonial Office. There a friend of his father's must have removed the personal letters and forwarded them using British postage. "From my parents," Kit explained to Adrian, trying not to sound as disappointed as he felt.

The latter wasn't listening. He'd ripped open his own letter and was scanning it excitedly.

"Good news?" Kit asked.

Adrian smiled and nodded without taking his eyes off the page. "It's from a wizard girl I met over the summer. She's agreed to meet up with me in London next week when we're on leave. She wants to see a play, she says, and would love to go dancing...." Adrian flipped over the page to continue reading happily.

"Well done," Kit commented, sick with envy.

Adrian tucked his letter into his tunic pocket as they mounted the stairway to the briefing room that was already abuzz with excited voices. The photos had been pinned to the large board at the back. White writing at the foot identified the aircraft to which the photo belonged. The crews were clustered around looking for their own results and pointing at this and that.

The gunnery master rapped sharply with his cane on a desk at the front of the room to get their attention. "Take your seats, gentlemen! Sit down! Quiet!" Reluctantly, the crews drifted away from the back wall with the photos and settled onto the chairs facing forward. Forrester led his crew to sit in the front row. Moran sank down in the row behind them, and his crew joined him, Peal to his left and Osgood on his right. The chatting slowly faded away

"We have some interesting results today. One of you got in excellent shots — and this is the astonishing thing — on two different fighters. In fact, the results are so good, that we're crediting you — unofficially, of course — with two kills."

Levesque jumped up with a hoot of triumph.

"Don't make so much noise, Levesque," the gunnery master reprimanded with a frown.

Levesque sank back into his seat still grinning with confidence. Forrester gave him a thumbs up.

The gunnery master took four photographs from the speaking roster. These had not been posted on the back wall. He pinned them up on the main board, where the map for operations would have hung had they been here for an operational briefing. "Here," he narrated as he tapped one photo with the tip of his cane, "in the first photo, you see the fighter just coming into the gun sight." He shifted his pointer. "The second photo shows the fighter more centred than before with the gun sight bang on the cockpit. If using live ammunition, this would almost certainly have killed the pilot of the fighter — provided it was a full two second burst, of course."

He turned to the second pair of photos. "Here you see the first shot is from 300 yards and a bit to the left, but the second — and this is the remarkable thing — is from just 150 yards and spot on that starboard engine. Very good shooting. The most astonishing thing here is to see the range closing that much between the first and second shot without the gunner losing his focus. Usually, the fighter is closing, and the bomber is evading fire, disrupting the gunner's ability to refine his aim. I don't know if this was courage, luck, or something else, but these two fighter kills were made without suffering a single hit in return."

Moran turned to look at Osgood in amazement; he'd done it. Osgood lifted his chin and his eyes glittered with pride over his swollen and bruised face.

"Who was it?" Someone called from the back of the room.

The gunnery master was smiling now. "Flying Officer Moran with Sergeant Osgood at the guns."

Forrester turned around and tossed at Moran. "More fool you for not taking my bet!"

Moran just laughed.

That evening, the Australian cornered Kit in the bar of the mess.

"What's the trick, mate?"

"Trick?"

"Your wet dick of a gunner didn't turn into a wonder boy overnight. Hitting one fighter might have been luck, but not two. You pulled some trick out of your sleeve. Let me in on the secret."

"You're wrong, Forrester." Kit told him levelly. "It was my gunner's idea, and I didn't think it would work. It did today, but I'm still sceptical. So, we'll test it again on the next fighter affiliation exercise."

"What?"

Kit knew that Nigel would as soon kill him as share his secret with the hated Levesque. "It's just a different means of coordinating our actions to get better results."

"What does that mouthful of baloney mean?" Forrester challenged him, his blue eyes icy cold now.

"It means I'm not going to tell you."

"Look, mate, I know Levesque has been a bit of a twit with his bragging, but — bottom line — we are on the same side in this war, remember?"

That, unfortunately, was the point, and Kit knew it. This manoeuvre might plausibly save Forrester, his entire crew and a precious Lancaster from being shot down one day. He settled on, "I'll tell you what, Forrester: you get a grip on that clot Levesque, get him to belt up and lay off Osgood, and *then* I'll let you and Levesque in on the secret — guaranteed before you go on ops, but not before Levesque eats a little crow."

Forrester thought about the offer for only two seconds. Then he held out his broad hand. "Deal!"

They shook on it.

At the end of the sixth week of training, they received a week's leave starting from the end of a daylight exercise on Friday afternoon. Kit was dreading this week because he'd avoided making any plans in the silly hope — held right up to the last minute — that Georgina might get in touch and could meet up. Now it was too late to impose on any of his other acquaintances in England. Having no plans forced him to face the fact that Georgina had effectively ditched him, Kit glumly reflected as he returned his flying kit to his locker. She had not written once since he'd stayed with her parents, not even to answer his letter to her, and he was not going to humiliate himself by begging her to see him.

Adrian broke in on his thoughts. "I'm not going to depart for London until tomorrow morning. What do you say we take the rest of the afternoon to go and see Tewkesbury Abbey at last?" They'd been talking about visiting this architectural tourist attraction for weeks.

"I'd love to," Kit replied, smiling across at Adrian. "Except, I was just thinking we ought to do something as a crew before we go our separate ways." Don's crew had spent much of their free time together. "Maybe we could all go to Tewkesbury together — if you have room for all of us in your car?"

"No problem on that score, Kit, but I'm not sure the others would be interested in visiting a medieval market town and abbey. Stu maybe, but the other two?"

"Let's ask them." Kit countered, and turned to call out to Terry and Nigel, who were just about to leave the crew room. To Adrian's evident surprise, all three Sergeants jumped at the chance of a joint trip to Tewkesbury. There was a dash to change out of battle dress, and three quarters of an hour later they passed out of the main gate crowded into Adrian's ageing, black Humber.

It was a twenty-mile drive to Tewkesbury, which took them nearly an hour on the winding country roads. On the way they talked mostly "shop." Eventually, however, the conversation turned to their plans for leave. Stu was looking forward to spending a week with his parents in Manchester. "Can't wait to sleep in late and have breakfast in bed," he confessed.

Nigel too planned to go home to his Mum. "My twit of a younger brother has signed aboard a merchant vessel. Mam's all in a tizzy about it, him being only fifteen and all. I've got to go and sort things out." He sounded dutiful rather than pleased at the prospect of a week in Liverpool.

Adrian was hoping to meet up in London with the young lady who had written to him. He was cagey about details, however. Recognising the relationship was new and fragile, Kit chose not to ask too many questions.

"What about you, Skipper?" Nigel asked.

"I don't know. This looks like a nice town." He observed, distracting their attention. "Maybe I can find a guest house or small hotel and spend the week here."

They all knew his parents were in Nigeria, and if anyone was surprised by his lack of plans, they didn't say. Even so, Kit turned swiftly to his wireless operator to direct attention away from himself. "And how about you, Terry?"

"Here we are!" exclaimed Adrian, before the young Sergeant wedged between the other two in the back could answer. They parked and went in.

Adrian led the way, pointing out the more interesting features to them all. Kit found the symmetry, the scale and yet astonishing lightness of the abbey inspiring. "What a project!" he exclaimed, flashing a grin at Adrian. "There must have been thousands of workmen — masons, carpenters, tilers, glazers and whatnot. Coordinating all that and getting the timing right would have been a huge logistical and management challenge. It must have cost a fortune, too. How did they finance something like this?"

"I haven't a clue. Let's get a guidebook."

They found the tiny gift shop near the entrance and bought the small guidebook printed on flimsy paper, only to be disappointed by the sparse details on the construction. While leafing back and forth in search of the information, a slight, elderly man with thinning hair introduced himself as one of the vergers and asked if he could be of assistance. They told him what they were looking for, and he admitted that not much seemed to be known about the construction. "However, I do know a bit about the history, if you'd like a guided tour?"

Adrian and Kit looked at one another and nodded. "Yes, please."

The verger seemed delighted and proved to be a knowledgeable and cheerful guide. Kit and Adrian were genuinely interested, while the others tagged along docilely until the verger got to the great stone porch. Here he paused and gestured towards the open field falling away before them. "Out there is where the Battle of Tewkesbury took place, and —"

"What battle was that again, sir?" Terry asked.

"Tewkesbury, 4th of May 1471."

"Wars of the Roses, wasn't it?" Stu spoke up like an eager schoolboy.

The verger beamed back like a pleased schoolmaster. "Exactly. When Edward IV crushed the army of Lancaster under the Lancastrian Prince of Wales and the Duke of Somerset. Most of the men of Lancaster were slaughtered there in what we still call Bloody Meadow. Those strong or fleet enough to reach the abbey begged the right of sanctuary."

"How many made it here, sir?" Nigel asked.

"Hundreds. They flooded in and covered the entire nave, the aisles, the ambulatory. On their heels were the knights of York, led by King Edward himself. He rode onto this porch." The verger pointed at the badly worn flagstones. "Accounts say his horse's shoes struck sparks. But the abbot barred his way. Holding up the altar cross, he begged the Yorkist king not to besmirch his victory by shedding blood in a church."

"And did he spare them?" Stu asked eagerly.

"Well, most of the commoners were spared, but the Lancastrian leaders were dragged out, tried and executed."

At the end of their tour, they thanked the verger sincerely and returned to the car, but by mutual consent, they decided for tea in Tewkesbury rather than returning to RAF Moreton-in-Marsh straight away. They walked along the high street until they found a tearoom in what Adrian claimed was a sixteenth century building. By chance there was a bookstore next door with a used book on English architecture featuring Tewkesbury Abbey displayed in the window. Kit told the others to go ahead, while he darted in to buy it.

When Kit re-joined the others at a large round table in the window alcove, Nigel was saying, "I never understood the Wars of the Roses. What were they about anyway? Why did anyone care if the House of York or Lancaster held the crown? They were all English, weren't they?"

Adrian and Stu competed with one another to provide an answer, talking about Henry VI's madness, his French queen, the importance of patronage and various things that Kit found unenlightening. Terry muttered, "I wonder if five hundred years from now anyone will understand what we're fighting about?"

"How can you say that?" Stu protested. "We're fighting in self-defence!"

"Are we?" Terry asked back, his unwavering eyes framed by his spectacles. "I mean, maybe we were fighting in self-defence in 1940, but Jerry hasn't been trying to invade for years now, has he?"

"And what do you call the V1s?" Stu asked rhetorically, while Nigel snapped, "He's bloody well sinking our ships day and night! Hundreds of sailors die every week, you silly sod!" Nigel's tone was so hot it nearly set the air on fire, and it took Kit by surprise. Nigel and Terry had always got along well up to now.

"He's occupied practically the entire Continent too!" Stu continued in a superior, know-all tone that was bound to rub the other sergeants the wrong way.

"Are we fighting to free the frogs, then?" Terry shot back.

"It's not just the frogs," Adrian tried to explain in a more conciliatory tone. "As Stu said, the Nazis have occupied half of Europe — Norway, Denmark, Holland, and Belgium, as well as France, and not to mention Poland, Czechoslovakia and now the western part of the Soviet Union. Wherever they go, the Nazis bring terror and oppression."

"We're fighting for democracy and the British Empire," Stu concluded proudly.

"I'm not fighting for no British Empire!" Nigel countered angrily. "I don't give a tinker's damn about the flaming British Empire. And if we're fighting for democracy, then we need more of it right here in England! But I won't never forgive the effing Nazis for what they've already done neither!"

The smouldering fury in Nigel's words singed the air again, so much so that even Terry, who'd begun this argument, seemed stunned. Kit knew there must be an ugly story behind such vehemence. He would have liked to know what it was just to understand Nigel better, but Nigel had to want to tell him. He also registered that Stu had started puffing himself up for an indignant rebuttal and decided it was time to intercede.

"We don't have a lot of choice about fighting this war," Kit declared just as Stu opened his mouth. "The Germans started it, and it's no hoax that only a few hundred of our colleagues stopped them from invading after Dunkirk. Nor is what they've done to London, Liverpool, Portsmouth and all our other industrial cities anything less than murderous. Until the Nazis have been crushed, they will continue to threaten us, which means we have to keep fighting until we've finished them off. Hopefully that's sooner rather than later. As to what comes after, I agree with you, Nigel: we should strive for something better than what we had before."

As he spoke, Kit remembered the Reverend Reddings expounding on his hopes for a new Jerusalem in England's green and pleasant land. It made him sad because his personal Jerusalem had already faded into the mists of obscurity with Georgina's silence. He was relieved that the waitress chose this moment to bring their tea and buns.

The following morning buses were laid on to Gloucester and Oxford railway stations. Forrester had already headed out with his entire crew on their way to the fleshpots of London, or so they claimed. Adrian left first thing, taking Stu and Nigel to the station to catch early trains, but Kit was in no hurry and enjoyed a leisurely breakfast before going out to catch one of the RAF buses for Gloucester. Terry approached him at the bus stop and timidly asked if he could borrow the guidebook from the abbey. Kit replied, "Of course," then noted that Terry was in battle dress and had no luggage with him. "Aren't you going anywhere, Terry?"

Terry shrugged in embarrassment. "Nowhere to go, sir. I'll stay here."

Kit didn't think that was the best way to relax and rest from the intense training regime. "I don't have anywhere particular to go either," he admitted. "That's why I bought that book on English architecture. I looked through it last night and decided to see some of the more important monuments, starting with Edward I's castles in Wales."

"That sounds very interesting, sir."

"Why don't you come with me?" There seemed no point in them both being alone.

"Sir? Are you serious? You wouldn't mind me tagging along?" Terry sounded both astonished and excited, but then had second thoughts. "I can't afford posh hotels, sir."

"Nor can I. We can find affordable places like Youth Hostels or the YMCA."

Terry perked up at once. "You're sure you wouldn't mind spending your leave with me, sir?"

"If you get on my nerves, I'll tell you."

Far from getting on his nerves, Kit liked traveling with Terry. Since Terry didn't have an agenda, Kit could do what he wanted. Based on the architecture book, he selected what would try to see each day, found the best way to get there on their budget, and, after seeing the attraction, found a place to spend the night. They ate at "British Restaurants" and other unpretentious places where they could get a soup, main course, pudding and tea for just a shilling and thruppence. Kit appreciated that Terry didn't drink more than a pint or two in the evening and showed no interest in girls. What made travel with Terry fun, however, was the fact that young wireless operator had seemingly endless curiosity. His mind was like a sponge that sought to absorb anything and everything that came near it. He also asked some intriguing questions.

At Conwy Castle Terry surprised Kit by declaring, "I suppose Hitler will be remembered as one of Germany's greatest leaders."

"What on earth are you talking about? He's a madman."

"Yes, I suppose," Terry replied, weighing his head from side-to-side uneasily. "But we think of Edward I as a great English King because he subdued Wales and Scotland, don't we? How's that different from what Hitler's done for Germany by conquering Poland and France and all the rest?"

"In 1940, Hitler might have seemed great to the Germans, but we've got him on the run now. Germany is retreating from its occupied territories while we systematically destroy industrial and military capacity inside the Reich itself. By the time we've forced him to surrender, Hitler will be seen as one of the worst leaders Germany ever had."

"So, everything depends on winning?" Terry pressed him. "If Hitler had won the war back in 1940 or 1942, he'd be called a great leader, but if he loses that he'll be declared a disaster?"

"Well, no," Kit countered, uncomfortable with that notion, "After all, more and more evidence is coming to light about terrible atrocities — things worse and on a scale far beyond anything we saw in the last war. So, even if he had won the war, he'd still be a murdering, racist madman!"

Then Kit had a second thought and with a sheepish grin he admitted, "But I suppose, if he were to win the war, he'd be able to tell people how to write the history books, so future generations might not cotton on to just how bad he was." Kit's grin widened. "That's another reason why we have to win the war, Terry: So, we can write the history books our way."

After five days, they felt they had "done" Wales, and Kit suggested they go to York to see Rievaulx and Byland abbeys. Deep inside, Kit knew it was also because he wanted to go back to Yorkshire. He was considering calling the Reddings. If he was in York, he could claim he was "just in the area and wanted to see how they were doing." Maybe they would have something to say about Georgina that would explain her silence.... Or maybe he would simply make himself miserable by finding out that there was no reason for it besides indifference to him.

Kit and Terry got into York in the late afternoon and found a small hotel. It was a little pricey compared to where they had been staying, but Kit was getting tired of Youth Hostels and offered to cover the difference for Terry. They then went out to see York Minster before dinner. They had almost finished with their self-guided tour when Kit noticed someone waving at them from the far side of the nave and recognised the Reverend Reddings.

Kit waved back and at once Reddings squeezed his way between the folding chairs that had been set up in the nave for some special event. "Flying Officer Moran! What a remarkable coincidence. What are you doing here?"

"Just sightseeing. This is my wireless operator, Terry Tibble. Terry, Reverend Reddings is the father of an old friend."

They shook hands, Reddings smiling warmly at the sergeant as he asked, "Are you from these parts, Sergeant?"

"Oh no, sir. I've never been here before in my life. I was born in Birmingham and didn't get much chance to travel up to now. Flying Officer Moran was kind enough to take me along with him."

Reddings turned back to Kit. "Why didn't you let us know you were so near?"

"I was planning to call tonight," Kit assured him, unsure whether he would have had the nerve or not.

"How long are you here for?"

"Just tonight and tomorrow. Leave runs out at midnight on Sunday."

"I'm sorry it's such a short trip. Are you staying in York?"

"Yes, at the White Boar Hotel."

"That's a lovely hotel. I often stay there myself. And you're alone?"

"Just the two of us, yes."

"Then would you let me buy you both dinner? I've got a couple of things I need to do first — we have a church conference over the next two days, with seminary students coming in from around the country — but I should be done by six. Shall I collect you at the White Boar at seven?"

Aside from good food and company, an evening with Dr Reddings would enable Kit to get the answers he wanted about Georgina. Then again, that might expose him to humiliation in front of Terry. Uncertain, he glanced at his wireless operator, who answered his look with "I'm happy with whatever you want."

Kit decided to take a chance. "That's very generous of you Reverend Reddings. We'd be delighted to."

At seven-thirty, they found themselves in a tiny but pleasant restaurant with an exceptional menu of meals based on off-ration items. They talked about their trip at first, Terry enthusiastically describing all the places they had been and the things he'd learned. It pleased Kit to see how readily Terry, widely viewed as antisocial and "wet" in the RAF, opened up to the vicar. Then again, in his own quiet way Reddings was good at making people feel at ease with him. Even so, it astonished Kit when Terry boldly asked: "Being a priest and all, sir, could you explain to me how the Church justifies war?"

"Now that is a question that has occupied theologians for centuries, Sergeant." Reddings replied candidly, without a flicker of surprise. He removed his glasses and cleaned the lenses with his handkerchief as he explained comfortably, "There are some churchmen and theologians who do not believe it is ever justified. The majority, however, believe there are both just and unjust wars. The latter are anathema, but the former are necessary."

"But how do we know the difference?"

Reddings replaced his cleaned glassed and looked directly at Terry as he answered. "Just wars are best defined as wars of self-defence, such as the current conflict."

"But didn't we declare war on Germany?" Terry asked back puzzled.

"Only after Germany invaded Poland, an innocent country which had not committed an act of aggression. Christian theology does not define self-defence narrowly as the defence of oneself, one's family, or nation, but rather the defence of helpless, weak and oppressed people generally." Reddings appeared to be enjoying the conversation, as he continued with evident conviction, "In my opinion, even if only a little of what is coming to light about Nazi atrocities is true, then there has rarely been a more justified war in the history of mankind than this present conflict."

"But haven't we done some terrible things too?" Terry asked.

Kit held his breath, uncomfortable with the direction this conversation was going. It wasn't that he hadn't asked himself similar questions, but he was now in command of a Lancaster and Terry was a member of his crew. He had a responsibility to ensure that Terry did his job well, and doubts of this kind might undermine morale.

Reddings was already answering the question, "Are you disturbed by our policy of area bombing, Sergeant?"

"Sometimes, sir," the sergeant admitted with an apologetic glance in Kit's direction.

Before Kit could intervene, Reddings continued, "That speaks well for you, young man. I am bothered by it too. I keep asking myself if we truly must imitate our enemies in order to defeat them? And if so, how can we ever end the cycle of violence and counter-violence?"

Kit's unease mounted. While he respected the clergyman's opinion, he didn't think RAF aircrew could afford to ask these kinds of questions. Yet it was hard to interrupt without seeming both rude and dictatorial. Terry was, after all, off duty.

Reddings was reflecting, "I worry about the escalation of force we seem to be witnessing. Doesn't it undermine our moral fibre to engage in acts that kill the innocent along with the guilty? Don't we risk so much destruction — both physical and ethical — that we will not be able to rebuild when the guns fall silent? In other words, can one truly build Jerusalem among the dark, satanic mills?"

The clergyman's reference was lost on Terry, who now looked to Kit helplessly, implicitly asking him to respond. That gave Kit the opening he needed to answer forcefully. "They hit us first, sir, and they've hit again and again — most recently with these V1 and V2s. All we've done is fight back with what we have. The bombing offensive may be a blunt weapon, but it was the only one we had until the invasion in June. Navigation systems, target marking and bombsights that enable us to hit only the military targets would be wonderful, but we don't have them."

The reverend spread his hands apologetically. "Quite right. I'm sorry. I didn't mean to criticise you or your colleagues in any way. On the contrary, without your sacrifices, God knows, Hitler would not be in retreat. It's just that sometimes I fear — no, let me just say that I *pray* the price will not be *too* high. I pray that when the last bomb has fallen there will be something left on which we *can* rebuild a new world. In short that there will be a second chance for humanity."

"Amen to that," Kit exclaimed, and was surprised to hear Terry seconding him in an earnest tone.

Reddings bowed his head and added his own heartfelt "Amen." Then he smiled at them and remarked, "And where such spontaneous prayers arise, I find cause for hope. Now, puddings? Or shall we partake of what they have the audacity to call 'coffee' nowadays?"

As they waited for their mock coffee, Kit nervously realised he was either going to have to ask about Georgina soon or miss the opportunity altogether. Yet the very act of asking would reveal he'd heard nothing from her, which he found intensely embarrassing. He gathered himself for the question, but the arrival of their drinks gave him an excuse to procrastinate further.

Tiny packages of sugar and powdered milk tottered precariously on each saucer as the waitress set them before the guests. As she withdrew, Reddings coughed awkwardly, turned to Kit, and asked, "Won't you be seeing Georgina at all during this leave?"

Kit was momentarily relieved that Reddings had raised the topic, but then realised that he was still going to have to be honest. He tried to sound resigned rather than bitter as he answered candidly, "She hasn't been in touch with me since I reported to the OTU, sir. That rather gave me the impression that she wasn't particularly interested in seeing me again."

Terry hastily decided that he needed a smoke and left the table, for which Kit was grateful.

Reddings, meanwhile, poured himself a second cup of the mock coffee and then remarked. "I'm very sorry to hear that. I certainly wouldn't want to interfere in something that is not my affair, but for what it's worth, Mrs Reddings and I think highly of you. I also had the impression that Georgina was much happier during your brief visit than at any time since Don was killed. Would you object to my telling her that we met?"

"She's your daughter, sir."

"Yes, but I wouldn't want to put you in an awkward situation; that is, do anything that could make your life any more difficult than it is already." When Kit said nothing, he added. "If you tell me that you'd be happier never to hear from Georgina again, then I will respect that and say absolutely nothing to her."

Kit caught his breath. Was that really what he wanted? Never to hear from her again? She seemed to have forgotten him completely, but he certainly hadn't forgotten her. He still hoped for her letters every time Adrian collected the mail. "I'm not happier forgetting her, sir. I just don't want to keep hoping for something that can't be."

"That's all I wanted to know," Reddings answered earnestly. Then he smiled and turned to gesture to Terry that he could return to the table.

Changing trains in Birmingham New Street Station, they ran into Nigel. He seemed surprisingly glad to see them. Together they claimed a corner of one of the compartments, and Nigel shared some home-made toffees while Terry excitedly recounted their tour and described the places they'd been and things they'd seen. When they finally reached Gloucester, it had started to drizzle and dusk was coming fast. They boarded the station bus and Kit ended up sitting with Nigel while Terry was across the aisle. Surrounded by so many other RAF aircrew, Terry withdrew back into his habitual shell like a turtle. He pulled his head down and took out a book to read, evidently to discourage conversation.

Kit turned to Nigel, who hadn't been given much chance to say anything yet. "Were you able to straighten out the problem with your younger brother and have a good leave?"

"My brother?" Nigel asked puzzled.

"When you left, you mentioned something about him wanting to sign aboard a merchant ship—"

"Oh that. He'd already shipped out, so there was nothing I could do about it. Lied about his age, of course. Can't say I blame him. Me mam's got a new boyfriend and he's worse than me dad." Nigel's outrage was raw, and although his nose was almost back to its normal size, Kit thought he had some new bruises on his jaw. The teenager was complaining bitterly, "The bastard doesn't contribute a farthing to the household but expects my mam to wait on him hand and foot. Drinks too much too."

"I'm sorry to hear that," Kit replied, thinking his young gunner had a lot on his plate. Hopefully, he'd be able to concentrate on his job once he was back at the station.

"Ah." Nigel took a deep breath and then added, "I suppose it's better you know about all of it, sir. I got into a fight with the bastard and threw him out of the house. He called the police and...." He took a deep breath. "I got arrested, sir. I expect they called the Station, and I'll be on charges — again — when I arrive."

It flashed through Kit's head that when he'd pictured being skipper, he hadn't thought about these kinds of problems. He also wondered very briefly if Adrian was right to question Nigel's suitability for his crew, but he dismissed the thought. He'd taken the lad on, and it was now his job to look after him as best he could. It was this responsibility that made the role of skipper more challenging than simply flying a kite. To Nigel he admitted, "I honestly don't know how things like this are handled, but if there's any way I can help, I will."

Nigel's expression cleared a bit. "Would you, sir? I swear I won't let this interfere with the job. I didn't take to drink or anything — not after seeing the way that bastard quaffed it down and then spewed it up all over the place for me mam to clean up!" He was shaking his head in disgust.

Kit could sympathise, and promised, "I'll see what I can do."

Kit parted from the two sergeants at the main gate. Although he knew there had not been enough time for Reddings to have any influence on his daughter, he stopped to see if, by pure chance, he had any mail. The only letters were from his parents. After that he went see the station adjutant about Nigel. The adjutant told him all charges had been dropped already, but advised, "Maybe he shouldn't go home on his next leave." Kit emphatically agreed.

At the officer's mess, Kit was surprised to find Adrian had already returned and was reading a paper in the anteroom. "Adrian! I didn't expect you back until the last moment."

Adrian looked up. "Oh, hello Kit. Have a good leave?"

"Surprisingly pleasant. And yourself?"

Adrian shrugged and smiled self-consciously as he declared, "It certainly had its moments." Then he paused, scratched his head, and admitted, "But it didn't go anything like I expected, and I'm not sure what to make of it, actually."

"Come on. I'll buy you a drink and you can tell me about it."

Adrian grabbed his cap and willingly joined Kit. Kit bought the first round and they settled at an empty table together. "So, what happened?" Kit prompted.

Adrian stretched out his long legs with a sigh. "It was sheer chaos and confusion from the moment I pancaked in London. You remember the letter. I thought I was meeting up with a very streamlined piece of nice called Cynthia, but she showed up with her friend Julia, and of course I didn't want to be rude. So, I called a friend of mine to see if he wanted to join us. We went to school together, but he's flying a desk with the Admiralty after being wounded in the Med. He graciously agreed to join us — only to start charming Cynthia clear out of her knickers. All right, I don't know if he got *that* far, but I was more than a little browned off! But there was Julia, and while she isn't the corker Cynthia is, she wasn't entirely humid. In fact, she was a terrific dancer, one thing led to another, and..." Adrian downed the whisky in a single swig and announced he needed another, looking around for an orderly.

"Don't leave me in suspense! And what?"

"I think I got myself engaged."

"Congratulations!" Kit grinned and clapped him on the back.

"Well, that's just it, actually. I'm in a bit of a muddle about it and I'm not entirely sure congratulations are in order. What I mean is, I'm more than a little nervous about how my mother is going to take it. I hope you won't think me a toffee-nosed snob or something, but I fear Julia isn't the kind of girl she would approve of. You're jolly lucky your old lady's in Africa somewhere! By the time you introduce a girl to her it will be too late for her to protest."

Kit laughed easily with Adrian, but he was sad too. He was certain his mother *would* have loved the girl he wanted to introduce to her, but Georgina seemed determined to ensure he would have no reason to ever do that — unless Reverend Reddings somehow prodded her into writing to him after all. What was the expression? Hope dies last of all.

Chapter 6
Failing

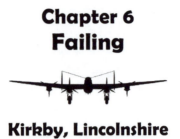

Kirkby, Lincolnshire
3 October 1944

Georgina sat in her tiny office fighting back tears. Miss Townsend had just reprimanded her for failing to maintain discipline in her classroom, adding in an ominous tone that unless she saw a dramatic improvement in Georgina's performance her assessment was going to be "below average".

That would have been bad enough, but the previous week Georgina had discovered that two of the boys she had particularly taken under her wing, the cheeky little Bertie and his freckle-faced friend Lew, had been lying to her. Bertie had claimed he was an orphan of the Blitz, while Lew had said his Dad beat him every night when he came home drunk from the pub. Neither story was true.

Miss Evans, who had been evacuated with the boys and knew both families well, had set Georgina straight. "Bertie's family is very much alive and well! In fact, his Mum has come to visit twice. As for Lew's Dad beating him, that's utter nonsense. He's a teetotaller and one of the mildest men I've ever met. The boys have been taking advantage of your appalling naivety and competing in making up these silly tales! Not only have they been laughing at you behind your back, but – and I'm sorry to have to say this to you Georgina, but it's better you know — the entire class thinks you're soft in the head!" Georgina felt a perfect fool.

The gloom of the rainy autumn day penetrated her office and she felt overwhelmed. It was nearly eleven months since Don had been killed. She had tried to refashion her life around being a teacher, but today that seemed like a cold and empty alternative. She could hardly make a career in education if she was no good at it!

Georgina had dreamed about being a teacher ever since she'd been in grammar school but, as she played absently with the pens on her desk, she reflected that she wasn't at all like her favourite teachers. They'd been so sure of themselves, kindly and understanding but firm and no-nonsense too. She let them pass in review mentally and concluded that she was no better than a rag-doll replica of her childhood heroines.

She glanced at Fiona's most recent letter that lay open on her desk. It mocked her. Fiona was a raving success: the girls she coached at tennis won all their matches, her debate team took first prize in the regional competition, the skit performed by her troupe was voted best by the entire school. Indeed, she'd already been offered a permanent position, while Georgina had no doubt that Miss Townsend couldn't wait to see the back of her.

Georgina didn't question that Fiona deserved her success. She could picture Fiona in the classroom: her lipstick and nail polish an immaculate bright red, her dark, bobbed hair bouncing with her vigorous and decisive movements, her tone cheery, her pose self-assured and her voice authoritative. The first paper aeroplane that flew would be firmly crushed in her fist and the "aircraft manufacturer" marched off to the headmistress on "charges." Fiona would have had no difficulty maintaining discipline at Kirkby Grange, and she would never have been taken in by the boys' lies either.

Fiona had willingly shared the secret of her success in her last letter. Georgina needed only skim down the page to find the phrase she was looking for: "*Don't try to be friends with your pupils, G. Don't care about being liked.*" (She had underlined "care" twice.)

But Georgina *did* care. She wanted to be the best-loved teacher in the school. Full of enthusiasm at the beginning of term, she'd used exactly those words in her first letter to Kit after coming to Kirkby Grange. That letter still lay inside her drawer, unsent, along with nearly a dozen others. Writing to Kit about what she was doing and learning, about her hopes and problems, had become second nature; so much so, that she hadn't been able to stop just because she'd decided to break off contact with him.

The decision not to communicate with Kit had not come easily, and several factors had fed into it. First, her mother had innocently reminded her that most of her pupils at the school, as evacuees, had had little or no contact with their families since the start of the war. "They have been forced at a very young age to stand on their own two feet and face life without the crutch of loving parents." Her mother hadn't meant to influence Georgina's relationship with Kit, yet her words had made her feel guilty for using Kit as an emotional "crutch" throughout most of this past year.

Then Fiona had responded to some mention of Kit with the words: "You can't have your cake and eat it too. You can't say you don't want a relationship with him, and then write to him twice a week."

The *coup de grace*, however, had been delivered by Philippa. Her advice about avoiding emotional involvement with aircrew and made it impossible for Georgina to blithely send her letters off to Kit as if they didn't matter. She forced herself to admit that she couldn't send and receive letters week after week without being sucked more deeply into a relationship. So, although she hadn't stopped writing them, she had stopped sending the letters she wrote.

The very fact that she didn't intend to actually mail the letter, however, made it all the more tempting to pour out her misery with the ink of her pen. Yet she stopped herself. She had no right to complain to *anyone* — not even a piece of paper — about a reprimand from Miss Townsend. The headmistress had been right. Her pupils had been loud and unruly, running about, shouting, and throwing paper aeroplanes at each other. She had completely lost control of them, and they had ignored all her pleas to quiet down and pay attention.

Instead of feeling sorry for herself, it was time to start facing facts. One of which was that she was not a born teacher. Indeed, she must seriously question if she could successfully finish training and earn her living in the profession at all. Maybe it would be better just to admit she'd failed?

No! She dismissed these defeatist thoughts vigorously and sat up straighter. Throwing in the towel now would be a betrayal of Don. He had been adamant about the importance of her completing training. "Your identity cannot be simply as my wife and dependent. You need to be someone in your own right." She was not going to quit at her first setback.

Lots of people had trouble learning their chosen trade. Just this past spring, she remembered, Kit had almost failed in flying training. Georgina started frantically opening the drawers of her desk until she found the thick bundle of Kit's letters tied neatly together with ribbons. They were in chronological order, and the letter she was looking for had been sent somewhere in the middle of his time overseas. She pulled a thick letter postmarked 21 April out of the bundle and opened it. Yes, this was it.

"*Dearest Georgina,*" Kit wrote, "*Forgive me for not writing last week. It was a bit fraught. I knew before I started flying training that only two out of every five trainee pilots actually earn their RAF wings, but like all young men I assumed I would be one of the lucky ones. It wasn't until I got here that I started to have my doubts. I think I mentioned that I was having a little difficulty getting a feel for things in the air. Did I also write that one instructor gave up on me entirely? I was assigned a new instructor two weeks ago. Unfortunately, he was just as frustrated with my incompetence as the first. I couldn't seem to do anything right. Because so many candidates have already washed out, we aspiring pilots have learnt that when the CFI (Chief Flying Instructor) takes the instructor's seat you're about to get the boot. That happened to me last Thursday.*

I'm sure you can imagine what a horrible moment that was for me. After being given this chance to rehabilitate myself, the thought of failing again was almost unbearable. When I saw the CFI waiting for me, my mouth went dry and I felt numb all over. It was as though sounds came from a great distance, and I was seeing things through a fog while everything happened in slow-motion. The CFI seemed particularly intimidating because he's not a South African Air Force instructor like the others, but a regular RAF pilot. He also has a whole fruit salad of medals on his chest and walks with a cane because he injured his knee bailing out of a Wellington.

Anyway, the CFI walked out to the aircraft with me, chatting cheerfully about the South African weather and the food and suchlike, which I suppose was meant to put me at ease, but didn't. We reached the aircraft, but rather than climbing aboard, he turned to me, nodded towards my tunic, and said, "Tell me about that DFM."

I was totally unprepared. I mean he had four times as many ribbons — everything but the VC, it seemed. I mumbled something about remaining with the pilot when he nursed a damaged Lanc back to England with wounded on board. He made me tell him the whole story and then asked if I'd ever been at the controls of a Lanc. I had to admit that Don let me do a little flying so I could help in an emergency.

You will hardly believe this — at least I didn't — but the CFI burst out laughing and declared. "That's probably your problem. You have to stop thinking of this flimsy, wood-and-canvas construction as in any way similar to a Lancaster. Except for both having wings, they are entirely different beasts. Think of this crate as a bicycle. Now show me some circuits and bumps."

So, we climbed into the Hawker Hart, I started it up, and taxied to the start of the runway. Just when I got the green light for take-off and was about to throttle forward, he called over the intercom: "Bicycle. Think bicycle" After that, *every* time he asked me to do something, he repeated the word "bicycle" before I could respond. By the end of an hour's flight, I wasn't only doing everything to his satisfaction, I was enjoying flying as I hadn't since those first couple of times back in the UK.

After landing the CFI climbed out grinning, and I later learnt that he gave a terrible rocket to the instructors for not taking the time to find the root of the problem. So it looks as though I'll be allowed to stay on the course for at least another few weeks. It's still a long way to go to my wings' exam, but now that I have the CFI on my side, I think I have a fighting chance. In retrospect I wonder if the South Africans wanted me to fail? Well, after that flight test, the CFI isn't going to let them do it *without a frightfully good reason!"*

Georgina caught her breath. When she'd first read that, she had been baffled as to why instructors might want to fail any trainee. Now, she knew it had been sheer racism.

She refolded his letter, returned it to the envelope, and slipped it back into its place in the pack. Rereading Kit's words brought him closer to her again. She realised just how much she missed *his* letters, missed hearing *his* news. Their correspondence had never been a one-way street. The letters had never been all about her.

Georgina keenly missed knowing what and how Kit was doing. Just last week her father had written to her that he'd run into Kit in York. He'd been pleased to discover that Kit spent his leave visiting cathedrals rather than going to nightclubs and equally impressed that he'd been traveling in the company of a sergeant. He'd assured her that Kit was "looking well", yet she remembered Don saying OTU training was intense and could be dangerous. Don had also told her it was where a pilot selected his core crew and had explained the importance of crew chemistry.

Don had been willing to die for his crew, and Georgina did not doubt that they would have done the same for him. Kit had been explicit in saying he *should* have died in Don's place. Now Kit had teamed up with four other young men and they were bound together by that same loyalty. How had Shakespeare worded it? *We few, we happy few, we band of brothers, for he who sheds his blood with me this day, shall be my brother....* She felt a stab of sadness to think that she knew nothing about the young men who were now Kit's 'brothers.' It was as though she had lost something of Kit to them, as if he had distanced himself from her.

The need to write to Kit seemed so overwhelming that Georgina tossed aside her earlier resolutions. She found some clean writing paper and yanked the top off her pen. Then she stopped herself. What was she doing? After six weeks of silence, she couldn't just write! A letter out of the blue would only confuse and upset him at a time when he needed to concentrate on training. Just because she desperately wanted to be in touch with him was no excuse to upend his life again. What was it her father had said his letter? "Kit's a very fine and sensitive young man, Georgina. It would not be right to toy with his emotions."

No. The decision not to correspond with Kit had been correct. The break was necessary to protect them *both* from becoming more deeply attached to one another. It wasn't about misleading Kit (as Fiona thought) or playing with his emotions (as her father implied). It was sheer self-defence, as Philippa had understood so well. She couldn't deal with losing the man she loved again, so she mustn't fall in love in the first place. She could not allow herself to feel the same way about Kit that she had felt about Don. And the only way to ensure *that* didn't happen was to keep her distance — at least until the war was over. Maybe then, if he still wanted her, if he was still alive....

She made herself return the bundle of Kit's letters to the lower drawer, berating herself mentally: "Focus on your profession, G. You're failing as a teacher. You can't maintain discipline in the classroom. Your pupils lie to you for fun. You are likely to get a bad assessment. You can't afford to start up a hazardous relationship. It's time for you to concentrate on your own life and your own goals. How are you going to turn things around here at Kirkby Grange?"

For a second she felt close to tears again, but she fought them back. She was tired of crying, tired of feeling sorry for herself, and tired of feeling helpless. Obviously she had made mistakes. Miss Townsend considered her a foolish traitor to her class, while Miss Evans thought she was a spoiled and naïve "do-gooder." They were united in thinking she was incompetent and more trouble than use. But there was no reason why she couldn't learn — just as Kit had learned to think "bicycle" in that training aircraft. If only, rather than judging her negatively, someone would give her a few tips the way that Chief Flying Instructor had helped Kit....

Inspiration struck. She would write to Kit's mother! It sat awkwardly with the decision she'd just made, of course... yet he'd spent that week with her parents and had apparently been happy enough to go for dinner with her father in York. She could send the letter via the Colonial Office since there was only one District Officer in Calabar, Nigeria. She would tell Mrs Moran candidly what a mess she had made of everything and ask for her advice. Because it took weeks for letters to reach Nigeria, she supposed any reply Mrs. Moran made would come too late for this term, but Georgina didn't think anything could salvage her reputation with Miss Townsend or Miss Evans anyway. It would be enough if she had a letter before the start of next term, when she would go to a new school and be able to make a fresh start. Besides, simply writing everything down would help her put things into perspective. Last but not least, Kit's mother might send news of Kit and mention to him that she had written.

Georgina turned to the fresh sheet of paper in front of her and addressed it to Mrs Moran. She opened her letter by introducing herself and apologising for her impudence in writing to a stranger. She explained how she, Georgina, had come to know and admire Mrs Moran through Kit's descriptions of her. She hoped that Mrs Moran wouldn't mind helping her a little as she struggled with mastering their common profession. The words flowed easily as she pictured Mrs Moran in her head. Her mental image was based in part on the photographs Kit had shown her, but even more on what he had written and said. Georgina's Mrs Moran exuded love and acceptance combined with an appreciation of music and literature and a down-to-earth sense of humour.

As she wrote, Georgina lost track of time. When she finished the long letter, it was already growing dark. She rushed to pull on her hat, coat and gloves before running down the stairs to her bike.

It was a gloomy evening with low hanging, threatening clouds. Georgina hoped it wouldn't start to rain during her half-hour trip to Kirkby village. Her coat wasn't waterproof, and she regretted for the umpteenth time not bringing her ancient oilskins from home. Nowadays nobody had new clothes anymore, so who would notice the ripped-out seams under the arms?

The darkness was closing in on her. Even in peacetime country roads were poorly lit, but the blackout meant that no light shone from the farmhouses along the route either. Their dark silhouettes increasingly became lost in the rising mist. The light on the bicycle was useless, and the inevitable happened: Georgina hit a bump or a stone and the bicycle jolted so sharply that she lost her balance and toppled over. She wasn't so much hurt as unnerved by the fall. She picked herself up, dusted herself off, and started pushing the bicycle along the side of the road, afraid to ride it any further.

She had a second fright when a car barrelled up the centre of the narrow road towards her, apparently unable to spot her in the gloom. In panic, she jumped to the side. The ditch fell sharply away from the road, causing her to fall again. As she got to her feet, she stared after the disappearing car in anger and frustration. The number plate identified it as USAAF, and the driver hadn't even slowed down to ask if she was all right! Straightening her coat and skirt, all she could do was continue to plod on, pushing the bicycle.

At the sound of another car approaching from behind her, she moved quickly off the road long before it could reach her. She stopped and turned to watch it pass by. About five yards beyond her, it screeched to a stop and backed up. The window rolled down and a male voice from inside the vehicle asked, "Aren't you Philippa Wycliffe's roommate?"

"Well, yes," Georgina admitted, trying to see into the car. The driver had leaned across the front seat to roll down the passenger window, but he was too deep inside for her to make out anything but a pale blur under what might have been a peaked cap. "Who are you? Do I know you?" The warnings of a lifetime about not getting into cars with strange men buzzed about in her brain.

"Oh, we've met once or twice. I'm an old friend of Philippa's. What on earth are you doing walking along a country road in the dark? I could have hit you!" Georgina found his reproachful tone condescending.

"Well, it's too dark to ride the bike and I haven't got any other means of transport," Georgina told him pointedly. "I assure you I can manage."

"Don't be ridiculous." The driver's door swung open and a tall, lanky man with a lean, hawkish face stepped out. He was wearing RAF uniform and had three stripes on his sleeve, which Georgina found totally intimidating. "We can put the bicycle in the boot," he told her, and before she could find grounds to protest, he had done exactly that — although the front wheel was still sticking out and the boot wouldn't close properly. Then he came around to the passenger side and opened the door for her. Georgina docilely climbed in.

As he settled behind the steering wheel again, he asked, "Cigarette?"

She shook her head vigorously.

"Mind if I light up?"

"No, of course not."

He put a cigarette in his mouth and struck a match to light it. In the light of the flame, Georgina finally recognised him — and remembered their last encounter. She had arrived to find Philippa showing this officer the door, while he had been pressing his attentions under the influence of too much alcohol. Philippa had finally slammed the door on him and turned to Georgina indignantly declaring: "If they survive sixty-some ops they think they're demi-gods! Well, he can bedazzle and bamboozle the silly WAAF on his own station and call himself 'Steeplechase' or whatever the RAF have come up with, but he's just Yves to me!"

Georgina had been impressed by Philippa's fortitude and listened sympathetically as she expressed her outrage at his shocking behaviour. Now, as Georgina sat beside him on the dark, lonely road, she remembered with increasing discomfort all the things Philippa had said. "He's a very successful, very glamorous Wing Commander. CO of a squadron, DFC and Bar, DSO, and heaven knows what else. He's had more girlfriends than I can count! Fools all of them. No, Yves Gorel is the last man who's going to turn my head and add me to his collection of conquests!" Georgina had heartily approved of her attitude at the time.

But Georgina had since learned that Philippa wasn't quite as virtuous as she seemed that evening. In fact, Georgina had been discomfited to discover that Philippa was carrying on with a much older, married man. She had no idea how *far* Philippa had gone with him, but she showed no compunction about letting him take her out to the kind of expensive restaurants that mere mortals could not afford. Nor did she hesitate to accompany him to the theatre and concerts, either. By far the worst moment, however, had been when Georgina had come upon them snogging rather passionately on the sofa in the sitting room. Georgina had backed out red-faced. She wasn't sure Philippa had seen her, but it had embarrassed her deeply. It didn't help that the object of Philippa's attentions, aside from being old enough to be her father, had been identified by Mrs Kennedy as Sir Howard Edward Dean, a Parliamentary Under Secretary whose ATS driver took him about the countryside in a Rolls Royce.

The Wing Commander beside her shook out the match, darkening the interior of the car again and making Georgina uncomfortable until he switched on the engine. He put the car into gear and started driving much too fast for Georgina's comfort. It was several moments before he remembered to introduce himself. "I'm Yves Gorel, in case you've forgotten the name."

"Georgina Reddings," she answered.

"Thanks for reminding me." He tossed her a smile.

"Are you stationed near by?" Georgina asked cautiously, as the Wing Commander navigated the winding country road with undeniably impressive skill.

"Coningsby, if that means anything to you."

Georgina had heard of Coningsby, it was further away than East Kirkby or Woodhall Spa, but still here in east Lincolnshire. She made a vague reply of "oh, yes," before asking, "And you've known Philippa for some time you said?"

"Ever since she and my sister shared a room at boarding school. My sister is getting married in two days' time and half the country will be there, but I know Gwen — my sister that is — wants Philippa to come early. Philippa will be her only bridesmaid."

Georgina started to put two and two together. Philippa had mentioned that she would be away for several days starting tomorrow in order to attend her best friends' wedding. But she also remembered Philippa mentioning that Sir Howard was taking her out to dinner tonight. A thought occurred to her, and Georgina asked rather abruptly. "Wing Commander Gorel? Is Philippa expecting you?"

"No, not really, but she's to be Gwen's bridesmaid and doesn't have a car, never mind access to petrol, so I thought I ought to swing by and offer her a lift."

"Oh."

"Why?"

"I don't know. Maybe I'm wrong, but I thought she said something about going out to dinner tonight and taking the train in the morning."

"Going out to dinner? Tonight?" Yves looked over sharply and there was an edge on his voice that made Georgina think she would not like to be someone on his squadron when he was angry.

"Yes, but maybe I'm getting confused."

"Did she say *whom* she was going out with?" Gorel pressed her.

"No, of course not. She moves in vastly different circles."

"Meaning parliamentary circles, perhaps?" Gorel asked acidly, and Georgina registered that he knew, or at least suspected, what was going on.

Georgina shrugged helplessly and tried to diffuse the tension. "Everyone she goes out with seems glamorous to me. I'm a just a vicar's daughter, and an apprentice teacher."

"There's nothing wrong with either," Gorel informed her with unexpected gentleness.

When they reached Mrs Radford's house they found only the housekeeper, Mrs Kennedy, at home. Mrs Radford was seeing to a sick cow, and Philippa had indeed gone to dinner "with a gentleman friend." Gorel again asked for a name, and Mrs Kennedy replied, "Goodness me, sir! Do you think I'm a gossip? It's not my place to keep an eye on Miss Wycliffe's social life. I don't know who the gentleman was, I'm sure."

Gorel was evidently put out, but he collected himself quickly and turned to Georgina. "How about my taking you out to dinner? Maybe Philippa will be here when we get back."

Georgina was not the least bit happy with this proposal. She explained that she was very tired and pointed out that she was not dressed for dinner.

"You can change while I get your bicycle out of the boot," Gorel dismissed her objections.

"I really don't think... I mean, I'm not like Philippa —"

"Just what the blazes has Philippa been saying about me?" Gorel asked sharply.

"Oh, nothing."

"You do know that is the *most* insulting thing you could possibly have said?"

"Well, I mean, nothing bad, just that you were the brother of her best friend and that she'd been very keen on you as a debutante."

"*That* was certainly ages ago," Gorel noted caustically. "Come now, what's the problem? Why not let me buy you dinner?"

"It's nothing personal," Georgina tried to explain. "I haven't wanted to go out with anyone since my fiancé was killed. It's been less than a year."

"You're not going out with me. I'm buying you dinner. I plan to eat what's on the menu, not you."

Unable to find a reply to that, Georgina capitulated and said she'd go and change. Soon she was back in the car with Yves Gorel, who she rapidly discovered could be very charming when he wanted to be. He was the perfect gentleman with her, and people turned to follow them with their eyes, the girls often with a degree of jealousy. Yves cut a good figure in his tailored uniform with DSO, DFC and bar. Georgina understood perfectly that he was using her to find out more about Philippa's activities and feelings and tried not to betray her roommate in anyway. Yet no matter how hard she tried to resist the feelings, she found Yves' attentions flattering and uplifting. Such is the frailty of women, she concluded dolefully.

At roughly eleven o'clock he brought her back to the Radford house. Mrs Radford's car stood in the driveway and a Rolls Royce was parked in front. Yves insisted on seeing Georgina to the door, and although she offered her hand and then turned her back on him, he pushed in behind her. From the hallway, they saw the ATS driver reading a paperback in the kitchen. The girl glanced up and sprang to her feet at the sight of Yves' uniform. He ignored her, his eyes already focused on the open door to the sitting room. He moved swiftly and walked in, switching on the light as he entered. Sir Howard and Philippa were on the sofa together and sprang apart when the light shattered the romantic mood. Philippa had let down her hair and removed her shoes; Sir Howard had shed his dinner jacket.

"Yves! How dare you burst in here!" Philippa demanded.

"I just brought Miss Reddings home, and we thought we'd have a nightcap," Yves lied.

While Philippa's eyes shifted to Georgina standing helplessly behind Yves, Sir Howard indignantly spluttered, "Just who do you think—"

Philippa cut him off, unable to curb her own anger: "You beast! You've been using poor Georgina to spy on me!"

"I didn't come to spy on you. I came to offer you a lift to my parent's home tomorrow."

"Expecting to spend the night here, no doubt! I've made other arrangements."

"About the lift, or about whose bed you'll be sharing?"

"That's enough!" Sir Howard ordered in a voice steeped in authority. "You are out of order, young man—"

"Don't patronise me, Sir Howard! I'm not a 'young man' anymore. I'm an *old* man. One who's lost too many friends because you and men like you were too arrogant to negotiate with Germany in good faith in 1919, too selfish to prevent an economic collapse in 1929, and too stupid to stop Hitler *before* we got into this bloody war."

"How dare you!" Sir Howard puffed himself up into dignified outrage, "I'll have you—"

Mrs Radford swept into the room and demanded to know what was going on.

"This arrogant young man—" Sir Howard started to explain with a dismissive gesture in the direction of the RAF officer.

"Wing Commander Gorel DSO—" Gorel started to introduce himself.

"I don't care who either of you are!" Mrs Radford forestalled further explanation. "Both of you get out of my house! Now!" She pointed to the front door, and with surprising docility both men filed outside. For a moment Georgina could hear their angry, albeit lowered, voices outside. Then Mrs Radford began lecturing her lodgers about taking advantage of her hospitality and disrupting the entire neighbourhood. She threatened that if anything like this happened again, she would throw them both out.

Outwardly subdued, Philippa apologised, assured her nothing like this would happen again, and announced that she was going to bed. Georgina followed her up the stairs to their attic room. There Philippa turned on Georgina and asked how Yves had wormed his way into the house. After she explained, Philippa drew a deep breath and declared: "You are too naïve for words, Georgina, but I know Yves can be very persuasive, so I don't blame you. He's a beastly man."

They left it at that, but as Georgina climbed into bed she found herself sympathising far more with Yves than with Sir Howard. Or was she just soft on anyone wearing RAF blue? No, she concluded. Sir Howard was married. If anyone was using anyone else, it was he. Yes, he was attractive in the way a mature man can be — particularly dressed, as Sir Howard always was, in flawlessly tailored three-piece, pin-striped suits and clothed in the aura of power. But naïve as everyone seemed to think she was, even she could see that the politician was only playing with Philippa.

Georgina remembered how her father had expounded on the connection between sexual and political power in the minds of men. She hadn't quite understood what he was talking about at the time, but it all seemed to make sense now. Sir Howard wanted the much younger and stunningly attractive WAAF officer not because he cared about her but because she was a symbol of his own virility. Based on her father's thesis, he needed a visible symbol of sexual power in order prop up his political position. Yves, on the other hand, was desperately in love with Philippa — or so it seemed to Georgina. It seemed odd, she reflected, that someone as savvy and wise as Philippa couldn't see both men for what they were.

Chapter 7
Fog

RAF Moreton-in-Marsh (OTU)
October 27, 1944

The eight crews of B-Flight were alerted for a night training exercise. At the briefing they were told they were to fly across Wales almost to the Irish coast, then turn and fly south past Land's End, before making a third turn, this time east into the channel, and finally, when level with Bournemouth, they were to turn inland and return to base. This being a moonless night, flying over the blackened landmass of England and Wales as well as over the sea, while navigating through a series of turns, made for an exercise which replicated operational conditions — except for the availability of the navigational aid known as Gee on the entire flight and, of course, the lack of enemy action.

The total route was 677 miles, shorter than most operations against targets inside Germany, but the weather looked set to be all too authentic. The forecast threatened gusty winds and decreasing visibility, and while the clouds already reported over Ireland and Cornwall were not expected to reach the station before all aircraft had returned safely, Moran knew from experience just how unreliable weather forecasts could be. Then again, the estimated flying time was just three hours and forty minutes, and conditions were excellent for take-off.

Sunset was 17:42 and 'start engines' was 17:45, which meant it was still daylight when Moran's crew were dropped off beside the familiar Wellington, P-Peter. They were fully kitted up in three pairs of gloves — silk, wool and leather — and double-thick socks inside flying boots as well as Irvine jackets. Already chilly on the ground, at the designated flying altitude of 15,000 feet it would be bitterly cold. The modest cockpit heating system might keep the four crewmen in the nose from freezing, but Osgood in the tail turret would need all the layers of his padded clothing.

Moran led the way up the ladder and into the aircraft with Peal right behind him, lugging his heavy case full of navigational equipment. Each man settled into his respective position and started pre-flight checks. In the absence of a flight engineer, who would not join the crew until they flew the four-engine "heavies," Babcock stayed in the cockpit to go through the checks with Moran. They started their engines on time, but Moran noted that Forrester had already eased out of his dispersal and was taxiing toward the head of the runway. Forrester liked being first in everything.

Moran was fourth for take-off. The green light flashed at him, and he took his feet off the brakes to allow P-Peter to start rolling down the runway towards the lingering sliver of salmon-coloured sky. When the air speed indicator read 120 mph Moran pulled back on the control column and the Wellington gracefully took to the air. He switched off the navigation lights and at 135 mph retracted the undercarriage. Beneath their feet the wheels clunked into position.

As on operations, all aircraft involved in this exercise flew independently of each another. Formation flying was impossible in the dark with aircraft that doused their navigation lights shortly after take-off to avoid being seen by enemy fighters and anti-aircraft. Instead, each navigator had responsibility for plotting the course and correcting as necessary. There was no "follow-my-leader" night flying in Bomber Command either in training or on operations.

Although visibility was good on the ground and at cruising altitude, a layer of high cloud blocked out the stars above. The horizon was only faintly discernible, and the blackout rendered the ground featureless. Moran depended almost entirely on instruments for flying.

After roughly twenty minutes of flying in complete silence, Moran started to worry: this particular exercise tested the skills of the pilot, navigator and wireless operator, but the gunner and bomb aimer were basically idle. It would be easy for Osgood and Babcock to start daydreaming. Moran didn't want them forming that habit because it would be deadly on operations when survival depended on seeing the night fighters before the night fighters saw them. Switching on his microphone he advised: "Pilot to gunner and bomb aimer: Look for other aircraft. They're out there. You've got to learn to see them in the dark. Report anything you see to me."

"Aye-aye, sir," Osgood answered promptly, followed by a less enthusiastic "All right, Skip," from Babcock.

Partly because he had no flight engineer yet and partly from habit, Moran kept his eyes on the fuel gauges. It was good habit. Operational sorties could take them to the very limit of their aircraft's range and fuel leakage or excessive consumption could be fatal. The sooner he knew about a possible fuel problem, the more options he had to resolve it. Training drummed this in by only allocating a moderate buffer beyond what was necessary for the scheduled flight. But Moran also used fuel consumption to estimate progress and help him know roughly where they were in his mental map. He always compared his estimates to those of the navigator, who he'd instructed give him an ETA to the first turning point every ten minutes. He wanted Peal to develop the habit of confirming their position frequently and regularly.

After they had been flying for roughly forty minutes, Peal reported: "Navigator to pilot: the wind appears to be increasing from the west. We're three minutes behind schedule."

Moran increased engine power, and the Wellington vibrated more intensely as it increased air speed. It almost seemed to be whining ominously.

Shortly afterwards, the intercom clicked on again. "Bomb aimer to pilot: aircraft off our port bow."

Moran's first assumption was that he was overtaking F-Freddy, that had taken off immediately before them, but then Babcock added. "He's flying south, Skipper! It must be Forrester or Crowley."

"Pilot to rear gunner: Can you confirm?"

"Gunner to pilot: Yes. It's Forrester all right. He just flashed his letter at us."

Moran could picture the Australian grinning and saying something rude about laggards, but he didn't care.

"Navigator to pilot: 60 seconds to turning point."

They made the turn and started flying across the wind. It buffeted them, making straight and level flight difficult. Moran started weaving gently, both to replicate operational conditions and because it reduced the strain. Below them, a thin layer of cloud slowly moved in to obscure the sea. The white, breaking crests of the waves that had relieved the utter darkness were gently blotted out until the men on P-Peter found themselves encased in mushy darkness. Peal fed Moran course adjustments at regular intervals to compensate for being blown eastwards.

"Pilot to gunner: Any sign of other aircraft?"

"No, sir."

"Pilot to wireless operator: Are you picking up any signals?"

"Ah, do you want to hear Irish music?"

"Very funny, Terry!" Peal noted sarcastically.

"I don't know. It might help me stay awake," Babcock suggested.

"No natter on the intercom," Moran reminded them. Silence descended until Moran asked a few minutes later, "Pilot to navigator: what's our ETA to the next turning point?"

"Another twelve minutes, sir."

Moran's nerves were on edge. He told himself it wasn't anything rational, only the result of similarities to his last operational flight: the high winds, the sense of being alone in the night sky. He mentally derided himself for being clapped out. He needed to master his nerves — NOW. Then again, the weather forecast had been iffy at best, and the increasing winds were driving the bad weather before them faster than originally anticipated.

Moran remembered one night during his first operational tour when, returning from a raid on Dortmund, they'd found England blanketed in fog. Landing had only been possible using SBA (Standard Beam Approach), which was essentially an audio aid that guided pilots to within a couple of hundred feet from the start of the runway with sound signals. It was extremely difficult to use, and pilot after pilot had lined up on the runway too high or too late. That meant that at the last moment they aborted and went around again, and all the while other returning aircraft stacked up above them, waiting their turn and using up fuel. When their fuel gauges registered almost empty, Don diverted to an airfield fitted with FIDO. Officially "Fog Investigation and Dispersal Operation," FIDO was installed at only a few of the airfields in East Anglia and Lincolnshire. It consisted of petrol pipes pierced with holes that lined both sides of the runway. When turned on, the petrol spewed from the holes into the air like water from a punctured hose and was then ignited to burn off the fog in the immediate vicinity. Landing in a tunnel carved out of the fog between columns of flame was not a very comfortable experience, but it had saved their lives. Three of the station's aircraft had crashed in the fog, and the toll at other stations had been equally high. More aircraft had been lost that night to fog than to enemy action.

Peal called another course adjustment and Moran checked fuel consumption. They had just passed the half-full mark. That was as it should be. The last two legs of their flight were the shortest. But turbulence was becoming more noticeable, making it harder hold course and altitude.

"Navigator to pilot: Five minutes to next turning point."

It would be good to get the wind behind them, Moran told himself. If only it weren't also blowing the clouds eastwards. The cloud cover stretched as far as he could see in all directions now.

They reached the turning point and swung onto an east-by-northeast course that took them up the English Channel. Moran instructed Tibble to listen for more radio activity as they approached the busy port cities of the south coast. He didn't expect anything particular; he just wanted to keep Tibble focused. To his surprise, only moments later Tibble's voice crackled over the intercom: "Wireless operator to pilot: Met is reporting low cloud and decreasing visibility all across the West Country."

Damn it. "Pilot to wireless operator: how low? What's the ceiling?"

"Twelve-hundred feet but deteriorating, sir."

"Pilot to navigator: ETA to next turning point?"

"Thirty minutes, sir."

They droned onwards, relying on instruments until Peal called up the course change to put them on their last and shortest leg. If Peal had plotted their position correctly, they were less than fifty miles from Moreton-in-Marsh. It was now 20:55 and they had been flying for a little more than three hours. Based on Moran's mental calculations, they had roughly another fifty-five minutes of fuel left. That left them a buffer of about 40 minutes; but if that cloud cover sank too low....

"Pilot to wireless operator: What's the latest weather?"

Tibble answered nervously, "Patchy fog developing in the valleys, sir."

Moran was increasingly grateful for those three practice landings on SBA. His hands were sweating inside his three pairs of flying gloves. He took one hand off the control column and flexed it open and closed several times to try to relax his muscles. He repeated the procedure with the other hand. Then he drew a deep breath and descended slowly until he was skimming the tops of the clouds at 5,500 feet.

He levelled off, hesitant to enter the cloud. At least up here he could see a horizon. He could not fly above the muck forever, though. They had less than 45 minutes of fuel left. They were going to go through that cloud one way or another — controlled or uncontrolled. The sense of "visibility" and safety he had above the cloud was an illusion. Still, irrationally, he clung to it.

"Wireless operator to pilot: I'm picking up a lot of chatter from the Marsh, sir. Aircraft have been diverted there from Honeybourne. It sounds like Honeybourne is closed due to a prang."

"Thank you, wireless operator." Moran checked his watch. It was now 21:07. He was three minutes from Moreton-in-Marsh. He ordered Tibble to contact Flying Control and report in. He found himself checking the fuel gauges again and made himself stop: they still had a buffer of forty minutes flying time left.

"Wireless operator to pilot: Aircraft landing at the Marsh are on SBA. There are six aircraft ahead of us."

"Roger." Just one minute behind schedule, at 21:11, they were in the circuit at Moreton-in-Marsh. Moran throttled back and adjusted the fuel mixture to reduce consumption. He tried to do the maths in his head but found he could not concentrate fully. Still, a crude estimate gave them fifty minutes of fuel if he maintained a lean mixture. That should be more than enough.

Moran was given orders to orbit the airfield at 4,000 feet. At that altitude they were in the muck and blind, with other aircraft circling below and, presumably, above them. Moran's neck and shoulders were starting to cramp, and his calves were aching. He wriggled to loosen his shoulders, but there was little he could do for his legs.

The tension wasn't confined to his body; he could feel it like static in the air around him, and in the uneasy dipping, lifting and tipping of the aircraft as the rest of the crew shifted their positions. Babcock, in particular, couldn't seem to lie still up in the nose. He was probably trying to see something — anything — around them. Moran feared any unexpected sound or sight might ignite panic. He had to do something to defuse the tension. "Pilot to crew. We're over the Marsh and the airfield is open, but there are quite a few aircraft stacked up and all have to make an SBA approach. That takes time. I'm going to turn on the intercom so you can hear the communications with Flying Control. That way you aren't left in the dark about our progress."

They all listened as F-Freddy started an SBA blind approach into the airfield, and heard the pilot, Sergeant Crowly, abort after breaking out of the cloud already halfway down the runway but still two hundred feet above the ground. Moran kept his eye on the clock and noted it took Crowly four minutes to line up on the runway again. Moran looked at the fuel gauges. Even at only 100 mph and on a lean fuel mixture, he calculated that they were now down to forty minutes of fuel, and they still had F-Freddy and three other aircraft ahead of them.

O-Oboe reported in and was ordered to circle above him. Moran recognised the voice of the pilot; it was Sergeant Walter Perry — a nice bloke, whom Moran found congenial. Perry, sounding less calm than usual, reported that he was very short of fuel. Flying Control answered that all the aircraft were running low on green stuff, and he must wait his turn. Moran hoped that Perry had remembered to adjust the fuel mixture. It would be so easy to forget about that in a situation like this and without a flight engineer. In these conditions a pilot had his hands full just flying without worrying about the engines. Moran only remembered the latter because for much of his RAF career he'd been responsible for the engines instead of the flying.

F-Freddy touched down safely on its second attempt, and V-Victor was cleared to land. The stacked-up aircraft were told to descend five-hundred feet. Moran was now fourth for landing and circling at 3,500 feet.

At this rate that was roughly 15 minutes away. They'd be down to just 20 minutes of fuel, which was cutting it a bit fine. Hopefully, nothing would go wrong—

Even as the thought hung in Moran's mind, an explosion ripped through the air, shaking the aircraft like flak. Instantly a red glow started to spread under the cloud layer below them.

"My God! What was that?" Babcock cried out in alarm.

"V-Victor, I believe," Moran told him emotionlessly, as he tried to remember who had been flying V-Victor. He had a horrible feeling it had been Pilot Officer James, a likeable and conscientious young pilot. His own throat became parched with fear. This was a nightmare, and it was only getting worse. Yet the worst thing would be to show any nerves to his crew.

A female voice came crisply over the intercom. "This is Moreton-in-Marsh Flying Control! The airfield is closed. Repeat: the airfield is closed. All aircraft divert to Stanton Court. Repeat: all aircraft divert to Stanton Court."

Peal promptly provided a course. He had obviously anticipated the possibility of diverting; Moran made a mental note to praise him for that — if he had the chance. Stoically, he turned onto the new course, careful to maintain altitude. He had aircraft above and below him all going to the same destination. Stanton Court was 27 miles away; sixteen minutes flying time.

As soon as Stanton Court Flying Control came on the radio, Moran realized the situation here was worse that at the Marsh. This OTU had also had a night exercise and three of their aircraft were in the circuit already. Sergeant Pilot Perry in O-Oboe again reported he was extremely short of fuel and requested priority landing. Again, he was denied.

On ops, Moran remembered, they were told that if they could not land safely, they were to point the aircraft towards the North Sea, put it on autopilot and then bail out. But bailing out in zero visibility had its own dangers. Moran knew of one crew that had been forced to this extreme, but only six of the seven men survived the jump; the wireless operator was killed when he broke his neck colliding with something in the fog. It might still be preferable to crashing, but he was also aware they were too far from the sea for the aircraft to make it on autopilot. It might crash into a farmhouse, a village or town. Moran couldn't bring himself to take that chance.

One of the Stanton Court aircraft made an SBA landing, and Moran had just descended another five hundred feet when an explosion ripped through the sky and again the clouds turned a murky red. "That's not on the airfield!" Babcock exclaimed in alarm.

"Jesus! Do you think O-Oboe ran out of fuel and crashed?" Osgood asked anxiously.

"There's no point in speculating," Moran cut the discussion short, all too sure that Osgood was right. Perry. He dared not think about it. "Navigator: I want a course to Colerne. Wireless operator: tell Stanton Court to give our slot to someone else. Then put a Darky call out and see if you can raise Colerne." If his mental calculations were correct, they were down to just fifteen minutes of fuel, and it would take him the better part of that to reach RAF Colerne.

Moran was going against orders they'd all heard, and it surprised him that none of his crew voiced the slightest objection. Instead, the alacrity with which Peal and Tibble responded and the pitch of their voices underlined that the tension was becoming nearly unbearable. Moran knew he had to keep them occupied. "Tibble, what is the reported cloud base?"

"I'll check, sir."

"As soon as you have it, tell me, and then check again. Understood?" Moran was careful not to sound angry or upset. In his head he heard Don's voice; Don had never once been flustered or excited.

Less than a minute later Tibble nervously cried out: "Just four hundred feet, sir!"

"That's plenty of room, Tibble. Nothing to worry about." Moran lied. "Babcock. I'm on instruments. I need you to be my eyes. If you see anything that is about to kill us, give me a chance to save us by telling me which way to fly. No need for 'bomb aimer to pilot' in this situation. Just shout 'up', 'right', or 'left.' Understood?"

"Understood, Skipper." Babcock sounded calmer.

"Peal? Is the course still 165?"

"Yes, Skipper."

"Good. Here we go." Moran drew a deep breath and cautiously descended. Both fuel gauges were now in the red.

He broke out of the cloud at four hundred feet, but patches of fog crouched like puddles on the otherwise black landscape beneath him. He could not remember if Colerne was situated in a valley or more on a rise. He hoped the latter.

Tibble's breathless voice crackled through the intercom. "Skipper! Colerne has responded! They'll fire a flare and we're already cleared to land!"

"Babcock, watch for that flare," Moran responded, concentrating fully on not flying into the ground while simultaneously trying to spot somewhere to put the crate down safely if he had to. That was a fantasy. In this darkness he couldn't see the contours of the land, let alone ditches, streams or stone walls — all things that would shatter an aircraft flying at 75 mph. Anyone inside would be turned into unrecognisable lumps of muscle and bone. He could not reduce speed further without stalling, however, unless he lowered the flaps and undercarriage. If he lowered both, he could reduce the stalling speed to 65 mph, but at the price of increasing fuel consumption and delaying their arrival at the airfield.

"Flare!" It was Babcock. "Ten degrees to starboard, Skipper."

"Got it!" Moran corrected his course slightly as a flare path lit up the darkness. It wasn't exactly clear. A light mist clung to the ground blurring the lights, but he could see the path of darker grey between the fuzzy lines of light. Even as he lowered the undercarriage, he ordered, "Crash positions, everyone."

Babcock scrambled back up into the cockpit and strapped himself in just as they cleared the perimeter fence. Moran was too high, and he side-slipped to the left and then the right to reduce altitude before putting on full flaps. By then, he'd used up half the grass field that served as a runway. He had to stall it or go around again. He didn't have the fuel to go around again. He throttled back and dropped the Wellington onto the ground. It protested loudly by creaking and screeching, and it bounced up twice before kindly deciding to stay on the ground.

They were hurtling toward the end of the runway, and Moran frantically tried to apply the brakes equally, terrified of yawing violently or putting a wing in and cartwheeling. At the last minute, he swung hard onto the perimeter track, heard a crash and felt a jolt as the tail hit something. Probably the Chance Light. "Osgood? Are you all right?"

"Yes, sir — but we just lost the port tail plane"

His first prang, Moran registered. He was bound to get a red endorsement in his logbook for that, but at the moment he didn't give a damn. He focused on taxiing down the perimeter track toward the signalling ground crew. They directed him to a dispersal point and motioned for him to cut his engines. He gladly shut them down and breathed in the silence.

It was a moment before he could summon the energy to take his feet off the pedals. He was only now conscious of how stiff he was.

Behind him Peal remarked in his precise Oxford accent, "Well, that was a sobering experience."

"And no one was even shooting at us!" Tibble added.

They all laughed, and that felt good.

Moran released his straps and unclipped the oxygen mask. His face was rubbed raw. Using the handle riveted over the control panel, he pulled himself out of his seat. It hurt to straighten up. "I have to report to Flying Control, but the rest of you can —"

"We'll wait for you, Skipper," Peal cut him off, seconded by a murmur of assent from the others.

As Moran dropped onto the tarmac, a Flight Sergeant appeared out of the darkness. "Any damage besides the tail plane, sir?"

"Not that I know of, but if you can find any fuel left in the tanks you can drain it into a thermos and give it to me as a souvenir."

The Flight Sergeant laughed appreciatively and gave him a casual but sincere salute.

Moran made his way to the tower and up to the first floor to report to the Flying Control Officer. The tower was darkened, of course, but he identified a Flight Lieutenant by the faint light of the instrument dials. He appeared to be the most senior officer present. Moran saluted.

"Are you the pilot of the Wellington that just landed?"

"Yes, sir."

"Where were you supposed to land?"

"Moreton-in-Marsh, but another aircraft crashed on landing, and we were told to divert to Stanton Court. Unfortunately, aircraft were stacked up there as well, and one went in full bore, so I thought I'd look for someplace less crowded."

"Yes," the Flight Lieutenant replied. "In the last hour, a total of three aircraft have crashed, another two have pranged on landing, and one crew has bailed out. Given you got down safely and saved lives by reducing the queue at Stanton Court, I don't think you need to worry too much about that tail plane. We should have it repaired for you by the morning anyway."

"Thank you, sir. Do you think we might be able to spend the night here?"

"Of course. The squadrons are on the Continent and the messes are nearly empty. In your shoes, I could do with a stiff drink."

"Thank you, sir." Moran responded automatically, but he was thinking it would be better to have a drink or two together as a crew. They couldn't do that if they went to their respective messes. He decided to ask, "Could you recommend a nearby pub? Three of my crew are sergeants."

"I can do better than that. I'll lay on transport and a driver for you. Just wait out the front. It won't take five minutes."

Twenty minutes later, they found themselves comfortably seated before a blazing fire in the *Black Horse*. They were still in flying kit and their arrival aroused the curiosity of the landlord, who wasn't used to bomber crews, but he made them welcome, offering to find them a bite to eat despite the late hour.

It was warm enough for them to open their flight jackets, unwind their scarves and peel off their layers of gloves. Adrian bought the first round, including a double whisky for Kit. The others modestly stuck to beer.

As the alcohol flowed, their tongues loosened. Stu was the first to admit, "I was a bit worried up there, Skipper."

"That makes two of us," Kit quipped back.

"Five!" The others corrected almost simultaneously, and they all laughed.

As the laughter faded out, Terry asked shyly, "Have you been in a situation like that before, sir?"

"Not as skipper, but bad weather is something we'll have to contend with. Ice, electrical storms, high winds, cloud and fog are all likely to be encountered at one time or another. Which is why, Terry, I'd like you always to be on top of the weather."

"I'm sorry, sir—"

"That wasn't criticism, Terry. You did an outstanding job tonight. You all did," Kit added looking around the table somewhat unnerved by the way they were hanging on his words. "Every exercise is carried out so we can learn from it. We can all learn from it. Including me. If you think I did anything wrong up there, I want to hear it from you."

"If you want to know what I think, Skipper," Stu started off at once, "if you'd done anything wrong up there, we'd be all be so much strawberry jam by now."

They laughed, but then Terry ventured another question. "Why did you ask for a Darky Call specifically to Colerne, Skipper? Wasn't Abingdon closer?"

"Abingdon is an OTU, and I thought it might also have aircraft stacked up. With the amount of fuel we had left in the tanks, flying in circles was not an option with a future in it. Colerne, on the other hand, is a day fighter station. I suspected they would have no aircraft airborne and counted on receiving immediate clearance to land."

Sergeant Perry's pleas for precedence still rang in Kit's ears. He would not want to be one of the Flying Control officers who had denied O-Oboe permission to land — assuming O-Oboe was one of the aircraft that had crashed. Then again, they had all been short of fuel, and if O-Oboe had been given precedence, who was to say that one of the others wouldn't have crashed? There was no simple answer to a situation like this. Kit bought the next round.

Stu seemed to be reading his thoughts, however, as he piped up with the next question. "Why don't they give us more fuel, Skipper? If we'd had more fuel, it wouldn't have been so dangerous."

"You bloody fool!" Nigel snarled, taking them all aback by his abruptly aggressive tone. Nigel had never forgiven Stu for not supporting him in the brawl, yet they had managed to remain polite with one another up to now. Before Kit could intervene, Nigel growled, "Do you think aviation fuel falls from the sky like rain or that it just bubbles up out of the ground? Every sodding gallon of that green stuff has to be brought from America or the Middle East by ship!"

"I know that!" Stu snapped back. "But —"

"You don't know an effing thing!" Nigel insisted raising his voice. "People like you don't have a flaming clue about what it's like for sailors, working four hours on and four hours off, while—"

"That's enough, Nigel!" Kit laid a hand on his arm.

Nigel shook off Kit's hand and continued furiously, "— while the bloody U-boats lurk unseen all around you until one of them pounces and that aviation fuel explodes under your backside—"

"Nigel! I said that's enough." Kit insisted.

"Don't any of you realize how many men die at sea to bring us that flaming fuel?" Nigel was very worked up.

Kit changed tactics. "You're right, Nigel. Practically every gallon of aviation fuel has to come through a gauntlet of U-boats. That why it's rationed and why training stations don't have unlimited supplies of it. Priority is always given to operational stations, and station commanders are expected to be miserly with it. Sometimes we'll be sent on sorties at the extreme range of our kites and there won't be any buffer, or not much. Even for less distant operational flights, aircraft are only issued enough fuel for the briefed route plus a moderate reserve."

"What's a 'moderate' reserve?" Adrian asked with a barrister's insistence on precision.

"We usually had roughly one hour extra flying time which could be stretched by flying on a lean mixture to ninety minutes or more."

"And that's what we had tonight?"

"No, we had about forty minutes," Kit admitted.

"That seems like a bad call when three aircraft crashed for want of fuel," Adrian observed frostily.

Kit agreed, but as skipper he felt he should not allow doubts about their leadership to take root. "Things would have been all right, if the weather hadn't closed in unexpectedly like that."

"Somehow," Terry murmured, "I never thought the weather might kill me. I always knew Jerry might get me, but not the English weather."

"Me neither," Nigel agreed. His jaw was set, and Kit could sense he was trying hard to get control of his emotions. "I volunteered for the RAF and for aircrew, so I *wouldn't* killed by the weather. I said to myself: in the RAF you won't find yourself paddling around with the ice floes after some flaming U-boat has sunk your ship out from under your arse. I thought, in the sky, it's a clean death. Here one minute and gone the next. None of the agony of slowly starving and freezing to death in a ruddy lifeboat." The young gunner's expression was forbiddingly grim.

"I just wanted to *be* someone," Terry spoke up again. "For once in my life I wanted to be someone special, someone other people looked up to."

This confession astonished Kit. Usually, men who volunteered for aircrew for the alleged glamour of it didn't fare well. Yet Terry had done well so far, especially today. Kit sensed a determination in him that would get him through anything. Maybe wanting to prove he wasn't worthless wasn't the same as being attracted to the glamour?

Terry's remark, or the alcohol and decompression from the tension of the flight, triggered a confession from Stu as well. "I fancied myself as a fighter pilot. One of the older boys from my church choir flew in the Battle of Britain. He's buried in the churchyard. It even says on his tomb 'One of the Few.' I heard he lasted something like two weeks on his squadron. Not very long." He sounded pensive.

"It was the Blitz that got to me," Adrian picked up the theme. "I was up at Oxford when it started, but when I came home for Christmas—" He shook his head. "London just wasn't the same. Smoke and dust hung in the air, and the whole city *smelt* different. It wasn't just the broken gas and sewage pipes or the smell of unwashed bodies on the buses and in the shops. It was more than that. I can't explain it exactly, the whole city smelt dusty, dirty and battered. You'd turn a familiar corner and suddenly be confronted by shattered buildings, broken glass and masonry, or wrecked vehicles surrounded by puddles of leaking oil. Sometimes dirty bandages and discarded clothes fluttered in the gutters, or dazed people stumbled around sorting through the rubbish for something to salvage from their former life."

Adrian shook his head. "So much has been written about how the Londoners 'took it' — and, of course, they did. But it hurt and it made us angry, too. At least it made me angry. What bloody right did the Germans have to blow up our city and destroy our way of life? What right did they have to disrupt our simple, peaceful pleasures — shopping, walking in a park, going to the theatre or out to dinner? What right did they have to shatter our homes, shops, workplaces and churches?"

"Or sink our ships!" Nigel lashed out again. "Submarine warfare is cowardly! They can't be seen or heard, and they don't attack warships — just innocent merchantmen. Bastards, that's what they are. Bloody bastards!" Clearly, Nigel had been hit hard and personally by the war at sea. Even Stu, whose relationship with Nigel had remained strained since the fight with Levesque, understood and looked both anxious and concerned, glancing at Adrian for guidance. Adrian looked at Kit.

"If you tell us what happened, Nigel, maybe we'd understand better," Kit prodded gently.

"Me brother." Nigel's voice almost broke. "Me older brother, who was more a father to me than that drunken bastard, who called himself me dad. Danny always looked out for us, worked extra jobs, hid the money so me dad couldn't drink it all away. January 1941 a U-boat got his tanker amidships." Nigel was not looking at any of them, just staring at a spot on the table and speaking in a tight, angry voice. "It blew up and went down in less than five minutes. Fuel all over the surface. Burning. Two lifeboats got away, but one caught fire and went down. The other managed to pull two men out of the water, but they'd swallowed too much oil already and were puking their guts out. Others were too badly burnt to be touched let alone manhandled inside the boat, and there were too many of them in it already anyway. They didn't have enough water or rations and it was freezing cold. When the sun came up, they saw icebergs on the horizon. And after that one by one they died. Miserably. From injuries, the cold, the oil-contaminated rations. By the time the Navy finally found them, only three were left. Danny wasn't one of them. His mate came to tell me about it, and that's when I decided I would bomb the effing hell out of Germany!"

Whatever the others thought, they nodded out of respect for their crewmate. Nigel downed what was left of his beer in a single guzzle, and Kit signalled the landlord to bring another round.

"What about you, Skipper? Why did you volunteer for aircrew?" Terry put the question to him, his eyes fixed earnestly on his skipper.

Kit shrugged. "I didn't like watching other men risk their lives, while I sat around safe. I felt I had to do my part or I wouldn't be able to look at myself in the mirror." It sounded to Kit like a propaganda newsreel, yet it was true.

"But surely you proved you were as good as anyone with your first tour as a flight engineer," Adrian was quick to note. "Why the second tour?"

"Was it because you wanted to fly?" Stu asked.

"Or command?" Nigel spoke up, his voice still strained but somehow calmer too.

Kit was in dangerous waters. He did not want to tell them that volunteering for flying training and a second tour of ops had been his ticket out of the humiliation and degradation of being posted LMF. He thought they would lose all respect for him if they knew that. Trust too. If he told them he'd refused to fly in November 1943, they might wonder if he would fail them at a critical moment in the months ahead. He opted for a half-truth instead. Shaking his head to Stu and Nigel's questions, he told them solemnly. "Nazism is based on racism. I detest racists and want to eradicate them from the face of the earth."

"Are you Jewish?" Stu asked surprised.

"No, but killing people because of their race is unchristian, immoral and horrifying." Kit's tone told his subordinates that the discussion was over.

"True," Adrian agreed, defusing the sudden tension. "I'll get this round." He pulled out his wallet as the landlord delivered their refills to the table.

When the drinks were distributed, Stu got to his feet, pint in hand. "I want to propose a toast." They waited expectantly. "To the best skipper in bomber command: Kit Moran!"

"I wouldn't —" Kit started to protest, but the others drowned him out as toasted him loudly with raised glasses.

By the time they returned to Colerne they were all blotto and giggling ridiculously at almost anything. Kit registered that he was no less sozzled than the rest of them, which he shouldn't be. Don had never been this drunk, he reminded himself — at least not in the presence of his crew.

And yet, as Adrian and he helped each other up the steps to the officers' mess, he thought maybe it wasn't such a bad thing either. This flight, the shared confidences, and the excess alcohol had pulled them together. That was a good thing. By the way Stu and Nigel had been holding each other up, he hoped that even that latent friction had been laid to rest as well.

Going into the circuit at Moreton the following morning chased the last fumes of alcohol and high spirits away. The burned-out wreck of V-Victor lay like a corpse beside the runway. Smoke also drifted up lazily from another crash site over the rise of the nearest hill in the direction of Stanton Court. The faces of the ground crew were marked by shock. This was a training station: they weren't used to losing several crews in a single night. "Good to see you back, sir," P-Peter's ground chief greeted Moran.

"Which crews bought it, Chiefy?"

"The crews of U-Uncle and O-Oboe were lost entirely; only the gunner and bomb aimer got out of the flames of V-Victor."

Moran knew he would never forget the sound of Sergeant Pilot Perry's requests for priority landing in O-Oboe.

Moran was yanked from his thoughts by the Flight Sergeant who added, "Uh, and, Pilot Officer Forrester is on jankers, sir."

"What?" Moran couldn't believe his ears. "Forrester? On charges? Whatever for?"

"Landing without a green, sir. Put his crate down after the airfield was closed. Used the other runway to avoid the fire engines and meat wagons on the main runway."

Moran nodded. He could sympathise. After all, Perry had followed orders and he and his crew had got the chop. If Perry had done as Forrester had, maybe he and his entire crew would still be alive.

At Flying Control, Moran was ordered to report to the Station Commander. There the adjutant asked him to wait in the anteroom. He could hear angry voices on the other side of the door. Abruptly, the door crashed open, and a red-faced Forrester stormed out. He seemed surprised to see Moran, but drew up long enough to say, "Glad to see you made it, mate!" before adding in a loud, furious voice over his shoulder, "No thanks to these buggers!" Then he was gone.

Moran was waved into the Station Commander's Office and saluted the Group Captain. The latter was as flushed as Forrester and one hand nervously played with a button of his tunic. Moran could see he was agitated, but he had little sympathy. He had sent them out knowing the weather was deteriorating, and he had not authorized extra fuel in case fog developed. He had consciously risked what had happened. The pressure to get crews trained rapidly fostered this kind of risk-taking, Moran supposed, and, as they had discussed last night, aviation fuel was a precious resource that should not be wasted. Even so, what harm would there have been in issuing a little more fuel under the circumstances?

"Well, Moran," the Group Captain opened in a hostile tone. "Just like Forrester, you disobeyed orders and simply did as you pleased."

"If that's the way you see it, sir." Moran kept his tone polite and correct, but there was no mistaking that he was not intimidated.

"What's that supposed to mean?" The Group Captain snapped back belligerently.

"Stanton Court was stacked up seven deep. With only fifteen minutes of fuel remaining, I made the decision to divert to another airfield. I don't regret my decision and I'm perfectly happy to tell the inquiry that. Sir."

The Group Captain gazed at him with a hard, hostile expression for a moment, but then seemed to change his mind. He shrugged and remarked, "All right. We'll leave it at that for now. But don't think this incident will be forgotten."

Chapter 8
Mistakes

Kirkby, Lincolnshire
Thursday, 16 November 1944

The discovery of three apples on her desk made Georgina smile. She inspected them carefully, but just like the first offering last Monday, they did not look worm infested. When that first apple had appeared she'd immediately assumed it was some sort of practical joke. She did not risk biting into it, but instead carefully cut it open. To her surprise, it had been perfect. After lunch, she'd announced to the class that she'd enjoyed it very much and thanked "whoever" had left it for her.

Then yesterday a sullen girl, whom Georgina had believed utterly uninterested in everything related to school, had offered to darn her stockings. That had been embarrassing on two counts: first, because Georgina had hoped no one would notice the little run in her black cotton stockings, and second, because she was perfectly capable of darning her own stockings. Yet Georgina recognised instantly that for a girl unwilling to risk being caught filching apples from someone else's orchard, skill with a needle was all she had to offer. Georgina accepted the gesture in order to make the girl feel useful and appreciated.

The incident also gave her an idea. At a time when clothing coupons were so short that they barely covered the acquisition of a single dress a year, Georgina had provoked jealousy at the teaching college and Kirkby Grange for having "so many frocks." A full wardrobe had become an unpatriotic crime. Miss Evans had gone so far as to insinuate that Georgina was either buying clothing coupons on the black market or forging them, neither of which was remotely true. Georgina had simply mastered the art of making her own clothes — with a little help from her maiden aunts.

At the end of the last war one of her father's unmarried sisters, Aunt Emma, had set up a dress shop. She started modestly with repairs and alterations, but as her confidence grew, she started to design clothes. Her sense of style won her a number of well-heeled clients, until the war put an end to this growing business. Aunt Emma retained her independence and avoided industrial conscription by specialising in tailoring officers' uniforms, but she hadn't lost her ability to design and sew. So, war or no war, she continued to share her designs with Georgina and had taught her niece how to sew. Georgina outfitted herself not only with modified hand-me-downs from her aunts but, using Aunt Emma's patterns, transformed old tablecloths, bedspreads, and raw silk pillowcases among other things into garments. She learned how to get the absolute most out of a yard of fabric, how to cannibalise two worn suits to make a new one, and how to make an old dress look new just by putting in a new pair of sleeves or adding a different collar, pockets or trim. Her outfits looked expensive but were all self-made, leaving Georgina's ration coupons for shoes, stockings, rain gear and other items that she could not make herself.

Up to now Georgina had used those sewing skills merely to satisfy her own vanity. Miss Evans' false insinuations, however, made Georgina realize she possessed skills that were especially valuable to girls from poorer backgrounds. She therefore suggested to Miss Townsend that she offer sewing classes at the weekends. To her surprise, the headmistress readily agreed, adding, "I must say, I hadn't expected such initiative of you, but that is a very good idea. You may start at once." It was the first word of praise Georgina had received since coming to the school and it made her think maybe she was going to succeed after all.

She had just started to collect her things to go to the last class of the day when the door crashed open and a breathless boy burst in without knocking. "Miss Reddings! Miss Reddings!" The little boy, in his short trousers and sweater, hung on the handle of the door catching his breath. "You're to report to Miss Townsend straight away, Miss!" He gasped out. "There's a telephone call for you!"

A telephone call? In the middle of the week? That couldn't be good news, Georgina thought as she hurried to the headmistress's office. Could her brother's ship have gone down? No, it would be all over the news if *HMS Illustrious* had sunk. But her father might have been in an accident, or her mother, or something could have happened to Teros or Hester. Or Kit... "Oh, God, no."

She reached the headmistress' office and burst into the anteroom almost as precipitously as the boy messenger. The door to Miss Townsend's office stood open and the headmistress waved her in irritably.

At a gesture from Miss Townsend, she closed the door behind her and advanced to stand in front of the headmistress' solid oak desk. Miss Townsend purred into the receiver in an uncharacteristically fawning voice, "She's here now, sir." With these words, she handed the receiver across the desk to Georgina, accompanied by the stage-whispered explanation, "It's the Parliamentary Under Secretary Sir Howard Dean."

What on earth could he want, Georgina wondered as she took the heavy receiver and put it to her ear. "This is Georgina Reddings."

"Thank goodness I was able to reach you! I've been trying to contact Philippa for two weeks. She's not taking my phone calls. The housekeeper and Mrs Radford both refuse to put me through to her — allegedly on Philippa's instructions. I'm most distressed, Miss Reddings. I must know what is going on. I expect you to give me an honest answer."

Bullying bastard, Georgina thought. "But of course, Sir Howard. Why would I ever deceive you?" Georgina's voice resonated with such angelic innocence that Miss Townsend rolled her eyes. Sometimes, it was useful to have been brought up a vicar's daughter, Georgina realised.

Sir Howard cleared his throat. "Quite. So, what *is* the matter with Philippa? Why won't she take my phone calls?"

"I'm very sorry, Sir Howard, but I *honestly* don't know." Georgina kept up her charade of 'sweetness personified,' "I agree that recently she *has* been acting strangely. I'm very worried about her myself, but I simply cannot explain her behaviour to you. I don't have any idea what the cause of it might be." Georgina might have adopted an artificially sweet tone of voice, but she wasn't being dishonest; she hadn't a clue what had got into Philippa of late.

A moment of dead silence answered her. Georgina could sense Sir Howard's frustration, but he could hardly call her a liar without being ridiculously rude. "Well. I suppose I'll just have to find someone else who *can* help me, then." He concluded in a huff. "Good day, Miss Redding." He hung up.

Georgina leant across Miss Townsend's desk to replace the receiver.

"Would you mind telling me what that was all about?" It was not a question.

"My fellow lodger in Kirkby Village has not been herself recently, and Sir Howard is worried about her."

"Sir Howard, a Parliamentary Under Secretary, takes an interest in your fellow lodger?" Miss Townsend sounded as though she thought she was being taken for a fool.

"Well, Philippa Wycliffe's father is an important financial backer of the Conservative Party, Ma'am. Philippa moves in much better circles than I do," Georgina explained, again striving to look demure and angelic.

Miss Townsend snorted and dismissed her with a wave of her hand.

Georgina hurried back to her class. It was past time for it to start and, of course, in her absence the pupils had run wild; she found total chaos on her arrival. Two boys were chasing each other around the room shrieking in delight. Several others were scuffling, and one boy had climbed onto her desk and was evidently imitating her to the delighted giggles of the rest. Getting things back under control took her full attention.

Only as she cycled home could she focus on Philippa again. Philippa had been irritable and terse for about ten days. At first, Georgina thought nothing of it. While Philippa had a temper, it usually flared up and died down quickly, so she was confident that Philippa would get over whatever was bothering her. When Philippa's bad mood stretched into a second week, however, Georgina became worried that something more serious might be afoot. Based on her experiences at school and college, Georgina suspected "boyfriend problems," and since Philippa's bad temper coincided with a notable absence on Sir Howard's part, Georgina concluded that Sir Howard's ardour for Philippa had cooled.

Today's phone call scuppered that complacent theory, which meant there had to be another explanation for Philippa's behaviour. As Georgina made her way along the country lane, her imagination started to run away with her. Remembering an incident in her father's parish, she wondered if Philippa might be pregnant. For a woman of Philippa's standing, such a development would be far more scandalous and catastrophic than for a farm girl, particularly if Sir Howard, a married man, were the father. She would be forced out of the WAAF for a start, and her reputation and marriage prospects would be ruined. Georgina knew she could never ask her roommate directly about something so delicate, but maybe she could coax Philippa into confiding in her?

She stowed her bicycle behind the house and entered by the kitchen door, determined to try to get Philippa to talk. Instead, Mrs Kennedy pounced on her with the alarmed exclamation, "Miss Reddings! Something's terribly wrong with Miss Wycliffe! She's on nights, as you know, which means she usually sleeps until about four pm, when she likes me to wake her with a cup of tea. But today when I tried to bring it to her, I found the door locked. I knocked and she growled — that's the only word I can use for her tone! — she growled at me to go away. When I told her she'd be late, she told me – a snarl it was this time — that it was shift change and she didn't need to be back at the Station until tomorrow morning. Which is all very well, I told her, but I still needed to tidy up, as I always do, before you come home. You can't imagine what she did next: she threw something at the door! A slipper or shoe, I think! I heard it thud! And then she, very rudely, told me to go away again." Mrs Kennedy was indignant.

"Oh, dear," Georgina hurried up the stairs to the attic. As the housekeeper had warned, the door was locked from the inside. Georgina knocked. "Philippa? It's me, Georgina. Please open the door."

Silence answered. She called louder and knocked more forcefully. "Philippa?"

Still no response. Georgina went back downstairs and reported to the housekeeper, asking "Where is Mrs Radford?"

"Oh, she's dealing with a case of colic at Highbourne. Could be gone all night she said."

"I'm...I'm afraid that Philippa might be sick or have hurt herself." Georgina's imagination had gone into overdrive, remembering tales of unwed mothers aborting their babies or killing themselves from shame.

"I'll call the carpenter." Mrs Kennedy responded with new vigour as she too acknowledged this was a crisis. "You keep trying to wake her," she ordered.

Half an hour later, the carpenter clomped up the stairs and hammered with his fist on the wood beside the handle to test it. To the surprise of all, this provoked an outraged curse from the other side of the door.

"Philippa? Are you all right?" Georgina called relieved yet concerned.

A groan answered her, followed by a thud and the sound of retching. "Oh God," Philippa's voice moaned.

"Let us in so we can help you, Philippa!" Georgina urged.

Shuffling approached the door from the inside and the carpenter, with a tip of his hat, withdrew discreetly. A moment later the key turned in the lock and the door was yanked open. Philippa stood swaying in front of them with her dressing gown gaping open and the smell of vomit wafting from it. "Oh, God!" she gasped. "I'm going to be sick again!" She turned away, cupping her hands in front of her face and vomited into them.

"Get her down to the bath. I'll clean things up." Mrs Kennedy directed.

Georgina put her arm around Philippa's waist to guide her down the stairs to the bathroom on the floor below. As she turned Philippa, she noticed two empty gin bottles on the floor. Well, that explained her state, Georgina registered. It also made her a little nervous — she'd never dealt with anyone suffering from such an excess of alcohol before.

In the bathroom Philippa barely managed to wash her hands before she collapsed beside the lavatory. She threw up into it, and then leaned back against the wall with a groan as Georgina pulled the chain. Georgina decided she had to get Philippa cleaned up since the smell was making her feel sick too. She helped Philippa remove her dressing gown and underwear. These she put into the tub and ran water over them to rinse away the worst of the mess and smell. Meanwhile Philippa tried to wipe herself clean with a flannel then dry herself off with a towel. In the process she stopped more than once, apparently dizzy. "My head!" she exclaimed. "It feels like it's been whacked by a propeller blade!" A moment later she groaned again, then remarked, "Now I know what they mean when they talk about hangovers."

Mrs Kennedy went by with the bucket and mop, "All cleaned up," she announced into the bathroom cheerfully.

"Could you put the kettle on?" Georgina called after her. Then she ran upstairs to fetch her own dressing gown. The latter was a little too small for Philippa's fuller figure, but better than nothing on a chilly night like this. With Philippa covered, Georgina persuaded her to come down to the kitchen for tea and toast to settle her stomach.

Philippa did not resist. She seemed content to surrender to Georgina's care. The edginess had transformed into something much heavier. Philippa seemed weary and aged, as if she were sixty-five rather than twenty-five.

In the kitchen the kettle's whistle softened to a whimper as Georgina and Mrs Kennedy settled Philippa by the stove with a cup of tea in front of her. Mrs Kennedy then excused herself. It was nearly eight o'clock and she had to get home. Georgina, although grateful for her help, was also glad to see her go. She now had a good excuse to ask Philippa what was wrong, and Philippa was more likely to open up if it was just the two of them.

Georgina put slices of bread in the toaster and margarine and jam on the table. Since she'd had no dinner, she helped herself hoping her example would encourage Philippa. It did. Philippa took a piece of bare toast and started nibbling on one corner of it.

"Sir Howard has been very worried about you," Georgina opened the conversation cautiously.

"Oh, really?" Philippa asked back listlessly.

"He rang me at Kirkby Grange today, hoping I could tell him what was wrong. He seemed very upset."

"Oh, I'm sure. It must have disturbed his social calendar, not having me at his beck and call," Philippa agreed indifferently. It would have been more in character if she'd spat this out as a snide quip, but she didn't. The words simply formed a weary statement of fact. It was as if Philippa wanted to snap but didn't have the energy.

Georgina reached across the table and laid her hand on Philippa's. "What is it, Philippa? Have you broken up with Sir Howard?"

"Broken up? With Sir Howard? Why should I do that? He's such a gentleman, such a perfect gentleman..." Her tone rang flat, mocking

133

almost, and then she added, with a vehemence that made Georgina flinch, "Not like that beastly Yves!"

Georgina was taken aback. Had the RAF officer done something really vile to earn Philippa's outrage? Had he pushed things too far? "Has Wing Commander Gorel done something?" Georgina asked, picturing a cruel letter, hurtful gossip or a public scene.

"*Done* something?" Philippa asked back in a tone of mock astonishment. "Yes, I suppose you could say that. Wing Commander Yves Gorel, the invincible, immortal "Steeplechase," DSO, DFC and bar did indeed *do* something — he attacked an Me109 with a Lancaster. A Lancaster against an Me109! Brilliant, what? I suppose you might say that's *doing* something."

"I don't understand," Georgina stammered, confused as much by Philippa's tone as by her words. Philippa sounded bitter and angry about something that Georgina would have categorised simply as an act of foolhardiness.

"Several crews reported that two Me109s attacked one of the squadron aircraft. One set the port outer engine on fire and then continued diving, but the second was still pumping lead into the wounded Lancaster, having already killed the rear gunner. Yves wheeled around and took his Lancaster in under this persistent Me109, and his mid-upper gunner managed to shoot it down. Terrifically valiant, of course — except that it made him a sitting duck for the second Me109. In the end both Lancasters went down. That was nine days ago. Some parachutes were seen, so it wasn't until last night, when I was on duty, that I learnt Yves wasn't one of the survivors. He was found burnt to a cinder in his cockpit."

The anger was gone. Philippa closed her eyes and leaned her head against the back of the chair, tears streaming down her face.

"Oh Philippa!" Georgina jumped up and went around the table to put her arms around the WAAF Officer. Those horrible days after Don's death came flooding back to her. Her sympathy was not feigned as she murmured, "I'm so sorry!"

Philippa answered by breaking down completely and sobbing miserably in Georgina's arms. "I thought — I thought," she gasped out between sobs, "I thought, if I just didn't let myself get *involved* with him — if I had someone else — if I called him names — I thought — it wouldn't *hurt* so much!" She broke down again, and all Georgina could do was hold her, feeling her pain so sharply she was close to tears herself.

After a few minutes, Philippa pulled away and wiped at her face with a tea towel. "I was such a stupid fool. Such an idiot!" She shook her head again and again, wiping her nose with the tea towel in between shakes of her head. "All I did was make it worse. I haven't just lost him, Georgina. For the rest of my life, I'll also feel guilty for being so beastly to him in his last months, when I could have been making him happy instead."

Long after Philippa had fallen into an exhausted sleep, Georgina lay awake in bed gripped by growing panic. Suddenly, chillingly, it was so all so clear: she was in danger of making the same mistake. She had been keeping Kit at arm's length to protect herself from pain. She'd told herself she didn't love him because she didn't love him the same way she'd loved Don.

With razor-sharp clarity she saw that didn't matter. She didn't love her mother the way she loved her father, or her father the way she loved her brother, or love any of them the way she'd loved Don, but that hardly meant she didn't love them. Each love was as unique as the object of love. She would never love anyone exactly as she'd loved Don, but to deny her love for Kit was absurd. She did love him, intently and powerfully — and he had a right to know.

"Oh, God," she prayed. "Don't take him away from me before I have a chance to tell him I love him!" She knew all to well that training accidents could be fatal. Why, just last week Philippa had told her — without betraying any details, of course — that several training aircraft had been lost on a single night due to an abrupt change in the weather. For all she knew Kit was among them, already dead. Oh, God, please not that!

The panic was increasing not easing. Georgina almost got out of bed to write a letter to Kit immediately but turning on a light would disturb Philippa. Besides, a letter would take days to reach him, days in which he might die. She couldn't risk it. She must ring him first thing in the morning. But she didn't have a telephone number. No matter, Philippa would be able to find it and pass it on to her — assuming Philippa was fit to work tomorrow. Georgina looked over at her snoring roommate and pleaded mentally: Please go on duty tomorrow! Please!

Chapter 9
Endings

RAF Moreton-in-Marsh (21 OTU)
16 November 1944

It was announced that Course 73 would end with a "gardening" — sea mine-laying — sortie. It had become increasingly common to allow crews still in OTU training to take part in operations of this type. The RAF leadership believed it built up morale and confidence in novice crews, while simultaneously taking some of the pressure off the remaining operational Wellington squadrons of Coastal Command. The risks to the crews were deemed minimal now that the Royal Navy had re-established firm control of the English Channel and the northern reaches of the Bay of Biscay.

Yet even if Bomber Command crews tended to view these operations as milk runs, they had their challenges all the same. For a start, unlike roads, railways, and canals, sea lanes looked identical to the geography around them. In the absence of visible surface features to help identify the target, precise navigation was essential. Furthermore, the actual "sowing" of the mines had to be undertaken from just 1,500 feet and at a steady speed of 180 mph. Although these two characteristics made it an ideal exercise for training navigators and pilots, the cost of the ordnance meant it could not be wasted either. Only the five best crews from Course 73 were selected; Moran and Forrester were among them.

The target was the approaches to the U-Boat pens at St. Nazaire, just to the South of Brittany. The distance was short, roughly four hundred and thirty miles, almost all of it over Allied-controlled territory, and the risk of German anti-aircraft fire arose only directly over the target. For Kit's crew, the operation had an added benefit: targeting Nigel's nemesis, the German U-boats.

The crew briefing was at 15:00, and they climbed out of the crew bus beside the weary but familiar Wellington P for Peter at 15:50. The sun hung low and golden in the Western sky, and the air was already chilly.

Moran's crew acted keyed up and even a little jittery. "Isn't it supposed to be good luck to pee on the tailwheel before take-off?" Babcock asked, heading in that direction. The others followed him.

Going up the ladder into the Wellington, Tibble stopped abruptly to ask Osgood if he had his lucky bosun's whistle.

"Right here in my pocket," Osgood assured him, patting the right breast pocket of his white flying suit.

"What about the coffee? Aren't we supposed to be issued a thermos of coffee each?" Peal asked looking around, as if expecting it to appear out of thin air. Hot coffee on operations was one of the perks of aircrew.

"Got 'em," Babcock indicated the heavy canvas bag weighing down his right arm.

Moran just shook his head and continued into the cockpit to get strapped into his seat. "Gardening" did not feel like an operation to him. He'd never flown a mine-laying sortie on either of his earlier tours, while the diminutive, twin-engine Wellington just didn't seem aggressive or powerful enough to him to be classified as a "real" bomber — not after flying so many hours flying in Lancasters. As Moran strapped himself in and started the pre-flight checks it felt like nothing more than another training exercise — which was just as well since tonight's flight would not count towards their tour of duty either.

Take-off was timed for twilight to enable them to be over the target after the onset of darkness but before moonrise; on 16 November 1944 this converted to a take-off from Moreton-in-Marsh at 16:30 to put them over the target at 18:45. Although Kit started the engines bang on time, Forrester still beat P-Peter to the head of the runway. He so took off in M for Mike immediately ahead of Moran.

Moran didn't care. He turned onto the runway and breathed in the beauty of the luminous twilight around them. The green light flashed from control, and he throttled forward, conscious of how comparatively sluggish the Wellington seemed when weighed down with six mines. It took almost the entire runway to get airborne, and once in the air the Wimpy struggled to gain altitude. Not that that mattered — they didn't need a lot of altitude since they were flying over friendly countryside. Moran banked gently around to the south, silently admiring the strip of rose-coloured sky lingering on the Western horizon and the wisps of clouds glowing like burning embers against the waxing night.

For roughly a quarter of an hour as they droned across the blacked-out English countryside, Moran held Forrester in view ahead of him. From the tail Osgood reported that he could see all three of the aircraft from Moreton-in-Marsh that had taken off after them. But the earth was rotating inexorably. Gradually, even the reflection of sunlight on the bellies of the clouds was doused. The darkness intensified; the other four aircraft faded from view.

Apparently alone now, they continued into an increasingly cloudless night sky. Breakers disintegrating into white swirls against the black shores of the island kingdom crisply outlined the English coast. A duller grey interrupted by squiggles of white appearing and disappearing at irregular intervals marked the Channel where the wind had evidently whipped up white horses on the crests of the waves. P-Peter flew over three convoys, and each time Aldiss lights blinked angrily at them, demanding ID. Tibble dutifully flashed the letter of the day to avoid being shot at by the Navy. The sight of so many Allied ships in the Channel gave Moran a feeling of satisfaction. Those merchant ships represented Allied dominance and progress towards victory.

Not long afterwards, P-Peter left the Channel behind to start over the darkened landmass of France. When last Kit had flown operations almost exactly a year ago, this had been home to scores of Luftwaffe fighter squadrons and bristled with anti-aircraft batteries. Now the flak was silenced, and the Luftwaffe had been driven back to defend the Reich. These days the RAF flew as safely here as over England itself.

Throughout the flight, Peal diligently took fixes every ten minutes. The wind was very light and course corrections were minimal. On schedule, they started their descent to the "bombing" altitude of 1,500 feet. Ahead of them the Bay of Biscay shimmered faintly, a lighter shade of silvery grey.

Just as they entered their run, Babcock reported, "There's an aircraft ahead of us, Skipper."

"What is it? Another Wellington?"

"I think so, Skip."

"Think so, bomb aimer? How many hours of aircraft identification have you had?"

"It's a Wellington," Babcock decided.

"Forrester?" Moran asked.

"Can't be sure, Skipper, but I'd put my money on it."

Now that Babcock had drawn his attention away from his instruments, Moran could faintly decipher the other Wellington and felt a flicker of annoyance. He'd expected Forrester to have completed his run before he started. He would have preferred not to have Forrester ahead of him, flying the same altitude, course and speed, while they both released six mines over a twelve-mile run. Moran didn't fancy drifting into Forrester's slipstream. He briefly considered circling around to give Forrester time to complete his mine drop before commencing his own, but the German flak apparently hadn't spotted them yet. The longer they waited, the more likely it became that Jerry would wake up. Moran decided that the buffeting of Forrester's slipstream was the lesser evil.

Moran opened the bomb bay doors and told Babcock to direct him. He had just released the second mine, when Osgood broke over the intercom excitedly. "U-boat! One of the bastards just surfaced! Right behind us. If you could just—"

"Pilot to rear gunner: we're on the bomb run and cannot — repeat cannot — manoeuvre. If you get him in your sites without course changes, you have permission to fire."

"Steady, Skipper!" Babcock warned. "Steady!"

The guns started chattering furiously, and a flash of light lit up the sky to port.

"The bastard's firing back!"

"What did you expect?" Moran asked his gunner laconically, while trying to remember what calibre of gun the U-boats carried. He decided it didn't matter. Almost any kind of gun could hit them at their present altitude, and a lucky shot might hit something vital, but they were also rapidly increasing the distance. A newly surfaced U-Boat would have wet decks and there was a considerable swell running in Biscay left over from last night's storm. The U-Boat's next shots confirmed Moran's assessment, exploding even farther away than the first.

Babcock reported "Mines gone!" and Moran immediately pulled back on the control column to start climbing and turning back toward England.

As they reached 5,000 feet, Moran levelled off. All was silent and dark. Again, they appeared to be completely alone in the sky as they crossed liberated France. The Channel beckoned, and beyond Moreton-in-Marsh, and the *Green Man*, where the crews of Course 73 not selected for this sortie were probably already ordering their first rounds in the end-of-course celebration.

Moran clicked on his intercom. "Well done, everyone!" He was a little taken aback by the cheers that answered him. Part of him wanted to warn them this had been a milk run, and real operations were going to feel different, but why spoil the mood?

"Isn't it time for that coffee?" Peal asked.

"Coming!" Babcock answered and a moment later he emerged from the nose with four thermoses clutched in his arms. He passed one to Moran and continued down the fuselage to hand one each to Peal, Tibble and Osgood. Moran unclipped his oxygen mask and let it hang down beside his face as he took a sip of the warm, sweet liquid. It might be weak and watered down with milk, but it was still real coffee.

"I haven't tasted coffee this good since before the war!" Peal announced, clearly enjoying his first taste of operational privileges.

"I've never had real coffee before," Tibble answered.

They landed at Moreton-in-Marsh at 20:38 without incident. The ground crew welcomed them cheerfully with words of congratulation, and a crew bus awaited them. After returning their parachutes and Mae West lifejackets, they crossed to the ops building and climbed to the de-briefing room on the first floor. They exchanged brief greetings on the stairs with Forrester's crew as the latter hurried out, already done with their debrief and anxious to join the party at the *Green Man*.

At the top of the stairs an airman ticked their names on a list as they reported in, and another handed a mug of tea laced heavily with rum to each of them. Intelligence officers waited at tables spread around the room to debrief the crews.

It was only when Kit tasted the rum-laden tea that memories flooded over him. Suddenly he was back with his old crew at the end of a long sortie over Germany. An instant later, like a kick in the gut, he realized that most of them were dead — the aggressive Canadian gunner Bob, the ever competent and mature navigator 'Sailor,' and the introverted wireless op Les, while Reggie was a cripple. Only the cheeky half-Yemeni bomb aimer Hamad with his nearly incomprehensible Geordie accent was still flying. Yet what hurt most, of course, was the reminder that Don wasn't with him, that Don would never be with him again.

For a second that seemed impossible, unreal. Then, with disbelief, Kit realized it was nearly a year since Don had been killed. With shame he registered that in all that time he had not once visited his grave. He had been posted LMF at the time of the funeral and after that Don's father had told him he was unwelcome. Yet the anniversary of their last flight together would fall next week, during seven days' leave. Instantly, Kit knew he had to alter the plans he'd made to stop himself from thinking about Georgina. He had to pay his respects at Don's grave on the anniversary instead. He owed it to him. No matter how hard it was to get there —

"Flying Officer Moran?" It was the WAAF intelligence officer at the wooden table where the rest of his new crew already sat. She was looking at him puzzled.

Kit recovered himself and joined them.

The car park at the *Green Man* was already overflowing, so Adrian suggested the others go in to find a table while he found somewhere to park. Terry, Stu and Nigel climbed out of the back, but Kit stayed with Adrian. As they started back to the pub on foot from the parking place Kit ventured, "I have a big favour to ask, Adrian."

"Of course, Kit. Feel free."

"You'll be with your parents in London this coming week, won't you? Will you be needing your car?"

"No, why? Would you like to borrow it?"

"It will be the anniversary of my skipper's death next Thursday. I'd like to visit the grave, but he's buried in a village up near the Scottish border and I haven't got a clue on how to get there by public transport, much less how long —"

"You're welcome to my car, Kit, but I'm not sure about petrol rations—"

"I can work something out," Kit answered evasively. As a former fitter, he knew that, although totally illegal, RAF ground crew could usually be persuaded to siphon off fuel — if the price was right. He was confident he could organise some canisters of petrol for the journey before leaving Moreton.

They reached the pub and pushed their way through the thick black-out curtains. Inside, cigarette smoke hung in the air like a heavy fog. The noise level was almost unbearable, as voices and laughter all but drowned out the music from the radio. The crews that had not been selected for the gardening operation must have started early and were clearly well pickled.

Kit and Adrian shouldered and shoved their way to a large table where Stu, Terry and Nigel had managed to crowd in, clutching two empty chairs. At the other end of the table, another crew sported several misshapen caps, apparently soaked in beer as the aftermath of some sort of antics.

"I'll get the first round!" Kit announced without sitting down.

As he elbowed his way to the bar, he found Forrester — as usual — ahead of him.

Forrester turned and scoffed, "Oh, the U-boat boys! Did Goodie sink that U-boat?"

Forrester's tail gunner must have seen the tracer from their guns, Kit registered, and mentally admitted it would have looked a bit ridiculous shooting at a submarine with a machine gun. He tried to explain. "No, but he let off a little anger. He's got a grudge against U-boats." He hesitated, but then decided he should confront the lingering tension between the two of them head-on. Ever since Forrester had been given a red endorsement in his logbook for landing without a green on the nightmare evening of 27 October — which the participants of Course 73 called "Black Friday" — he had become more aggressive toward Kit. Now, they were going to start training on Lancasters at the same Heavy Conversion Unit (HCU) a week from now. "Look, Red, can't we lay this to rest?"

"What?" Forrester answered with a pretence of innocence.

"Your resentment over the fact that you got a red endorsement in your logbook on Black Friday and I didn't."

"Yeah, sure — if you can tell me one good reason why I got that endorsement and you didn't! We both disobeyed orders!"

"I can't answer that, Red. I don't endorse the logbooks, the CO does."

"Well, I can!" Forrester snarled. "Because you're a Pom and I'm a Colonial, that's why."

Kit could identify with Forrester's resentment. He'd been in his shoes. But he also thought Forrester was wrong. "I can understand why you feel that way, but actually I'm not as 'Pom' as you think I am." He paused and then admitted, "I'm classed as coloured in South Africa."

"What?" Forrester swung around and gawked at him.

"My grandmother was a native South African. Black."

"Are you stiffing me?"

"No. Furthermore, I admire you for landing without a green given the circumstances in which you did it. I wish I'd had the courage to do that — and that's precisely what I told the inquiry panel. I've already told you about pausing in the corkscrew and throttling back to let your rear gunner get in a good shot. I still think it's risky, but it seems to work. I'm perfectly willing to admit you're a more natural pilot than I am. Whether I like your crew as individuals or not, I recognize that they're a first-rate team. Now, can we bury the hatchet?"

Forrester seemed to think about this for a moment, and then he grinned and clapped Kit on the shoulder so hard it jostled him. "You're all right, mate!"

"No more rivalry?"

"Ah, no." He shook his head. "I didn't say that. I can't stop myself. It's just the way I am. But don't take it wrong, mate. We can be friendly rivals."

"I can live with that, but for Osgood's sake, will you at least keep Levesque reined in?"

"I'll do my best." Forrester offered his hand on that, and Kit readily took it. Forrester continued in a markedly friendlier tone, as if he were trying to build bridges, "What are you doing this coming week?"

"We're sight-seeing on our way to London as a crew, and then we'll have a night on the town together before going our separate ways on Sunday."

Forrester nodded. "Yeah, we plan to paint the town red and hit the fleshpots on Saturday night too. Then I'm going to visit friends of the family. Some old bloke my Dad met in hospital after Gallipoli." He grimaced to suggest this was a duty rather than a pleasure. "With any luck I'll get away after a day or two and find myself more satisfying entertainment. What about you?" He swung his hips from side-to-side suggestively.

"I'm meeting up with the widow of the navigator on my old crew on Sunday. She's now a WAAF—"

Forrester grinned and winked. "Don't break your wrists trying to get her twilights off too fast!"

"No, it's not like that; we're just having lunch. She's a friend and I want to see how she's coping. On Monday I'll be traveling up to my old mid-upper gunner's farm. He lost an arm and was invalided out. He lives there with his parents and his son."

Forrester nodded but he didn't appear interested in such mundane activities, and Kit preferred to avoid the Australian's no-doubt coarse contribution to his planned visit to Don's grave. Instead, he clapped Forrester on the shoulder and parted with, "Have a good time, Red. See you at Swinderby!" Then, collecting the five mug-handled glasses waiting for him, he wriggled his way through the crowd at the bar back to his waiting crew.

The next morning, Kit had to organize the extra petrol before collecting his bags from the mess. He succeeded in obtaining two large jerry cans full to the brim, but was running late, and the rest of the crew was already waiting by the gate while Adrian brought his car round. Just as he went to sign out, the clerk at the desk called over to him. "Flying Officer Moran? There are three messages for you." As he spoke, the clerk removed three folded pieces of paper from one of the pigeonholes behind the desk.

Kit frowned but took the messages. The first was logged in at 15:10 yesterday, when he'd been at the pre-ops briefing. It said simply: "Miss Reddings. Will call back." The second had the same message repeated at 18:46, when he'd been over the target. The final message was logged at 21:05 and read: "Miss Reddings. Please call back." A number was provided on the line below.

What irony! Last time he'd had leave he'd made no plans, hoping until the very last minute that Georgina might contact him so they could spend some time together. Now, when he'd given up all hope and had made other plans, she reached out. But why? Why would she ring him now? After all this time? And where had she got his number?

Kit was wary, but he couldn't ignore the request. Leaving his bags by the door, he went to one of the phone booths, put in the necessary coins, and dialled the number.

After only two rings, Georgina answered sounding a little breathless. "Hello? This is the Radford residence."

"Georgina. It's Kit Moran. You asked me to ring you back." Kit kept his voice neutral, even a bit cool. He did not want her to think that he was desperate to talk to her.

"Oh, Kit! I'm so glad!" She sounded very relieved. "When you didn't get back to me yesterday, I started to think — to fear — that.... Never mind. It doesn't matter what I thought. Kit, we have to talk. I mean meet." The words seemed to tumble over one another in her eagerness to get them out. Kit couldn't decide if she was excited or anxious. "I have something to tell you, but I want to say it face-to-face. Not over a telephone. Is there any way we could see each other? Soon?"

"I'm about to go on leave, with my whole crew." His tone reflected his reluctance to upend his plans for her. Kit did not want Georgina to think that she only had to snap her fingers and he would drop everything to come running.

"Oh." She sounded disappointed but persisted. "But if you're going on leave next week, surely we could meet up some place? Where will you be and for how long?"

"We have seven days, and we're starting in London."

"Couldn't I meet you there?" She asked enthusiastically, adding brightly, "We could have lunch together tomorrow?"

Part of Kit felt uncontainable joy because of her apparent eagerness to see him again, yet another part was angry still. She made not a hint of an apology for three months of total silence. Dashing her hopes, he explained, "I've already arranged to meet Kathleen Hart for lunch tomorrow." Since Georgina knew Kathleen, Kit knew he did not risk sending a wrong message.

"Oh. I'm glad you'll be seeing her. Please give her my regards." Georgina's words were perfectly correct, but Kit could hear the disappointment in her voice nevertheless — and in her next plea, "What about later in the week, then? I could try—"

Kit cut her short. "I'm going to Reggie's farm for three days and then up to Hobkirk. I want to visit Don's grave on the anniversary of his death."

He heard Georgina catch her breath and instantly regretted blurting it out like that. Georgina might have hurt him, but that didn't give him the right to be unkind. Her grief for Don was real, and he should have known that reminding her of the anniversary no bluntly would cause her pain. As soon as he let his anger drop, he considered that her silence probably hadn't been so much indifference to him as a desire to just cool things down a bit. She had probably only wanted to signal to him that she wasn't ready for a new relationship — or hadn't been. Had enough time passed for her to risk getting closer now? If so, he be shooting himself in the foot to be too hard on her just out of stubborn pride.

"You're going to Hobkirk?" She asked timidly on the other end of the phone. "Next Thursday?"

"Yes, my navigator has lent me his car so I can drive up from Reggie's farm." Kit very much wanted to see Georgina again, but he had pictured being alone with Don during this visit. He didn't want Georgina standing between them.

On the other end of the line, Georgina asked uncertainly, "Kit? Couldn't I come with you?" She paused but did not give him time to answer before adding apologetically, "I was planning to ask my father to take me there, but if you're going anyway wouldn't it make sense for us to go together?" When he still did not answer straight away, she added, "Please?"

Kit could hear the tears in her voice, and his heart melted. Yes, he wanted time alone with Don's memory, but surely that took second place to helping Georgina? Don would certainly have wanted him to help Georgina.

"Please, Kit," she pleaded again, a choked-back sob audible on the other end of the line.

The fact that she didn't take his answer for granted was the final straw. Kit didn't have the heart to say no, even as he warned himself that she'd said nothing to indicate she had changed her mind about him — or rather, about them. Just because she was willing to risk meeting again didn't mean she was ready to fall into his arms. Maybe she was just having a new crisis and needed a shoulder to cry on? Maybe he should resent that — but he didn't. He realized that even if that was all this was about, he wanted to help her if he could. "Yes, we can go together," he answered her at last. "Where—"

"I can get myself to York, if that would help? You could pick me up there. Is that all right?" She still sounded unsure.

"Yes, of course." The telephone started beeping, an indication that Kit's coins had almost run out. Hastily, they agreed on a place and time just as the connection cut off.

Kit returned to the front hall to retrieve his bags and noticed with amusement that his step was lighter. So much so that he allowed himself a short little African jig. The realisation that he would be seeing Georgina in less than a week made him happy. Ridiculously happy. Love makes fools of all of us, he thought, but he left the mess smiling.

London
17 November 1944

Their day together as a crew went well. They started with a tour of Kenilworth Castle, where Adrian's enthusiasm quickly infected the rest of them. They spent longer there than planned, yet still reached London in time to see a matinee performance of "This Happy Breed" at a cinema near Piccadilly Circus. They feasted on fish and chips together, washed down with plenty of beer, before seeking out a night club. Terry opted to bail at this point, asking Adrian to drop him at a YMCA instead, but the remaining four went on to one of the many clubs popular with the RAF.

Mobs of RAF and USAAF crowded the premises and filled the dance floor, but girls in satin, silks, and velvets held near parity with the numbers in uniform. The brass band wailed and a female singer in a sequined dress cooed melodiously above the benign rumble of voices and laughter. They joined the happy throng, squeezing in at a tiny round table, and soon the cocktails flowed.

By 1 o'clock in the morning, despite the large numbers of more glamorous Americans, Nigel and Stu were secure in the arms of their dance partners. Kit had had enough drinking, dancing and chatting, but since he was staying at Adrian's home he could not just slip away. Fortunately, his host returned to their table without a girl and sank down wearily in his chair.

"Adrian, you look knackered, and I've had enough. Why don't we pay up and go?"

Adrian roused himself. "Shouldn't we wait for Nigel and Stu so we can drop them off at their lodgings first?" he protested, looking around the still-crowded dance floor for the remaining members of the crew.

Kit leaned a bit closer to his navigator, "Adrian, they're dancing with their lodgings."

"Oh," Adrian blushed and hurriedly signalled for their bill.

They collected their greatcoats from the cloakroom and abandoned the over-heated, smoky interior for the crisp, cold air of a late-November night. The stars pricked the dome of the heavens overhead, and they paused to look up. "Before the war," Adrian remarked with a deep breath, "you could never see the stars in London. There were too many city lights, too much coal smoke too."

They found their way back to Adrian's car, but Adrian had some trouble getting the key in the door.

"Shall I drive?" Kit offered.

"Would you mind?"

"Not if you direct me. I don't know London."

"No trouble at all."

Kit got in behind the wheel and Adrian sat beside him. The streets were empty except for the odd taxi. Kit drove slowly and cautiously, unused to driving in an urban area in the black-out.

"Did you plan this, Kit? Nigel and Stu..."

"Let's just say I didn't want Nigel going back to Liverpool where he got arrested on his last leave. As for Stu," Kit shrugged, "Let me put it this way: there's a story that in the midst of the Battle of Britain some WAAF OC complained about the behaviour of the pilots to the CO of a Hurricane squadron. He allegedly he replied that it would be a shame if his pilots died virgins. I share that sentiment. Not that I think we're all going to die, but we can't ignore the odds."

"So, you've been to places like that before?"

"The nightclub?"

"Yes."

Kit looked over at Adrian briefly, then returned his attention to driving as he answered. "You may not be aware that I originally mustered as a fitter and spent the first two years of the war as an erk."

"You? But why?"

"When I went to the recruiting office, they said so many had signed up for pilot training already that I might not be called up for nine months or more. I was 19, bored in my job, and in a hurry to do something 'exciting.' So, I agreed to muster as ground crew."

"But...wasn't that... I mean, well, awkward? With your background...."

"I've always been the odd man out, Adrian. Being an erk was arguably the first time in my life I was able to submerge myself in a crowd."

"But...it must have been a bit of a rough crowd, surely?"

"Yes and no. The war had just started. Young men from all walks of life had rushed to volunteer with the RAF and we were all thrown together. All of us were experiencing service life for the first time. It seemed like a great adventure, and I was happy to be part of it. Dissatisfaction didn't creep into my consciousness for another couple of years. By then the novelty of being surrounded by other immature young men had worn off, and that's when I volunteered for aircrew. Yes, I wanted to prove to myself that I was brave enough to risk my life, but I was also looking for the company of men with higher ambitions than the next party. When I met my skipper, I recognized how much I'd been deceiving myself about fitting in. It was good to be back amongst people who shared my interests and views. Nevertheless," he paused to toss Adrian a grin, "those two years as an erk were definitely an education!"

"Did you have many girls?" Adrian asked back seriously.

"Plenty of girls were happy to go out with us. We passed the word among ourselves about which ones were 'snobby' or 'difficult' and which were 'easy' and 'out for a good time.' We were all in our teens, remember. Few of us wanted to get serious just yet. All we wanted was a quick thrill. It was intoxicating at first." He paused and remarked with a rueful smile. "I suspect Stu may be experiencing that thrill for the first time."

Adrian laughed nervously. "Yes, I suppose so. And Nigel?"

"Nigel's the son of sailor who grew up in the slums of Liverpool. He may be the youngest member of our crew, but I'll wager he's had more girls than the two of us put together."

Adrian tittered uncomfortably, "That's not hard, Kit. I've only had one girl, Julia."

"She must be a wonderful girl," Kit surmised gently.

Adrian nodded, but he didn't meet Kit's eye and his expression was more worried than pleased. They dropped the subject.

The next morning Kit slept in late, and by the time he came downstairs Adrian's parents had already left for a charity event. Kit met Kathleen for lunch and was both heartened and slightly saddened to see that she was very much getting on with her life. After she had rushed off to return to her unit, he walked slowly back to South Kensington. He'd had little chance to get to know London, having never lived in or near it. All his other visits had been like now, on a short leave with other young men. This was the first time he could remember being alone in the great city, so he enjoyed just soaking in the sights and sounds of the capital of the British Empire.

By the time Kit reached the Peals' white, terraced house, he barely had time to freshen up before cocktails; Adrian's older sister and her husband had been invited to join them for dinner. The grandfather clock in the hall struck half past seven as Kit stepped off the carpeted stairs in his best blues and polished shoes. Laughter bubbled out of the drawing room, and Kit paused in the doorway to take in the scene before him.

A stunningly beautiful young woman in a black, velvet dress, high-heeled shoes and what appeared to be real silk stockings was sitting beside Adrian on a sofa. She was smoking a cigarette in a holder and Adrian looked diminished beside her. Kit surmised she must have made quite a splash as a debutante. Standing before the coal fireplace with its elaborate brass grille was a short young man with longish, dark, curly hair. He wore a full, pre-war evening suit and heavy gold cufflinks that reeked of affluence. He was speaking to an older version of Adrian — a slender man, with longish, wavy, receding blond hair and a classically handsome face. The elder Peal also wore dinner attire complete with a winged collar, bow tie, white waistcoat and gold cufflinks that gleamed when he flicked the ash of his cigarette into the fire. Mrs Peal was absent.

Feeling Kit's gaze, Mr Peal turned his head and smiled with his mouth but not his eyes. "Ah, you must be the mysterious Flying Officer Moran whom Adrian has told us so much about."

"Nothing too terrible, I hope," Kit answered with a quick glance at Adrian as he advanced deeper into the room. He felt as though he was entering the lion's den.

The elder Peal laughed politely as they shook hands. "Nothing negative at all. Adrian thinks the world of you. Told us all about your DFM, and that you've done a tour already and all that." Whatever that meant.

Kit opted for the safety of an apology. "I'm sorry I missed you earlier, sir."

The elder Peal waved his words aside. "Oh, I was young once too. Let me introduce you to my son-in-law Gregory Durand and my daughter Stephanie. Flying Officer Moran is Adrian's pilot — or skipper as you like to say?" The latter remark was directed at Adrian.

"That's right. Like the captain of a ship, he commands the aircraft and crew in the air," Adrian explained.

While Kit shook hands with Adrian's sister and her husband, the elder Peal continued, "Adrian mentioned that your father is in the Colonial Service." Although not stated as a question, it was clearly intended to prompt a reply.

"Yes, sir. He's the District Officer in Calabar, Nigeria."

"Sounds interesting. Winchester Old Boy, Adrian said. One of my partners went to Winchester and thinks he remembers him. Said he was good at rowing."

"That will be him," Kit confirmed, knowing that his father had indeed been good at the sport in school.

"I must say, I was surprised to hear he didn't send you to his alma mater." Again, it was a statement that was also a question.

Kit had observed that there was far less racism in England than in South Africa and, in retrospect, he knew he would probably have fared better in an English school than at St. Andrews in Cape Town. However, he had no idea what factors had induced his parents to send him there at the time. Possibly nothing more complicated than finances. As Peal senior was still looking quizzically at him, he opted for an answer that he thought would be uncontroversial. "I know he has fond memories of school, but we have no family in England."

"None? No grandparents or aunts and uncles?" The elder Peal sounded astonished.

"My father's family are all in India, sir, and my mother was an only child. Her parents lived in South Africa."

"I see," Peal's tone suggested the opposite of his words. "Adrian went to Shrewsbury as did my father and I. It is a tremendous advantage in life to have not only a good education, but a network of friends built up from childhood."

"I take your point, sir. My apprenticeship was arranged by one of my father's friends from Winchester, but my father wanted me nearer family."

"It seems to me that a boy's future should not be put at risk for the sake of mere sentimentality. I find it hard to believe—"

"Richard! This isn't a cross-examination!" Mrs Peal admonished her husband as she arrived on the scene. "Besides, dear, you're being a terrible host. This is supposed to be a cocktail hour, and poor Flying Officer Moran doesn't have a drink yet." It was only because Kit knew she was American by birth that he thought he detected a faint hint of an accent; Mrs Peal was now very British in her manner, dress and tone. Her husband looked annoyed for a moment but then pulled a smile onto his face and graciously asked Kit what he wanted to drink. The others were drinking whisky, so Kit asked for one as well before turning to thank Mrs Peal for her hospitality. Mr Peal turned the conversation to hunting. "Adrian tells me you done a number of safaris."

"Yes, rather normal where I come from," Kit pointed out.

"Big game?"

"Sometimes. Once my father and I brought down a bull elephant that had started trampling down gardens and huts. Good bit of excitement."

"I can imagine," the elder Peal finally seemed impressed.

Kit remembered that his father claimed to have taken up safari hunting to increase his standing with his peers. Yet he had also come to disdain men who came out from Europe in order to prove their manhood by killing African game. Kit found himself saying out loud, "My father killed a man-eating lion once too, but mostly we hunted gazelles and ostrich because they are plentiful and good meat. He taught me to disdain the trophy-hunters, men who only hunt for the sake of their own ego." Peal senior quickly changed the subject after that, and the conversation went on to other topics.

Kit glanced once or twice at Adrian to check whether his forthright replies might be causing offence, but his usually eloquent navigator seemed to be resolute about staying meekly in the background. At the stroke of eight, the family moved into the dining room. Here the only lighting came from the candles in the chandelier. The china was Royal Doulton, the crystal Waterford, the linens Irish, and the modest but exquisitely presented meal was served by a uniformed, balding butler.

The elder Peal dominated the dinner conversation. In stark contrast to Rev Reddings and Kit's own father, Peal was dismissive of any opinion that did not conform with his own, no matter who voiced it. He was condescending to both his wife and his daughter. At one point making disparaging remarks about women who possessed "the hubris" to go to university with the aim of taking up a profession. "By all means go there to meet an intelligent and well-qualified husband, but no woman should have the gall to think she can actually compete in government service, the professions or in private enterprise," was his verdict. Peal also complained bitterly about a female law clerk at his firm who "broke down in tears over the slightest criticism." Kit could easily imagine why.

Kit welcomed the end of the meal. The gentlemen retired for cigars and port in Mr Peal's study; a room characterized by heavy, dark furniture, oriental carpets, and Victorian wallpaper. Cigars were passed around. Kit cautiously took one, conscious that he'd never smoked one before and suspicious that the others guessed it. Carefully imitating what they did, he smoked while Mr Peal declaimed on the declining morals of the working class.

"I should know!" he insisted, although no one had dared to challenge his right to pontificate. "I see them in the courtroom week after week. But the worst of it is this growing attitude of entitlement. They think they've won this war and that we owe them something for saving our hides, as they put it. Labour is both feeding such sentiments and going to reap the benefits, I tell you."

"But Mr Churchill is very popular," Durand ventured to point out cautiously.

"That won't make the least bit of difference when the shooting stops!" Peal pooh-poohed his son-in-law's objection. "Mark my words: Churchill is going to lose the first general election after the war."

Kit didn't have any strong political opinions, so he held his tongue and waited impatiently for the return of the ladies. On their arrival, the political discussion ended, and Stephanie put a record on the gramophone that lightened the atmosphere. Nevertheless, Kit was not sorry when the Durands announced it was time for them to leave. Kit presumed their departure would enable him to excuse himself shortly afterwards. Unfortunately, Adrian jumped up instantly to see them out, and Mrs Peal disappeared to check on something in the kitchen, leaving Kit alone with Mr Peal.

As if he had been awaiting just such an opportunity, Mr Peal pounced on Kit. "So, how is Adrian doing? An honest answer now!" Hi voice was anxious, and yet demanding — as if he were in a courtroom, Kit thought, instantly resenting being cross-examined like this.

Yet he answered without hesitation, "Adrian is first-rate, sir. The best navigator on the course."

"Well, I'd expect that, but the boy's always been a bit over-sensitive. Not like his brother." Peal nodded in the direction of a photo of a young man who looked like a larger, heavier and altogether more robust version of Adrian — wearing the uniform of a paratrooper lieutenant. "Adrian fancied himself an artist for a while, and then he wanted to study art history, of all things!" His father rolled his eyes. "It was only after I threatened to cut off his allowance that he agreed to read architecture instead."

"He seems to have taken to it whole-heartedly. He gave us a first-rate tour of Kenilworth Castle yesterday," Kit replied. "His explanations enabled me to see things I would not have noticed on my own, and they ignited an interest on the part of the sergeants that hadn't been there to start."

"Yes," His father answered absently, not really listening. Frowning into the fireplace he complained, "But he was never good at sports. Didn't like them much. Fencing was his only sport. Fencing!" Peal made it sound as if it were not a sport at all. "His mother and I worry about Adrian," Peal continued. "He's never brought a girl home to meet us, and...."

"I don't think you need worry on that score, sir," Kit gladly defended Adrian's manliness. "I happen to know he is seeing someone. I'm sure he'll introduce her to you in due course."

"Oh, that's good!" His father brightened. Even so, as voices in the hall indicated that they would soon be re-joined by Adrian and his mother, Peal leaned in urgently and asked again, "And he's all right in the air, you say?"

"He's top notch, sir," Kit stressed, just as the door began to open.

Chapter 10
Memories

York/Scotland
Thursday, 23 November 1944

Although Kit thought he'd left Reggie's farm with plenty of time to be punctual at his rendezvous with Georgina, heavy rain soon set in, slowing his progress sometimes to a crawl. By the time he finally reached the sandwich shop beside the railway station in York where he had arranged to meet Georgina, he was an hour behind schedule. No sooner had he entered, still shaking the rain off his cap, than Georgina jumped up and waved to him from one of the booths. Her expression was one of utter relief. She must have been afraid that he would stand her up, he registered as he hurried over. "I'm sorry I'm late," he apologised. "I hope you didn't stand on ceremony and had something to eat?"

"No, I was waiting for you," Georgina admitted.

His slow progress this morning and the low, dark heavens promising more rain made him worry about reaching Hobkirk before dark. He wanted to get back on the road as quickly as possible, so he looked around to catch the waitress' eye before sitting down.

Only after he'd settled opposite Georgina did he notice that she had gone to considerable effort to look nice for him — or was it for Don? Of course, she was still dressed like a vicar's daughter on her way to a funeral, in a trim, dark suit and white blouse, but rather than binding her hair up in a ponytail or bun, she had rolled it smartly away from her face yet let it fall down at the back. Brushes of rouge on her cheeks and the colour of her lipstick brought out the green in her eyes more vividly — and Kit hadn't seen her wear lipstick since Don died. She wore a pearl choker, too, but it was the sight of his ebony elephant earrings dangling from her ears that delighted him. She wasn't wearing *those* for Don, he thought, and his heart wanted to take flight. He held it back. Don't jump to wild conclusions, he told himself, yet he couldn't stop himself from smiling and telling her, "You look lovely."

"Thank you! So, do you!" Her whole face became luminous with happiness. Her expression put Kit in mind of the way she used to look up at Don — and that reminded him that, whatever might have changed between Georgina and himself, they had a duty to the dead first. "We can't linger, I'm afraid," he warned. "I don't want to be driving on country roads in the dark, and we're four or five hours away from Hobkirk by my reckoning. We'd better order right away, and we'll have to eat in a bit of a hurry."

The waitress arrived, took their orders and withdrew. Still preoccupied with the journey ahead, Kit warned, "We're going to have to stay overnight in Scotland, so I've booked two rooms at a hotel in Hawick. I hope you understand that I can't, and won't, go back to Ashcroft Park, but if you would prefer to stay with the Selkirks —"

"No. I want to spend the time with you, Kit. There's so much to say. So much I want to tell you. I —" she cut off as the waitress arrived with their sandwiches. When they were alone again Georgina concluded, "We'll talk about those things later, after we've honoured Don. But first, please tell me about Kathleen and Reggie and your new crew."

Kit nodded. "I was surprised by how well Kathleen has settled into WAAF," he reported. "She seemed so — I don't know — calm and confident."

"Yes. She's been a sterling example of courage in the face of loss," Georgina agreed.

Hearing her implicit self-criticism, Kit reminded her gently, "We all have to find our own way of coping with grief."

Georgina drew a deep breath, "Yes, I suppose you're right," she admitted and then asked, "And Reggie? How is he doing?"

"Not so well. It's hard to be a farmer and a father with one arm. And you know the divorce is final?"

"No! That's terrible! How can any decent woman divorce a man after he has suffered such a terrible injury? It is utterly unchristian," the vicar's daughter was emphatic.

Kit was more understanding. "Reggie was a first-rate gunner and crew member. He's a loving father to his boy Toby and dutiful son to his old father, but from the day I met him until the day he lost his arm, he was unfaithful to his wife — and not with one girl but with anyone he could cajole into bed with him. The marriage was on the rocks before he was wounded, and his wife was threatening divorce before I ever met him. His injuries don't change any of that. Why should a neglected and betrayed woman bind herself to a cripple?"

Georgina had no ready answer and her expression became troubled as she thought about it.

"It wasn't the divorce that upset me," Kit continued, "but seeing him struggle with his handicap. It made me wonder if Don and I really did him a favour bringing him home."

"Don't say that, Kit! You and Don flew that badly damaged Lancaster back to England because Reggie was severely injured and afraid to bail out. You got the DFM and your commission for your part in that – or are you questioning the King's good judgement on both counts?" she teased slightly before adding more forcefully. "The important thing is he's alive! He'll learn to cope with his handicap. He can watch Toby grow up and be a father to him. You must never doubt that life, no matter how impaired, is better than death."

Georgina sounded passionate about the topic, but Kit had a horror of being crippled or handicapped. He could not bear the thought of being anything less than whole and was even more repelled by the thought of being dependent on others. Watching the way Reggie needed help getting washed, getting dressed, cutting his meat, and so on throughout the day had stunned Kit. He did not think he could cope with such a situation. He would rather have been dead.

Kit called for their bill, helped Georgina into her overcoat and then pulled on his own, before they made a dash through the rain to the car. As they left the city and drove north the drizzle became a downpour, forcing Kit to concentrate completely on the driving while Georgina navigated for him, a map spread across her knees. It was only when they turned onto the calmer A-1 main road towards Scotland that Georgina got a chance to ask again about Kit's crew.

He answered readily, regaling her with tales of crewing up, and about Forrester and the unintentional rivalry that had evolved between them. He told her how much he liked Adrian and how well they got along. He talked, too, about his trip with Terry, and how his young wireless operator's thirst to educate himself sometimes led to mad but thought-provoking questions. He confided in her about Nigel being thin-skinned and quick to quarrel, and about his feud with U-boats. When she asked about Stu, however, he found himself struggling to say anything beyond that he seemed spoilt and immature.

Georgina encouraged him with so many questions that it was more than an hour before he realised that he'd been doing all the talking and insisted, "I've said enough about myself. Tell me about your teaching. Is it going well?"

"Well... not entirely," Georgina admitted. "In fact, I got off to a very bad start. The children mocked me, my fellow teachers don't take me seriously, and the head thinks I'm all but worthless."

"What?" he asked incredulous, taking his eyes off the road to gaze at her.

Georgina didn't dare meet his sudden stare, but she did try to explain. As the drenched, November landscape swept steadily past, Georgina recounted to Kit both her difficulties and the first little signs that things might be turning around. As the inside of the windows steamed up, obscuring the world outside, Kit was inexorably drawn into Georgina's world. With sparse yet strategic questions he kept her talking, and as the afternoon wore on she impressed him with how well she had faced her disappointments. She related her problems with a degree of self-deprecating humour that repeatedly made him laugh. It sounded to him as though she had already grown into a better teacher than she gave herself credit for. If nothing else, despite their less than model behaviour, Georgina retained a palpable commitment to her pupils.

At one point Kit felt compelled to point out, "I hate to tell you this, Georgina, but schoolboys are rotten little sods to apprentice teachers everywhere in the world. My friends and I were no better. You really don't want to know about the tricks we played on them, and I confess I was particularly horrible."

"I don't believe you," Georgina professed, and then asked with a giggle, "What did you do?"

"Oh, one of my favourite tricks was to put snakes in their wardrobes. Because my father had served in the bush, while most of the others came from families who lived in civilized places like Jo-burg or Harare, I developed a very acute eye for which snakes were poisonous and which were not. I would shamelessly allege the opposite of the truth when I discovered the harmless snakes which I had planted. Once I even pretended one had bitten me and faked a swoon; it caused quite a panic."

"You horrible thing!" she told him, and they laughed together. As the laughter died, Georgina ventured, "I hope you don't mind that I've written to your mother asking for her advice."

Kit looked over so sharply they nearly went off the road. When he'd recovered, he looked at her sidelong and noted in a low, serious voice, "You know, you risk giving my mother a mistaken impression of our relationship by writing to her like that. She's bound to think there is more between us than there is."

"I hope not — Kit! That was the turn off to Hawick!" Georgina had visited Don's home more frequently than Kit and knew the way better. Because of an army convoy on their tail, however, Kit couldn't stop and back up. He had to continue until he found a place where he could pull off the road and then turn around.

Eventually, they got back on their route, but they had left the main roads behind, and nothing was signposted. Georgina needed to concentrate on navigating and Kit on driving. The closer they got to their destination, the more absorbed they became in their separate thoughts about Don.

After a long silence, Kit asked, "When was the last time you visited?"

"In the summer, before you returned and term started."

"You stayed with the Selkirks?"

"Yes, of course."

"If you'd rather do that now—"

"No."

In Hawick, Kit pointed out the *Black Swan*, the hotel where he had managed to book two rooms for them. Yet, although dusk was closing around them rapidly, there was no question of stopping for the night just yet. Both Kit and Georgina were determined to visit the grave on the anniversary of Don's death. It would have seemed selfish and insulting to put their comfort and convenience ahead of honouring the date.

At Georgina's direction, Kit turned into the narrow lane to Hobkirk. By the time they reached the churchyard it was pouring with rain. Georgina scurried into the enclosed side porch of the small neo-Gothic church to tie a scarf over her head. A service had apparently just ended because candles still burned on the altar and the smell of incense lingered in the air. As the worst of the rain eased, they left the shelter of the porch and started towards the lines of gravestones, Georgina leading. Even in the semi-darkness the new, white marble RAF marker stood out in a row of grey, lichen-covered graves.

Abruptly Kit froze. Two people stood side-by-side before the grave already. He knew instantly that they were Don's parents, Colonel and Mrs Selkirk. Too late he realised that they, naturally, also wanted to honour the anniversary.

Georgina looked up at him, startled by his sudden halt.

"You carry on. I'll wait in the church until the Selkirks have left."

Georgina looked toward the grave, only now seeing the older couple. She seemed torn between staying with Kit and continuing. In the moment of her indecision, the Selkirks turned away from the grave and started towards them. Kit instantly retreated into the side porch, leaving Georgina alone outside.

Before she could decide what to do, Colonel Selkirk caught sight of her. "Georgina? Is that you?" He hurried forward, dragging Mrs Selkirk along in his wake. His voice boomed out in the soggy stillness of the churchyard. "We've been thinking about you, my dear, and wondering what had become of you."

While the Selkirks closed the distance, Georgina stood uncertainly before the church with an invisible Kit behind her. The colonel bent to kiss her on both cheeks and Mrs. Selkirk embraced her, remarking with feeling, "We've missed you, Georgina, why didn't you write or ring?"

"I started my apprentice teaching this autumn," Georgina waffled lamely. "I found it quite overwhelming, much more difficult than I'd expected. I'm afraid I've neglected everyone."

Don's mother moved in to take Georgina's hand. "No matter; you're here now. But why didn't you tell us you were coming? You know you're welcome at Ashcroft Park any time."

"I came at very short notice," Georgina tried to explain.

"Surely you can cancel your hotel reservation? And if not, at least join us for dinner." Colonel Selkirk took command, laying his hand on her elbow as though he were going to propel her directly to his car.

"John," Mrs Selkirk stopped him, "Georgina hasn't had a chance to visit the grave yet. We can wait in the church while Georgina has a moment alone with Don."

"Of course, of course." The colonel realised his mistake, and Kit started looking around for a place to hide.

Georgina intervened. "It's not necessary for you to wait, Colonel. I'm afraid I really can't join you this evening."

"But why ever not?"

"Because I'm here with someone else." Georgina hesitated only a second before adding, "I'm with Kit."

"Kit? Kit Moran? That coward!" Selkirk frowned and raised his voice to ask, "Why are you with him?"

Kit had long known the colonel's opinion of him, yet the words and tone still stung like a whiplash. He recoiled, but Georgina sprang to his defence. "Kit was Don's best friend, Colonel. And Don did not make friends lightly. That alone should tell you that there is more to Kit than what you *think* you know. He's here because he wanted to pay his respects, and —"

"I see, and now he's afraid to face us," Selkirk scoffed.

Kit's blood started to simmer, but Georgina was faster off the mark. She indignantly retorted, "He's not *afraid*, Colonel. He is respecting *your* wishes. *You* told him you never wanted to see him again." Kit heard Mrs Selkirk gasp; apparently, her husband had not informed her of what he'd said to their son's best friend.

Colonel Selkirk retorted, vigorously and unashamed, "And quite right too! Why would any decent person want anything to do with a lily-livered coward?"

"Kit is no coward, Colonel. He's a good man, and he's been a wonderful help to me throughout this past year," Georgina countered.

Mrs Selkirk spoke up, her voice strained with anguish. "We wanted to help too, child. It was just—"

Georgina cut her off in a gentle, reassuring tone, "It's all right, Mrs Selkirk. I understand. You just couldn't cope with my hysteria on top of your own grief. I don't blame you. But when I needed him most, Kit was there for me — despite his own problems, which were so much more serious than mine."

The colonel snorted derisively. "Problems stemming from his own lack of moral fibre! Still, I suppose he *is* the kind of man who's good at drying a young girl's tears. Doesn't take courage to do that, does it? But I thought *you* had more character than to befriend a yellow rat, let alone be seen in public with disgraced scum! Aren't you ashamed of yourself?"

Kit's anger boiled over and he took a step forward, but Georgina answered before he had left the shelter of the church. "Kit is every bit as good a man as Don! I'm not *ashamed* to be with him, Colonel!"

"You little hussy!" The colonel hissed at Georgina.

Now Kit's anger truly erupted, and he stepped out into the open to confront Selkirk face-to-face. "You have no right to insult Georgina, Colonel. Belittle me all you like, but not Georgina."

Selkirk caught his breath and took a step back. Despite the near darkness, he registered that he was facing an officer — one wearing wings. "What are you doing in that uniform? You've been court martialled and demoted to aircraftsman!"

"No. The RAF did not share your assessment of me. I was sent to flight training and I'll soon go operational as a Lancaster skipper."

"But — but you were LMF —"

"When I tried to explain things, you wouldn't stop shouting long enough to listen."

"I —" The colonel fell silent, too perplexed to know what to say.

"I'm so glad to hear that you weren't punished, Kit," Mrs Selkirk gasped out. "I never thought you deserved punishment." She sounded as if she was close to tears.

Georgina swiftly stepped forward and enclosed the older woman in her arms. "It's all right. I'm sure Kit understands."

"Yes," Kit seconded her, but he maintained his distance.

As the colonel continued to splutter, Mrs Selkirk pulled herself together and drew back from Georgina. "Thank you, dear. I wish you all the best. Both of you," she addressed the latter remark directly to Kit. Then she turned to her husband. "Take me home, John. I'm not feeling well."

Kit and Georgina stood without moving or speaking until the Selkirks had returned to their car and driven away. The silence reverberated with all the things they felt yet dared not say. Georgina's words in his defence both humbled and uplifted Kit. Even if she hadn't meant everything the way it sounded, he would never forget that she had defended him so vigorously.

But they had come all this way for Don, and the darkness around them was growing even though the rain had paused. "We'd better go to the grave while we can still see it," Kit suggested. Together they walked through the wet grass to the white RAF marker. It read: Fl/Lt Donald Selkirk, Pilot, 1919-1943, Aged 24."

Standing at Don's feet, Kit's agitation over the exchange with Colonel Selkirk returned. "I'm sorry," he told his dead friend. "I'm sorry. That wasn't supposed to happen. I didn't want it to happen. I came here hoping to show you that your sacrifice hadn't been in vain. I wanted to show you that I have made something of myself. I came to promise I will be the skipper you would have continued to be, if only...."

Suddenly Georgina's hand found his and gripped his fingers fiercely. Tears streamed down her face and her lips trembled. Without hesitation he put his arm around her shoulders and held her closely. He'd never dared do that before, but today he sensed she needed comfort more than she needed to maintain a distance. After what she had just said about him, maybe...They would have to talk about that. Later. For now, holding her felt right and good.

He was a sorry when, with a nod, she drew back and suggested in a tight voice, "Let's go to the hotel and have some dinner."

They didn't speak on the drive back to Hawick. Georgina wiped her face with her wet scarf and put some powder on so that she didn't look as though she'd been crying when they arrived at the hotel reception. Kit was relieved to find that the hotel, which he had had to book without knowing anything about it, was respectable and comfortable. Yes, it was chilly and rundown in the way everything was in Britain after five years of war, but it was not sordid as he had feared. Rather it exuded rustic charm and the receptionist welcomed them with enough warmth in his heavy Scottish brogue to make up for the lack of heating. He commiserated about the weather and told them the hotel restaurant would open shortly. He also volunteered other useful information about baths, hot water and breakfast. There was no wink or any insinuation that Georgina and Kit might be there for an illicit tryst. They signed for their respective rooms and received their separate keys. They were on different floors. They separated, agreeing to meet for dinner in half an hour.

Kit came down first and selected a table for two as close as possible to the only source of heat in the room – an open fireplace. As he settled in, he noted mentally that this was the first time the two of them had been to dinner on their own. They'd done a lot of double dating when Don was still alive, and after his death they mostly went for consoling, long walks together before Kit had left for Africa to begin pilot training. During her weekend visit when he was staying at the Reddings' they always dined as a family. He and Georgina had never been alone together in an atmosphere anything like this.

She appeared in a stunning, three-quarter-length green cocktail dress that matched her eyes. Aside from the fact that cocktail attire was almost extinct in wartime Britain, Kit had assumed that Georgina would continue to wear mourning. He stood and pulled out the chair for her, tongue-tied in his confusion. Georgina looked up at him. "Please sit down, Kit. You're making me nervous."

He sat down.

"I'm sorry I cried," Georgina announced, looking embarrassed and pained. "Please forgive me."

Kit reached across the table and took her hand. "Georgina, there's nothing to be sorry about. Crying is your way of expressing grief, and that's why we came here today — to let Don know that we remember him and love him, that we are grieving still."

Georgina seemed to want to say something, but the waiter materialised seemingly out of nowhere, and she bit back her words. The man looked at least 70 years old, gaunt, and wrinkled with wispy white hair. His coat-tailed livery was threadbare, but he bowed deeply and offered them each a menu — on which most items had been crossed off. After they had placed their orders for steak-and-kidney pie, Kit resumed the conversation, anxious to get his feelings off his chest. "I'm immensely grateful for the way you defended me to the Selkirks, yet I want you to know that I'm also dreadfully sorry about the whole encounter. I should have known the Selkirks might visit the grave today."

"It's no more your fault than mine," Georgina countered. "I should have realised what was going on the moment we noticed a service had just been read in the chapel."

The waiter returned with their wine and uncorked it. After Kit had tasted and accepted it, the waiter poured for them both and withdrew. Georgina sipped her wine, her eyes turned inward, and Kit let her be. In the silence, he became conscious of the soft music playing in the background on a gramophone. He took in the gentle light of the candles on the tables, augmented only by the flames licking at the large logs in the fireplace. It could have been a such romantic evening — except that Georgina was emotionally still engaged to Don.

Abruptly, Georgina looked up and met his eye, "The saddest thing about what happened between you and Colonel Selkirk is that he's hurting himself more than anyone."

"I'm not sure. I think the person he's hurting most is Mrs Selkirk. I had so wanted to tell her about Don's last flight, how Don flew despite being mortally wounded. His loyalty to his crew was literally death-defying, enabling him to fly home and make a perfect landing despite having a cannon shell lodged in his heart. It was a miracle — and the Selkirks will never know their son was at the centre it."

"Yes, that *is* sad. And yet," Georgina countered, "I find it even sadder that in cutting you out of their lives they are doing exactly the opposite of what Don wanted."

Kit drew a deep breath. "I know."

"I'm not sure you *do* know," Georgina answered softly but firmly, looking up at him, her eyes shimmering with tears. "You see, Don told me that he wanted his parents to love you like a son."

"He wanted me to feel at home," Kit corrected.

Georgina shook her head. "No, Kit, it was more than that. He wanted you to be the brother he didn't have – and the second son his parents wanted and needed." She looked Kit straight in the eye. "He wanted you to fill the gap he knew he would leave behind in his parents' home — and hearts — when he was killed."

Kit stared at her a moment before noting dryly. "Well, I certainly failed at that task."

"You didn't *fail*, Kit!" She corrected him angrily. "Colonel Selkirk didn't give you a *chance*. Not once."

Yet again, Kit was taken aback by Georgina's loyalty. After a moment, however, he conceded, "To be fair, if I'd stayed on ops, the Colonel probably would have adopted me as his own, and we most probably would have become much closer. It's only because I was so pig-headed about not flying another op to Berlin the day after Don

163

was killed that all this happened."

"And what if Don had refused to fly? Do you think they would have told *him* they never wanted to see or speak to him again?"

"But that's the point. Don would never have refused to fly."

"Are you so sure about that?"

"Yes." He paused and then added, only half in jest, "If only because he knew his father would never speak to him again if he did."

Georgina looked at him uncertainly, a slight frown hovering on her brow, but then she shook her head ambiguously and pursued her own thoughts, "I'm beginning to understand that Don knew he was living on borrowed time. He tried to arrange everything to make it easier on those he knew he would leave behind. That's why he wanted me to finish my teacher training, and why he wouldn't talk about marriage before I turned twenty-one. He must have looked on me as a child."

"Georgina, he loved you intensely," Kit assured her, sensing her sadness.

"Yes, but he was so much wiser than me. I was so naïve."

"He loved you just the way you were. He'd seen enough cynical, embittered and selfish women."

Georgina nodded thoughtfully. "I suppose you're right. A lot of women have become embittered and cynical. My roommate in the billet at Kirkby seems like that sometimes. She's a WAAF officer, and the day we met she claimed that she'd broken her heart too many times already, so she wasn't going to let herself get involved with RAF anymore. That seemed so wise at the time. I told myself I would be the same. I told myself I wasn't going to risk falling in love again, or at least not before the end of the war, and certainly not with aircrew." She stopped and looked Kit in the eye.

He evaded eye contact, preferring to nod and looked away. He did not daring meet her gaze because he could neither suppress nor disguise his disappointment. Apparently, despite her spirited defence of *him*, she hadn't changed her mind about *them*. It was comforting to know that she thought highly of him and appreciated his help, but it hurt and saddened him that she was still determined to keep him at a distance. With a sense of profound loss, he realised he had to respect and accept her decision. Resigned, he answered, "I understand."

"Kit, no! That's not right!" Georgina countered with surprising emphasis, even urgency. "It's *wrong* not to love. It's *wrong* not to admit when you love someone — especially wrong to do it just because of the *job* someone has. Not loving someone because of the uniform they wear is nearly as bad as not loving them because of the colour of their skin!"

Kit wasn't sure he should dare believe what she appeared to be saying, so he just gazed at her uncertainly.

"Kit, I'm trying to tell you that I love you!" Georgina blurted it out with all the passion of her young heart. "I love you and I can't deny it or pretend it isn't true any longer."

Kit hadn't been prepared for that — not so soon after convincing himself that she was not ready to risk her heart again. As if he were rolling a Wellington, he felt strangely disoriented. Then the full import of her words hit him, and he asked cautiously, "Seriously? Do you mean that?"

"Yes, I do! It doesn't change what I feel for Don. I know you understand that. Don will always have a special place in my heart, but he's gone now. You're right here, and I love you."

It must have been his African blood, but Kit wanted to jump up and dance for joy. Obviously, that wasn't done in England, so he broke into a wide grin instead and announced ecstatically, "I think that calls for champagne."

"Yes!" She agreed, beaming back at him. "It does!"

He stood and came around the table to kiss her on the lips for the first time.

They were both a bit tipsy by the time they went to their separate beds. No sooner had the door clicked shut behind him than Kit indulged in a short victory dance. He could still hardly believe it. Like everyone who has ever been in love, he felt lucky and undeserving, elated and full of miraculous powers. At some point it crossed his mind that Georgina's love might make it harder for him to die, but he didn't want to think about that. Not now. Tonight he would wallow in the warmth of being loved and float weightlessly on the uplifting breezes of pure joy.

Chapter 11
Getting Closer

RAF Swinderby
No. 1660 Heavy Conversion Unit (HCU)
15 November 1944

Armed with Georgina's love, Kit felt invincible. Which did not mean he was not apprehensive. Pilot and flight engineer training, up to now separate, converged at Heavy Conversion Units. Thus, while the OTU had been a new experience, the HCU was not. In addition to going through HCU training as a flight engineer, Kit had spent six months as an instructor there. The very familiarity of the environment made Kit wary. He worried that memories would haunt him, and that he might have difficulty facing a Lancaster again.

With terrifying clarity, Kit's last flight in a Lanc remained fixed in his memory. Raging winds had ripped the bomber stream apart. Diverging decoy flares sowed confusion. Cloud cover trapped the beams of the searchlights and light of the fires, creating a lurid, luminous, red-yellow carpet below the belly of the bomber. Against this molten backdrop, the black bombers stood out crisply, perfectly silhouetted for the lurking Luftwaffe night fighters. The cracking shudder of canon punching into the Lanc's fuselage still tore Kit from his sleep some nights. He would never forget the sheen of sweat on Leslie's white face as he lay wounded, nor the image of Sailor bleeding over his charts. Through it all, Don had remained calm and in control — only to be declared dead on landing.

As he turned Adrian's car into the station and showed his papers to the guard at the gate, Kit searched the distance for the familiar aircraft silhouette, but saw only utilitarian buildings blocking the view to the airfield. The sentry returned his papers and saluted. Kit turned into the drive and started in the direction of the officers' mess. At last, he caught a glimpse of grass and beyond that tarmac and a paved dispersal. He put on the brakes and stared at the Lancaster sitting patiently in front of a hangar. It sat nose-in-the-air with its double-finned tail low to the ground and its hundred-foot wingspan stretching grandly to either side.

Instead of dread, a rush of affection suffused him. Despite suffering severe damage, their gallant Lancaster had brought them safely home. He smiled to himself. Most RAF trainee pilots fantasised about flighty, high-strung Spitfires and Typhoons or audacious, versatile Mosquitos, but Kit had long since given his heart to this majestic machine. The fighters were mere toys compared to it. Kit liked to think of the Lancaster as a four-horse chariot from which they hurled death like a modern-day Hector battling the arrogant, invading Achilles.

The officers' mess was functional rather than attractive, but at least it was brick-and-mortar rather than corrugated iron. It offered tall windows that let in the brittle winter sunlight. The officers' quarters were also housed in a solid, brick building and more spacious, with only two officers assigned to each room. Kit checked to see if Adrian was back yet, and when the clerk could find no one by that name registered, Kit told him to put Pilot Officer Peal in his room when he arrived. He unpacked rapidly and returned to the anteroom. It was six pm and drinks were being served.

Adrian arrived within the hour. He waved and came straight over, asking with a look of concern. "Everything go all right, Kit?"

"Yes, I brought your car back in one piece. No dents or scratches."

"That's not what I meant," Adrian protested. "Did you find the grave?"

"Yes, and I'm glad I went, even if the cemetery was in the middle of nowhere and it was raining cats and dogs. It was important to me. I can't thank you enough for the car. How about you? How was the rest of your leave?"

"I managed to get away for a day to see Julia." Adrian's smile was so wide Kit laughed out loud. "What was that quote from the Squadron Leader in in the Battle of Britain? That it would be a shame—"

"Never mind, since it clearly doesn't apply to you."

"There's still the problem with my parents, though," Adrian pointed out, looking down at his drink pensively. "Now that you've met them, I expect you can understand how difficult it is to take a girl home to introduce to them." Kit nodded to show he could see Adrian's point, and Adrian shrugged and changed the subject. "What about the rest of your leave?"

"It was —" What word could possibly describe what had happened? "Amazing" sprang to mind. Yet Kit feared that if he talked about Georgina the magic spell might break and her love turn to ashes. "— not what I expected. I met an old friend and we discovered that we wanted to see more of one another. A lot more of one another." He grinned.

"The kind of girl you'd take home to introduce to your mother?"

"Yes, actually. She's in teacher's college and my mother was a teacher.

I think they'd get on like a house on fire. In fact, the girl in question has already written to my mother without my knowing about it!"

"Cripes! I'm not sure I'd like it if Julia wrote to my materfamilias behind my back," Adrian muttered as though to himself. Kit burst out laughing and Adrian joined in. They ordered another round.

About an hour later Forrester arrived and made a beeline for Kit and Adrian. "Well, if it isn't Zulu Moran himself!" he declared in a loud voice that turned heads across the anteroom.

"That's not—" Kit started to protest, angry with himself for confiding in Forrester about his background. Adrian caught his eye and shook his head sharply. Kit understood. If he protested, he'd only increase Forrester's delight in this new nickname; by laughing, he rendered it harmless. So, Kit laughed and went on the offensive, "What happened to you? A girl take exception to your amorous advances?" Forrester had a black, swollen eye and a bad, jagged cut on his chin.

"Had to teach some snotty Americans a lesson," Forrester answered grinning. "Best fight I've had in years. What are you drinking?"

Kit and Adrian let him buy them a round, and Forrester pulled up a chair beside Kit. "So, give me the gen on the Lanc," he demanded.

Kit smiled and kept the tone light and bantering. "She's not at all your type, Forrester. She's a lady. Steady, sedate, smooth, and sophisticated."

Forrester wasn't offended. "Think I can't handle a lady? I'll bet I solo on her sooner than you do."

"Save your money. You may need it to pay bail next time you decide to break things."

"I'll give you odds. If I solo first, you pay me ten bob, but if you do, I'll pay you a whole quid."

Kit didn't want his reacquaintance with the Lanc rushed by the pressure of competition. He shook his head. "No, thanks. I told you before I'm not a gambling man."

"I'll take the bet," Adrian offered his hand to the Australian.

Forrester shook it firmly. "Glad to see someone on Zulu's crew has balls. Bet's on then!"

"Your money, but for the record: it's not getting in the air first that counts but getting back again too."

Before turning in, Kit called over to the sergeants' mess to make sure the rest of his crew had arrived safely. They all had, and without arrests or other incidents.

In the morning, after the usual welcoming speeches from the Station Commander and Chief Flying and Ground Instructors, the trainee crews were given their introduction to the Lancaster. They had not yet seen any sign of the mid-upper gunners or flight engineers who would be joining the course. Rumour had it that they would arrive in the afternoon and crewing up might start as early as the following day.

After collecting and signing for a parachute and Mae West, the trainees were driven out to the dispersed aircraft in the back of a lorry. Moran's crew was assigned to N-Nan, an old, scratched and dented veteran that had evidently been repaired innumerable times. While the other members of his crew climbed up the ladder in a state of barely suppressed excitement, Moran walked over to the ground crew standing together under the nose. Opening a packet of cigarettes, he held it out for the men to help themselves as he asked: "Any particular gremlins I should know about?"

Amidst the murmurs of thanks, a flight sergeant gestured toward N-Nan. "Number one engine doesn't fire properly at first, but once it settles down it's fine. Number three takes marginally more revs for the same amount of power." A second member of the ground crew chimed in: "Nanny also has a tendency to yaw badly to port on take-off. Haven't worked out why. Otherwise, she's fine."

Moran thanked them and climbed aboard. Inside the fuselage he turned towards the tail and clambered over the aft spar and the Elsan toilet to check on Osgood. Opening the armoured doors and poking his head into the turret, he asked, "Comfortable?"

Osgood looked over his shoulder startled by the intrusion. Then he grinned and nodded. "It's got wizard visibility, Skipper."

Moran made his way forward, glancing up at the still empty mid-upper turret, clambered over the main spar, and paused to check on Tibble and Peal. The wireless operator was clipping his jotted briefing notes beside his workstation, while the navigator had spread out his map and lined up his instruments, pencils and notebook in an orderly fashion. Rather than stopping in the cockpit, Moran dropped down into the nose. Babcock lay on his stomach checking the bomb site equipment. At the sight of Moran, he gave him the thumbs-up.

"Hello?" A voice called from behind, and Moran returned to the cockpit where the instructor had appeared. "Darby." He held out his hand. "Shall we get started?" It obviously wasn't a question. He raised his voice, calling into the nose, "Bomb aimer, come up here and watch this as well."

The instructor indicated Moran should take the pilot's seat but not strap in, while he folded down the engineer's seat. Babcock stood in the steps down to the nose.

The instructor addressed himself to Babcock. "Until a flight engineer joins the crew, you'll have to assist the pilot at take-off and landing. It isn't hard." Then he picked up the check list and started to show Moran each of the dials and instruments. He rapidly realised he wasn't telling Moran anything he didn't know. He looked back at him somewhat irritated. "What position did you fly before?"

"Engineer."

"Right. Do you feel you can handle it straight away, or do you want me to show you a couple of take-offs and landings?"

Based on the annoyance in Darby's voice, Moran opted for caution. "I'd rather watch you once or twice, sir."

They switched places and Moran took over his old role as engineer, handling undercarriage, flaps and throttles on two complete circuits while the instructor provided a running commentary on what he was doing. Babcock looked on with an expression of mild terror. Darby also pointed out features of the countryside as landmarks for navigation. After they touched down for the second time, the instructor motioned to Moran to swap places.

His hands feeling the vibrations of the giant aircraft that was now under his command, Moran cautiously taxied to the head of the runway and turned onto it. Positive excitement embraced him. In some ways this moment meant more to him than soloing on single-engine trainers. That, of course, had been a necessary prerequisite for this moment, but this was the real test. Even the Wellington had been like a fairground pony compared to a racing thoroughbred. Only now, with the four Merlin engines growling furiously and the whole aircraft humming around him, did Moran feel he had finally made it. He was a Lancaster pilot.

He held his breath as he waited for the green light from the caravan beside the runway. Finally, it beamed at him. He advanced the throttles and eased off the brakes. The Lancaster started to roll forward. She was light without a full load of fuel and bombs. Keeping her straight on the runway took sensitive use of the rudder, particularly due to the heavy port yaw the ground crew had warned him about. Yet she wanted to fly, and Kit had to resist the temptation to let her have her head. The instructor was calling out the speed to him. "Ninety-five... one hundred... one ten... one twenty." Now. He gently eased back on the control column as the instructor held the throttles at the stops. The Lancaster became lighter, striving for the air, the wheels only barely kissing the concrete. "One twenty-five... one thirty." Moran pulled her up. With a soaring sense of elation, they left the ground behind.

Like most pilots, Moran found the Lancaster a dream to fly. She was responsive without being over-sensitive, and she was gracious in her willingness to overlook moments of inattentiveness or excessive exuberance. After conducting the standard set of manoeuvres required, the instructor ordered Moran to land Nan back at the station. Unlike take-off, Kit had landed a Lancaster once before. It had been Don's idea; he'd said he wanted Kit to know how to do it "in an emergency." They had swapped places, and Don had talked Kit through the landing procedures as they returned to their station from a test flight. The experiment had not gone well. Kit had banked too steeply into the final approach, touched down with one wheel, overcompensated, and then bounced his way to the far end of the runway. There he'd slewed the big bomber around so hard it had gone off into the mud, crumpling one leg of the undercarriage. Don and he had received the worst ticking off of their lives, and Don very nearly got a red endorsement in his logbook.

Kit recalled that landing now as he lined up with the runway at Swinderby — not with apprehension, but rather with a sense of superiority and amusement. He'd had no pilot training before his last landing; now he had close to three hundred flying hours. He eased back to 100 mph, ordered flaps and undercarriage down, then pulled the nose up to settle onto the end of the runway like a great bird. It was a near-perfect landing.

As Kit turned off the runway onto the taxiway, the instructor started to gather his things together. "Not much point my staying here when I'm obviously not needed. Drop me there by the dispersal and then take her up again. Take half an hour or so to get familiar with the geography hereabouts, but be sure to land before," he looked at his watch, "11:00."

"Yes, sir." Moran tried not to show how pleased he felt.

"And Moran?"

"Sir?"

"Do try not to break anything."

Moran stopped the aircraft. The instructor squeezed his way past Peal and Tibble's station and down the length of the narrow fuselage. He opened the door and dropped down without bothering with the ladder. Tibble went aft to close the door after him. Moran continued on the taxiway. Just before he turned onto the runway, he switched on his microphone. "Pilot to crew: has anyone seen the instructor leave Forrester's Lanc yet?"

"Doesn't look like it, Skip," Babcock piped up.

Osgood answered more definitively, "Not bloody likely, Skip. He's still on board all right."

"In that case, I think the first round's on Peal tonight — when he collects his winnings."

Beaming, he turned onto the runway and could hear the laughter of his crew ringing through the Lancaster as he again got the green for take-off. He was now, at last, a Lancaster skipper.

Lincoln Diocesan Training College
27 November 1944

The Director of Assignments looked severely over the rim of his glasses at Georgina and told her pointedly, "We strongly advise against trainees spending their entire apprenticeship at the same school. The point of these apprenticeships is to give you exposure to real-life situations and diversity of experience will prepare you better for your future."

"I understand, sir." Georgina answered calmly. "However, I did not perform well at Kirkby Grange. It took me an inordinately long time to find my footing. I feel as though I was just starting to get into my stride and become useful when term ended."

"Well, you are not alone in having difficulty at Kirkby Grange." The director noted sitting back in his chair and removing his spectacles altogether to see her better. "The school has quite a reputation. Indeed, I seem to remember trying to dissuade you from going there in the first place."

"Very true, sir." Georgina's appearance of calm was a façade. Underneath she was terribly nervous, but she believed her best chance of talking the Director around was to own up to her weaknesses. "You were right to doubt my ability to cope. However, now that I'm making progress it would be a shame to stop. I'd like to bring things to a satisfactory conclusion rather than run away in the middle — so to speak."

"That's admirable, Miss Reddings, but we make every effort to ensure our trainees have only one difficult, and one easy, berth. Having survived Kirkby Grange, I've assigned you to Waverley, an excellent girls' school in Devon. It has spacious, modern facilities and generous on-site accommodation, so there'd be no more billeting."

My God, Georgina thought in horror. There was hardly anywhere in the whole country farther away from the bomber stations than Devon.

Oblivious to Georgina's distress, the director continued praising Waverley. "The headmistress is a lovely, cultivated woman, while the girls will give you none of the trouble the little monsters at Kirkby Grange did."

"They weren't that bad, sir," Georgina told him with a smile that was only partially forced. "I asked for a coeducational school because it's the kind of school I want to work at after I'm qualified. Lovely as Waverley sounds, it wouldn't be as relevant to my future work as returning to Kirkby Grange would be."

"I see. So, you still see your future at a co-educational school?"

"Yes, very much so."

"Even without doing an apprenticeship at a girl's school? Isn't that being a little hasty?"

"I went to girls' schools all my life, sir. I know what they're like."

"Hm. You certainly seem to have your heart set on this." He leaned forward and replaced his glasses as he looked over the lists in front of him. Georgina tried to look alert, obedient and confident all at once. The director, however, shook his head as he checked details, and her heart sank. "I'm sorry, Miss Reddings. I've already informed Fiona Barker that she will be going to Kirkby Grange after her comfy assignment last term. The only way I could countenance you returning there would be if you could convince Miss Townsend to take two apprentice teachers for the remaining terms." Looking back and forth over his lists, he muttered, as much to himself as to Georgina, "Although I could then give this posting at Waverley to Miss Abbot, who also had a terrible last term."

Georgina thought that talking Miss Townsend into two apprentice teachers might be difficult but at least it wasn't a firm 'no.' "Could you give me this week to try to arrange that? A second position at Kirkby Grange, I mean?"

"Until Friday? That would be December the 1st. No, I'll need something firm before that. You'll have to get back to me by tomorrow, Wednesday at the latest. If I haven't heard back from you by then, your assignment to Waverley will be final."

"I understand."

Rather than returning directly to her lodgings after her day of consultations at the College, Georgina cycled to Kirkby Grange to seek an interview with Miss Townsend. It was already seven o'clock, and the headmistress had retired to her flat. After only a moment's hesitation, Georgina decided to seek her out there. She wanted to resolve the issue of her assignment as soon as possible.

She approached Miss Townsend's door with considerable trepidation. As always when nervous, she pulled her hair away from her face and wrapped the end of her ponytail around the base to make a hasty bun. Then she tugged the cuffs of her blouse further down her wrists, noting with dismay how frayed they were.

In answer to her knock, the door cracked, then pulled open wide with a surprised exclamation of "Miss Reddings! I thought you had consultations at your college today?"

"I've just returned from them, ma'am. The college is preparing the placements for the next Spring and Summer terms, and I've come to request re-assignment to Kirkby Grange. The college will allow that, if you accept —"

"This sounds like a longer discussion than one that we should be having here on the doorstep. You'd better come in." Miss Townsend admitted Georgina and led her into the cosy sitting room. The neo-Gothic room was stuffed like a Christmas goose with old, plush furniture, rugs, books, paintings and porcelain figurines. Georgina caught a glimpse of a woman who was not as austere as the headmistress. She also spotted an oil painting of a younger Miss Townsend in hunting pinks beside a bright-eyed, chestnut hunter.

"Oh, do you hunt, Miss Townsend?"

"I used to," the older woman answered sharply. Then, noting Georgina's gaze, something in her softened. "That was my favourite hunter, Champagne. Painted in 1912." A sad look crossed her hardened face, and Georgina saw a flicker of regret and lost love. Miss Townsend turned to face Georgina with a raised brow, "Do I infer that you hunt yourself?"

"I was passionate about it before the war; a bit horse-mad really. I hope I've grown out of that, but I also hope I'll never stop having horses in my life."

"Hm. I felt the same, once. We used to have horses here, you know. Until we closed the boys' school. I was very sad to see them go." Miss Townsend sounded surprisingly melancholy, provoking in Georgina an unexpected twinge of sympathy for the headmistress.

"Did you never think of bringing them back?" Georgina asked. "I mean, now that we have the evacuees." The idea started to excite her. "Most have probably never been near a proper horse in their lives. They could learn so much from the noble beasts."

"We could never find grooms nowadays. Everyone's doing war service." Miss Townsend retorted with an irritated gesture.

"But we could look after them ourselves, Miss Townsend. My parents have looked after our three without any hired help ever since the war started. After all, learning to look after horses would be as good, perhaps better, for the children than learning to ride. We could start with just two or three horses and maybe a pony or two."

"That would only lead to terrible fights over who gets to ride, groom and everything else! To avoid jealousy, a school this size would need at least twenty mounts, and the expense associated with a stable that size is far beyond our capacity. The whole idea is utterly impractical!"

Georgina realised that it was because Miss Townsend would have loved to revive the stables that she was so angry she could not, so she docilely backed down. "I'm sure you know best, Miss Townsend. It was just a thought..."

Miss Townsend considered Georgina with an expression the latter could not read. After a pause she suggested, "Would you like some tea, Miss Reddings?"

Although the offer came as a surprise, Georgina instantly accepted. Given their tense relationship so far, she interpreted the invitation as a gesture of reconciliation — or at least a new start. "That would be very kind, ma'am."

"Have a seat, then," Miss Townsend indicated a sofa beside a low coffee table and disappeared calling "Maisy! Tea for two, please." She returned shortly and settled herself into the comfortable armchair at the head of the table. "Let's get back to the purpose of your visit." Miss Townsend faced Georgina squarely as she continued, "You said you want to return here for the remaining two terms. Whatever for?"

"Well, I got off to a very poor start—"

"You certainly did!" Miss Townsend agreed.

"But I had the feeling I was getting better by the end of term."

"Indeed, but you could hardly do much worse."

"No, and, you see, I felt that going to an easy school with all girls wouldn't do anything to make me a better teacher. Sticking it out here and getting to grips with the more difficult pupils, on the other hand, would be the best preparation for a career in the profession."

"Hm." Miss Townsend answered ambiguously.

When she said nothing more, Georgina felt compelled to fill the silence. "I really would like a second chance, ma'am, but the college insists that I must not be assigned to exactly the same class."

"That's good because I don't think Miss Evans could stand the sight of you." Miss Townsend paused and then asked not at all unkindly, "Just how far does your new-born self-confidence extend? Do you think you could take on older boys? Third Form perhaps? Or were you hoping to stay with little children?"

"I'd be delighted to teach Third Form," Georgina lied. She was not delighted by the prospect of older boys but had foreseen that this might be her only option. She certainly preferred older children at Kirkby Grange to children of any age at a school in Devon, where she and Kit would have no hope of seeing one another at the weekend, much less evenings.

Miss Townsend raised her eyebrows sceptically, but then turned away altogether as an aging maid brought in the tea. She poured for Georgina and invited her to help herself to some tinned shortbread. Only after the ritual was over did she speak again. "I'm not sure what I should say, Miss Reddings. Despite your poor performance in the classroom, I admit I was pleasantly surprised by your diligence. You have worked late and on many weekends. You've done a remarkable job with this sewing class you started. When you first got here, I'd expected you to be out drinking and dancing with the swarms of aircrew that infest the local pubs."

Georgina squirmed inwardly. She rather hoped her abstinent ways were about to change.

"Nevertheless, I'm going to be perfectly honest. I do not have much confidence in your ability to manage older boys. When even First Formers can make you dance to their tune, how are you ever going to cope with the older children?"

"I've learnt my lesson, Miss Townsend. I promise to be much firmer from the start."

"Hmph!" Miss Townsend considered her again. "I must say, I admire your pluck. You did not crumble as I expected you to, and you have indeed shown marked improvement over the last month." She paused again. "All right. You may go and talk to Mr Willoughby about the possibility of assisting him. I'll ring and tell him you are on your way. But," and the headmistress held a warning finger in the air, "it will be entirely his decision whether he wants you or not."

Mr Willoughby had been a Sergeant Major in the last war, and he'd lost a leg at Verdun. He walked with a cane, and lines carved by pain and disappointment marred his once handsome face. Up to now, Georgina's contact with him had been minimal, as all the male teachers from the Old Palace School of Bromley kept to themselves in the 'boy's wing' of the school. Advised by Miss Townsend of her visit, he offered her a seat and tea, but she declined the latter, explaining she'd just had some.

"Let's get to the point," he opened in his brusque, military manner. "I've never had an assistant teacher and I'm not at all keen on the idea. I'm particularly opposed to having a young woman with your background interfering in my classroom." Like Miss Evans, Mr Willoughby had worked his way up from a poor background and had a low opinion of 'daughters of privilege' such as Georgina. "Frankly, I don't know what I'd do with you."

Georgina started to panic but she was not prepared just to back down. "I've noticed that many of the evacuees don't spell very well, sir, and that's one of my strengths. I thought perhaps I could start a roll-a-word club—"

"Oh, that's just like you do-gooders! You want to turn everything into a game!"

Georgina looked down at her hands. The remark hurt because it was true. She did think learning ought to be fun. Yet sensing that a man like Willoughby would be more impressed by spunk than passivity, Georgina risked arguing with him. "It's a proven fact, sir, that many boys drop out of school simply because they don't like it. Doing something to make them enjoy — and take an interest in — learning is surely the first step to getting boys to stay in school long enough to get a school leaving certificate."

Mr Willoughby snorted and looked at her with a frown that was no longer entirely hostile. He seemed to be reconsidering her. After a moment, he announced, "I don't think turning learning into a silly game is the answer, but I concede we have an inordinate number of pupils whose performance is so deplorable that if they don't get *some* sort of extra help, half of them will be resitting this summer — which is not my idea of fun. I presume you can teach remedial English, but do you also think you could tutor 14-year-old boys in maths?" He looked over at her with a raised eyebrow.

"I'd enjoy that," she told him, trying to disguise her nervousness.

He snorted again. "I doubt it." He shook his head. "I'm not at all convinced that women can teach boys of any age, let alone 14-year-olds. Their hormones play up an awful lot at that age, you know?"

"I do have an older brother," Georgina tried to point out.

"I can just imagine!" He retorted in a tone that seemed to imply that any brother of hers must be effeminate if not outright homosexual. She rather wished he could meet Gerald but knew better than to say anything. All she could do was await his verdict. Finally, he announced. "I honestly don't think this is going to do any of us any good, but what have I got to lose? We'll give it a try, but if things go badly, as I suspect they will, you'll have to find a new assignment."

"Yes, sir. That's fair enough," Georgina told him levelly, trying to disguise her relief. She did not know how much time God would give her with Kit, but she was determined to see as much of him as possible, and that meant living close to where he was likely to be stationed. As for the boys, Georgina believed that she had learned her lessons and was strong enough to face them. If she could discover something as interesting for them as the sewing had proved for the girls, maybe she would succeed at making one or two of them interested in learning to improve themselves....

RAF Swinderby
No. 1660 Heavy Conversion Unit
1 December 1944

As soon as the mid-upper gunners and flight engineers arrived, the process of crewing up began again. As expected, Forrester tried to snatch up the men with the best reputations, but Kit also overheard him warning men away from "Zulu" Moran. That annoyed him, but by now he knew that he generally didn't like same men that Forrester did anyway. Instead, he charged his three sergeants, who shared the mess with the newcomers, with finding men they thought would fit into the crew.

The burden of identifying a mid-upper gunner fell on Nigel. He was in the same specialist instruction as the other gunners and so in the best position to judge their character and skills. In just two days, Nigel introduced Frank Roper to Kit. At nineteen, Frank was a year older than Nigel, and his father was a sailor too, but in Frank' case a petty officer with P&O serving on troop transports. Frank was short, stocky and self-assured without being cocky. What spoke most for him, however, was that he and Nigel had taken to each other so spontaneously that Kit accepted Frank would be an asset to the crew almost regardless of how well he could shoot.

Finding a flight engineer proved more difficult. Too different in background and personality to like the same kind of people, Stu and Terry recommended two different candidates. Kit agreed to fly with both, but he also had his own expectations for the role he'd once held himself. He took it as read that an engineer would make the same calculations in his head as he had done, such as knowing at all times how far they could fly at the current rate of fuel consumption. He also expected his engineer to be able to locate the control cables in the fuselage in the dark, to lower the undercarriage without hydraulics, and a variety of other skills he'd brought to Don's crew. Neither of the men his sergeants recommended could do these things, and Kit turned them down. It proved to be a mistake.

Flight engineers started avoiding him and teaming up with other pilots. Kit had set his expectations too high but would now be left with the dregs. After two days only three crews were incomplete, one of which was Kit's.

The following day, a burly Scotsman with flight sergeant stripes climbed out of a crew bus beside N-Nan and introduced himself to Kit with a smart salute. "Gordon MacDonald, sir. I've been temporarily assigned as your Flight Engineer, sir."

"How old are you, Flight?" Kit asked, noting the deep lines chiselled into his face. Stu had mentioned this man as one of the remaining candidates but been dismissive based on his age.

"Thirty-five, sir. That's why most of the lads call me 'Daddy.'" He grinned as he admitted this.

"How long have you been in the RAF?"

"Twenty years. Joined as one of Trenchard's brats in '24."

"Fitter?"

"Yes, sir."

"That makes two of us, Daddy. The fitter part, that is. I was never a Halton Apprentice. Welcome aboard." Except for Adrian, who already knew, the rest of Kit's crew gaped at their commissioned skipper in astonishment. They had not dreamed Kit had once been a lowly erk.

"Ah, sir?" Daddy MacDonald stopped Kit as he turned to mount the ladder into the aircraft.

"Yes?" Kit waited expectantly.

"The other engineers are saying, like, you expect your engineer to do a lot of maths in his head. Well, I thought I'd better tell you straight up that I can't do that, but I've got a very clever wee pencil here." He pulled the stub of a pencil from behind his ear. "And a pad of paper here," he tapped the left breast pocket of his battle dress, "and I'll do the calculations by hand. They'll be right that way, skipper."

"Fair enough," Kit told him. "Let's prepare to start engines."

By the end of that first flight Kit knew Daddy was an asset. The older man was conscientious, meticulous and utterly unflappable. Kit rolled the Lancaster to prove to himself that he could do it, but it was also a private victory roll for getting this far: a Lancaster skipper with a complete crew. He wished Georgina could have been below to see it.

As the dust fell back from the ceiling to the floor Daddy asked in a calm voice, his face utterly impassive, "Do you do that a lot, sir?"

"I don't plan to do one ever again," Kit answered honestly.

"In that case, sir, I won't ask for a transfer after all."

The rest of the crew burst out laughing, adding their agreement with loud shouts of "hear! hear!"

Foster Clough, Yorkshire
First Sunday in Advent
3 December 1944

Edwin Reddings pulled over to the side of the road and stopped the car. Sudden and intense head pains like a hammer on his forehead nearly incapacitated him. He removed his wire-framed glasses and pressed a hand to his brow. Images abruptly filled his head with terrifying clarity. "No, stop! Please!" He pleaded. "I don't want to see any more!" God was not listening.

Fortunately, it was over in a matter of seconds. The images faded, and Edwin was left breathing deeply and shakily. The pain started to drain away. He'd had maybe a dozen of these visions over the last two decades, and he hated them. They left him frightened and emotionally drained. He was far too shaken to drive, so he started methodically cleaning his glasses to regain his composure.

The first time he'd experienced one of these visions had been in 1919. He'd been a 22-year-old subaltern in the Duke of Wellington's West Riding Regiment and returning from a party irresponsibly inebriated. He was feeling smug and devil-may-care because the war was over and he was still alive. It was a foggy evening and, conscious of just how plastered he was, he drove with drunken determination behind a lorry, convinced that as long as he followed the taillights he would stay safely on the road.

Then suddenly he was thrust off the road by an invisible force that seemed to push the car aside like a toy. He struggled with all his strength to stay on the pavement, but he wasn't strong enough. The car went off the road and skidded to a halt to the sound of flying gravel. The engine cut out. The terror generated by that encounter with the paranormal was enough to sober him instantly. Yet as he waited for his breathing and pulse to stabilise, the image of a horrible accident invaded his mind: a lorry had collided with a sports car and the drivers of both vehicles were badly injured. The lorry driver was hanging halfway out of the window and dripping blood from a smashed and lacerated face. A woman had been flung from the passenger seat of the sports car and lay in the ditch beside the road, her bones shattered and moaning in agony.

The twenty-two-year-old Reddings had fought in Flanders. He had seen plenty of dead and dying. Yet that vivid image of a car crash after the utterly unfathomable experience of being pushed off the road by an invisible force made his hair stand on end. He concluded that the accident had happened on this stretch of road and the ghosts had pushed his car aside to tell him of their tragedy.

Frantic to flee this haunted spot, the young officer restarted the car and pulled back onto the road. Although nothing unnatural stopped him, without taillights to follow, he had to drive much more slowly. All he could do was crawl through the fog in second gear, following the broken white line dividing the two lanes until he came around a curve to see the accident from his vision *in front of him*. Reverting to his training and experience as a frontline officer, he jumped from his car, pulled his first aid kit from the boot, and rendered what assistance he could. The driver of the sports car was beyond help, but he got the woman and the lorry driver into his car and drove them to the nearest town, where the police took over.

Only when he finally got to bed did it occur to him that the lorry in the accident had been the one that he had been following. Had he not been forced off the road by that invisible force, he would himself have contributed to and been a victim of the accident. Furthermore, without the premonition of the accident, he might not have spotted the woman in the ditch in the dark. There might have been four casualties instead of one; certainly, the woman would have died. It was his personal epiphany.

Not being a professional soldier, Edwin had planned to finish reading law when his demob papers came. Instead, he transferred to theology and four years later obtained his Doctor of Divinity followed by seminary and ordination. In all that time he did not have a second vision of any kind. Only after he came to his parish did it happen again. Seeing the death of a neighbour's child in a swimming accident had been less dramatic, but the horror of seeing a child drown before his eyes while being utterly incapable of taking any action had been emotionally devastating.

In today's vision the casualty had again been one of his parishioners, the ne'er-do-well son of the village grocer. The boy's parents would be devastated by his death, while Edwin was more appalled by the intuitive knowledge that he'd died with a great deal of guilt and hatred in his heart. Bob Crofts would not rest easily in the Beyond, Edwin concluded with a deep sigh. He replaced his glasses, turned the key in the ignition and continued his journey home.

He was glad to reach the vicarage half an hour later. Amanda loved Christmas and for her it always began with the first Sunday in Advent. He knew before entering that the house would already be decorated with sprigs of holly and other evergreens. All would be hung with silver bells and garnished with gold ribbons. As he came through the back door, he could smell fruitcake in the oven and hear the cheerful sound of women chatting and laughing in the kitchen. So Georgina had made it home while he was doing his rounds.

He paused in the kitchen doorway to take in the domestic scene: Amanda wearing her apron was standing beside the sink and stirring something in a bowl while Georgina sat at the kitchen table chopping nuts. Georgina looked astonishingly happy, he noted gratefully. This time last year her grief for Don had banished all trace of Christmas cheer. Despite going through the motions of celebrating, the holiday had been miserable.

Amanda saw him first. "Edwin! You looked exhausted! What is it? Has something happened?"

Edwin shook his head. "Not really. Nothing I want to talk about." He gave Amanda a warning look and she understood instantly.

Georgina jumped up to give him a happy hug of welcome and exclaimed, "It's so good to see you, Daddy! I have so much to tell you, but you *do* look tired. Aren't you feeling well?"

"I'm fine. Have the horses been fed?" he asked, diverting attention from his emotional state.

"Yes, of course, Daddy!" Georgina answered in a mock-insulted tone. "Fed, groomed and they all have their blankets and water for the night."

"And are you on holiday now, or do you have to go back to that dreadful school?" He asked, pulling out a chair at the table and sinking down into it with relief.

"Oh, it's not that dreadful, Daddy. You know, it was mostly my own fault that I fell for the silly stories the boys told and let them run roughshod over me in the beginning. They were just children having fun. And my sewing classes have been a great success! More girls show up every time. I believe I've helped some of the girls who were uninterested in learning to, well, listen at least some of the time."

"That sounds very encouraging indeed!" Edwin smiled at his daughter, pleased by her attitude. There had been times this past year when he'd feared for her sanity. He had worried that she might crack and lose her reason altogether, or at a minimum be psychologically scarred for the rest of her life. He'd wondered if her naturally sweet and optimistic nature would become warped by the magnitude of her grief. Instead, his resilient daughter had found inner strength and fought her way back not only onto her feet but to her old self. Remembering that it hadn't just been the pupils who'd proved difficult, he asked, "And the staff? How are you getting on with the headmistress and Miss Evans?"

"Oh, I've learnt how to cope with the nasty ladies." She answered lightly with a tinkling laugh, before adding more seriously, "I don't think I'll ever like Miss Evans or vice versa. She resents people like us, whom she considers 'privileged,' 'spoilt,' 'smug' and 'self-satisfied.' But I've come to respect Miss Townsend. Yes, she's narrow-minded on many things, but she has had a very difficult time keeping the school going. It nearly closed down altogether. Taking in refugees saved it but coping with so many children from working-class backgrounds whilst managing a close-knit, resentful clique of teachers from a different school hasn't been easy."

"No, I should think not," Edwin agreed. "I'm very glad that you can see that."

"I'm not completely blind, Daddy," Georgina quipped back. "In fact, I've volunteered to return to Kirkby Grange for the rest of the year and will be teaching Third Form."

"Good gracious! Are you sure that was wise?"

Georgina laughed. "I doubt it was wise, Daddy, but it's what I want." Her smile seemed strangely impish, as if she were hiding a secret.

Edwin glanced at Amanda questioningly and was surprised to see his wife looked amused rather than concerned. She seemed to know something he didn't, but before he could ask to be let in on the secret Georgina asked solicitously, "Shall I get you some tea, Daddy? You really do look knackered."

"Frankly I think I need something stronger. What do you say I make us all hot toddies?" Amanda and Georgina readily agreed, so Edwin stood again and returned to his study to fetch the alcoholic ingredients from his drinks' cabinet. The last time he'd made these, he remembered, had been when Kit Moran had been staying with them. The thought made him sad. Moran struck a chord with him, and they had conversed easily about so many things. And how many other young officers spent their leave visiting abbey ruins and cathedrals? He'd mentioned his encounter with Moran in a letter to Georgina, but she had responded ambiguously. He supposed he shouldn't have tried to interfere, but he liked Moran so much that he was sorry to see her break off with him.

Back in the kitchen, the kettle whistled faintly as Georgina stirred honey into concentrated lemon juice. "You're looking very well, Georgina, if a father is allowed to make such remarks." Edwin sank again into his chair and removed his glasses. "I feared... well, you know, that the anniversary might put you in a gloomy mood."

"I can understand your trepidation, Daddy," she conceded, "but as I was telling Mummy before you came, I've decided I have to move beyond the pain. I'm sorry I was such a child last year."

"It's not your fault you were so young or that you loved so deeply," her father told her gently, his affection for her welling up.

Amanda took the screeching kettle off the stove and came to pour it into the mixer her husband had brought. As her parents concentrated on making the toddies, Georgina leaned her elbows on the table and cupped her chin in her hands. "Daddy?"

"Hm?"

"You get these visions sometimes..."

Edwin spun about sharply. How had she known? He looked at Amanda with an unspoken question. She just shook her head bemused.

Georgina was continuing, "But they've always involved strangers, haven't they? Or, well, people you only know distantly. You've never had them about someone close, have you?"

"What do you mean?" He handed her a mug of steaming alcohol.

"Well, Gerald, for example. Or Don?"

"Gerald is fine," her father answered firmly, causing even Amanda to raise her eyebrows.

"And Don? I mean since he passed away is there any way that you —"

"Georgina, your father's tired. You shouldn't—"

"It's all right, Amanda," Edwin told his wife before looking intently at his daughter. "I'm not a medium, Georgina. I can't contact the dead, and they do not speak to me. It's true that I sometimes have these visions — fortunately not too often. And sometimes I sense things that aren't entirely tangible. That's all. I have never had contact with those who have already gone on before us."

Georgina nodded solemnly. "I understand, Daddy. It's just…"

"What's bothering you, child?" He encouraged her.

"Well, Kit and I visited Don's grave on the anniversary of the crash—"

"You've seen Kit again?" Edwin was so pleased he couldn't help interrupting.

"I — I rang him. He was planning to visit the grave on the anniversary anyway, and he offered to drive me there."

"So that's why you didn't ask me to take you. I'd kept the day free and even had the car serviced. When you didn't ring, I assumed Miss Townsend hadn't given you the day off."

"Thank you for thinking of me, Daddy," she reached out and squeezed his hand once, but then continued with her thoughts. "When I was there, I had this powerful feeling that Don wanted me to move on. Do you think that's possible? I mean, is it possible that it was something real, not just me making excuses for what I want to do?"

"Georgina, if there's one thing I believe, it is that Don wanted you to be happy. You can't be happy by dwelling on the death of a wonderful young man. You can't be happy by denying yourself a future. Seeing how you grieved must have hurt Don terribly."

Georgina caught her breath. She had never thought of Don *seeing* her grieve. What a frightening thought! After being so selfless and brave himself, Don must have been disgusted with her lack of fortitude and courage. "Do you think…"

"Go on," her father urged her.

Georgina took a deep breath. "Do you think he'd be upset to know that Kit and I have fallen in love with one another?"

185

"That's splendid news, my dear!" Edwin proclaimed breaking into a broad smile. "I'm very fond of that young man and so is your mother." He glanced towards his wife, realising that this was the secret she and Georgina had already shared before his arrival.

"But what would Don think?" Georgina asked her father seriously, evidently still unsure.

"My dear, I can't imagine anyone Don would approve of *more*. Together you will never forget him, and that is the most the dead have a right to ask of the living."

RAF Swinderby
No. 1660 Heavy Conversion Unit
December 1944

The nerves and skills of the trainee crews had been tested throughout the first two weeks of December as the instructors cut engines on them unexpectedly and simulated other emergencies. They practiced "crash positions" on every flight, and on the ground their classes focused increasingly on first aid, emergency and survival equipment, as well as evasion and escape. As they moved into their third week the emphasis shifted back to bombing runs and simulated fighter attacks by Mosquitos from a Fighter Command OTU, but unlike back at Moreton-in-Marsh, most of the exercises were now at night.

When a blizzard smothered the whole of northeast England in snow on the 20th of December, all hopes of Christmas leave were dashed. Instead of getting in training all hands, officers and men, were put to shovelling the runways and taxi ways. Just when they had everything cleared, fog rolled in. They were kept standing-by in hopes of an improvement in visibility for another two days but remained grounded. They had lost three days of training and were informed that rather than ending at noon on 23 December as originally planned, the course would be extended by one more week to end at noon on 30 December.

Frank complained loudest. "That's not ruddy fair!" He told his crewmates at the local. "We've got a right to time off and holidays."

"Not any more you don't, laddie!" Daddy told the youngster bluntly.

"We're not slaves!" Frank retorted hotly. "We're free citizens —"

"In uniform!" Daddy reminded him.

"Look, this isn't arbitrary," Kit intervened before tempers flared further. "The HCU is supposed to give us 30 hours of flying in the Lancaster. If the weather closes down and we can't take off, then they have no choice but to extend the course until we get the flying in. If the operational squadrons were screaming for replacements, they might have shaved a few hours off the course, but this weather has closed down ops as well. We're here to learn something that could save our lives. Don't look at it as chicanery, Frank."

"But why couldn't we go home and come back after Christmas?" Stu asked. He sounded less belligerent than Frank, but resentful all the same.

"Because the Met is promising good flying weather tomorrow."

"As they have for the past three days! We could end up sitting around all day Christmas Eve and Christmas Day too!" Stu whined.

"We could," Kit conceded, "but what if they sent us home only for the weather to clear? We need to fly at every opportunity until we've clocked those 30 hours on Lancasters."

"They'll put on a fine dinner for us too, and the officers serve the airmen," Daddy tried to console the younger men.

"And why shouldn't they? What makes them better than us, anyway? Aren't we all fighting the same war? Aren't we taking the same risks?" Frank shot back.

"Officers are gentlemen, which is more than I can say for you, laddie!" Daddy rebuked him hotly.

"When this war is over, things are going to change in this country. I'm not going to take orders from anyone just because they're richer than me — and I'm not alone." Frank declared. "We're not going to recognise the authority of anyone who derives it from nothing more than being born to it!"

"That includes the king!" Stu gasped out, shocked.

"Does, doesn't it?" Frank thrust out his chin.

"Are you talking about me, Frank?" Kit fixed the gunner with his eyes. He was still leaning back in his chair, but he had crossed his arms in front of his chest tensely.

Frank pulled back startled. "Of course not, sir! You're not some toff! You earned your right to command."

"So, there'll be no mutiny on my aircraft?"

"No, sir! Of course not."

"Good. Then let's leave it at that. Until the war is over, we all obey the rules as they are. Agreed?"

A rumble of unhappy "yes, sirs" greeted him. This was evidently one night when drinking together was not going to console them, so Kit got to his feet. "Excuse me, I've got to make a phone call. See you tomorrow."

Back at the mess, Kit put a call through to Georgina to explain what had happened. He was sorry to miss Christmas with her and her family, but not until he heard the distress in her voice, did he feel bad. "Oh, Kit! That's terrible! We've all been looking forward to having you with us. Mummy went to so much trouble to scrape together enough sugar and margarine coupons to make a plum pudding because you said you liked them so much, and I've organized mounted carolling, where everyone with a horse rides to the more isolated farmhouses to sing carols. We always get invited in for hot drinks, and the horses get apples. It's so much fun!"

"I'm sure it is. I wish I could be there." Kit wasn't lying. Communal singing resonated with memories of his African childhood and the idea of going carol singing on horseback appealed to him.

Georgina continued over the phone, "My father's three sisters are here, as well, and they're ever so anxious to meet you. Not to mention the parishioners."

"Georgina, please give everyone my apologies, but there's nothing I can do about it."

"I'm sorry. I know," she sounded small and dismayed. "It's just that I ruined everyone's Christmas last year. I'd hoped to make up for it by being doubly happy this year — and I'd been so looking forward to sharing all our Christmas traditions with you."

"Georgina, I'm sorry. Really, I am. But there's nothing I can do. I can't come for Christmas. The only consolation I can offer is that I've heard the Royal Shakespeare Company has a special program in Stratford-upon-Avon over the New Year weekend — three plays, hotel and a "Tudor Feast" all inclusive. If you'd like, I could try to get us tickets?"

"I'd love that, Kit!" She brightened up. "I've heard about it, and I've always wanted to go. It's not too dear, is it?"

"I'm not promising front row seats, but I'll see what I can do."

"I'd be happy with the second balcony!"

"After the festival we can stay on in Stratford for a day or two and then spend the last weekend of my leave with your parents.

Would that suit you?"

"That would be perfect! Yes. Thank you, Kit. I really do understand about Christmas."

"Good. I'll let you know the details as soon as I have them."

"Before you ring off, would you mind just saying hello to my aunts?" Georgina pleaded. "I'm not sure they'll believe you really exist otherwise.".'"

"If you insist, and I'd like to wish your parents Happy Christmas as well."

RAF Swinderby
No. 1660 Heavy Conversion Unit
29 December 29 1944

On Boxing Day, the weather cleared and flying training resumed with a vengeance to make up for lost time. On the morning of Friday 29 December, the crews were briefed for a final long-distance, daylight training exercise. Once completed, they would go on leave and then move on to the final stage of training, "Lancaster Finishing School" at Syerston.

The exercise consisted of each aircraft dropping a different coloured dye marker within a triangle defined by three buoys on Loch Ness. They were told to make a "low level" run and to drop their canisters of dye at no more than 1,000 feet, before climbing quickly again to clear the mountains around the loch. The total distance was nearly 900 miles, which meant a flying time of four and half hours. The flight plan called for them to fly to Inverness and there turn southwest on their dummy bomb run. Once their canister was jettisoned, they could turn for home. The Chief Flying Instructor and Master Bomber would be circling the area in a Mosquito watching the operation and recording the results for each aircraft. The exercise would require precise navigation, precise flying and precise bombing, while the flight engineer needed to be on his toes due to the risk of icing and to keep an eye on the fuel levels. Only the gunners could relax and enjoy the ride.

As was his habit, Moran was the last to board the aircraft after a talk with the ground crew. Since this was a daylight trip the curtains were not closed around the navigator or wireless operator's stations, and Moran paused to look at Peal's maps.

"How high are the mountains around Loch Ness again?"

"Ben Nevis is a touch over 4,400 feet; most of the others are shy of 3,000 feet."

"What winds are forecast?" He asked stepping back to address Tibble.

"Out of the west at 15 to 20 mph but gusting higher."

"Be prepared to drop a flame float to test wind drift when we turn in over Loch Ness at Inverness," he told Tibble. Plugging in his intercom to a socket, he warned Osgood as well. "The wireless operator is going to drop a flame float as we turn onto the bomb run. You'll need to spot it and read deviation."

"Understood, Skipper."

Moran continued to the cockpit to find MacDonald held the checklist already, pencil in hand, awaiting the pre-flight cockpit check. They started their engines without difficulties two minutes ahead of time.

Babcock called up from the nose. "Bomb aimer to pilot: Forrester is already taxiing towards the runway."

"Roger," Moran answered.

There was a pause, and then MacDonald noted. "We're ready to go, skipper."

"I'd rather be one of the last on this trip," Moran answered and kept them at dispersal for another couple of minutes. They took off sixth of eight aircraft into a clear blue morning sky.

It was a beautiful flight over the snow-clad landscape. From their altitude of twelve thousand feet, it was impossible to see dirt or footprints; everything looked pristine and pure. Railway tracks, cleared roads and bodies of water looked black, forests grey. Gradually the landscape became more rugged.

Peal called in over the intercom. "Navigator to crew: we've left English airspace."

"You mean we're over enemy territory?" Frank asked aghast.

"Y' daft joker," MacDonald growled. "We'rrre finally hooome."

They left the Lowlands behind them and climbed up over the Cairngorms before sinking down toward the Moray Firth and then, at Peal's direction, turning southwest. Ahead of them stretched Loch Ness, clearly visible between its flanking hills.

Moran descended gradually to 1,000 feet and asked MacDonald and the gunners to keep their eyes on the aircraft ahead of them. He asked Tibble for the winds. "North by northwest. Gusting 20 to 25 mph, Skipper."

Ahead of him Moran could see Forrester's aircraft already climbing above four thousand feet and banking around to the south. Behind Forrester, Sergeant Pilot Taffy Owens had also finished his run and was gaining altitude. The other three aircraft ahead of them were still on their runs. They appeared to be badly buffeted by the winds and the loch was ruffled by choppy waves.

"Pilot to bomb aimer: Can you see the buoys?"

"I think so, but none of the dye markers are anywhere near them."

"Can you detect any sort of pattern to the misses?"

"They're all downwind of the buoys."

Their instructions had been to make the drop at "no more than 1,000 feet." Moran now suspected that this was not the optimal altitude. The instructors wanted to see if the bomb aimers or pilots could judge conditions for themselves and adjust their run accordingly. He pushed the column forward as he called over the intercom, "Wireless operator, launch the flame float." Tibble must have moved to the flare chute earlier because he could detect no changes in the trim of the aircraft and almost at once Osgood read off the degree of deviation.

As Moran dived, MacDonald looked over at him with alarm. "Five hundred feet, Skipper."

"Don't worry, Daddy. I'm not ditching."

The aircraft immediately ahead of them was climbing and Babcock reported. "He was closest so far, but still wide of the triangle."

Moran continued down to 200 feet before ordering: "Pilot to bomb aimer: master switch on. Take me in."

"Right. Right. Right. Right. Steadeeee. Steadeee. Left. Steadeee. Gone!" Had they been carrying a full load of bombs the Lancaster would have leapt up several hundred feet when they were released, but the dye canister was too light to make any difference.

Moran pulled the column back hard and asked for more power from MacDonald. The Merlins started screaming in protest as the Lancaster strained upwards.

"Got it!" Osgood called excitedly from the tail. "We're the first kite to lob the canister bang on target!"

"Congratulations, Babcock!" Moran replied, although his mind was preoccupied by the mountains around them. From his current altitude he had no chance of clearing Ben Nevis, rearing up to 4,400 feet beyond

Fort Augustus, but if he could climb to three thousand feet, he should be able turn south beforehand. To reach 3,000 feet he needed five minutes, during which time he was going to use up some 11 to 13 miles of loch. He should be able to make it. Alternatively, he could just keep flying down Loch Linnie and bank south from Oban, but that route would eat up more fuel and delay their return. It was cold up here, the day very short, and the risk of icing would increase as the sun went down. Moran opted for the shorter route. "Pilot to engineer: give me maximum boost, 3000 rpm, and 15 degrees of flap."

"Max boost, 3000, 15." MacDonald acknowledged.

The battle-weary Lancaster shuddered and strained, and Moran sensed unease from his crewmates as she struggled to climb. They weren't going to have a lot of room to spare, he registered, but he wasn't really worried. Less than ten minutes later, they scraped over the snow-capped mountains and Moran eased off on the power, reducing the noise and vibrations. Gently, he banked around to turn for home, and reminded Peal to keep track of airfields they could divert to on their way back. He had no reason to anticipate the need to divert — except for icing. It was just good practice always to have an eye on options, and there was no shortage of these when flying over Scotland and Northern England.

"What's that? Sorry! Mid-Upper gunner to crew: I can see what looks like a column of smoke rising from Loch Ness."

"Rear gunner to pilot: It's smoke from a fire on the side of the mountain flanking the Loch."

In the dead of winter after heavy snow? Then a chill ran down Moran's spine as he requested: "Pilot to Wireless operator: Are you picking up anything?"

"W-William just flew into the ground, Skipper. The CFI is calling for emergency services, but it doesn't sound good."

It didn't make sense. They'd had perfect visibility. Part of Moran wanted to turn around, fly back, and see what had happened, but there was nothing they could possibly do. Seeing the crash site would not exactly bolster morale either. He held his course for Swinderby.

The loss of W-William with all seven men aboard cast a grim shadow over their final half day at the HCU. All trainee crews were called in to be briefed. Shortly before the crash, Pilot Officer Newton had reported by radio that he'd lost control of his elevators. They were, in his words, "fluttering like laundry on a line." Preliminary investigation of the wreck indicated that the elevator cable had snapped. The aircraft had been at

500 feet when the elevator problem was reported. What happened after that nobody knew. Clearly this was an extremely dangerous situation, but an experienced pilot would probably have mastered it. Kit thought he would have tried to ditch the Lancaster. They had a reputation for floating well, and while the water was bitterly cold, they were being watched and rescue would have been prompt. He could not imagine turning toward the high hills surrounding the loch with his elevators gone. The CFI suggested, however, that P/O Newton had hoped to crash land beside the lake, thinking perhaps this would be safer than on the choppy water. Whatever he had been trying to do, he'd miscalculated, and the entire aircraft had exploded on impact and everyone had been burned before rescue services could reach them.

The accident would be chalked up to "pilot error." The RAF always preferred to blame dead pilots rather than question the competence of living ground crew and instructors, much less station commanders.

As they left the briefing, preparing to collect their things and go their separate ways for the next week, Daddy caught Kit by the elbow. "If you have no objection, sir, I'd like permission to check the control wires personally before each flight. I presume that once we're on a squadron, we'll have our own ground crew and they'll look after us properly, but on training stations, trainees come and go too fast for the ground crews to care much. Just one rigger thinking more about his lassie than doing his job and this is what happens."

"You read my mind, Daddy. Thank you."

"I won't keep you any longer then, sir. I know you're anxious to see *your* lassie."

Kit couldn't deny it, and he obviously hadn't been able to conceal it either. Adrian was planning for a week with Julia. Nigel and Frank had decided to spend the week with Frank's mother in Southampton, and Stu was going home to his parents', of course. Which left Terry out in the cold. Before Kit could even open his mouth, Daddy read his thoughts for the second time. "I suggested Terry come home with me. The wife won't mind. She's used to me bringing m'mates home. Might even be a bit brassed off if I showed up alone. Been married 16 years and she doesn't find me exciting anymore."

"Did Terry accept?" Kit knew Terry could be prickly sometimes.

"Yes, he seemed very pleased."

"He's a good lad."

"They all are, Skipper. You included." The Scotsman smiled. "See you next week at 'Finishing School.'

Part II

Performing

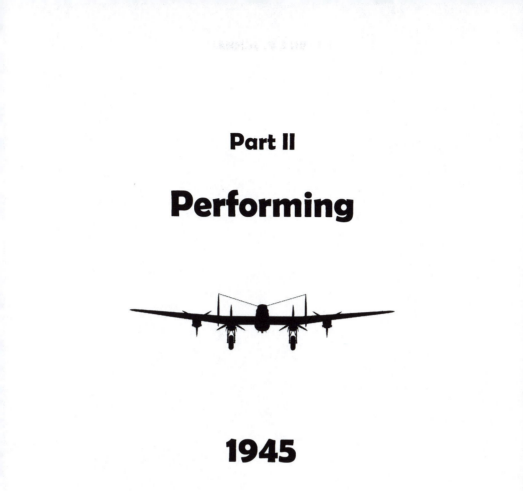

1945

Chapter 12
Commitments

Stratford-upon-Avon
1 January 1945

Georgina's trip from Yorkshire to Stratford-upon-Avon entailed many changes and turned into an all-day nightmare. Kit ended up waiting over three hours at the railway station for her. They barely had time to check into their hotel and change for the theatre before being swept up in the official program of the Royal Shakespeare Company's "New Year 1945 Festival." The Company had lost all their young male actors to the services, so male roles were played by men too old for conscription, or in the case of some minor roles, by women. Yet that did not detract from the magic they created. The world conjured up by Shakespeare's enthusiastic disciples readily absorbed Kit and Georgina.

Their package opened with "King Lear," followed, on New Year's Eve, by a tour of Shakespeare's birthplace, Ann Hathaway's cottage, and a lecture before a performance of "Much Ado about Nothing" in the evening. The day ended with a "Tudor-Style Dinner," where the waitresses wore period costume to serve a game-heavy meal accompanied by medieval music. This pageant lasted past midnight, when a horn fanfare and one glass of champagne served to each guest welcomed in 1945. The program ended on New Year's Day with a matinee performance of "Henry V."

Surrounded by ardent theatregoers, Kit and Georgina were swept up in the atmosphere. All the talk was of the performances, the cast, the costumes, the sets and Shakespeare himself. Enjoyment and excitement came simply from being together. Georgina bedazzled Kit each day with attire that was subtly elegant and understated, yet never failed to turn heads — and not just Kit's. When Kit asked her where she managed to find such wonderful clothes in wartime Britain, she let him in on her secret: "I make them myself — with the help of Aunt Anna, who went to Singapore and back in 1936. She returned with two steamer trunks full of raw Chinese silk and Indian saris."

It wasn't until after that final performance that they had time to focus on themselves. They went to a small Hungarian restaurant, recommended to them by other guests at the hotel, and enjoyed an exceptionally good, spicy meal, quite unlike standard British fare. Afterwards they walked back to the hotel holding hands. It was only half past nine, too early for bed. Since the lobby was practically empty, yet surprisingly warm and inviting with a blazing fire, Kit suggested they leave their overcoats upstairs and come back for a nightcap. Fifteen minutes later, they were settled on a sofa, with a bottle of white wine in an ice bucket on the coffee table in front of them. The waiter poured them each half a glass and withdrew.

"Your mother wrote me the most wonderful letter," Georgina announced, reaching out to take one of Kit's hands in hers.

Her smile was so captivating that it took Kit a moment to register what she had just said. His *mother* had written to her? Why? Of course, because Georgina had written first! "She answered?" Kit asked, sitting up straighter. "Why didn't you say anything sooner?"

Georgina leaned down and extracted the letter from her handbag. She didn't give it to Kit, but rather opened and read from it. "*The thing to remember about children is that they are people. Just like adults, they are neither all good, nor all bad. The best thing to do is to treat each child as you would an adult: as an individual. Search for the unique personality, conscious that it will be a mix of positive and negative traits.*' That is so wise! If I'd approached my pupils with this perspective last term, I'm sure it would not have been the calamity it was. And listen to this: '*If you can find out what makes a child happy or curious, you can reach him or her more easily than by playing on fear.*' I think that's beautiful — and just the opposite of what Miss Evans does!"

"Hm. Did she say anything about me?" Kit asked, reaching out for the letter.

"Of course!" Georgina replied with a saucy smile, while holding the letter beyond his grasp. "Just as you predicted, she assumed that I would not have written to her unless we were serious about one another, and she included some wise words of advice about how to handle you."

"Such as?" Kit wanted to know, with a touch of alarm. What was his mother doing interfering in his affairs like this?

"Nothing you need to worry about," Georgina told him pertly as she put the letter back in her handbag. Then she held out her glass for a refill of wine. Although still annoyed with his mother, Kit wasn't prepared to spoil the mood over it, so he reached forward to pour.

"Don't you think this would be the perfect time to tell me the romantic story behind your grandparents' marriage?" Georgina prodded, slipping more comfortably into the crook of his arm as they settled back with their refilled glasses of wine.

Kit squirmed. He didn't like the direction this conversation was going. It was only natural that a nice girl like Georgina wanted to get married. She and her parents had already shown great trust in his honourable intentions by allowing her to spend the week with him. The unspoken expectation was that they would soon get engaged. Furthermore, Kit had no doubts whatsoever that Georgina was the woman he wanted for his wife. The problem was that the thought of proposing sent him into a panic precisely because it implied making plans for the future. The closer he got to going operational, the more he was gripped by an irrational yet powerful fear that he would jinx his chances of survival by planning for it.

Georgina broke in on his thoughts. "Please tell me the story of how your grandparents met and married. It must have been almost like a fairy tale."

"What makes you think that?" Kit demanded in alarm, hastening to cool things down by adding, "It wasn't like that at all. According to my father, my grandfather married my grandmother to demonstrate to the mission community that Christ was not racist and that he, as Christ's vicar, did not discriminate based on the colour of a man's — or woman's — skin."

"Wasn't their marriage happy?" Georgina asked back, sounding severely disappointed.

"I wouldn't say that. It was a good marriage; it just wasn't particularly romantic." Kit felt he had to dispel Georgina's romantic ideas before she got carried away by them. He tried to sound as matter-of-fact as possible as he explained, "You have to understand, my grandfather went out to South Africa as a missionary accompanied by his Scottish wife, Victoria. She was the one who noticed that my grandmother came to every service and then stayed to sweep out the church and help in any way she could. It was Victoria who took my grandmother under her wing and taught her to read and write. Later, when Victoria became ill and bedridden, my grandmother nursed her as if she were her own sister. She looked after my widowed grandfather for almost four years before he married her — and, no, they were not lovers during that period."

"How do you know?" Georgina challenged him cheekily.

Kit wriggled uncomfortably, again, and answered with a stubborn, "Well, that's what my mother says. Besides, my grandmother didn't become pregnant until more than two years after they were married, and no one was more amazed than my grandfather because he'd had no children with Victoria. He named my mother Dorothy from the Greek meaning a 'gift of God'. My mother was very well-loved by both of them, and in fact by the whole community. Of course, that only lasted as long as she stayed in the bush. Going to Pretoria for teacher training must have been a horrible shock for her."

"How did she meet your father? Was that more romantic?" Georgina asked hopefully, apparently determined to discover a great love story somewhere in his family history.

"Yes, I suppose so," Kit conceded, his resolve about deterring romantic thoughts was weakening under the onslaught of Georgina's big, green eyes and the warmth of her body against his own. "My grandfather came to Pretoria seeking something from the Colonial Administration and my father was the junior official at Government House detailed to take care of it. As they finished their business, my grandfather invited the nice young civil servant to join him for dinner with his daughter. My father says he was most reluctant to accept because he expected some dried-up old maid several years older than himself — he just couldn't think up a polite excuse fast enough to decline. He was astonished and enchanted to find a vivacious, quick-witted, and beautiful young woman of twenty-two."

"And it didn't matter to him that she was half-African?"

"Well, if one believes the story the way my father tells it, he fell in love at first sight, and after that her smiles were the only thing that mattered to him."

Georgina beamed, much happier with this narrative, until she remembered his caveat. "Don't you believe your father?"

Kit smiled faintly. "I don't believe in love at first sight — or I didn't until I saw you and Don together. As for my mother's race not mattering, I think my father was in a rebellious and provocative mood at the time. He'd come to Africa in defiance of his father's wishes, and he was on the verge of breaking with his family altogether. He wanted to take a stand for justice and equality. I believe he was captivated by my mother, and he certainly loved her deeply. But she was also his way of rebelling."

"That sounds so — I don't know — calculating," Georgina concluded, an expression of sadness, diffusing her fire-lit face.

She was so lovely in that moment, that Kit found it hard to concentrate on the conversation. He would have preferred to kiss her than to answer, but he restrained himself. He made himself focus on the tale of his parents, and abruptly something clicked in his mind, as if a door had opened enabling him to see something he had not seen before. Of course, he'd *known* the story of how his parents had met all his life, but for the first time he empathized with the traumatized young man his father must have been.

Suddenly, he knew that in 1920, his father had been as lost and disoriented as he had felt after Don's death. Embittered by his war experiences, his father had collided violently with his pompous sire, a general in the Indian Army. He'd fled the noxious family environment by joining the Colonial Service and requesting a posting to Africa. Yet he was a complete stranger both to the African continent and the mentality of the hide-bound Colonial Service. In that first year, he had been insecure and intensely lonely. Then quite unexpectedly, he'd been confronted by a lovely, open-hearted woman undistorted by the manners and prejudices that characterized colonial Indian and South African society. With a sense of wonder, Kit realized that his mother had been as much a lifeline to his father as Georgina was to him.

Aloud Kit corrected himself to Georgina. "No, there was nothing calculating about it at all. He simply fell deeply in love. Truly nothing else mattered to him except capturing my mother's heart and then making her as happy as he possibly could. Any ulterior motives were entirely subconscious — or invented by me." He cast Georgina a sidelong, apologetic smile.

A victorious grin transformed Georgina's face. "You see!" She declared triumphantly. "I knew there had to be —" The approach of the waiter made Georgina bite her tongue.

"I'm afraid I'm closing the bar now," the waiter explained diffidently. "Will you be requiring anything else, sir?"

Kit was surprised to realise they were the last people left in the lobby. He lifted the bottle from the bucket. It was still almost half full. "No, we're fine, thank you."

"Then, if you don't mind, sir, I shall retire. Please just leave everything where it is when you go to your rooms. I would, however, ask you to ensure that the fire is out and that the embers are scattered before you go up to bed. Is that all right, sir?"

Kit glanced at the fire. It was slowly dying. "Yes. I'll take care of that."

"Do you have your room keys? Or should I bring them to you?" The waiter glanced in the direction of the deserted reception desk.

Kit checked his pocket. He had his key. "Georgina?"

"I've got mine in my handbag."

"Very well then. Good night, madam. Good night, sir." The waiter disappeared down a corridor and Kit refilled their glasses.

Rather than resuming what she had been saying, Georgina kicked off her shoes and lay back against his chest, settling into the crook of his arm with a contented sigh. He put his arm around her shoulder, savouring the feel of her soft body moulded with his own. He wanted her intensely, yet his situation was different from what his father's had been when he had found the woman he needed. Kit simply couldn't overcome his superstitious fear that planning for a future would put a premature end it. He remembered Georgina mapping out her life with Don and the way she'd talked exuberantly about all the things they would do, the places they would go, the children they would have. Don had indulged her. "Whatever you want, Georgina," he had told her with his gentle smile.

Don had not cared what Georgina planned because none of it had been real to him. Georgina had created the mirage, not Don, and he had allowed her to do so because it made her happy. Yet he had known all along that he would not survive. While Kit did not share Don's sense of fatality, he knew the odds of surviving another 30 ops. He could not know if he would be lucky or not, so the only way to ensure survival would be to turn and run. He'd done that once before, on the night after Don was killed. He would not do it again. He was determined not only to go back on operations, but to be as good a skipper as Don had been. That meant never shirking his duty and it meant doing all in his power to save his crew. He could not allow Georgina to place all her faith in his survival, as Don had done. He was not an actor, he reflected, thinking of the plays they had just seen.

"Kit?" her voice came pensively to him. "Do you realise that you've never told me that you love me."

"Do you doubt it?"

"No, but I'd like to hear you say it all the same."

"I love you, Georgina." He bent and kissed the top of her head. She twisted around to meet his lips, and he kissed her again more passionately.

She settled back in his arms, sipped her wine, and asked in a soft, purring voice. "Why do you love me, Kit? You're not like your grandfather, are you? You're not just trying to make a point by being with me, are you?"

"No, of course not. Anyway, what point would I be trying to make?" That you're as good a man as Don, an evil voice said in the back of his head. Kit dismissed it. To Georgina he declared, "I never wanted to fall in love with you. You belonged to Don. I didn't fall in love with you until after he was gone."

"Was it because I stood by you when you were temporarily posted LMF?"

"In part, I suppose, but not *just* that."

"What else then?"

Kit had never thought about *why* he loved her. He didn't know why.

Did anyone know why they loved someone? He could not pretend it had been love at first sight; he had been distracted by the flashier Fiona, and besides Georgina had eyes only for Don and vice versa. He supposed his love *had* been ignited that day in Torquay when she had vehemently rejected his suggestion that he should have died in Don's place. When he was feeling worthless, she had told him he mattered. Then by turning to him in her grief, she had made him feel useful. As long as she needed him, his life had a purpose. Ultimately, she'd made him want to keep going, if only so he could be a shoulder she could cry on. Such an explanation was hardly romantic, however. Kit feared she might be hurt to think he'd fallen in love with her only because of his own needs rather than because of special qualities in her.

But then an image flashed through is mind: it was that night at the Selkirks' when Mrs Selkirk had played Chopin by candlelight. The Colonel was snoring, Don's sister Maggie and her friends were talking in sign language, Fiona sat looking politely bored and even Don looked distracted, but Georgina had become enraptured by the music. In that instant, Kit had sensed depths in her that he had failed to notice earlier. He had caught his breath and told himself that still waters run deep. He had felt a sudden and powerful longing to get to know her better but had angrily rebuked himself because she was engaged to Don. Yet, in retrospect, that had been the moment he had fallen in love.

But why? He couldn't even properly describe what he had been thinking and feeling. He decided on a teasing half-truth instead. Laughing gently, he bent and kissed her behind the ear as he whispered, "I love you because you remind me of my mother." By then, however, Georgina had already drifted off to sleep.

Kit re-awoke with a start, embarrassed that he had fallen asleep. He had no idea how long he had been sleeping, but the fire had died. Only a few embers glowed weakly, and the room was chilly. Georgina still lay cuddled in his arms, sleeping with deep, soft breaths. His hand stroked her side to gently wake her, but the feel of her ribs through the soft silk dress set his senses on fire. Suddenly every nerve was awake. Georgina was so delicate, fragile and vulnerable, that a surge of protectiveness swept over him — yet she was vibrant and energizing too.

He bent his head to kiss her forehead, and she stirred in his arms. With a soft "hmm," she turned into him more. He adjusted his position on the sofa to make them both more comfortable and kissed her again. She lifted her face to meet his lips, a gentle, languid smile suffusing her face. Her half-closed, green eyes glowed like the runway signal lamp, granting him permission to proceed. The invitation electrified him. He started kissing and holding her more intensely, afraid that the moment might slip away — or she might change her mind.

Georgina, murmuring that she mustn't tear her "irreplaceable" silk dress, sat up and removed it altogether. Kit responded in kind. When he encountered difficulty with her bra, Georgina helped him with a soft chuckle that reinforced the encouraging look in her eyes. Not once did she try to stop him, or hesitate, or become passive. She was an active partner, to the very end. Yet to the last, a corner of Kit's mind expected her to cry out Don's name. She didn't, only gasped out his.

Very gradually the ecstasy receded and the sizzling emotional heat cooled, making room for reason to return. Kit sank softly from the unearthly heights and as he touched down again, he realised they were lying naked on a couch in a hotel lobby with their clothing scattered on the floor around them. Anyone might walk in at any moment. "Georgina!" He whispered in alarm. "Georgina! Wake up! We have to go. Before someone finds us here."

"Yes, of course," she answered dreamily. Then she drew a deep breath, opened her eyes and sat up. She found and pulled her dress over her naked body without bothering with her underwear. She collected all the bits and pieces of the latter in her arms and, carrying them along with her shoes and handbag, led the way up the stairs. Kit pulled only his trousers on and carried everything else. At the door to his room, she turned and kissed him once, before continuing down the hall to her own room.

"Good night!" he called softly, anxious not to awake any of the other guests.

"Good night, Kit Darling!" She answered in a gentle voice. "See you in the morning."

Kit closed the door behind him, all thought overwhelmed by a sense of wonderment and well-being. He made no attempt to fight his feelings. He simply pulled off his trousers, fell into bed, and let a sound and untroubled sleep embrace him. For once, he slept free of nightmares, doubts or fears.

Georgina closed and locked the door behind her. First, she hung up her dress and put away her underwear. Then, with a flannel, she wiped herself clean at the tiny bedroom sink. Finally, she slid between the fresh, crisp sheets of the hotel bed and lay thinking.

Something momentous had just occurred but she didn't quite know what to make of it. Her mother would be distressed by her lack of self-control, but she had not lost control; she had made a conscious choice.

Fiona would be contemptuous of her for letting herself get 'caught,' but had she been tricked in any way. Her Aunt Lucy would say her behaviour had been vulgar, yet she did not feel tawdry. Miss Townsend and Miss Evans would dismiss her a "fallen woman", but she did not feel demeaned. She had surrendered her virginity and could never again be considered 'pure,' yet she did not feel defiled. By the doctrines drummed into her since childhood, she had unquestionably committed a sin, yet she felt no guilt.

Instead, she felt gloriously happy and uplifted. Yes, there was a shadow of regret for not having shared such intimacy with Don. Then again, he had not asked it of her, so she need not reproach herself for denying him. They had been so sure that they would marry and have a whole life together in the future. There hadn't been any rush...

How naïve she had been! So trusting in the benevolence of God and in the power of love. She had never thought "it" would happen to Don, and Don had indulged her. He had told her he was lucky, and she'd taken that to mean what she wanted it to mean: that he would survive. Yet Don had known better. He simply hadn't wanted her to worry. He had wanted to protect her, to give her the security of the engagement and the promise of a future together, because he knew it made her happy. Yet, he had refrained from claiming her because he knew in his heart that he wouldn't live long enough to fulfil their dreams of a future together. Georgina felt tears forming and she whispered into the darkness. "Dearest Don, you were so good to me."

As the tears fell, her grief reached a crescendo of pain so intense that she felt Don's presence, as if her pain had dragged him from his grave. He laid his hand on her shoulder and suddenly the pain was gone, replaced by a sense of incredible benevolence and peace. Don was gone, but she had Kit. The thought of Kit filled her with joy. He was a good man — loving and caring like Don, but lively and fun-loving, too. He needed her as much or more than Don ever had, and he loved her with his whole being. In return, he deserved her full and unrestricted love.

She took a deep breath and prepared to sleep in the certainty that she had done the right thing. Smiling, her last conscious thought was that her father would understand and approve because she had acted not out of lust — but love.

When Georgina didn't appear for breakfast at the arranged time, Kit started to get nervous. When she still wasn't down after half an hour, he was too distressed to drink another cup of tea. He left the breakfast room and nervously paced around the "scene of the crime," the lobby. After an hour, he knew he had to find out what was wrong. Georgina might be ill, he supposed, but he didn't believe that. He was certain she regretted what they had done and was in tears or angry. Maybe she had already checked out and left him here? He looked over at the key rack. With relief he saw the hook for Room 16 was empty. Presumably, Georgina was still in her room, then. Should he ask the receptionist to ring up and see if something was wrong? No, that would be cowardly. He took the stairs two at a time and stopped outside Georgina's room. He drew a deep breath and then knocked very gently.

There was no response. He knocked again, louder, and called softly but intently. "Georgina? Are you upset with me?"

In answer, the door swung open, and Georgina stood before him in a dressing gown, her hair wrapped in a towel. She beamed up at him, "No, Kit Darling! Why ever would you think that? I'm sorry I'm late. I forgot to set an alarm and slept in. Then I wanted a bath before coming to breakfast. Please forgive me." She went on tiptoe to give him a kiss.

Kit was so relieved that she wasn't angry, he wrapped his arms around her and clung to her for a moment.

"Just give me ten more minutes," she begged as she pulled away with a smile. "You can order a fresh pot of tea. I'll be right down."

True to her word, she was down shortly afterwards, dressed in yet another smashing outfit, her hair partially rolled away from her face but the rest loose and wavy as it hung down to her shoulders. Kit's pulse quickened at the sight of her, and he stood to pull out a chair. She settled down with a smile for the whole room. Indeed, she radiated so much happiness that the other guests smiled back, even a gloomy couple in the corner.

The landlady came over at once, "Good morning, Miss Reddings. Flying Officer Moran was starting to worry about you." She winked at Kit.

"Understandably so!" Georgina assured the landlady candidly. "I'm over an hour late."

"Now, would you like baked beans and stewed tomatoes with your scrambled eggs?"

The eggs were powdered, of course, and shook her head. "No, thank you. I think I'll forgo the eggs altogether today. Toast and jam are all I need. And tea of course."

"A fresh pot is brewing right now." The landlady assured her and withdrew. Georgina turned her attention to Kit, smiling still.

Kit reached his hand across the table to take hers and lowered his voice as much as possible. "Georgina, I want to you know that I didn't plan last night. I didn't even expect it. It just — happened."

"I know. I was there, remember?" She quipped back in a whisper, then laughed and squeezed his hand. In a more normal tone she added, "I'm not upset, Kit. I feel wonderfully happy. I'm so glad that before we go to my parents' we have another three days," she dropped her voice again to add, "— and nights — together."

He was the one who blushed. "I was thinking...." His voice trailed off as he lost his nerve.

"Thinking is always a good thing, my father says," she encouraged playfully.

He drew a deep breath. Last night changed everything. It was not fair to indulge his superstitions. He owed Georgina the commitment they both wanted. "Yes, I mean I was wondering if you wanted to go together to look at rings."

"Rings? Did you get a promotion? You need to buy a second stripe for your sleeve?" With a finger she traced the lone ring on his tunic sleeve.

"No, of course not! I meant an engagement ring."

"Did you?" She looked at him as if utterly astonished. Suddenly, Kit feared she was going to turn him down despite last night.

Georgina dropped her look of feigned surprise and leaned across the table to give him a brief kiss on the lips. "I'm sorry, Kit Darling. I shouldn't tease you — you just looked so very serious, and I feel so light-hearted. I think you've awakened some sort of impishness in me — at least this morning! I'd be delighted to wear your engagement ring. I can't think of a more pleasant way to spend a rainy morning in January than finding the right one."

"Meaning you will marry me, if I don't—"

She put her hand to his lips. "Don't say it. Don't *ever* say it out loud. I will marry you, Christopher Moran. I promise you, I *will* marry you."

Chapter 13
Trying Again

Foster Clough, Yorkshire
6/7 January 1945

The weekend with her parents went very well. Obviously, Georgina and Kit slept apart and gave no hint that things had been otherwise for the past four days. Indeed, much as she cherished the nights they'd had together, Georgina would have felt very awkward sleeping with Kit under the parental roof in her girlhood room with its single bed, horse show ribbons and menagerie of stuffed animals.

What mattered was that her parents seemed genuinely pleased that Kit and she had become engaged. Her mother, perhaps, had a few doubts. When they were alone in the kitchen together, she asked with concern, "Are you sure you're ready for this?"

Georgina countered, "What do you mean, Mummy? Ready to love again? Or ready for grief again, if something happens to Kit?"

"Well, both," her mother answered uncomfortably.

"I'm certainly ready for love, and is any woman ever ready to lose the man she loves?" It was a rhetorical question. After letting it hang in the air for barely a moment, Georgina told her mother firmly. "I'll deal with the grief if and when it comes — but not now."

That put an end to the discussion.

Georgina's father, on the other hand, had shown no reservations whatsoever. On the contrary, Edwin embraced Kit with exceptional warmth. He'd liked Don too, of course, but their relationship had been characterized by wary respect tinged with uncertainty. There was none of that between Edwin and Kit. Instead, there seemed to be some natural bond between them. Georgina sensed it coming into the study to tell them dinner was ready and finding them with their heads together over a book. She noted it again when they went out for a walk together and returned deep in conversation. As they approached the vicarage, they kept stopping to extend the conversation and delay their return. They both gestured to underline whatever they were saying, yet laughed together frequently too.

When it came time to leave, Edwin announced he was giving Kit his car "as an engagement present." Kit immediately refused, saying it was far too generous a gift.

"Look, it's fourteen years old and it breaks down all the time. Since Gerald joined the Navy, you are the only who knows how to coddle it along. I either I have to take it to a garage, where repairs cost a fortune, or it sits in the drive like a lame carthorse. It's high time I found a car that I can rely on. Meanwhile, you need wheels so you can get about — as much for Georgina's happiness as your own. So please take the wretched thing off my hands, so I can find something better!"

Put like that, Kit could only thank him and accept. Obviously, getting petrol was going to pose a bit of a challenge, and he presumed he might well have to resort to the aircrew black market. Yet having a car meant that Georgina and he could see far more of each other. It also meant they didn't have to leave until after Sunday lunch, and that Kit could drive Georgina back to Kirkby before continuing to Syerston and "Lancaster Finishing School."

Kirkby Village

Mrs Radford invited Kit in to have a cup of tea before he continued on his way, but he said he mustn't be late "for school." He and Georgina kissed only fleetingly at the door of the house before he drove off for the final stage of training.

It was hard to see him go after this monumental week. Georgina felt depressed as soon as the door shut, but she looked forward to sharing developments with Philippa. She felt certain the sophisticated WAAF officer would both approve of what she'd done and have advice for her. She turned back to Mrs Radford, "What shift is Philippa working this week? Will she be back soon?"

"I'm so sorry, Georgina, but Philippa has been posted to the Middle East. It was very sudden, but a great honour, I gather. She is joining Air Marshal Park's staff in Cairo." How like Philippa, Georgina thought enviously. "She left a letter for you. It's on your dresser in the attic," Mrs Radford added.

Georgina thanked her and went upstairs. The attic seemed

empty, impersonal and much too big without Philippa's presence. Georgina supposed she would soon have a new roommate. Most probably Fiona, in fact, since Fiona was taking her old place at Kirkby Grange. Georgina didn't mind that. If nothing else they knew each other's habits already, but it wouldn't be the same as with Philippa. She'd liked and learned so much from the WAAF — not to mention that it would be a bit awkward explaining to Fiona about Kit. Georgina resolved not to worry about that until tomorrow and turned to Philippa's letter instead.

Dropping down on the soft, bouncy bed, Georgina began to read:

Dearest Georgina,

The only thing I regret about this sudden transfer is that I will not see you before I go. (I do hope we will meet again after the war, however!) This transfer is a wonderful opportunity and one I been dreaming about for ages. It seems almost like a wink from heaven, since, as you know, I was shattered by Yves' death and want nothing more to do with Sir Howard. My existence had become nearly unbearable, and I was not performing well on duty. It was only a matter of time before I made some terrible mistake —maybe one that cost lives.

I couldn't risk that. I had to get away, and I said as much to a friend of mine in the Ministry. He looked into things and discovered there was an opening on Air Marshal Park's staff in Cairo. A few words were said in the right ears and — bingo! — I had orders for Cairo.

I can't tell you how excited I am. Cairo has a splendid reputation as warm, exotic, and civilised, while Air Marshal Park is a <u>dream</u> CO. I've never heard anyone say anything bad about serving under him.

But, to be honest, I would have gone anywhere as long as it was too far away for Sir Howard to follow me and there was nothing to remind me of Yves. Going to Cairo is like being reborn. It is an opportunity to start life all over again with a clean slate. It is a chance to see the world not as the dreary, dreadful place it has been these last five years, but as something fresh and new and exciting.

Since I won't be needing winter things in Cairo, I've left a drawer full of jumpers and cardigans that you can keep. I also left the rabbit-fur mittens you loved so much, and my woollen scarf.

All I ask is that you remember me when you wear them!

I'll write as soon as I've arrived and give you the correct address for writing back. Letters will probably take forever, but I'd hate to lose touch altogether. I enjoyed sharing a room with you and wish you all the best for the future. Just don't let any RAF officer — least of all one still flying ops — steal your heart again! Women's hearts are too fragile for what the RAF does to them.

All for now. I'll write to you with my impressions of Cairo as soon as I have some!

Philippa

Georgina folded the letter together and put it back in its envelope. She set it on the dresser and looked down at the ring Kit had given her. Conscious of Kit's limited financial resources, she had selected a far more modest ring than Don had given her. Rather than a large, flashy diamond, it was a simple gold band with three diamond chips embedded in a row. Georgina liked the fact that in addition to being affordable, the diamonds could be hidden altogether just by twisting it on her finger until they faced her palm. When she did that the ring looked like a simple wedding band.

Georgina's father had once told her that in the Early Middle Ages the Church recognised marriage as the commitment of two people to love one another exclusively unto death. There had been no need for the sacrament or for witnesses, much less registry and celebration. "It was the act of commitment before God alone that made a marriage," he explained.

Georgina turned the ring inwards now, closed her hand into a fist, and whispered, "I am *already* married to you, Christopher Moran. And you to me."

Kirkby Grange
9 January 1945

Reporting back to school the following morning proved more difficult than Georgina had anticipated. She'd expected to be buoyed up and refreshed by the holidays. Instead, like a schoolgirl, she felt depressed to be "back at school." Riding her bicycle in her tweeds, mittens and bulky woollen hat made her feel utterly dowdy. Surely this girl in heavy socks and woollen hat couldn't really have made love naked on a hotel sofa to an RAF officer?

At Kirkby Grange, she parked her bike, deposited her outer layers of clothing in the 'cloak room' and continued to her little office. On her desk was a carbon copy of the Third Form weekly schedule, which she took with her to the teachers' common room for the weekly staff meeting. She was early as usual and could select a seat at the back. Here she looked over the schedule while the other teachers drifted in. The last people to arrive were Miss Townsend with Fiona in her wake.

Georgina caught Fiona's eye and waved in welcome, igniting an answering smile and wave. She realised she was glad to see her old college friend. With so much in common— a shared profession and work at the same school — they'd have lots to talk about and, once she got through the awkwardness of telling Fiona that she was engaged to Kit, they would surely have fun together.

Meanwhile, Miss Townsend welcomed everyone back for the spring term and made various announcements. Eventually, she introduced Fiona and noted, with a gesture in Georgina's direction, that "Miss Reddings will also remain with us for the rest of the year and will be assisting Mr Willoughby in the Third Form."

After the staff meeting, Mr Willoughby took Georgina with him to introduce her to his pupils. He pointed out the children she would be tutoring, five boys and three girls in English and seven boys in maths. "All boys for maths?" Georgina asked in surprise.

"Of course. Girls don't need to be good at maths. Not these girls anyway. They'll all be married when they turn sixteen, and mothers not long after."

Georgina didn't like that dismissive attitude, but she decided not to challenge Mr Willoughby, at least not on the first day. At the lunch break she chose to look at the school records of the children she would be tutoring rather than join the mob in the dining hall. She then started a letter to Kit, but before she could finish the bell rang.

At the end of the school day Miss Townsend summoned Georgina to her office and asked her to help billet Fiona, to which Georgina readily agreed. After leaving the head's office, the girls embraced enthusiastically. "You look so fit, Fiona!" Georgina exclaimed. Fiona had always been chic, but she also tended to plumpness. She appeared to have lost weight and looked very trim.

"It was all the sports I did," Fiona admitted with a laugh. "But what has happened to you? You look absolutely smashing! Transformed! I don't think I've ever seen you look better — despite the fact that I've seen you in that old dress at least a hundred times! I love the way you're wearing your hair, too. It looks, I don't know, a bit like the women in the services, only more feminine. Has something happened?"

"I'll tell you all about it later," Georgina postponed the awkward conversation. "First, let me take you to your new home and introduce you to Mrs Radford, Bobby, Paddy, Sissy, Duchess and Grace."

"Good heavens! Are there that many lodgers?" Fiona gasped, taken aback. "I thought you said it was a private residence, not a boarding house!" She sounded alarmed.

"Didn't I warn you?" Georgina feigned surprise. "Bobby and Paddy are the collies, and Sissy, Duchess and Grace are the three cats."

Fiona laughed appreciatively. "But that's wonderful! I've always wanted dogs and my mother would never let me have one!"

They left together chattering about pets, the school and a thousand odds and ends they had forgotten to share by letter.

As expected, Mrs Radford was perfectly happy to have Fiona move into the space vacated by Philippa. After Fiona unpacked, they had a light supper together, but when Mrs Radford withdrew to read the newspapers and listen to the radio, Fiona suggested to Georgina that they go to a pub for a drink or two. "Or do you still only go to pubs in a large group?" Fiona's tone implied that she considered Georgina's previous behaviour unsophisticated.

"Oh, I don't mind going to the *King's Head*. Everyone knows me there, and I feel quite safe." Her words astonished her; she hadn't been conscious of her transformation until she said it out loud.

"Wonderful! Then let's go there," Fiona agreed eagerly.

"Not so fast, Fiona. I'm not sure *you'll* like it there."

"Why ever not?"

"You won't like the customers."

Fiona looked nonplussed for a moment, then laughed. "You mean they're *all* RAF."

"More or less."

"That sounds *marvellous!*"

"I thought you couldn't stand going to RAF watering holes," Georgina reminded her.

"Oh, you know, when we were in Lincoln the RAF was *everywhere*, and the other girls were so silly about them."

"Which made you contrary," Georgina grasped the situation at once.

"Exactly! The way the others fawned disgusted me, so I couldn't bear to imitate them. After four months at a rural girls' school, where the only men I laid eyes on wore Wellingtons caked in manure, the sight of aircrew would be nothing short of divine!"

"Alright then," Georgina agreed, and they went to the hall to put on their coats, hats and gloves.

"Do you happen to know the phase of the moon?" Georgina asked, pulling on the rabbit-fur mittens Philippa had left her.

"The phase of the moon?" Fiona asked back baffled. "What are you talking about?"

Georgina didn't answer directly, just stepped through the black-out curtains and stood on the front steps searching the fathomless winter sky. Despite some clouds crouching on the horizon to the west, the moonless heavens were swept clean and littered with vivid stars, but there was no moon. "Sorry, Fiona," Georgina announced. "Clear visibility. No moon. There won't be many aircrew at the *King's Head* tonight."

"I'm not following you." Fiona admitted.

"They'll be flying ops tonight. Come to think of it I did hear them droning overhead throughout most of the meal. I'm just so used to it now, I tune them out. Never mind. They'll be back in swarms tomorrow or the night after."

As Georgina had predicted, the *King's Head* was almost empty except for one table of locals preparing to leave. Georgina and Fiona ordered and went to sit at a corner table. As they hung their outdoor clothes over the backs of their chairs, Fiona remarked for a second time, "You really are looking remarkably well, Georgina."

"Oh, you should have seen me a week ago," Georgina countered with a wicked grin. "I looked *much* better then." That had been her first night with Kit. It seemed so unreal somehow.

"Why? What was happening a week ago?" Fiona asked surprised.

She had to get this over with some time, so Georgina took the plunge. "I was in Stratford-upon-Avon for the Royal Shakespeare Company's New Year's Festival — with my fiancé."

"Marvellous! That — Wait! Did you just say what I think you said?" Fiona asked flabbergasted. "You've become engaged *again*?"

"Yes!" Georgina beamed and held out her ring for Fiona to admire. Inwardly, however, she braced for the deluge. Fiona was not going to approve. In fact, she would probably indulge in one of her self-righteous lectures.

True to form, Fiona sputtered, "I don't believe you've done this! How? Why? Do you need a ring to make you feel whole?"

"Of course not," Georgina responded patiently. "I could have done without the *ring*, but it was important to him." She looked down at it affectionately.

"I don't mean the ring," Fiona clarified. "I mean, why do you feel the need to be attached to some man?" Before Georgina could answer, Fiona declaimed, "I was so proud of the way you ended your pathetically dependent relationship with Kit Moran. I thought you'd finally started to have a life of your own."

"I *do* have a life of my own," Georgina answered firmly, starting to get annoyed despite her best intentions. "My life simply includes the man I love. There's nothing wrong with that, Fiona. It's the most natural thing in the world."

"Includes? And what happens when you want to do something that he doesn't want you to do? You haven't had a life of your own yet, why on earth do you want to subordinate yourself to the wishes of some man?"

"I'm not *subordinating* myself to anyone. On the contrary, I feel very lucky to be loved by someone so good. He's certainly never asked anything of me. He's done all the giving in fact."

"I'm sure, but don't tell me he doesn't just want to get inside your knickers," Fiona scoffed.

Georgina burst out laughing, and then covered her mouth with her hand as she giggled. Fiona glared at her uncomprehending. Georgina managed to get herself under control but replied in an amused voice, "What's wrong with that Fiona? What could possibly be more natural than for people who love each other to want intimacy? Sexual attraction and ultimately consummation is the essence of romance. Are you saying you *never* want to sleep with a man?"

"Don't be ridiculous! There's nothing wrong with me! I just want to be loved as a mind and person first. I don't want to be a mere sexual object."

"Nor do I, Fiona — and you know it." Every trace of laughter had vanished. Georgina was deadly serious.

Fiona backed down enough to admit, "I know *you* don't want to be a sexual object," before continuing in indignation, "but that not the point! The point is that most *men* care about nothing more than a quick 'party.' Then it's toodaloo to you!"

Annoyed at the hypocrisy of her friend wanting to go to a pub to meet aircrew and then coming out with a statement like this, Georgina gestured at Fiona's outfit and hair. "If you don't like being looked on as something sexual, why do you go to so much trouble to look good? You could wear dreary, baggy clothes, flat shoes, and go without lipstick and make-up, couldn't you? What with clothes rationing being so strict, it's *easier* to look run-down, faded, and threadbare than not! It takes a lot of effort to look smart, and you go to that effort, don't you?"

Fiona shook her head, tossing her short dark hair out of her eyes. "Yes, but you're wrong about why. If I dressed like something the cat dragged in, I'd never be respected as a professional. A woman *always* has to look good in order to be taken seriously. Looking my best is about being my best. It's not about attracting a man. I don't need a man to make me happy."

"Neither do I," Georgina insisted firmly, meeting Fiona's eyes.

"Then why can't you live without one?" Fiona asked.

"I *can* live without one, but I *choose* not to because it would be wrong to deny or ignore love." Georgina paused and then added more gently. "If you ever fell in love yourself, Fiona, I'm sure you would feel exactly the same way."

"Maybe." Fiona conceded, but she didn't sure.

Meanwhile, Georgina realized she had to understand something. "What are you looking for in love, Fiona?"

"What do you mean?"

"Well, for example, you must have told me a hundred times that you *liked* Kit Moran — but you didn't love him. I don't understand that," Georgina admitted. Although she didn't doubt Kit's love for her, she realised that she wasn't going to be able to share a room with Fiona over the coming months without understanding better what *her* feelings for him had been.

"What don't you understand?" Fiona asked bewildered.

"Why didn't you fall in love with Kit?"

"Love isn't rational, Georgina. It simply wasn't there with us — but if you must have a reason, then one thing that really infuriated me was that for all that he pretended to respect my opinion he wasn't willing to take my advice. Behind that façade of geniality is one of the most pig-headed men I've ever met. Once Kit makes up his mind about something he's not open to reason. I warned him about volunteering for a second tour, but he went ahead anyway — and look what happened? Then after his own actions landed him in trouble, he expected me to put the pieces back together again. In a way, 'though, that's so typically male, isn't it? They want to have everything their own way. They want to do whatever they like, and we're supposed first to applaud them. Then when things don't go as expected, were expected to stand by them while everything goes wrong. Well, I'm not made like that."

"No, I can see you're not," Georgina agreed in a neutral tone. "So just what *do* you want in a man?"

Fiona took a deep breath as she considered the question. When she answered Georgina could see that she did so in earnest, not just to score points in an argument. "I've given this a lot of thought. In the end, I think that the most important quality is equality. A full partnership. I want to be able to earn as much as he does and pursue my own career rather than play second fiddle to him. I want a man who'll share the housework and child-rearing with me, rather than expect me to do it all. I want a man who loves me for my mind, not just my body, and who takes my advice seriously. Is that really so much to ask? So hard to imagine?"

"No," Georgina agreed, nodding seriously. "It doesn't sound at all outrageous to me — just a little unrealistic in this day and age. Now, aren't you curious about my fiancé?"

"Oh, of course!" Fiona seemed to realise she'd been rude not to ask earlier. Perhaps she regretted her tirade too. In a tone designed to be conciliatory, she urged, "Tell me all about him!" Before Georgina could answer, however, she had a new thought: "It's not Mr Willoughby, surely?" Her face lit up. "Of course! That's why you wanted to be re-assigned to Kirkby Grange! And to the Third Form! He *is* very distinguished looking. I like his moustache. But how like you to take on a man with only one leg. Have you seriously thought about what that means for—"

"Fiona." Georgina cut her off, laughing. "Calm down and give me a chance to say something! It's not Mr. Willoughby — or anyone else at the school. It's Kit."

Fiona looked blank.

"Kit Moran."

"But — I thought — you said you'd broken off contact with him." Fiona sounded bewildered.

"I did, for three months, and then I recognised what a terrible mistake I'd made. I asked him to meet me, and he agreed. It didn't take us long to realise how we felt about each other. It was wonderful," Georgina insisted, but Fiona was still gaping at her, making Georgina uncomfortable. "Why are you looking at me like that? You just told me what a stubborn, pig-headed fool he was to ignore your advice. You can't be jealous."

Fiona shook herself out of her thoughts. "Jealous? No, of course not. But Georgina.... Didn't you say he'd earned his wings and was back in Britain for operational training?"

"Yes. He's at Lancaster Finishing School right now."

"Oh Georgina! After the hell you went through when Don — how can you do this? I mean: to yourself?" Fiona's gaze was beyond shock and disbelief; it was full of fathomless pity.

"Do you honestly believe," Georgina countered in a slow, serious voice, "that just to save myself emotional pain — I should deny love to a good man? Especially one who may only have a few more weeks to live?"

Chapter 14
Assignments

RAF Syerston
Lancaster Finishing School
20 January 1945

His time with Georgina overshadowed the following two weeks at "Finishing School," and Kit found the training simply more of what had gone before, only more intense and more complex. Georgina's love, on the other hand, completed the long process of recovery from his near collapse of the previous year. It meant more to him that she had agreed to marry him than that she had slept with him. The latter might have any number of explanations. Her willingness to marry him, on the other hand, unequivocally meant she wanted him in her future. It was this latter thought that gave him a self-confidence he'd never known before. Even Forrester noticed it, complaining that he was getting "cocky," to which Kit only laughed.

The course ended on Friday the 20th of January. As at the HCU, Moran and Forrester's crews had performed best overall. Osgood was still angry with his skipper for sharing the anti-fighter manoeuvre they had worked out, but Forrester had muzzled Levesque enough to prevent the rivalry between the gunners from igniting again. Meanwhile, Frank had more than held his own against Forrester's mid-upper gunner. Adrian still ranked first among the navigators, while Forrester's bomb aimer Wright had the overall best bombing results, particularly from 15,000 feet or above, but Stu's bombing was consistently among the top results otherwise. There was no measure for flight engineers as such, but Kit had complete confidence in Daddy, while Tibble's final score was only a couple of percentage points behind that of Forrester's wireless operator. All in all, Kit believed they'd done well and were as ready as they could be for operations.

Late on Friday afternoon, an announcement blared over the station tannoy that squadron assignments had been posted on the large notice board outside the adjutant's office. While the pilots crowded around trying to find their names, the crews collected in a larger but equally anxious group on the periphery. The nervous excitement of the others, including Kit's crew, took tangible form in the jostling and joking.

Kit appreciated what they were going through. Most of these men had been in training for eighteen months or more, but at last training was over. They were about to face "the real thing." Within the week, even days, they would be flying operations. They naturally wondered what it would be like and if they would measure up.

Kit thought he knew the answer to both those questions already, so the assignment didn't worry him. He did not believe that certain units were either "lucky" or "unlucky." In his experience even squadron commanders had little impact on squadron casualties, performance or morale. The AOC of Bomber Command, Air Vice Marshal Harris, set the targets, and good COs flew with their men, dying just as easily and as frequently as other experienced crews. Bad COs left the flying to others and survived, but their behaviour did not materially increase the losses of the others.

The noise and excitement around him intruded on his thoughts. Adrian pushed his way through the crowd to ask, "Aren't you going to find out which squadron we're on?"

"I can wait until the throng is little thinner," Kit answered, gesturing with his head.

Around them, some men were openly celebrating, while others looked upset. Friends noted if they were staying together or being separated. Numbers were bandied about. "Is 432 Squadron with 1 or 3 Group?" "Does anyone know where 105 Squadron is stationed?"

Kit was not worried about such details. Over the last year his doubts about himself had gradually melted away. He had gained his wings, and with them a sense of professional pride unlike any he had known before. He'd been given a chance to see his parents again, as an adult. Most miraculously, in these last twelve months he had been allowed to win Georgina's love. Kit was boundlessly thankful for such unexpected gifts. He accepted that he might now pay for them, but this past year of grace could never be taken away.

Kit supposed he was becoming more of a fatalist. He had done and would continue to do all within his power to do his job effectively and to keep his crew alive, but he could not shield them from everything. If he had once felt he *ought* to die, Georgina had cured him of that madness. Yet not even her love could protect him. It was better to accept the odds were stacked against them and enjoy each moment to the fullest. He felt a surge of gratitude to Georgina for being willing to contribute to the richness of what might be his last months — just in case fate did catch up with him.

"Zulu!" Forrester's voice demanded his attention. "We're in trouble."

"Why?" Kit asked back flippantly, certain it was just one of Forrester's jokes. Then he saw Forrester's face. The Australian looked genuinely alarmed.

"We don't have assignments. It just says 'Report to CO.'"

Frowning, Kit pushed his way through the remnants of the crowd and rapidly found his name on the blackboard. Forrester was right. No squadron number had been chalked in beside it, only the order to report.

"What's the matter?" Stu asked bewildered, speaking for his entire crew. The crowd had thinned out leaving only a score of men standing about, Forrester's and his own crew among them.

"I'll tell you when I find out." Kit answered, sympathising with their distress. Adrian looked worried, Daddy unhappy, Terry shaken, and the gunners confused. "Go on to the *Friar Tuck* without me. I'll catch you up," he assured them.

"But we were going to celebrate our assignment," Nigel protested. "If we don't have one—"

"They aren't going to send us home after all the time and money they've spent on training us. It's probably just some bureaucratic cockup," Kit assured them. As he spoke, he mentally considered possibilities. Was he being posted to Training Command as an instructor? Were they all being sent overseas? The former would mean his crew got a new, unknown skipper, which seemed unfair. The latter would mean being separated from Georgina, just when he had counted on savouring every minute together. She'd gone to so much trouble to get herself reassigned to Kirkby Grange so they could be close.

Forrester, meanwhile, had gone down the hall and was already pounding loudly on the CO's door. He let himself into the CO's office already complaining, "The assignments board—"

"Ah, Forrester. Is Moran with you?"

"Yes, sir," Kit answered, catching up.

"Excellent. Shut the door, would you? Have a seat." The senior officer gestured towards two chairs with his pipe.

They sank down, Forrester edgy, Moran apprehensive.

"I have a request here to recommend the two best crews to a particular squadron, but I don't have the authority to make an assignment because, technically, you must volunteer and apply."

"Pathfinders!" Forrester guessed, his face lighting up with excitement and satisfaction.

Kit did not share his enthusiasm. Pathfinders flew 45 consecutive operations rather than 30 and casualty rates were reputedly higher than in Main Force.

"It's a bit more than that, actually," the Wing Commander told them, managing to look both amused and serious at the same time.

"Well, don't keep us in suspense!" Forrester pressed him.

"The Air Ministry has finally carried out their threat to force a number of long serving crews off 617 Squadron. The new CO has asked us to help refill the ranks."

Forrester whistled. "The Dambusters!"

"That's correct."

"What forms do I have to sign?" Forrester wanted to know.

"You're sure you don't want to think about this a bit?"

"Not a chance. Just show me where to sign."

"What about your crew?"

"They'll be tickled pink," Forrester assured his commanding officer.

The Wing Commander made no further attempt to dissuade him. He passed the papers across to Forrester with a glance at Moran. Kit maintained his silence, so the CO focused on Forrester. In five minutes the formalities were completed, and Forrester left with a grin and a "See you at Woodhall Spa, Zulu!"

After the door closed, the Wing Commander turned to Kit. "What about you, Moran?"

"I'm honoured that you thought of me, sir, but I don't think I'd fit in at 617."

"Why ever not?" The Wing Commander sounded genuinely astonished.

"From what I've heard, sir, the chaps in 617 — like Forrester — are men who live for flying and bombing and nothing else."

"I'm not so sure about that. They have a pretty wild reputation in their off-duty time too."

That fitted Forrester too, Kit noted mentally, but he confined himself to saying, "Undoubtedly, but that's to balance the intensity of their commitment to duty. I'm determined to give my best to the war effort, sir, but there is a difference between being dedicated and being addicted. I've heard that some of 617 aircrew have flown more than 100 ops."

"I take your point, Moran, but those are precisely the chaps who have been forced off the squadron."

"Leaving the men with 90 and 80 ops still there. I'm simply not in that class. I'm a sprog pilot with barely 350 flying hours altogether."

"And the best record in low-level bombing I've seen in six months. You've also shown exceptional independent thinking and initiative on two separate occasions during training. You aren't just one of the pack, Moran."

Kit had worked hard to be among the best and he was proud of what he and his crew had achieved. Even so, he'd never suspected it would lead him into this kind of ticklish situation. "I'm honoured, sir, but I just can't see myself fitting in at 617," he insisted stubbornly.

The CO appraised him, tapping his pipe thoughtfully. "That wouldn't be because you think it's a suicide squadron, would it? Because it's not. They took heavy losses on their debut operation, and that received a lot of press attention. Since then, however, their casualties have stabilised."

"I'm not afraid of ops, sir, but whereas I view operations as a necessary job to win the war, the crews on 617 reputedly look on them as some sort of high-risk sport, rather like motorcar racing or ski jumping or whatever. I've heard some of them go along as supernumeraries even when they aren't slated to fly. The gen is that the crews of 617 think ops are 'fun'."

"I think that's putting it a little strongly, Moran. You mustn't fall for our own propaganda, which — as you must know by now — overstates the "devil-may-care" attitude and keenness about hitting at the enemy of all aircrew. I believe that far from being out of place, you'd fit in well at 617. They are assigned special duties for which they prepare carefully, meaning they fly less frequently than either Main Force or Pathfinder squadrons. When they do fly, however, it is to strategic targets of exceptional importance."

Mentally, Kit added "and difficulty." But that wasn't the issue. The kind of precision bombing for which 617 was famous appealed to Kit enough to be worth the greater risks involved. Furthermore, he was no less flattered than Forrester that they had been selected. Yet the man who had commanded 617 longer than any other, Group Captain Cheshire (one of the most highly decorated officers in the RAF including a VC), had been scathing about anyone touched by LMF. Kit didn't want to go to the squadron only to be thrown off again because someone found out about his past. Then again, 617 was based at Woodhall Spa, only twelve miles away from Kirkby and Georgina. "How many operations is a tour with 617?" he asked.

"Forty-five."

"I need to discuss this with my crew."

"Yes, I think that's best. Perhaps you should also have a talk with 617's new CO, Group Captain Fauquier? He's the one to address your reservations to, and if anyone can lay them to rest, it will be he. Would you like me to arrange that?"

"Yes, sir. I'd appreciate that very much."

It was easy to spot his crew at the *Friar Tuck* because they sat together in a sober and tense group while around them the others celebrated and animatedly discussed the future. As Kit joined them, Stu announced, "Forrester's bragging about being posted to 617 Squadron. Is that right?"

"I told Stu they only take experienced crews." Adrian answered in an irritated voice. Stu got on Adrian's nerves when his "know-all" attitude showed too much. With an annoyed frown at the bomb aimer, Adrian insisted, "Forrester's line shooting!"

"They've just forced a number of the veteran crews off the squadron and are recruiting new crews," Kit admitted, sitting down.

"What? Seriously?" They gaped at him. In fact, they appeared to be holding their breath in anticipation of what he was going to say next.

When Kit didn't respond, Nigel burst out, "You mean we're going to 617 too?"

"No, not necessarily. We have to volunteer, and I didn't want to do that without consulting you."

Adrian and Terry nodded appreciatively. The gunners exchanged a look of disbelief, and Stu exclaimed in awe, "But Skipper! 617! They're the *best!*"

"They are also known known as the 'death or glory boys.'" Kit tried to dampen the enthusiasm. "Furthermore, a tour with 617 Squadron entails signing on for 45 ops," he added solemnly.

"Skipper! They're *legendary*." Stu insisted, his eyes alight.

"It is definitely an honour, Kit," Adrian seconded him. "I can't say I'm not chuffed. And aren't they stationed at Woodhall Spa, where the officer's mess is housed in the old Petwood Mansion Hotel?"

"That's hardly a reason for committing to fifteen more ops than on a Main Force squadron," Kit countered in evident irritation.

Terry piped up next, sitting straighter as he declared with pride, "This is an opportunity to be part of history, Skipper."

"Every squadron is part of history, Terry. Every one of us is part of history already."

"But this is different," Terry argued.

Nigel and Frank were grinning at each other pleased as punch, so Kit turned to his last hope for caution, the older and steadier Daddy MacDonald. "What do you think, Daddy?"

The flight engineer concentrated on lighting his pipe. Finally, he shook out his match and looked straight at his skipper. "I don't see as it makes much difference what squadron we're on. The flak and the fighters don't discriminate as far as I've heard. As to forty-five versus thirty missions, my guess is the Germans aren't going to last much more than six months, and we're probably in it that long no matter where we go. What's holding you back, Skipper?"

"A squadron like 617 with a high sense of its elite status is not going to welcome sprogs. We're going to be scorned and disdained."

"Sprogs are disdained regardless of squadron — until they've proven themselves by putting a few ops behind them," Daddy replied. "That's just the way it is."

"Up to a point, but at 617 the situation will be extreme. Some of their crews have more than two tours behind them already. That means the experienced crews aren't 10, 20 or 29 sorties ahead of us, they're 65, 75 and 85 ops ahead of us. I also suspect they don't want inexperienced crews at all, and this is a Group or Ministry idea being forced on them."

"Well, in that case they'll have to lump it, won't they?" Daddy pointed out. A long-serving veteran, he'd had to 'lump' a lot of things he hadn't liked in the course of his career.

"Besides, we'll have Forrester and his crew to keep us company in the sprog corner." Stu pointed out cheerfully.

Kit looked around the table for someone who shared his reluctance, but he found no one. "You are unanimously in favour of applying to 617 Squadron?"

"Yes!" "Absolutely!" "Roger!" "Aye, aye!" They were giving him the thumbs up, Frank and Nigel each with both hands.

Kit shook his head. "Very well. But calm down, all of you. I'm going to have a talk with 617's squadron commander before I make a final decision. I'll let you know the outcome before the weekend is over."

Openly disappointed, the others looked at one another baffled, but they recognized there would be no point in arguing. Moran was their captain, and his decision would be final whether they liked it or not.

RAF Woodhall Spa
21 January 1945

At 13:10 the next day, Moran turned into the gatehouse to RAF Woodhall Spa, home to 617 Squadron. The corporal at the gate directed him to the admin block housing the offices of the station and squadron commanders, and punctually at 13:30, Moran knocked on the door of Group Captain J.E. Fauquier, CO 617 Squadron.

Fauquier called "Come In," and Moran stepped inside. He had made every effort to look his best and delivered a smart, parade ground salute.

Already thirty-five, Fauquier was a good-looking man with a broad face and wide-set dark eyes under reddish brown hair. He wore a small moustache and a "fruit salad" of decorations — DSO and two bars, DFC. Moran had managed to shake from the grapevine the additional information that Fauquier had thousands of civilian flying hours amassed before joining the RCAF. Furthermore, the Canadian had been an instructor in Canada for two years before being sent to the UK to help form No 405 Squadron RCAF. Appointed to 617 the previous December, he had taken a reduction in rank from Air Commodore to Group Captain in order to be able to fly operations.

"Thank you for taking the time to see me, sir. I'm sure you're very busy —"

"I'm never too busy to talk to my pilots, Moran. Take a seat. Smoke?" He offered Moran a cigarette, which Moran declined.

"I expect it is unusual for pilots who have been recommended to apply to 617 to request an interview, sir."

"Unusual, yes, but sensible, nevertheless. I gather you have some reservations about joining us?"

"Yes, sir."

"Do you want to expand on that?"

"617 is rightly viewed as an elite unit, sir. Your aircrew are all of the highest quality, and the vast majority have proven this not just in training but on many operations. I don't believe that I have skills that exceed those of experienced replacement pilots you could recruit from any active squadron."

"Skills? Probably not. But that's not the only thing that counts. Many pilots with other units have already developed a fixed mind-set. They think they know it all. Pilots straight out of training are more open-minded. The fact is 617 needs fresh blood. That's why I'm here, and it's why I want a few crews straight out of training. I'm also looking for airmen untainted by cynicism, men who'll bring enthusiasm to the job."

"Pilot Officer Forrester and his men will certainly do that. And, I admit, my own crew were very excited to hear of this opportunity and keen to join. Unanimously, I might add." Moran admitted. "But in my opinion, sir, they are over-estimating their capabilities. We are simply too inexperienced to face the demands placed on members of 617 Squadron. We would be a weak link in the chain, detracting from the strength of the squadron as a whole."

Fauquier's eyes focused on him intently trying to see beyond his words. "The WingCo at Syerston mentioned that you were modest and told me you questioned whether you would fit in. That is to your credit, but I think your doubts are misplaced. First of all, we train our sprog crews very carefully before we take them along on operations. Every new pilot — regardless of where he comes from or how many flying hours or sorties he's flown elsewhere — flies Second Dickie with me personally before he takes his own crew on an op. That's why my Lancaster is still fitted with two sets of controls. Furthermore, we don't only fly against the high-profile targets that get attention in the papers. We do many routine ops, mostly marking and illuminating for Main Force. In short, you'd have plenty of opportunity to gain experience and confidence before tackling something dicier. That said, it's not strictly true about you being so inexperienced, is it?"

Damn, Kit thought, *he's pulled my personnel files.* Not one of the COs at the training units had bothered to do that. Kit answered cautiously, "I've never commanded a Lancaster on operations, sir."

"No, but you've flown 36 complete ops, and you're wearing the DFM," Fauquier countered. "Furthermore, assessments of your flying have gone from 'average' in advanced flight training to 'exceptional' at the HCU. You were chosen by the Lancaster Finishing School to apply. That says to me that you continue to learn while many others who have learned to fly easier and faster have plateaued. That's what makes me believe you have the potential to be a valuable member of this squadron."

"Thank you, sir. But, as you mentioned a moment ago, fitting into a squadron isn't all about flying skills. It also has to do with sharing attitudes. Every squadron has its own character and ethos. I think you'll agree that 617 Squadron has a markedly different character from the squadrons of Main Force or even the Pathfinders?"

"Yes, Moran, it does. We believe in getting the job done, not just counting ops. We want maximum impact with minimum casualties — and that applies to casualties on the ground as well as in the air. We've beaten up factories in advance to warn the workers to get out. We've bombed marshalling yards and other military installations without dropping one bomb outside the perimeter fence. We aim for high-precision bombing to ensure there is no — and I mean no — unnecessary casualties. I don't deny that we take risks, but never suicidal risks. I was a banker in civilian life, Moran; I'm good at calculating risk."

Moran found himself attracted both to Fauquier's blunt honesty and to the kind of operations he was describing. Yes, Main Force was *supposed* to bomb legitimate military and industrial targets, but the reality was that neither the navigational equipment nor bombsites were accurate enough to ensure results. It was why they had long ago given up even trying. Instead, night raids targeted cities, causing massive civilian casualties. The phrases 'area' and 'saturation bombing' better described their activities. Harris had even invented the term 'de-housing' to justify the destruction of residential areas. The term was meant to imply this wanton destruction of dwellings was a legitimate means of waging war by undermining the morale of Germany's population, particularly the industrial workforce. In the worst raids, the ones that started fire storms, thousands of civilians, some claimed tens of thousands, regardless of age, sex or job, were incinerated.

"Your reservations wouldn't have anything to do with what happened to you on November 23, 1943, would they?" Fauquier asked softly into the silence.

Moran was relieved that the group captain had broached the subject. It was better this way than if he'd had to raise it or if they'd continued to tip-toe around it. Meeting Fauquier's eyes, he answered, "Yes, sir, they would. I believe 617 has a record of treating cases of LMF particularly harshly."

"Possibly. I've only been on the squadron six weeks. However, let's be clear about this. I've read your file, including your CO's report on the incident. You didn't suffer from LMF. You suffered from bloody-mindedness."

The assessment caught Kit so by surprise that he laughed. Then fearing this might be misinterpreted as not taking the incident seriously, he cut himself off. Soberly, he admitted, "I was undoubtedly being bloody-minded, sir."

"If I'd been your commanding officer, I would not have expected you to fly after just two hours' sleep — that's stupid and often leads to accidents. When I sent you back on ops, it would not have been with a sprog crew; they deserve someone particularly calm, not someone just off a dicey-do with fatal consequences. Instead, after you were rested, I would have asked you to fly as my flight engineer. Would you have refused to fly?"

"No, sir." That was not bravado. Kit knew that if he'd been given only a day or two to come to terms with Don's death, he would have flown with any skipper he respected; and he already respected Fauquier.

"Right. So, what we have here is a command failure combined with some bloody-mindedness on your part, not a case of LMF." Fauquier let that sink in, while Kit nodded mutely and thought: My God, why hadn't anyone else seen it like this? Why hadn't he seen it himself? Because everyone had been so quick to tell him he was "LMF" — until Dr Grace refused to confirm the diagnosis.

Fauquier continued. "Now you know my opinion, does it change yours about joining the squadron?"

"Yes, sir," Kit answered with a smile and a surge of relief. This wasn't just about laying his ghosts to rest, it opened up new prospects as well. Kit could now allow himself to become genuinely excited about the prospect of joining the most famous Lancaster squadron in the RAF. "I'll sign the application forms as soon as I'm back at Syerston."

"No need. You can complete the formalities here. One thing we're not in this squadron is sticklers for bumf! I'll inform the messes to expect the arrival of you and your crew tomorrow night. We can take care of the red-tape sometime next week." He stood and held out his hand. "Welcome aboard, Moran."

Kit took the outstretched hand. "Thank you, sir. I'm genuinely honoured that you would go to so much trouble over just one sprog pilot."

"We were all sprog pilots once, Moran. But more importantly, there's enough inhumanity in this war to make it essential that we treat each other with mutual respect, don't you think?"

Kit answered with a heartfelt "Yes, sir!"

Chapter 15
Second Dickey

RAF Woodhall Spa
6 February 1945

Moran had never trained so hard in his life as he did in his first fourteen days with 617 Squadron. Precision bombing constituted the raison d'être of 617, and their standards called for bomb placement within 50 yards of a target from an altitude of anywhere from 50 to 20,000 feet. To do this they used a new, semi-automatic bombsite, the SABS, which Babcock was struggling to master. The SABS required a longer bomb run, which meant more straight-and-level flying. That would be nerve-wracking when under attack, but Moran resolved to cross that bridge when he came to it. In addition to the bombing exercises, the gunners had to keep in practice and so did Peal, so they seemed to be constantly flying. Whenever in the air, squadron policy required the flight engineer to record fuel levels, engine temperatures, revs, oil pressure and more every fifteen minutes. Some men would have groused, but Daddy seemed to enjoy being kept busy.

By the end of each day, they were exhausted, but the messes at Woodhall Spa provided the necessary atmosphere for rest. The Sergeant's mess had the advantage of being a solid brick building with central heating rather than a Nissen hut as at many stations, while the officers' mess was famous for its luxury. It had been built as a mansion and then used as a luxury hotel, "the Petwood," before being converted into the officers' mess. The sprawling mock-Tudor structure sported a half-timbered exterior, wood-panelled interiors, a grand central stairway with elaborately carved banister, and seemly countless leaded windows. The ceilings were high, the floors polished or carpeted, and the large fireplaces were well fed with wood to provide a warm and cosy atmosphere. In addition to the bar and two lounges, there was a billiards room and library. The surrounding grounds offered a tennis court, swimming pool, golf course, and walking trails among towering rhododendron bushes and old elms. There was even a cinema in a converted wooden pavilion. Altogether, the facilities and grounds were so expansive that it was possible to escape the inevitable conviviality of the mess — if one wanted. Moran welcomed both the opportunities to mix with his new comrades and to retreat as needed.

Although he rang through to Georgina each evening, he found he needed the time alone to rest and gather his energy for challenges of the next day.

Then suddenly there was a hiatus, at least for the crews, as the squadron's Lancasters underwent a major refit. First, the bomb bays were modified to carry a single 12,000-pound bomb that was fitted with fins to make it spin. To be able to carry such a payload, the Lancasters received more powerful Rolls-Royce Merlin engines. Then two extra fuel tanks replaced the rest bed. The extra weight of the fuel and the bomb combined, however, exceeded even the capacity of the new engines, so the mid-upper turret and the forward machine guns were also removed, as was the armour plating behind the pilot's seat. As these changes took shape, the crews speculated on the target. There were many guesses from Berchtesgaden to Danzig, but the only certainty was that it was very far away.

Finally, a notice was posted with the twenty crews selected for the operation. The Order of Battle listed Forrester among the twenty pilots, his first op as skipper, and Moran as "Second Dickey" to Fauquier. Neither notification was surprising. Forrester had flown Second Dickie to Fauquier on a raid against the Bielefeld aqueduct just a few days earlier. It had been unsuccessful, but Forrester still made a "big deal" of the fact that he was going operational first. In the mess he patronisingly bought a round for "you poor non-operational sods" and "commiserated" with Moran and Peal about Babcock. "The school-boy just can't get the hang of the SABS, can he?" Forrester rubbed in the fact that Moran's high altitude bombing results remained unsatisfactory.

"There's nothing wrong with Babcock," Moran insisted, as he lifted his pint in a toast to Forrester with a "Here's to you, Red!"

Putting his glass back on the table, Kit remarked casually, "But I do worry about you, you know."

"Me? Whatever for?"

"Well, given the fuel load, the target must be a long way away, and we never fly straight there and back. The way your navigator Riley tries to do dead reckoning blind, you're as likely to bomb Switzerland or Sweden as Germany."

"It's about time the Swedes got off their backsides," Forrester responded, downing his beer in a single swig.

"Couldn't agree with you more," Kit agreed, drinking more slowly. "It's not the Swedes I'm worried about, Forrester. It's what Fauquier will do to you if you cause an international incident."

"It'll be too late by the time he finds out." Forrester quipped back with a laugh.

"Not too late to tear a strip off — and then I'll have no one to buy me pints here in the officers' mess because you'll be a sergeant again."

"Fat chance, Zulu!" Forrester countered, clapping him on the shoulder before climbing over his chair to go and get some sleep prior to the operational briefing at midnight.

The aircrews stomped stoically up the stairs to the briefing room. Some, like Moran, had tried to rest. Others hadn't bothered. All seemed half asleep and untalkative, but after the darkness and silence of the night outside, the garish lighting of the briefing room jarred them, and the station staff buzzed with excitement. Fauquier's flight engineer caught sight of Moran and gestured to him to join the rest of the CO's crew. Moran was grateful for that simple gesture of solidarity. With them, he sat down in the front row.

Shortly afterwards, the crews were called to attention and Fauquier entered with the Station and Base Commanders as well as Air Vice Marshal Sir Ralph Cochrane, the commander of Five Group. Slight and high-browed, Cochrane looked more like an accountant than a military leader. His expression was sour, underlining his reputation for lacking a sense of humour. If he was here tonight, the raid must be important, Moran surmised.

The senior officers told the crews to sit, and Cochrane stepped forward. His uniform was immaculate and his tone as crisp as the creases on his trousers. "Well, you all know by now, is that this op must be important, but what you don't know is that tonight's operation has been ordered by the Prime Minister personally. You may have heard rumours — although hopefully you haven't — that the German battleship *Tirpitz* used the terrible weather of the past few weeks to slip her moorings and disappear for a number of days. She has, fortunately, been located again, deep inside Tromso fjord." The *Tirpitz* was the terror of the Royal Navy and Moran knew that more than thirty attempts had already been made to sink her using bombs, mines, torpedoes, and even mini submarines. Even 617 had made a previous attempt, in which they'd flown first to Russia and then struck from landward, but without success.

Cochrane snapped his fingers, and the curtain was drawn back to reveal a map of the North Sea between Scotland and Norway. With a crack that made Moran wince, Cochrane hit his wooden pointer on a dot at the very top of the map. "That is where the beast is now! In range of your modified Lancasters after you take on a full load of fuel at Lossiemouth.

No more nonsense about flying to Russia to refuel as on your last attempt. You, supported by No. 9 squadron, will fly up the North Sea as you can see here." He pointed to a piece of yarn stretched between pins that paralleled the Norwegian coast until it made an abrupt right-hand turn and crossed overland. "We've identified a gap in the German radar here between Trondheim and Torghatten. You'll nip through there and cross into Swedish airspace." His pointer continued to follow the yarn pinned to the map. "Up the central valley until this pass here. You'll cross that at 100 feet to avoid German radar and continue straight on to the target, taking it from the south. We have no reports of Luftwaffe fighters anywhere within two hundred miles, which is why we have no worries about removing the mid-upper turret and forward guns." He paused to let this sink in, and a wave of satisfied nodding rippled across the room. Above the rows of uniformed men, smoke wafted lazily from scores of lighted cigarettes that burned bright and then faded as men inhaled or let out their breath.

"The flak, of course, will be considerable, and the *Tirpitz* has its own armament, as you well know, but you'll be using Barnes Wallis' Tallboy bombs and bombing from 18,000 feet. The weather, as you'll see in more detail in the later briefing, is predicted to be ideal, or at least as good as it gets at this time of year. Now although sunrise over the target is around 10 am GMT, the problem is that its angle is so low that the valleys and fjords are in shadow for much of the day. Good ground visibility over the target only starts at 11:45, and we'll lose it again at 14:58, although you'll have twilight of sorts until 16:00. To make maximum use of that window of better visibility, you are scheduled to be over the target at noon. We'll hold the detailed meteorological briefing and the briefings for wireless operators and navigators in Lossiemouth during the refuelling stop, so that's it for now. However, remember the PM wants the beast destroyed. Belly up, is how he put it. I expect you to go in and do the job! Good luck to everyone!"

The AVM departed. Fauquier took over with instructions for the flight up to Lossiemouth, noting as he finished, "We'll be flying low until right before going over the target for the bomb run, and icing should not be a problem, but it is bitterly cold at these latitudes nevertheless. Dress warm, take extra thermoses of coffee, tea or cocoa — and some extra relief bottles as well." That got a laugh from the crews.

Fauquier closed with, "I'll take off at 2 am and the rest of you follow at one-minute intervals behind me. On arrival at Lossiemouth, navigators and wireless ops go directly to the detailed briefing. Pilots, engineers and rear gunners can stop in at the messes for a smoke."

In the little time left before the crew buses left for the aircraft, Moran decided he should put on another layer of underwear. He returned to the mess, and had barely finished dressing again, when Forrester burst in on him.

"Mate! I need a favour! My wireless operator just called over from the Sergeant's Mess to say Riley's throwing his guts up. Some kind of food poisoning. Since you're flying Second Dickie with Fauquier and the rest of your crew is stood down, can you lend me Peal? Otherwise, they'll scratch us altogether and send the back-up crew instead!" He sounded panicked by the thought of being left off what promised to be a high-profile operation.

"You'll have to talk to Peal, Forrester. I don't own him." Adrian's room was two doors farther down the hall.

"Yeah, but he said he wouldn't go unless you approved."

"Then you've already talked to him?" Kit was slightly annoyed, but he'd come to expect things like this from Forrester.

"Yeah. He's keen to go. Getting kitted up right now — subject to your approval, of course."

"In that case, good luck," Moran replied.

"I owe you one, mate!" Forrester shot back with a grin and disappeared.

They flew up to Lossiemouth without incident. While the navigators and radio operators attended their briefing, the pilots collected in the anteroom at the mess. Moran felt isolated with none of his crew around him. He could have joined Forrester and Peal, of course, but the former was joking loudly — too loudly, Moran thought — and he didn't feel up to fending off jabs about still being Second Dickey. Instead, he sat quietly and eavesdropped on some veteran of pilots talking about the last attempt on "the beast" in September of the previous year. According to press reports, 40 Lancasters, 20 from 617 Squadron and 20 from 9 Squadron, had flown to a Red Air Force base near Archangel and, from there, refreshed and refuelled, launched an attack on the *Tirpitz* from landward.

Listening to pilots who had flown that op, Moran learned that it had not gone as smoothly as the newspapers made it sound. His colleagues complained about non-existent radio signals that should have helped guide them in, and about the utter lack of landmarks in the seemingly endless forest. They joked in retrospect about watching their fuel drain away with nothing in sight but trees and snow as far as the eye could see. Several mentioned being shot at by Soviet anti-aircraft but, as someone else reminded them, "the Royal Navy do that all the time, too!"

"Do you remember Knilans landing with the branches of that tree still sticking out of the nose!" they laughed. "The whole crew still had pine needles in their hair at the briefing!"

Abruptly, an announcement came over the tannoy. Transport was waiting outside to take them out to their refuelled aircraft. With a collective murmur, the pilots finished whatever they were drinking — none of it alcoholic before an op — and pulled their flight jackets back on.

Moran latched onto Fauquier's flight engineer. "Were you in on the last attempt to sink the beast?"

"Yes, I was flying with Tait then." Group Captain Tait had been Fauquier's predecessor as CO of 617 Squadron.

"How did it go?"

"Overheard some of the chaps reminiscing, did you? Don't worry. As far as engaging the *Tirpitz*, things didn't go badly at all. We lost no aircraft or crew to enemy action, although two crews went down over the arctic, one far off course. We don't know the reason. Could have been icing or another technical failure." Now the engineer paused and shook his head in disgust. "Bloody costly trip in terms of aircraft, though. We lost twenty Lancs, eighteen of them to the appalling conditions over there. On the flight over only half of our aircraft could even find the airfield, Yegodnik; the rest crash landed wherever they could. Ten were patched up again, but we had to cannibalise two other Lancasters to do that. And while the long-suffering ground crews were working around the clock to make the kites serviceable, we were living in lice-infested bunkers and entertained with Soviet propaganda films showing German atrocities against the Russians. I've never been so glad to leave a place in my life!" He laughed. "When Knilans returned to Woodhall Spa, he made a show of stripping naked in the driveway and burning every piece of clothing he'd worn on the trip!"

Moran sympathised, but the most important message was "no losses to enemy action." For such an audacious undertaking, that was encouraging. After all, 617 had lost eight out of nineteen aircraft on their debut raid.

Just before 6.00 am, in pitch darkness and snow flurries, Fauquier led the squadron into the air. The new, more-powerful Merlins screamed in protest as he pushed them through the wire to get the overloaded Lancaster off the ground. To the former flight engineer Moran, they sounded as though they were tearing themselves apart, and his fingers itched to ease back on them. Fortunately, he wasn't flying; they barely cleared the end of the runway and staggered into the air, gaining altitude agonisingly slowly.

They flew out over the North Sea and after levelling off at just 2,000 feet, Fauquier turned the controls over to Moran and lay his head back to 'get a few winks' — or pretended to anyway. From this altitude, by the light of the stars alone it was easy to see how rough the North Sea was. At one point they passed over a northbound convoy. The heavily laden merchantmen wallowed in the deep troughs of the waves, partially submerged. Around them the escorts battered their way through the frothing crests, flinging sheets of water upwards as their sharp bows cut into the lead-grey seas. The gusty wind blew the spray and spume backwards, drenching everything topside and making the superstructures glisten.

At the designated turning point Fauquier took the controls again and banked the big black kite onto a course of due east as they crossed over Norway. Not a single search light greeted them. No gun fired at them. There really *was* a gap in the enemy defences, Moran concluded in wonder. Usually, such promises proved illusory.

Fauquier stayed at the controls until they crossed into Sweden. They knew exactly when they crossed into Swedish airspace because the Swedes greeted them with half-hearted bursts of flak. These appeared designed to indicate they were not sleeping, but just as clearly to send the message that they meant no harm either. With the RAF blatantly and consciously violating Swedish airspace, Moran conceded that his joke about Fauquier "tearing a strip off" for causing an international incident had been seriously misjudged. Forrester would probably take the mickey out of him about it when they got back.

They turned again to fly up a broad valley between two mountain ranges. For a second time Fauquier turned the controls over to Moran, but rather than pretending sleep he worked his way back to the Elsan toilet. They were still flying low to deceive German radar. Gradually the sky brightened. Slowly and almost eerily the Norwegian glaciers to port turned a pale pink. Below them headlights beamed as they wound along on twisting roads. Shortly afterwards, a whole town appeared, like scattered diamonds on a velvet cloth. The beautiful sight encouraged Moran to hope that the time when all of Europe would be free of blackouts was not so far away.

They flew on, and a dawn from a low sun shone on the ordered, peaceful life of northern Sweden in the snow below them. Finally, the navigator warned, "Fifteen minutes to marshalling point."

Fauquier took over the controls again. Moran received permission to stretch his legs, and after a quick pee, climbed up into the astrodome to get a good look around. Streaming out behind them in an irregular gaggle flew the other Lancasters of both 617 and 9 squadrons. They started slowly circling an invisible point in the sky like a huge mobile while waiting for the stragglers to catch up. Moran identified Forrester's Q for Queen among the melee. Peal would be conscientiously doing his calculations, so there was no point in waving, but mentally Kit mentally wished them luck.

Eventually the wireless operator reported that all aircraft of both squadrons were on station. The navigator gave Fauquier the next course as they started laying on altitude to climb over the Norwegian mountains toward Tromso. Gradually, the ground rose to meet them and sides of a pass closed in on them. At the one hundred feet they had been briefed to fly, they left Sweden behind. Beyond, as the ground sloped down again towards the Atlantic, they continued to climb towards their bombing height of 18,000 feet. This was the altitude at which the "Tallboy" bombs were supposed to be most effective.

"Happy?" Fauquier asked, glancing over at Moran.

"Pleasantest sight-seeing tour I've had in a long time."

The Canadian laughed briefly before adding, "I hate to tell you this, but that's probably about to change."

"All good things come to an end."

As they passed through 10,000 feet, Fauquier notified the crew and they clipped their oxygen masks over their faces. Below them, the mountains were still falling away, but contrary to the forecast, cloud hovered over the Arctic. It didn't obscure everything, at least not yet, but Moran thought it might make the bomb runs tricky. Soon the German defences came to life and the first bursts of flak blossomed in the sky ahead. It looked harmless and almost beautiful at first, but Moran knew better. With relief he registered no excessive apprehension. He'd always felt tension as they headed into flak; a man would have been mad not to. Yet now, as before, his anxiety did not reach a magnitude beyond his capacity to control or conceal.

The German anti-aircraft gunners started to find their range and the flak crept closer to them. Although it buffeted the Lancaster, the heavy load meant it only caused the aircraft to stagger rather than bounce about the sky. Then, with a near deafening bang, something punched them in the belly. The Lancaster was whipped upwards a hundred feet or more as filthy brown smoke engulfed them. It was like nothing Moran had ever experienced before. Involuntarily he exclaimed, "Christ! What the hell was that?"

"The *Tirpitz*." Fauquier answered calmly. "Among other armaments, she has eight 15-inch guns with a range of 17 miles. Happily, they underestimated our altitude."

"You mean they're firing at us with ordinance designed to sink a battleship?!"

"That's one way of wording it."

"Well, I suppose the good thing is we won't feel any pain when it hits us," Moran observed, drawing a deep breath and crossing his arms.

"Exactly," Fauquier answered with a quick grin in his direction.

The next shell exploded precisely at their altitude. Fortunately, it was leading them by about 500 feet; that increasing cloud cover had its advantages, Moran thought to himself. Not only was the target becoming veiled from view, so were the bombers. The German gunners were just as blind as the bomb aimers, and that forced them to set their guns based on what they *heard* rather than saw.

Now Fauquier started the bomb run, eliminating the option of evasive action. The shore batteries were hurling volleys of light flak at them as fast as possible, and the *Tirpitz* was firing with all her guns. The bursts of the shells continued to go off precisely at 18,000 feet and were now just tens of yards ahead of them, forcing them to fly into the smoke and debris. The smell of cordite soaked in through the very rivets of the bomber as it shuddered, trembled and jinked in the shock waves. Moran found himself senselessly counting the seconds, thirty, thirty-one, thirty-two, thirty-three....

"Eight-tenths cloud, Skipper," the bomb-aimer called up. "I can't see the target."

"Right. We'll go around again and give someone else a chance in the meantime." Fauquier banked away from the target and swung down the fjord. Moran returned to the astrodome to watch the other aircraft make a pass at the target. He found Q for Queen in the queue and watched as it flew steadily through the gauntlet of anti-aircraft and heavy naval artillery fire. Q-Queen released the bomb on its first run, but even with his limited visibility as the ragged clouds plodded across the sky, Moran could see that it fell wide.

Watching these bombs was like nothing Moran had experienced on his previous tour. Aside from the fact that he'd never taken part in a daylight operation, these Tallboys differed dramatically from the standard 500 lb bombs and 2,000 lb 'cookies' Moran knew. Because of the fins, rather than tumbling over themselves as they dropped, they spun like gigantic bullets. Even after leaving the aircraft, they continued forward with their sharp noses pointed towards the target. He saw one hit the water, sending up a tremendous plume of water that visibly rocked the battleship. Shortly after D-Dog's bomb run, a column of smoke rose up through the clouds, suggesting at least one hit had been made. Yet roughly half the attacking aircraft turned away without releasing their bombs at all. The only good news was that the battleship's 15-inch guns were still firing too far ahead of the bombers.

When they were lined up again, Fauquier took them back in for a second run. The aircraft was pushed up, down and sideways by the air pressure of the explosions going off nearer and nearer to them. Pieces of shrapnel clattered on the metal skin and the smell of cordite again seeped into the cockpit. Moran had nothing to do but count the seconds as they flew straight and level. Again, the bomb-aimer reported he could not see the target in his site, and they aborted to go round yet again.

The flight engineer, who was dividing his time between watching the instrument dials and looking out the starboard side of the cockpit, flicked on his microphone. "Flight engineer to pilot: E-Easy has been hit. Port inner has packed in. Landing gear and flaps are down. I can't tell if that's hydraulic damage or if he's signalling that he wants to land."

"That's Bill Carey, isn't it?" Fauquier associated the pilot with the aircraft. "Is he on fire, Engineer?" he asked.

"Not that I can see, sir. He's turning back toward land."

"Right. Understood."

They made their third run at the target, and finally the bomb-aimer felt he could see enough to drop the bomb. On release, the Lancaster bounced upwards, pressing them down on their seats, and then they seemed to float for a second when it stabilised. As Fauquier turned away from the target, the rear gunner reported: "Near miss, sir! Maybe twenty yards off her stern. I could see her rudder and propellers when she lifted out of the water as the detonator went off. The water around her stern is still frothing with turbulence. There may be underwater damage to her steering gear."

"May be, yes," Fauquier retorted dryly.

Unlike Moran's previous ops, the release of the bomb did not also release them to fly for home. Instead, Fauquier started stooging around as he requested the wireless operator to find out how many aircraft had not yet delivered their bombs. Moran looked at his watch and saw they had been over the target for more than thirty minutes already. In Main Force, time over target rarely exceeded ten minutes. Moran reminded himself he could have opted to go to Main Force, instead of letting himself get flattered into this madness. The just rewards of vanity, his mother would surely to tell him — if she had the chance. He drew a deep breath to calm himself down; his ribcage seemed strangely smaller than normal....

"Wireless operator to pilot: Hamilton's got a hang-up, sir."

"Remind me what aircraft he's flying, Wireless Op?"

"H for How — or, as he says, Hamilton, sir."

"Pilot to crew: Can anyone see H for Hamilton out there?"

"Tail gunner to pilot: I've got him in sight, port astern low."

Fauquier banked around and slid in beside the aircraft with the bomb stuck partway in and partway out of the bomb bay. Over the wireless, Fauquier told the pilot that he would fly alongside him to help draw the flak — and the 15-inch guns, Moran mentally noted — while Hamilton made another attempt to release the bomb.

Moran understood that there was no question of Hamilton landing with the bomb in this position. Just as obviously, if they were going to try to shake it loose, then doing so over the target made the most sense; the Tallboys were custom-made and frightfully expensive to produce, after all, and one didn't want just to toss them in the drink. On the other hand, over the Arctic Sea no one would have been shooting at them. As for the CO flying alongside an aircraft on the bombing run to draw off some of the enemy anti-aircraft fire, that was a squadron tradition going back to Guy Gibson VC, and the original raid on the dams. As they started into the gauntlet yet again, Moran again questioned if he'd made the right decision by joining this 'death or glory' squadron.

When the bomb failed to drop and H-Hamilton swung out to go around once more, Fauquier turned to Moran and asked casually: "Do you want to do the next run with him?"

"Certainly, why not?" Moran retorted without irony. If they were going to fly through the barrage again, he'd rather be at the controls than just watching the flak and the shells chasing them. At some point soon, the German gunners were bound to work out what they were doing wrong with those 15-inch guns....

Fauquier conspicuously leaned back with his hands linked behind his head to demonstrate his confidence in Moran — for three more bomb runs. Finally, on their overall seventh run over the target, Hamilton's bomb finally came unstuck. It shot through the cloud to splash harmlessly beside the battleship.

There was now only one other aircraft still circling the target, and the tail gunner identified it as the one flown by Pilot Officer Buckham, who had the job of photographing the results of their efforts. He was just waiting for the rest of them to clear off. Fauquier took control of the aircraft back from Moran and turned west to cross the Norwegian coast as quickly as possible, before turning southwest over the Norwegian Sea and setting course for Scotland.

Flak from the outer islands of Norway bracketed and buffeted them as they flew over. With a sound like gravel thrown at a Nissen hut, a near miss produced a sprinkling of holes in the skin. These soon lowered the inside temperatures to well below freezing, but they had sustained no serious damage. Finally, the glistening Norwegian Sea spread out below them. The sun just peered across the Western horizon, turning the water gold as it began to set. It was only just after 1 pm, but above the Arctic circle at this time of year it barely rose more than ten degrees above the horizon, even at noon.

As the danger of enemy action receded, the tension that had enveloped Moran like a too tight-fitting vest eased. As they sank back below 10,000 feet, they could unclip their oxygen masks. Mugs of hot cocoa and coffee were handed out. With their masks hanging loose beside their faces they drank, those in the cockpit shouted jokes at one another over the droning of the four engines. The bomb aimer came to join them, complaining about how cold it was in the nose.

It *was* bitterly cold, and Moran looked at his watch, trying to calculate how much longer they would be trapped in this icebox. Out of habit, he checked the fuel gauges. They had consumed two thirds of the fuel and still had most of the North Sea to cross. They'd spent 50 minutes over the target and had been flying for over seven hours already.

"What are our diversion 'dromes, sir?"

"There's a Coastal Command airfield on the Shetlands. Short runway straight into a mountain. We should be OK to get to Lossiemouth though," Fauquier replied.

"Should be," Moran answered dryly.

Fauquier laughed. "I'm beginning to like you, Moran."

"Beginning?"

They landed at Lossiemouth with some ten minutes of fuel left. "I told you we were fine," Fauquier noted.

"Since we had tail winds," Moran muttered.

"Did we?"

"You mean you didn't notice?"

"Bloody-minded, didn't I say? Bloody-minded."

While still taxiing to dispersal, Fauquier called the tower asking for the status of the squadron's other aircraft. He was told that seventeen were back at Lossiemouth, but two had put down on the Shetlands. One of the latter was a write-off from flak damage, but the crew were all right and were hitching a lift with the other Lancaster that had simply been low on fuel. The latter would proceed to Lossiemouth forthwith and be ready to return to Woodhall Spa in the morning. This made E-Easy piloted by Flying Officer Carey the only casualty. As his Lanc had not been on fire, he and his crew might well have succeeded in putting it down safely either in Norway or — if they were lucky — in Sweden. It wasn't a bad outcome for 617 — except that they hadn't sunk the *Tirpitz*.

"Well, let's debrief and get something to eat before a short kip and the trip back to Woodhall Spa," Fauquier suggested after he shut down the engines, leaving only the ringing in their ears.

Moran got to his feet feeling stiff all over. A hot toddy before bed wouldn't be such a bad idea. He would find Adrian and see how he'd fared over a drink or two. Moran was glad to have this flight behind him. It reassured him that he could handle operational flying without undue inner tension.

He climbed down the ladder in Fauquier's wake, parachute slung over his shoulder. Suddenly Forrester was in front of them shouting, "Peal's a bloody coward! He froze and nearly got us all killed! If my bomb aimer hadn't taken over the navigation we'd have drowned somewhere out there! I won't fly another mile with him! I want him off the squadron—"

"He's my navigator, Forrester!" Moran broke into the flood of indignation. "You've got no right to—"

"Shut up, both of you!" Fauquier cut them off. "We don't discuss things like this at the top of our voices in front of ground crew on the tarmac. Follow me."

He led them back toward the Mess, found the first empty room, and slammed the door behind them before confronting Forrester. "Now, start over again in a reasonable tone of voice."

"As soon as the first burst of flak went up, Peal turned into a bag of shitless jelly, literally shaking and unable to calculate a single thing. I didn't need a course for the run, so I ignored him until we'd dropped our load, but when it was time to turn for home, I asked for a heading and he didn't answer me. The wireless operator tried to shake him out of his daze, but he just covered his head with his arms. My bomb aimer had to take over the navigation with the help of the wireless op. Peal's worthless, and I won't fly another mile with him."

Fauquier didn't say anything for a moment. Then, softly, he responded. "You don't have to. My navigator can fly back to Woodhall Spa with you tomorrow, and Peal can fly with me. Now go to the debriefing hut and report to the intelligence officers, but without mentioning this to them or anyone else."

Mollified, Forrester started to withdraw. As he reached the door, he paused to remark to Moran sincerely, "Sorry, Mate. I know he's become your friend, but he's a worthless coward the moment flak opens up. The sooner you get rid of him the better."

"I'll be the judge of that," Moran answered tersely.

"Suits me fine. Won't be my neck," Forrester retorted and was gone.

Fauquier said nothing for a moment or two, then he suggested, "I don't need you at the debrief, Moran. Why don't you go and find Peal? Hear what he has to say for himself and tell him he'll be flying back to Woodhall Spa with us."

"Yes, sir. And, sir, I'm willing to fly with him no matter what."

"I thought you might feel that way. We'll see."

Adrian did not report to the debriefing room, nor did he join the others getting their meal of bacon and eggs. He was not in the anteroom drinking either and he had not gone to bed. Increasingly alarmed, Kit started to fear he'd walked off the station AWOL. It was with relief that he found Adrian in the toilets, sitting on the floor with his face in his hands. Kit went down on his heels beside him. Adrian smelled of urine.

"I'm ropey. Washed out. Done. LMF."

"You're none of those things. But you do need a bath. Come on. I'll find you a clean pair of trousers, while yours go to the laundry. Then we'll go and have a drink together."

Adrian looked up at him with fathomless eyes, but he let Kit pull him to his feet and lead him to the bathroom. Kit found a batman and asked him to sort out the trouser issue. The man readily agreed noting, "Not the first time this has happened, sir. Not to worry."

By the time they reached the anteroom, most of the others had already turned in, but Fauquier appeared to have been waiting for them. When he saw them, he nodded once to Kit in acknowledgement and then withdrew.

"What's going to happen to me, Kit?" Adrian asked miserably as he sank down into one of the deep, leather chairs at a corner table.

"First, you fly back in the CO's Lancaster with me. Then we get 48 hours leave, and you come with me to Kirkby to meet Georgina. After that, we'll be operational and you're my navigator."

"Why did you want me to fly with Forrester?" Adrian asked, looking at him with large, uncomprehending eyes like a dog that has been beaten and doesn't know why.

"I didn't!" Kit protested. "I told Forrester it was your decision, but he said you were keen to go — only wanted my permission."

"The bastard! I said I didn't want to fly but he told me you wanted me to — that it was your suggestion!"

"That's not true, Adrian. I swear."

"I believe you." Adrian took a deep breath. "It's just — you can't imagine what it was like on Forrester's kite. The crew talks the whole time using the foulest language I've ever heard in my life. They compete with one another for the raunchiest jokes and the crudest insults. They even talk back to Forrester — albeit only in jest; they jump when he gives them an order. But after six hours of that constant chatter, my nerves were frayed. And then the flak hit us. One burst went off so near I thought I was already dead." Kit suspected it had been one of the 15-inch guns rather than flak, but he said nothing, letting Adrian continue. "It left me deaf for half a minute and — I snapped. I just snapped." He dropped his head in his hands, his long fingers with their signet ring combed through his blond hair. Kit noticed they were shaking.

Adrian lifted his head and looked straight at Kit. "You can't imagine what happened next: Forrester's wireless operator hit me. He slapped me across the face twice and shouted at me to 'snap out of it.' It made me feel — I don't know — like a child. I just folded up into a ball with my arms over my head and waited for it to be over."

In Kit's mind he heard Fauquier saying: "command failure." To Adrian he said, "You're never going to have to fly with Forrester again. That's a promise. Now, what are you drinking?"

Adrian shook his head. "What difference does it make? I'm washed out."

"Not yet, you aren't," Kit answered firmly. Then he went in search of an orderly and asked for two hot toddies.

Kit wanted to give Adrian another chance. Yet in the pit of his stomach, he knew Adrian's behaviour had been qualitatively different from his pig-headed refusal to fly because he was pissed off with his CO, Group and Butch Harris. Kit knew that he *could* have flown but *chose* to protest instead. Adrian, on the other hand, appeared to have been un*able* to operate effectively under fire. If that was the case, he endangered all of them. Kit knew that his responsibility to the rest of the crew might have to take precedence over his loyalty to Adrian — and that made him inwardly sick.

Chapter 16
Challenges

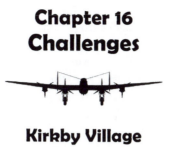

Kirkby Village
7 February 1945

Georgina's strategy with the children in need of remedial instruction was first to break down their resentment of the extra lessons they were being forced to take. That entailed making the lessons fun, and in some way relevant to the children's lives. Remembering Mrs Moran's advice about finding out what made a child happy or curious, she spent the opening session with both groups just trying to get to know the children and what motivated them.

Sometimes over grudging resistance, she dragged information out of them. Luckily several of the boys were keen on engines. Since her brother Gerald had shared that interest at their age there were plenty of books on the topic at the vicarage, and she resolved to bring some of them to school. These books had pictures and diagrams, unlike the books in the school library, and could form the basis of her lessons with those boys. The fact that nearly all the boys were mad about the RAF gave her another lever: when she mentioned that she was "pretty sure" she could arrange for them to meet a pilot from 617 squadron it was quite clear that she'd scored a bullseye.

In contrast, two of the girls appeared exclusively interested in boys, which Georgina found rather sad. Nevertheless, both were already in her sewing classes. She thought they would warm to the English lessons if she let them write their essays about fashion or film stars.

Her unresolved problems boiled down to two pupils, one boy and one girl. The boy spent most of his time doodling naked women and male sexual organs. Knowing she mustn't show shock, Georgina had taken a medical textbook on human reproduction from the library and presented it to him, telling him that reading and copying the text would be his weekly English assignment. After that he remained a sullen sod, but he stopped doodling in her presence. The girl, Battie, on the other hand, completely baffled her. She sat hunched in her chair, never responding to questions, and consistently submitted incomplete or blank assignments.

Georgina was so frustrated by this behaviour that she approached both Mr Willoughby and Miss Townsend about the girl. Miss Townsend was dismissive. "That one's a waste of time, Miss Reddings. She's not even from the Old Palace School: her mother enrolled her in the evacuation scheme on her own and she first went to the village school. She was billeted with local families but none of them wanted to keep her. As soon as she turned eleven, the local school board dumped her on us for the sole reason that we have the dormitories."

Mr Willoughby's assessment was no better: it amounted to, "The girl has the brain of a peahen. Too thick to take anything in. She belongs in a factory where she turns the same lever all day long and doesn't have to think."

Georgina was outraged by such attitudes. Even so, she remembered that Mrs Moran had warned her, "You won't be able to reach every child. We, too, are only human, and we aren't going to like or be liked by everyone. Do your best, but don't spread yourself too thin. You mustn't have 'favourites,' but don't overcompensate by lavishing all your attention on those children who respond least, either."

Maybe Battie was in that category, Georgina thought as she unfolded the ironing board and plugged the iron into a socket. Maybe Battie was just one of these children that she couldn't reach or who didn't want to be reached. Then again... Her mind started to wander. It was hard to concentrate on Battie when she hadn't heard from Kit in three days. Up to now he'd phoned regularly, so three days of silence in a row could only mean one thing: Kit was operational.

In the next room, Mrs Radford was listening to the BBC Home Service as she did every night. Georgina unconsciously started listing as the announcer intoned, "...*Yesterday, twenty aircraft of 617 Squadron made a second attempt to sink the German battleship* Tirpitz, *causing damage to her steering system and making other hits but failing to send her to the bottom.*" Georgina gasped and turned toward the doorway. "*One of our aircraft failed to return. Meanwhile, Main Force squadrons...*"

Georgina wasn't listening any more. Not already! Surely, not already! There was still so much to say to him, to do with him.

The telephone was ringing in the hallway. Georgina tensed, suddenly terrified it was the Station Adjutant ringing with the news Kit was missing. She ran into the hall without even unplugging the iron. "Hello!" She gasped into the receiver.

"Hello, Georgina. It's me. Are you all right?" Kit had evidently picked up on the alarm in her voice.

She almost exclaimed "Thank God!" but stopped herself just in time. She knew she mustn't let him see just how much she worried about him. She pulled herself together and tried to sound light-hearted. "Yes, yes. Of course. We were just listening to the BBC and heard that 617 attacked the *Tirpitz* yesterday! Were you on the raid?"

"Only as Second Dickie." He sounded strangely sober, Georgina thought, and she curbed her attempt to sound cheerful. Kit was continuing, "Georgina, I have a favour to ask. My navigator and I need to decompress a bit. There's a Red Cross dance in Boston tonight and we'd like to go. Do you think you could talk Fiona into joining us? Just this once. Tell her I promise not to make a habit of it, but Adrian doesn't have time to ask his girl to join us. It would be more fun as a foursome. Like old times. Do you think she'd mind?"

"No, I don't think so. I'll twist her arm, if she hesitates." Georgina improved her answer with a laugh. "What time do you want to pick us up?" She looked at her watch again. At quarter past nine, it was already late, and it was a Wednesday night. She was going to have a long night, little sleep and a rough day tomorrow, but there was no question of saying 'no.' For all she knew, this might be their last evening together.

"We'll pick you up as close to ten as possible," Kit promised.

"We'll be ready. See you then!"

They hung up, and Georgina went into the sitting room where Mrs Radford and Fiona both waited expectantly.

"Kit flew on the *Tirpitz* raid — as Second Pilot to the CO. He's coming to take me out to a dance and his navigator is with him. Would you like to join us, Fiona?"

Fiona raised an eyebrow. "Are you sure Kit wouldn't mind?"

"It was his suggestion."

"In that case, why not?" She jumped up eagerly.

As she went upstairs to change, Fiona's emotions churned. She'd told Georgina that she didn't love Kit, and that was true. Yet she acknowledged to herself that she felt jealous of Georgina. Watching Georgina glow whenever Kit phoned and hearing her talk about him and the things they'd done together made Fiona feel strangely forsaken.

What about Georgina appealed to men so much? She was pleasant looking in a pale, wishy-washy sort of way, but she wasn't stunningly beautiful. She was intelligent, but hardly a witty conversationalist, much less a genius. Fiona conceded that she had a flair for fashion that she could indulge because one wealthy aunt had a trove of pre-war fabrics and another was a dressmaker, but her figure was flatter and less curved that Fiona's own. Fiona just couldn't grasp what made men devoted to Georgina — in a way they never were to her.

She opened her wardrobe and ran her hand across the utility dresses and make-overs hanging inside. Georgina's words about dressing in baggy clothes, flat shoes and wearing no make-up echoed in her head, and she knew her own answer had been disingenuous. She *did* want male attention, but she wanted men to like her for what she was — self-confident, ambitious, and career-oriented. She wasn't going to give up everything just to cook and clean for some man, but neither did she want to spend the rest of her life alone or, worse, exclusively among females. She thought back to the teachers at her last school, to Miss Townsend and Miss Evans. She did not want to end up like them.

She started looking through her wardrobe for something flattering. If she was going to a dance, then she wanted to stand out. It had been fun flirting with the RAF that came into the *King's Head*, but so far she'd garnered not a single serious invitation. The young men seemed a bit preoccupied when they came to the *King's Head* — so often still in dirty battle dress, their faces chaffed from the oxygen mask. There was something almost desperate yet distracted about the way they latched onto anything female. Maybe a good dance would put them more in the right frame of mind?

She thought back to the time when Don, Georgina, Kit and she had been a foursome. They'd gone to the flicks and concerts, plays and dances together and had a wonderful time. In retrospect, it had been one of the best times of her life, and she wanted to recapture that mood.

Georgina was brushing out her long hair and putting on a pair of earrings. She was nearly ready to go.

Fiona turned back to her wardrobe and removed a red-satin, three-quarter length dress with a V-neckline and a broad, black collar. It was a hand-me-down from her elder sister, but she'd had it fitted and it looked good on her. She regretted not having enough time to put on fresh nail-polish, but it was too late for that. A car pulled up outside and doors crunched shut; male voices wafted up on the evening air.

"I'll go down and greet them," Georgina tossed over her shoulder as she left the attic.

Fiona pulled on the dress, brushed out her hair vigorously, re-touched her make-up and put on fresh lipstick. Then, grabbing a shawl, she started down the stairs as voices filtered up from the hallway. She could see Kit clearly as Georgina held out her hand to the other officer, who stood partially obscured by the banister. Kit's eyes caressed his fiancée as she smiled and chatted to his navigator. He had never looked at her like that, Fiona acknowledged with a pang of jealousy, yet it vindicated her decision to break up with him too. He had loved her no more than she him. And yet... he had never looked as good as he did tonight either. He looked so mature and self-confident in his Flying Officer's uniform. What a difference a year could make!

The others looked up the stairs expectantly. Fiona pulled herself together and put on a broad smile as she held out her hand to Kit. "Lovely to see you, Kit." Before he could say more than "You too," she turned to the second RAF officer and gave him her hand with a self-assured, "Fiona Barker." Focusing properly on Kit's friend for the first time, she noted he was very good-looking, albeit in a slightly dreamy, artistic way.

He took her hand. "Adrian Peal. How do you do, Miss Barker." His uniform was exquisitely tailored, his hands manicured, his shoes polished, and his accent was pure Oxbridge. Fiona could just picture the way her social-climbing mother would drool over him if she brought him home.

Kit was eager to get on their way, and the ladies hastened to put on their winter coats, gloves and hats before going out into the cold night. At the car, Adrian held the back door open for Fiona, before going around to get in the other side. As Kit turned the key in the ignition, something clicked in Fiona's head. Turning to Adrian, she asked, "You aren't by any chance related to the barrister Sir Arthur Peal, are you?"

"Yes, he's my father. Do you know him?" Adrian sounded alarmed more than pleased.

"Oh, no! I just happened to be reading about him in today's paper. What a coincidence, don't you think?"

"He was in the news?" Adrian sounded horrified.

"Yes, for getting an acquittal in a high-profile murder case that everyone thought would go the other way. Didn't you see the papers?"

"We've been rather busy," Kit remarked from the drivers' seat, and Fiona heard the edge to his voice. She ignored Kit and focused on the more receptive Adrian. "If you're interested, I can clip the articles and send them to you? They were most adulatory."

"Oh, don't go to any trouble," Adrian replied evidently embarrassed. "My father gets a lot of publicity."

"Are you also interested in the law?"

"Not at all. It's too grim and depressing. Besides, how could I ever live up to my father's expectations or reputation? I thought it better to read something totally unrelated."

Fiona found his modesty appealing. She also liked the fact that he was not making the least attempt to sit nearer or put his hand on her knee or the like. She hated men who tried to get physical before they even knew her; such behaviour only underlined that she was nothing but a 'skirt' to them, rather than a human being with a mind.

In the front seat, Georgina enthusiastically regaled Kit with stories of her special pupils — as though he could possibly be interested. It took Fiona aback when Georgina asked Kit if he'd be willing to visit the school. And even more so when she turned to look into the back seat to include Adrian with the words, "I thought maybe you could *all* come to the school to talk about flying Lancasters. You could each talk about your respective trade. They'd love that, Kit." She turned back to him. "So many of the boys are fascinated by flying and Lancasters — especially 617 Squadron, that they've all heard about. They hear and see the aircraft in the skies overhead all the time, but most of them have never met anyone who actually flies one. It would really motivate them, don't you agree Fiona?"

"The kids would love it. I'm not sure if Miss Townsend would approve. Miss Evans certainly wouldn't."

"Mr Willoughby likes the idea," Georgina countered. "I think he can talk Miss Townsend into it — if you'd be willing to sacrifice some of your precious time off?" She looked from Kit to Adrian.

Kit laughed, "Of course, if it helps you out."

Adrian looked less comfortable with the idea. "I'm not sure they'd be interested in navigators," he waffled.

"All the more reason to tell them how important your work is, and how difficult," Georgina contended. "Everyone has heard of pilots and gunners and bomb aimers, but not flight engineers, navigators and wireless operators. Yet it's the latter three trades that will be needed after the war." Georgina's enthusiasm bubbled up ever more forcefully. "It's so important to expand their minds, to show them that there are opportunities out there other than working 'down the pit' or at some factory or on the land. If you could spark interest in navigation in just one of the boys, it might make all the difference between a life of drudgery and a life — well — up amongst the stars!"

Kit laughed out loud, and Fiona moaned, "Don't be so melodramatic, Georgina."

"If you think it's important, of course I'll come," Adrian agreed diffidently.

"Wonderful!" Georgina threw him a smile from the front seat.

"We won't be able to commit to anything, you understand," Kit warned, "and I don't guarantee the others will come."

"I understand. But now that I know you're willing *in principle* I can work on getting Miss Townsend to agree," Georgina sounded very pleased with herself, Fiona thought, slightly annoyed.

As none of them knew Boston they had some difficulty finding the venue of the advertised dance, but eventually they located it and parked the car. By then it was so late that the crowd had thinned considerably. Or maybe the quality of the band, or the fact that it was a Wednesday night, had inhibited the turnout. As it was, there were perhaps one hundred and fifty people in the large venue, and most of these were Americans with local girls; the RAF was poorly represented.

Kit took Georgina onto the dance floor at once. Fiona followed them with her eyes, remembering how Don danced so gracefully that he and Georgina seemed to float. Kit couldn't dance like that, but Georgina obviously didn't mind. As she watched, they paused and Kit did a ridiculous little jig of some sort that set Georgina laughing in delight. Then he took her back into his arms again, excluding the rest of the world from their bubble of happy intimacy.

Adrian, however, seemed reluctant to ask Fiona to dance. Was she really that unattractive? By the looks some of the Americans were casting her, no. Then something else occurred to her. What if Kit had made negative comments about her to his navigator? "Did Kit say something about me?" she asked bluntly.

"What? No. I mean, only that you'd been a twosome for a while, but had gone your separate ways more than a year ago." As he spoke, Adrian fidgeted and looked more embarrassed and uncomfortable than ever. That convinced Fiona that Kit must have said more.

"Did he tell you why we broke up?"

"No, just something about you not being interested in a serious relationship — not that he suggested you were some sort of floozy!" Adrian hastened to add. "He said you were a nice girl — and I can see that for myself. On the other hand, you see, I'm — I'm not after a serious relationship just now." He floundered about like a drowning swimmer. "Not that I'm just after a party either. I mean — it's just — I think — I'm making a mess of this," he concluded abruptly, flushed with embarrassment. He avoided looking at her.

Fiona was not put-off by his incoherence and bashfulness. She thought it was rather endearing, in fact. Yet, she also sensed that something more was going on here than just a word of warning from Kit. Since she had no idea what it might be, however, she suggested, "Why don't you take me onto the dance floor before that American sergeant does," nodding towards the man who was making his way across the room in her direction.

"Yes, of course," Adrian instantly obeyed. Fiona found herself in his arms. He was almost as good a dancer as Don, and she felt a leap of joy. This was the way it was supposed to feel, she thought, remembering all the other dances she been to and all her different partners. Not once had she felt this same quiver of delight at the warmth of a man's hand on her rib-cage — very lightly, very politely guiding her to the rhythm of the music. She certainly hadn't felt this with Kit, she thought, as they glided past him and Georgina, who were hardly dancing at all as they laughed about something together.

Since Adrian appeared too shy to strike up a conversation, Fiona took the initiative, "You were saying in the car that you didn't want to read law, so what did you read?"

"Architecture."

"Oh, that's lovely. I have a cousin who read architecture."

Adrian seemed to pull himself together to make a greater effort to engage her. "You're studying to be a teacher, Kit said, at the same school as Georgina. Is that correct?"

"Yes, we've shared a room together for three years."

"And where are you from?"

He wasn't looking at her as he asked, Georgina noticed. His eyes were fixed somewhere in the distance. He really wasn't interested in this conversation or her, but she still made the effort. "Lincoln. My father's the Deputy Director at William Foster and Company, the tank manufacturer."

Adrian nodded politely but showed no interested. After their promising start this wasn't going at all the way Fiona wanted it to. Here she was dancing with a divine-looking partner from the "right" sort of background, but he seemed to be off in a different world. Fiona searched for some topic that might trigger interest in her — or at least what she was saying.

"My problem," she told Adrian as he looked across the room rather than at her, "is that I want the same thing that men want."

That got his attention! He nearly stumbled as he turned to look at her in disbelief. His eyes were a piercing, bright blue. "What?"

"No, I don't mean sex. I mean I want to be liked — and one day loved — for what I am. I don't want to have to deform myself to meet some ideal of what a woman should be."

"Of course not," Adrian agreed simply, looking away across the room again. He added wistfully, "but men shouldn't have to conform to some ideal either."

"Women don't expect men to be ideal. We tolerate almost any number of faults, weaknesses and obsessions."

"Just as long as they aren't LMF," Adrian noted under his breath.

"That's not true! I would have broken off with Kit whether he'd been LMF or not."

Adrian stopped dancing so abruptly that Fiona lost her footing and stumbled. Adrian stared at her. "What did you just say?"

"That Kit being LMF wasn't the reason I broke off our relationship."

"When was Kit LMF?" Adrian spluttered in disbelief.

Too late, Fiona realised that Adrian hadn't known. "Oh, my God," she took a step back, covering her mouth with her hand. "I shouldn't have said that," she confessed. Then, more forcefully, she added, "Please forget I said it." But that was impossible. No one could forget something of such import. Kit and Georgina would think she'd done this deliberately to discredit and hurt Kit. They would hate her and blame her for hurting his reputation, yet she had neither intended nor wanted that. "Please promise me you'll never tell anyone what I said. Please!" she begged hopelessly.

Adrian shook his head as though dazed. "Don't worry. I won't tell anyone. I just — I — maybe — maybe, I understand something now." He twisted away from her, and his eyes sought out Kit, still dancing in blissful oblivion with Georgina. Then he seemed to remember Fiona and turned back to her only to say, "I sorry. I don't feel like dancing. May I get you something to drink?"

"Only if we go together. I don't want to be accosted by one of the Americans." She slipped her hand through Adrian's elbow and clung to him. She was trying to work out why Adrian had mentioned LMF if he didn't know about Kit. Why had he said that was the one thing a woman wouldn't forgive? Surely, he wasn't...? No, he couldn't be. He was Kit's navigator. None of this made sense.

They reached the bar and Adrian asked what she was drinking. Fiona asked for cider, and Adrian ordered for her. When it came, he passed it to her, saying, "We were talking about what you wanted in a relationship."

"Oh, that's not important. I just wanted to get your attention."

He smiled softly. "Well, you have it. Tell me more."

"It's just —" suddenly she didn't feel as sure of herself as when she was lecturing other girls. In fact, she felt a little confused, but she tried to explain. "It's just that it seems to me that people — all people, men and women — have different talents and gifts. I mean, your father is apparently a brilliant barrister, but you are an architect. Another man is skilled as a writer or a mechanic or at mathematics. We seem to accept that each has a role to play regardless of their chosen field, but women — we're all supposed to good obedient wives and loving mothers. We aren't allowed to be anything else."

"It certainly has been that way in the past," Adrian conceded, nodding thoughtfully. "But I think that's changing. I know that I'd rather have a wife who can talk about something other than nappies or fashion." He tried to make it a joke but didn't quite pull it off.

Still, Fiona appreciated his attempt at understanding. "It's a little more than that, really," she tried to explain. "What I'd like is to follow my own dreams. I'd like a career and income of my own. I suppose what I'm saying, when you get down to it, I want to find a partner who understands me and loves me the way I am, with all my warts and pimples, ambitions and bad habits."

Adrian nodded seriously. "I think that is what we all want, but finding someone like that isn't easy — for men or women. Frankly, I don't think any woman could accept me with all my faults."

What faults could this exquisitely handsome, gentle and well-mannered man possibly be hiding? Fiona wondered. She could not believe his flaws were anything truly terrible. He probably set too-high standards for himself, and what he considered "weaknesses" were simply things that made him more human and interesting. Maybe, for example, he was *afraid* of being LMF?

Fiona found the humble and melancholy young man a thousand times more attractive than the self-confident and brash young men she had met at other dances. She felt a powerful desire to get to know Adrian better. His gaze had drifted into the distance again, so she called his attention back to her, "Adrian." When he looked down at her questioningly, she risked being very bold. "You'll never know if you can be loved faults and all unless you give me a chance to get to know you better."

For a moment, he seemed to want to smile, but then he shook his head. "No, there's no point in starting anything, because I don't think I'll be around here much longer."

Chapter 17
Boomerang

RAF Woodhall Spa
10 February 1945

After two days of bad weather, 617 was put on alert for an operation requiring six aircraft that had not been modified for the strike against the *Tirpitz*. When the crew list was posted, Forrester was again selected. Moran was not.

Moran immediately sought out Fauquier. Saluting smartly, he got straight to the point: "I noticed that I'm still not operational, sir. Is there a reason for that?"

"Of course, there's a reason," the squadron commander retorted forcefully but not harshly. "While I don't question your readiness to fly operations, Moran, I do have doubts about your navigator. Peal will be flying with me tonight, and according to how he handles himself, I will decide whether he stays on the squadron — or not. If he performs professionally, you'll be operational on the next sortie. If he goes to pieces again, you'll get a new navigator. Fair enough?"

"Yes, sir." Moran felt slightly ashamed of himself for having questioned Fauquier.

Fauquier spared him a smile. "Don't worry, Moran. Your time will come."

The verdict would come soon enough, but Kit still found the wait excruciating. Adrian was extremely nervous, and a cloud of gloom enveloped him. He seemed old and tired; the easy cheerfulness that had been so much a part of his charm during training had vanished. While kitting up, he kept dropping things and was absent-mindedly indecisive. He handed Kit his cigarettes and then took them back. He put on his silk gloves and took them off again. He changed scarves twice. He was, in short, a nervous wreck before he even went out to the aircraft.

Kit tried to encourage him. "You're a first-rate navigator, Adrian. You can do the job. Keep the curtain closed. Ignore the chatter on the intercom.

Focus on your work."

"I'll do my best, Kit. I know it would be hard on you to have to adjust to a new navigator."

"That's not the point. Do this for yourself."

Adrian looked at him strangely. He seemed to want to say something but held back.

Take off was 18:50. Kit put on his flight jacket and flying boots and went out to stand beside the runway. The ground crews of the participating aircraft and a handful of WAAF collected along the runway in a solemn little group. Bundled up against the cold and wind they kept to themselves, unspeaking, each lost in their own thoughts. Although today it fitted Kit's pensive mood like a glove, this was the standard ops send-off. The ground crews were invested in "their" pilots and planes, while many WAAF had boyfriends and fiancés on board the Lancasters. Until they returned, the role of all of those left behind on the ground would be helpless waiting while trying not to think about the chance that any given plane and its crew might not return. Kit turned up the collar of his Irvine jacket, so the sheepskin enclosed his ears and the leather underside held off the wind. He shoved his gloved hands into the pockets as deeply as he could.

Fauquier's plane, A-Able, turned onto the runway. The rotating blades of the four propellers caught the light from the flare path and formed ethereal silver disks in the darkness. Otherwise, the aircraft blended into the night. Painted a matt black, the hulking dark shape hung suspended between a pair of navigation lights, one on the tip of each nearly invisible wing. A tiny greenhouse lit by eerie bluish lights sat astride the barely perceptible fuselage, seeming almost to float above it. Inside, dark shapes moved.

To Kit's left a green light appeared. The earth beneath his feet started to vibrate as the engines changed their tone from a low growl to a high-pitched roar. The black thing started rolling towards him; the eerie lighting grew larger and the shapes inside became human heads. Fauquier and his flight engineer, Kit registered. Adrian was invisible behind the curtain of his workstation. The great winged monster whisked past and Kit could now see the glass bubble of the mid-upper turret crouched upon its long, black back like a jockey on a massive charger. Finally, A-Able lifted itself from the earth, and slowly, her engines still screaming, started to climb up the night sky. As the wheeled folded into the body like a bird tucking in its feet and the navigation lights went out, Kit wished Adrian luck with all the power of his mind.

Then the next aircraft, U-Uncle, turned onto the head of the runway. Kit, his fists jammed into his pockets and his shoulders hunched, watched all six aircraft take-off. Forrester in Q-Queen was last for take-off. Only after the Australian too had switched off his navigation lights and faded into the night did Kit return to the mess, still in his flight jacket and boots.

The murmur of voices punctuated by laughter oozed out of the lounge and bar, but Kit did not join the veterans. Instead, he went to his room. His roommate was flying, so he had it to himself. He set his alarm for two a.m., an hour before the bombers could be expected back, and tried to read one of the books Rev Reddings had lent him. He couldn't concentrate very well, but eventually he became sleepy enough to turn off the light and try to sleep.

When the alarm jangled, Kit pulled flying boots and flight jacket on over his pyjamas and climbed onto the back of lorry taking the intel and medical officers down to the airfield. As they arrived, the ambulances and fire-engines rolled out of their garage and took up their stations along the edge of the runway. WAAF chatted in subdued voices as they walked towards the hut where the parachutes were packed and stored.

After looking at and listening to the empty sky for a few minutes, Kit followed the intel officers to the ops centre. The black board showed the target — Leipzig — and listed the six aircraft of the squadron by number and code letter with the pilot's name and take-off times noted next to them. Beside one aircraft, X-Xray, a landing time had been recorded with the note: Aborted due to defective airspeed indicator/ice. So, they were facing ice out there; Kit didn't envy them.

The distant sound of engines drew him back outside. The temperature had sunk below freezing, but the air was clear and visibility excellent. Searching the sky, Kit identified the dark shape of a four-engine bomber and followed it as it banked around the airfield to line up on the runway. The flare-path switched on, and shortly afterwards the aircraft set down and rolled to the end of the runway with what seemed like an audible sigh of relief. The aircraft without damage always returned first, but Fauquier would shepherd the stragglers home — if he could.

Although he'd been trying not to think about it, Kit could no longer ignore his worries. What if Fauquier posted Adrian LMF? Who would replace Adrian as navigator? Was there an "odd bod" available on 617 who could immediately be assigned to him? Kit hadn't been here long enough to get to know everyone. One of the squadron members on leave or in hospital recovering from injuries might be a loose navigator who could replace Adrian, but it was unlikely. More likely they'd have to request someone from another squadron.

Kit resisted the thought of a new navigator, especially a stray posted from somewhere else. No matter how good an experienced navigator might be, Kit and his crew would have little time to get to know him and develop a rapport before going on operations. In six months of training, Kit's crew had coalesced into a well-working team, and Adrian and he had become friends. He did not want to fly with any other navigator.

But would he be able to trust Adrian fully, even if Fauquier allowed him to stay on the squadron? Wouldn't a trace of nagging doubt linger in his subconscious?

Two aircraft landed in quick succession, including Forrester. Then, after a gap of three or four minutes, the remaining two kites arrived together. One was flying on three engines and was being escorted by Fauquier, whose Lancaster appeared undamaged. Kit watched them land and taxi to their respective dispersals to be met by the waiting ground crews. The nearest crew climbed stiffly down the ladder, dragging their parachutes, and disappeared into the waiting bus to be taken to the debrief with the intel officers. Finally, Fauquier's crew emerged, but Kit couldn't bring himself to intrude on Adrian in front of everyone. He would wait until morning for the verdict. He returned to the mess.

A knocking on his door awoke him. "Kit!" It was Adrian's voice.

Kit dragged himself out of bed and opened the door.

Adrian stood in the hall grinning from ear to ear. His relief was like a halo around him. He seemed to be glowing. His bright, blond, good looks were boyish, as if he'd dropped ten years in the last 12 hours. He burst out: "I'm cleared to fly, Kit!"

Since Adrian still wore flying kit and there was no evidence of dawn, Kit concluded Adrian had not yet gone to bed. With a glance toward his roommate's still made-up bed, Kit also surmised that Adrian had not joined the others for a post-op pint, preferring to bring the good news to Kit. So, Kit gestured for Adrian to come in. "Well done! Come in and tell me all about it."

Stepping willingly into Kit's room, Adrian narrated in an excited voice: "We flew as Illuminator for Main Force squadrons. Fauquier's task was to drop the illuminators from 4,000 feet, and the other five 617 aircraft put down the Target Indicators. So precision was everything. I knew I had to do my absolute best and that I couldn't make the slightest mistake. I wanted to show that I could do it, Kit. The CO's navigator was splendid. He had me do the navigating and just verified with his own calculations.

By the time the flak started, I had calmed down so much that — I can't say I wasn't scared, but I didn't go to pieces either. Fauquier's navigator kept saying, 'Just navigate, Peal. Let the skipper and the gunners handle the flak. Your job is plotting the course for home.' It worked. I focused on the job, and we were spot on the target. The bomb aimer said so. Absolutely bang on!"

"Well done," Kit repeated. "I knew you could do it." He grinned, feeling a wave of relief. "Now go and get some rest. Drinks are on me tonight. We may be flying ops tomorrow."

They were — along with 19 other crews in the still-modified Lancasters. Everyone knew what that meant.

Frank intercepted Kit on his way to the ops briefing to complain. "It's not fair, Skipper. If you fly without a mid-upper gunner, it means you'll all complete your tour ahead of me!"

"Not necessarily. Other crew members may miss one or another sortie due to illness or leave. Or you may be able to fill in for the gunner of another crew when the rest of us don't fly. Who knows! Maybe Germany will surrender before our tour is over, and then you'll get away with having flown one less op than the rest of us."

"But this is our first sortie! We ought to be doing it together." Frank insisted

"I'd prefer that too, Frank, but I don't have any control over it," Kit reminded the teenager. "All I can suggest is that if you feel so strongly about coming along, maybe you can convince Nigel to give up his place to you." Kit glanced at the rear gunner as he spoke.

Nigel frowned and shook his head; his jaws were set stubbornly. "No chance!"

"That's final then, Frank. You stay behind on this one."

The rest of them continued into the briefing room. The map was the same, but AVM Cochrane hadn't bothered to come down to Woodhall Spa this time. Instead, the Station Commander opened the briefing. "You know the target. You'll be flying the same route as before. This time, however, you'll fly up to Lossiemouth and get a couple hours' kip while a meteorological Mossie takes another look-see at the weather. If we get a green, you'll get a final briefing before take-off. Sunrise in Tromso tomorrow is 09:42 and sunset 16:18. The solar angle to light the valley floors has improved even in just these few days, so the window of opportunity is a bit wider. We want you over the target at 11:00 this time, so take-off from Lossiemouth will be pushed back to 5:00. 9 Squadron will be backing you up again and will stage at Kinloss. A total of forty aircraft will take part, all with a single Tallboy each."

The crews nodded knowingly. No one seemed particularly agitated. After all, there had been no losses due to enemy action on either of the earlier 617 raids on the *Tirpitz*. Even Bill Carey, who been forced to crash land after the last foray, had put down in Sweden. He and his entire crew were now interned there but likely to be repatriated soon.

"I'm afraid I do have a bit of bad news, however," the Station Commander noted in a casual tone. Instantly everyone in the briefing froze. Lighted cigarettes burned until the ash fell off; not a boot scraped the floor. "Since our last visit, the Luftwaffe has moved two Me109 squadrons up to Bardufoss. That's only ten minutes' flying time away."

Moran felt a shudder run down his spine. Fighter opposition when they had no mid-upper gunner?

From the back of the room, a Canadian voice called out, "Did anyone warn the Luftwaffe that they are only allowed to attack from the stern?"

"Very funny," the Station Commander retorted sarcastically.

Nobody laughed.

Fauquier took over with the times for starting engines and take off for Lossiemouth and other details. When the preliminary briefing ended, they got to their feet but there was no rush for the exit. Most of the crews stood around talking and smoking. Forrester came over and offered Moran a cigarette. "Why don't they send some Mustangs with us? Surely, they have the range and would be able to hold off the Jerry fighters while we do our job?"

Moran accepted the light from the Australian. He inhaled and blew out the smoke before answering, "Good question, Red. Why didn't you ask it?"

"Me? I'm a Colonial and a sprog with a red endorsement in my logbook," he snapped back, before changing the subject, "Are you really going to fly with Peal?"

"Yes."

Forrester shook his head. "You're crazy, Moran. Suicidal."

"No, I'm certainly not that. I'm just—"

"Moran! Can I have a word with you?" It was Fauquier from the far side of the room, and Moran gratefully took his leave of Forrester. He went across to his CO, coming to attention beside him. Fauquier pulled him further aside and, facing the map with his back to the rest of the room, lowered his voice. "I think Peal is okay, and I believe we should give him another chance. However, if you have any problems, turn back. Do you understand?"

"Yes, sir."

"I'm serious, Moran. I don't want to risk a Lancaster, an expensive Tallboy and seven men because one of them loses his wool and gets lost in the dark and featureless snow above the arctic circle."

"I understand, sir."

"Can anyone else in your crew navigate?"

"My wireless operator has been teaching himself a bit about it using the H2S."

"Excellent." The Canadian paused and his eyes searched Moran's face. "It's still your call, Moran. If you tell me *now* that you don't want to fly with Peal, I can ask Knight to take your place on this sortie and find you another navigator within the week."

Moran felt his insides knotting themselves. It would be so easy. Throw Adrian to the wolves and he wouldn't have to face two squadrons of Me109s without a mid-upper gunner. "No, sir. Peal's my navigator. I've never personally had any problems with him, so I am happy to fly with him today or any day."

Fauquier nodded. "Well said. Good luck."

Outside Moran found MacDonald milling about with the other engineers and bomb aimers. "Can you find Tibble and ask him to join you and me at the aircraft ten minutes early?"

"Of course, Skipper. What's up?"

"I'm going to need your help with something the rest of the crew doesn't need to know about."

"Whatever you say, Skipper."

Moran left a message for Peal that he was going over to the kite early so he could get the "gen" from the ground crew. Then he hitched a lift out to his assigned aircraft, I-Item. He arrived while the Tallboy was being slowly raised into the bomb bay on the aircraft's wire winches. The armourer who'd brought him over, slung several ammunition belts over his shoulder and started towards the rear turret, while Moran walked in the direction of the nose. I-Item was an old and battered veteran of more ops than Moran took the time to count. He noted only that there were four rows of little bombs painted below the cockpit window and at least five of them were red instead of white. That meant she'd flown to Berlin — and back —five times.

Moran spotted the crew chief having a cigarette off to one side. He signalled the Flight Sergeant over. The sergeant ground out his cigarette and came over with a salute for the Flying Officer. Moran asked him, "Anything I should know about I-Item, Chiefy?"

"Well, sir. She's old friends with the *Tirpitz*. This will be her third visit to the beast. Trying to find Yegodnik airfield, she ran out of fuel and had to put down in a hay field. Squadron Leader Knilans managed that all right, but the next morning, not long after take-off, all four engines cut out on him. He had to dive to restart them and got so low that as he levelled off that he collided with a tree. Took three feet of timber right through the nose and shattered the cockpit Perspex. As you can see, we repaired all that." He pointed proudly to the newer panels of Perspex covering roughly two-thirds of the cockpit and virtually all the bomb aimer's "goldfish bowl."

"I'm surprised she could make it back to Woodhall Spa," Moran exclaimed with a bad feeling in the pit of his stomach.

"Oh, nothing vital was damaged."

"But why did the engines cut out in the first place?"

"The long flight over to Russia on lean mixture caused the spark plugs to clog. We replaced those while still in Russia and she flew against the *Tirpitz* the next day. She's perfectly serviceable now."

Moran nodded, but his uneasiness remained. He started pacing back and forth to keep his feet warm while waiting for MacDonald and Tibble to arrive. It was already bitterly cold, and a stiff wind was blowing out of the north. He could smell snow in the low clouds skimming only a couple hundred feet overhead.

Finally, his flight engineer and radio operator hopped out of a passing lorry and came towards him. They both looked concerned. He walked with them out of earshot of the ground crew, offering them cigarettes. "There's something you should know."

They waited. The wind made it impossible to light up.

"Adrian cracked on the last *Tirpitz* raid. That's why the CO took him on his aircraft to Leipzig. He was perfectly all right on that sortie, and I have every confidence in him. We all know that he's a first-rate navigator. I think what happened on the last *Tirpitz* raid was triggered by Forrester's style. That said, we have to take precautions just in case he does lose his wool. We must have a means of getting home without his help." Moran looked from one to the other. MacDonald was nodding, but Tibble looked frightened. Moran wondered if confiding in them had been the right thing to do.

"What are you proposing, Skipper?" MacDonald asked earnestly.

"He should be fine until the flak goes off, but when it does, Terry, you've got to keep him focused on the navigation. Ask him for a fix frequently — even if I don't have time to. Make him concentrate on his calculations, so he doesn't have time to listen to the flak. Can you do that?"

"I'll try, sir." The look on Tibble's face made Moran regret burdening him. Yet Tibble was the crew member who sat nearest and worked most closely with Peal. If anyone was going to have a chance of nipping panic in the bud it was the wireless operator.

"Also, I know you've been reading up on navigation and keeping an eye on the H2S."

"Yes, but not enough so I could navigate!" Tibble protested, terrified.

"Calm down, Terry. Adrian's probably going to be fine. Just use your interest in learning to keep him focused on his job."

Tibble nodded vigorously, looking a little calmer.

Moran turned to the flight engineer. "Daddy, I don't know exactly what I want you to do. Just be aware of the problem and do whatever you can to help Terry keep Adrian calm." Even as he made the request Moran asked himself what he was thinking. Neither Tibble nor MacDonald had flown operations. How could he know they wouldn't crack? He had never expected it of Peal, either.

The older Scotsman just said "Wilco, Skipper," and then the crew bus arrived with Peal, Babcock and Osgood.

The flight up to Lossiemouth was uneventful. Here, they were given beds for a few hours' sleep, before being woken at 2 a.m. They got a hearty "ops breakfast" of bacon and eggs, then picked up their rations of chocolate and biscuits and thermoses of coffee and tea. They were going to need them. It was starting to snow, and the ground crews were scrambling to de-ice the wings.

"You're going to have the devil of a time keeping things from icing up, Daddy," Moran remarked, as they climbed aboard. "Aye," replied the Scotsman, apparently unperturbed, as Peal and Tibble disappeared behind their curtain. When Tibble plugged in the intercom, Moran immediately ordered Osgood to test the heating to his fight suit. "I don't want you freezing back there!"

"Thanks, Skip. It seems to be working perfectly. Nice and toasty, so far."

MacDonald leaned forward and flipped on the wipers to keep the windscreen clear. A snow plough was moving up and down the runway methodically to keep the runway clear before any snow could accumulate.

MacDonald called for "contact" on number three engine, and after backfiring several times it settled into a steady rumble. So did number two, but number four kept stalling. Fauquier took off, followed successively by eight other Lancasters. By then, all the remaining aircraft except I-Item had left their dispersals to queue for take-off. Moran started to sweat despite the cold. He turned his attention to number one engine, got it running, and then tried number four again. As he did so, he glanced at the runway and verified there were just two Lancasters still waiting for take-off. He went through the start-up drill for number four again, and finally it caught. He gunned the engine. It belched black smoke into the frigid air, but otherwise seemed fine.

Moran and MacDonald rushed through the remainder of the take-off drill, waved the chocks away, and lumbered to the start of the runway. Not one of the other nineteen aircraft was anywhere in sight anymore. The green light beamed from the control caravan beside the runway, and Moran ran the engines up against the brakes. They sounded all right, so he eased the throttles back a little and then released the brakes. They started down the runway, snow blowing into their faces. Moran could feel the weight of the Tallboy and their extra fuel load in the handling of the controls and the sluggishness of the wheels beneath his feet. The Merlins protested and strained as they tried to drag the heavy crate forward. All the while heavy snowflakes smashed, melted and streamed down the cockpit glass.

MacDonald was reading the speedometer. "Ninety, ninety-five."

They had used up one third of the runway and were much too slow for take-off. The Lancaster did not seem to be developing any lift. She was stuck to the earth, tired and listless. Moran shoved the throttles through the wire but immediately felt I-Item start to sway to port as he did so. "Hold the throttles!" He shouted at MacDonald so he could return his right hand to the steering column. MacDonald grabbed the throttles, but his expression was one of sheer terror.

At last, the Lancaster started to bounce without actually leaving the ground. They were fast running out of runway. He either had to risk take-off or abort. Moran pulled the control column back, and the aircraft reluctantly left the earth. Yet everything about it remained sluggish and undecided. They were on the brink of stalling and crashing.

"Full flaps!" Moran ordered MacDonald as he put his own hand back on the throttles. They were vibrating so badly that they slipped back if not held in place.

The flaps popped them up but then the aircraft levelled off again.

Cautiously, Moran had MacDonald ease the flaps back to neutral, watching the altimeter tensely. The aircraft did not sink. "Full flaps!" he ordered again, and once more the aircraft leapt up a couple hundred feet. Moran shook his head. It was a ridiculous way to gain altitude, in steps rather than climbing steadily, but it worked for now. They were supposed to cross the North Sea at no more than a couple of thousand feet anyway. The problem would come crossing the Norwegian mountains and then attaining the bombing altitude of 18,000 feet. By then, Moran comforted himself, they would have used almost half their fuel load and the aircraft's weight would be back down below the authorised payload.

Moran settled onto the course provided by Peal and tried to unwind after the harrowing take-off. They were flying between the clouds and the agitated North Sea. White horses galloped in the dark beneath him, but their snarling and hissing were blotted out by the droning of the four Merlins. Gradually the snow stopped. The cloud cover thinned. Stars became visible overhead. It was roughly three hours from Lossiemouth to the point where they turned east to cross Norway. Once or twice Peal requested a modest change in course; otherwise, all was quiet.

Moran was conscious that they were as much as a quarter of an hour behind the others, but he simply could not flog any more speed out of tired old I-Item. He visualised the route in his head and could see no opportunity to cut any corners either. Cutting corners would only result in crossing the Norwegian coast sooner, presumably at a place where German defences was denser. It would also mean flying over enemy-held territory longer. That didn't make sense.

Peal called over the intercom. "Navigator to pilot: turning point in five minutes. You'll be steering 085." Peal's voice was very faint, and Moran presumed that he had unclipped his oxygen mask to have a drink of tea or something. Since they were flying at only 1,800 feet and oxygen was unnecessary there was no harm in that.

He checked his watch and noted the time himself. He had commenced the turn before Peal reminded him, his oxygen mask apparently still off. Moran made a mental note to tell him always to press the mask to his face when talking into the intercom, even if he didn't want to clip it on. For the moment, however, Moran's greater concern was "bouncing" this decrepit old crate up another thousand feet to avoid hitting anything when they made landfall.

Suddenly the land was there. It was rugged and black against a faintly lightening eastern sky. Moran instinctively pulled up a bit more and the Lancaster, although still mushy, responded. That was a relief! They moved over land. Someone had seen them and was firing anti-aircraft shells at them, but not very effectively. The tell-tale bursts of smoke were off to the side and behind. The flak batteries appeared to have been caught napping.

"Pilot to navigator: what altitude do I need to clear the Norwegian mountains?"

Only silenced answered. Moran's blood froze. Surely those two harmless cracks of enemy fire hadn't shattered Peal's nerves? He must have faced far worse flak than that on the sortie to Leipzig.

Trying to keep his voice very neutral and calm, he repeated, "Pilot to navigator: what altitude do I need for clearing the Norwegian mountains?"

Still nothing. Moran looked over at MacDonald. The Flight Engineer was looking back at him, his horrified expression reflecting Moran's feelings exactly. Unclipping his oxygen mask, Moran signalled MacDonald closer. The engineer came and leaned down so his pilot could speak directly into this ear. "Go back to Peal and find out what's going on."

MacDonald nodded and turned to push his head through the curtain of the navigator's workspace. Moran keep the Lancaster climbing as hard as he dared, trying to remember the altitudes on the map himself. MacDonald tapped him on the shoulder. He looked up. "Nothing wrong with Peal, sir. He gave you the altitude both times you asked."

"I didn't hear him. Tell him to put his mask back on."

"He's wearing it, sir. Maybe his mic's dead?"

Moran immediately switched on his own mic and called: "Pilot to crew: check in."

Dead silence answered him.

"Maybe it's my headset," Moran concluded. "You call the rest of the crew."

MacDonald switched on and called. "Flight engineer to crew: we may have intercom problems. Check in."

Moran watched MacDonald's face, while in his ears was nothing but the droning of the engines. MacDonald shook his head. "Nothing, sir."

"Go down into the nose and see if Stu's mic works."

MacDonald dropped down the steps into the nose, while Peal shoved his curtain aside, and came out to squat beside Moran. He had written down altitudes and courses on a chit of paper. Shouting over the engines, he said: "Climb to 4,700 feet and steer 110. Once we're over Sweden, we'll turn onto a northerly course, and you can pretty much choose your altitude for the next hour. I'm going into the astrodome to take a last star fix before it's too light for another."

"Well done, Adrian."

Peal smiled at him and nodded his thanks. He looked perfectly calm and confident.

MacDonald was back. "It's no good, skipper! Stu can't receive or send over the intercom either. The entire intercom must have packed up."

"Go back and ask Tibble to come forward. We've got time for him to try and fix it."

A moment later Tibble squatted down beside Moran and removed his mask. Moran explained the problem. Tibble nodded and moved back to his station purposefully.

The sky was definitely lightening. Meanwhile, although still sluggish, the Lancaster crept up to 4,700 feet. The mountains loomed ahead of them, but Moran could see a gap between two peaks, clearly the pass they were making for.

Peal nudged him and showed him a piece of paper with "09:18 turn onto 025."

Moran nodded and checked his watch. It was just after 9:00. Minutes later, they soared between the mountains drenched in pristine glaciers broken by jagged peaks. Then the land started dropping away below them, and lights were scattered across the plain ahead of them. They were over Sweden.

The clock crept toward 09:18 and Moran thought he heard some clicking in his earphones. Maybe Tibble was making progress.

Peal returned to Moran's side and called over the engines. "Steer 025."

"025." Moran automatically repeated, although Peal stayed beside him, his eyes on the compass as they swung onto the new course.

Tibble burst into the cockpit, sweat trickling down beside his leather helmet. "Skipper! There's nothing I can do! I've tried every trick they taught us. Unplugging, replugging, rewiring the socket. Everything. It's dead."

Moran gazed at Tibble. There was no mistaking the frantic look in his eyes. He appeared to feel personally responsible for this disaster.

"It's all right, Terry. It's not your fault."

Moran looked back out over the gradually lightening landscape below him. Everything from the slowly greying sky to the snow-covered earth was white — except for a weaving black line on which a few pairs of headlights crawled. The earth curved upwards on either side of them to form mountain ranges. Moran assessed the implications of the inoperable intercom. Visibility was excellent, so navigation to the target was probably not going to be a problem. Nor back again, because Peal could bring him the course changes by hand. But how would Osgood be able to warn him of approaching fighters or order him to corkscrew when needed? More importantly, how could Babcock lead him through the bomb run without a working intercom?

"Is the wireless working? Can you get a message to Fauquier?"

Tibble nodded.

"Tell him what's happened. Keep it very brief. Just our call-sign and 'Intercom u/s.'"

"Yes, sir."

Tibble left the cockpit to return to his workstation.

"What are you going to do?" MacDonald asked.

Moran shook his head to indicate he didn't know. If this had been their twentieth op, or their tenth, even their fifth, things would have been different, but it was their first. After Peal putting up a black on the first Tirpitz raid and given his own past, Moran was extremely reluctant to turn back.

Tibble returned. He handed Moran a notepad. On it he had written one word: "Abort."

Moran nodded, but he did not react at once. He stared ahead in the direction of the target. He could picture it: the massive battleship nestling against the sides of the fjord, looking too large to turn around in the narrow waters. She certainly couldn't go anywhere fast, and they would come at her one after another. Did he really need to communicate with Babcock? Couldn't he just fly straight and level as they got close and let Babcock drop when he wanted? Yes, they'd been drilled on the importance of precise bombing, but in this case wasn't a near miss better than aborting?

But a timely call from Osgood might make the difference between life and death — for seven men. The chances weren't very good to start with, so did he have the right to deny them even that small margin of safety just to prove something? And to whom? Fauquier had ordered him to abort. To carry on would be nothing but dangerous, insubordinate bloody-mindedness.

He looked up. MacDonald and Peal were both standing behind him anxiously awaiting his decision. He addressed Peal, "I want you to plot a course over Sweden to the Skagerak and from there out over the North Sea, avoiding Norwegian and Danish airspace altogether."

"Roger, Skipper." Peal returned to his desk to set to work.

Within a couple of minutes, he was back with the new course. Moran glanced at it and put the Lancaster in to a wide turn, taking them away from the target.

By the time they put down at Woodhall Spa almost seven hours later, and it was night again. The rest of the squadron had already landed, all of them, and the ground crews were in good spirits. The WAAF were laughing in the parachute hut when Moran and crew arrived, and in the debriefing room, they found the intelligence officers drinking the rum neat and toasting themselves and 617.

"Belly up — just as the PM wanted."

"We sank the *Tirpitz*?" Moran asked in disbelief.

"Capsized her! Have a look at these photos!" The intelligence officer drew Kit and his crew to the already developed films showing the great German battleship looking like a gigantic dead fish. There could be no doubt about the success of this attack.

"And everyone made it back safely?"

"Everyone. Not one casualty. What delayed you?"

"It's a long story."

In the mess, the party was already in full swing. There was loud music, loud laughter, and large quantities of flowing alcohol. Forrester was standing on a table guzzling beer. Kit's first instinct was to just go up to his room, but that wouldn't look good. He found Fauquier. "Congratulations, sir! I'm sorry we missed the show."

"I'm sorry you did too. Do you want to tell me what happened?"

Kit did.

"Any problems with Peal?"

"None at all, sir. He did a first-rate job plotting a course back that didn't take us through enemy airspace. We've brought the Tallboy back safe and sound, too."

Fauquier nodded solemnly. "Well then, have a drink or two."

"Don't mind if I do." Kit ordered a pint. He didn't need anything stronger.

Yet although he could drink, he couldn't join in the antics and the celebration. He hadn't been there. He hadn't contributed to the success. He was still a sprog pilot, a newcomer who hadn't yet earned his stripes in the squadron. Instead, Adrian and he found a side table and sat down together.

Adrian was looking almost slaphappy as he announced. "That was all right, Kit,"

"Yes, well done!" Kit assured him, although mentally he noted they hadn't been under attack today.

"I'm sure I can handle the flak when you're at the controls. I felt so much better today than when For—"

Like speaking of the devil, Forrester was suddenly standing unsteadily over them. He was swaying from the effect of too much alcohol imbibed too fast. Kit knew that when the Australian got drunk, he also got belligerent and bullying. Kit felt his muscles tense and mentally he took up a defensive stance, both feet planted firmly on the floor ready to stand.

Slurring his speech and splattering saliva, Forrester asked in a loud voice, "Lost your nerve again did you, Peely-wally?"

Kit jumped to his feet and faced Forrester eye-to-eye. "We lost our intercom not our nerves!"

"It was the thought of the fighters, wasn't it? But the joke's on you, Zulu! There weren't any!"

"Bully for you," Moran answered trying to keep his temper. "Now clear off!"

Forrester ignored Moran and instead bent to address himself directly to Peal. "Did you wet yourself again, Peely-Wally? Had to ask my friend Zulu here to turnaround so you could collect some new trousers, did you?"

Adrian seemed to be melting into the chair, his face pale with shame. Moran felt the urge to hit Forrester in the face — which, of course, was exactly what Forrester wanted. Instead, he pulled Forrester by the shoulder, trying to shove him away.

Out of nowhere, an icy-cold English voice cut across the noise of the room. "Forrester, did anyone ever tell you that your mouth can be connected to your brain — assuming you *have* a brain, that is." Astonished, Moran turned to find out who the speaker was. It was the other "Kit" on the squadron, Kit Howard, who had not only flown today, but was a veteran of over fifty other operations and held the rank of squadron leader. He was also, incidentally, heir to a peerage.

Forrester was taken aback just long enough for Kit to pull Adrian to his feet and walk out of the lounge. He didn't look back to see what happened, but he didn't hear any furniture breaking or the sounds of fists flying either. Howard trumped Forrester three-times over: in social rank, military rank, and — most importantly in this situation — seniority on the squadron.

In the coolness and relative quiet of the imposing hall, where the elaborately carved wooden stairs curved up to the next floor, they stopped. "Kit, maybe I don't belong here. On this squadron, I mean. Maybe I should just—"

"Go to bed, Adrian. You did a first-rate job today. Fauquier ordered us to abort, and the final decision was mine."

"But you...Didn't you..." Adrian didn't finish his sentence.

"What?"

"Never mind. Aren't you coming up?"

"No, I'm going to Kirkby."

"Oh."

Kit waited. When Adrian said nothing, he asked, "Do you want to come with me?"

"No, no. Go without me."

Relieved by the answer, Kit nodded and said good night.

Yet something was wrong when Kit reached Kirby. There were almost no cars parked in the village, and no bicycles either. All the houses and shops crouched dark and still behind their blackout blinds and curtains. Neither a sound nor shard of light escaped into the night. Nothing moved but a stray cat. After a moment of confusion, Kit realised he'd lost all sense of time. Maybe it was later than he'd assumed? He tried to read his watch but couldn't in the darkness. He reached over to open the glove compartment and groped around until he found his torch. He flicked it on and shone it on his watch. It was after midnight.

He couldn't possibly barge in on Georgina at this time. He should have rung her from the officers' mess at Woodhall Spa instead. But the telephones were situated near the lounge, and you couldn't have a conversation without half a dozen officers or orderlies walking past. Most of the time, other men eager to use the phones loitered nearby. They either talked among themselves or listened to what was being said.

Besides it was good to get away from the station. Away from the others, including Adrian.

Kit put the torch back in the glove compartment and pushed it shut. He folded his arms over the steering wheel and rested his head on them. He was physically exhausted and mentally drained. He'd flown over thirteen hours straight without a break — and all for nothing. A boomerang. It didn't count as a sortie.

The reality of being a Lancaster Skipper, Don whispered in his head.

Like a burst from a machine-gun going off beside his head, rapid-fire clicks shattered his sleep. Kit reared up disoriented. He couldn't remember where he was. What was he doing in a car? Then he saw Georgina was standing beside his window; at last, he remembered driving to Kirkby. Georgina was peering through the window anxiously and clutching a winter overcoat over her nightgown. Her face was ghostly in the darkness.

Kit waved to her, smiling automatically, and she stepped back as he flung the door open.

"Kit! Why didn't you come in? What's happened?"

He took her into his arms, but in doing so realised that she was in her bedroom slippers and shivering. He turned her in his arms so he could guide her back to the house. "Come. You need to get inside before you catch cold."

They slipped through the blackout curtains and into the front hall. It was chilly here, and Georgina led him into the kitchen, where a residue of heat from the oven took the edge off the air.

"Kit, what happened?" She pressed him again, her eyes wide with apparent alarm. "I heard the car but when no one got out, I thought — I thought it was Adrian coming to tell me — to say something had happened — but afraid to face me."

Kit pulled her back into his arms and held her closely. He shouldn't be putting her through this, he reproached himself, but he didn't ease his hold. He couldn't. He was too selfish.

"What happened?" She asked again, into the rough wool of his greatcoat.

"Wasn't it on the news already? We sank the *Tirpitz*."

"But Kit, that's wonderful!"

"Except I wasn't there. I had to abort due to problems with my intercom. I couldn't communicate with either my bomb aimer or my gunner. I *had* to abort, and, yet... It doesn't look good, Georgina. It's more than fourteen months since I agreed to go back on ops, and I still haven't flown one. Being second dickey doesn't count, and a boomerang *certainly* doesn't count. Fauquier took me on the squadron despite knowing about me being LMF. He must be having second thoughts by now."

Georgina pulled back and looked up at him. "I haven't a clue what Fauquier may or may not think, and I don't care. The question is whether *you* doubt yourself?"

Kit had to think about that, but then he shook his head. "Not really. I know I can do it."

"Good." She smiled gently. "Then go back, get some sleep and do it. Should I make you some tea before you drive back?"

Kit was so tired he would have rather stretched out on the kitchen floor and slept there and then, but he knew that he shouldn't and therefore couldn't do that. Instead, he accepted the tea, and left about twenty minutes later.

In the morning, his batman woke him with the news that Fauquier wanted to see him "straight away, sir."

His roommate was out cold, snoring. Moran dressed hastily and scraped a razor over his face more symbolically than effectively. The mess was a considerable distance from the admin building, so he borrowed a bicycle and pedalled through the cold, gloomy morning. At the CO's office, he knocked and saluted on entering.

"Oh! Morning Moran. Did my message get garbled in translation? I didn't mean to drag you out of bed, just that you should come over when you had a moment."

"I'm here now, sir."

"Yes. I thought you might want to know that the senior wireless tech confirmed your report. Your intercom was completely u/s. The damage was caused by water ingress into the wiring loom."

"I see." Moran tried not to sound resentful about being questioned.

Fauquier considered him. "When you sent the message 'intercom u/s', I thought it might be a code phrase for difficulties with your navigator. That's why I wanted to check with you again, since — in retrospect — yesterday in the bar hadn't been very tactful of me. *Did* you have any problems?" Fauquier looked at him with eyes that were focused and insistent.

"No, sir," Moran answered.

"None at all?" The group captain pressed him.

"No, sir." Moran repeated, while mentally noting that they hadn't faced any enemy action either — except those hasty and ill-aimed pot shots crossing the coast of Norway.

"In that case, nothing to worry about. Go get some sleep. We aren't flying for the next three or four days. All the bits and pieces we took out of the Lancasters to make them light enough for the flight to Tromso have to be put back in them again. Don't worry though, you and your crew will get your chance soon enough."

Chapter 18
The Most Dangerous Nazis

Foster Clough, Yorkshire
14 February 1945

The tradition had started at the end of the last war: every Valentine's Day, Edwin Reddings invited his three older sisters to tea. He made the gesture because they had neither husbands nor gentlemen friends to shower chocolates and flowers on them. Anna, Emma and Lucy Reddings were victims of the Great War, their prospective husbands having been slaughtered in four years of carnage, leaving all three spinsters. Amanda had chosen to be absent on this occasion and was using the day to attend to her duties as the local Women's Land Army representative. While she was off visiting her "land girls" to listen to their complaints and concerns, Edwin played host to his sisters.

As usual, Anna arrived first in her bottle green Women's Voluntary Service (WVS) uniform and its practical felt hat. She offered to help in the kitchen, but Edwin shooed her out. He didn't want anyone interfering with his chaos or observing his ineptitude. Anna, smiling knowingly, beat a hasty retreat.

Rather than taking a seat, however, she wandered about looking at things. She stopped before a photo of Georgina with her new fiancé, Flying Officer Moran. This was no studio photo and so less flattering than the formal engagement portrait of Georgina with Donald Selkirk, which it had replaced on the mantelpiece. Yet Anna decided she liked this snapshot better. Georgina was not gazing up adoringly at this young man the way she had at Don. Instead, she and her young man were laughing together. Anna approved of that.

In fact, it made her turn away, slightly saddened by memories of her own fiancé, Albert. They had met riding to hounds and had known each other three years before they finally became engaged in late 1913. Albert had been her friend, not her idol, a hard-working and serious businessman with a small factory producing component parts for the infant automobile industry. He also happened to be a reserve lieutenant in the Royal Artillery. He was called up at the outbreak of the Great War and was dead before a year had passed.

It seemed incredible to Anna that that was now thirty years ago. Pensively, she settled on the sofa, putting her handbag on the floor beside her. Life had turned out differently than the way she had then imagined it would, but apart from Albert's death she did not regret what had happened since. Anna had taken a position as a lady's companion when the war ended. In this capacity she had travelled first class to Singapore and back. The journey had lasted three years and included stops at scores of exotic places along the way. It had been an eye-opening experience to say the least, full of mild adventures and new impressions. Anna doubted if a life with Albert would have been as interesting. No, she wouldn't have wanted to miss out on her travels — or the very generous sum of money left her by her former employer. Anna was now considered "independently wealthy," and she rather liked things that way.

Someone was ringing the front doorbell, and Edwin called to Anna, asking her to answer. Willingly, she got up and found her sister Emma on the doorstep. It was snowing so hard that snow blew in on the ferocious wind. "Goodness gracious!" Anna exclaimed, as she struggled to shut the heavy door.

Emma shook the heavy snow off her hat, and then started to peel off and shake out her rest of her outer clothes. "What perfectly dreadful weather! Nothing was running on time!"

"And hasn't been practically since the war started," Anna concurred. The sisters embraced, touching cheek to cheek, and then Anna ordered, "Now let me see your latest creation."

Emma had coped with being left a single woman after the Great War by setting up a dressmaking shop and designing customized clothing for her clients. While her earnings did not come close to what Anna could draw from her portfolio, Emma had done well before the war, when she had more orders than she could fill. Her skills with a needle had also spared her from industrial conscription as they had been turned to tailoring officers' uniforms. In fact, there wasn't a regiment north of the Trent that did not depend on her. She kept her hand in fashion, however, by designing for Georgina, and she always wore her own creations. At Anna's command, she turned around so her elder sister could inspect the suit she was wearing.

"Not bad, given all the shortages and rationing," Anna noted. "If there were no other reason to wish this dreadful war over, it would be so we can all wear dresses with frills and flounces and puffy sleeves again. I'm so tired of uniforms!"

"So am I!" Emma agreed, as Edwin appeared at the far end of the hall wearing one of Amanda's aprons. Emma went to meet him halfway as he came to welcome her. "Lovely to see you, Emma!" They touched cheeks.

"Do you need any help, Edwin? It smells as though something's burning." Emma lifted her nose and sniffed the air.

"No, no! Not at all. Go and sit down. I'll be there with the scones in just a moment."

Together the sisters went into the sitting room. "You know, Emma," Anna started on one of her favourite topics. "It's time to start thinking about *after* the war. You'll be going back to women's clothing, won't you?"

"Definitely! I hope I never see another uniform as long as I live — unless it's being worn by a handsome young man!"

"Well, when the war's over, every woman in England is going to want a new wardrobe. Whether old or young, they are going to want to outfit themselves in new, pretty things. With your skills, you should be able to make a fortune."

"Oh, Anna! We've been through this before. I can only sew so fast and so much."

"Yes, exactly, which is precisely why you have to concentrate on the design and let others do the actual sewing. Do you realise that ten million women have been conscripted into war industries, and as soon as the war ends most of them are going to be laid off?"

"And be very happy about it too, I dare say!" Emma replied.

"Oh, I don't doubt that they'll be happy to leave the munitions and aircraft factories, but they will also have become used to an independent source of income. Many of them won't be happy just to sit around doing nothing or looking after their hubbies. The wonderful thing about sewing is that it can be done at home in as little space as it takes to set up a sewing machine. It's the perfect job for a woman with a family who wants to earn a little extra on the side. I'm absolutely certain you'll be able to find lots of women willing to work for you from home, so you don't need to expand your own premises. You can concentrate on design and customer relations, and before you know it, you'll be a famous fashion designer with business on a grand scale."

"Oh, don't be silly!" Emma waved the grand vision aside. "I don't know that I want that. Besides, women working from home might not be reliable, and if things are delivered late or not made properly, my customers will be rightfully indignant. I'll be quite —"

An insistent ringing of the front bell interrupted them. "That must be Lucy!" Anna exclaimed rolling her eyes. "I'll go and let her in."

Anna went to the door to admit their middle sister Lucy. Unlike Anna and Emma, Lucy had never found anything that made her happy in the years after the Great War, and her perpetual dissatisfaction had moulded her face into a permanently sour expression. It also made her quick to find fault with everyone else — especially her family. She was leaning on the doorbell.

"Good heavens!" Anna admonished, opening the door. "We heard you the first time!"

"It certainly didn't seem like it! Where were you? In the stables?" Lucy stomped into the hallway, leaving little mounds of snow on the mat. She removed her snow-caked hat and overcoat, shaking out the latter vigorously and getting Anna wet in the process.

Frowning, Anna moved out of range. "We're in the sitting room. Edwin will be joining us shortly."

Lucy, wearing her Air Raid Protection Warden's uniform, followed Anna into the sitting room, where they found Emma standing before the mantelpiece looking at the same photo that had attracted Anna earlier. "What's that?" Lucy asked at once.

"It's a picture of Georgina with her new young man, Flying Officer Moran."

Lucy made a beeline to the fireplace and snatched the photo out of Emma's hand. She peered at it intently and then declared dismissively, "Hmph! He looks quite ordinary to me. I can't imagine what Georgina sees in him. After the way she carried on after Flight Lieutenant Selkirk's demise, I would have expected her to take a vow of chastity and go into a nunnery — not go chasing after a new man and getting engaged again at the first opportunity. It's disgraceful the way that girl throws herself at men."

"Don't be ridiculous, Lucy!" Anna rebuked her. "Georgina is the last one to throw herself at anyone."

"Really? Then what is this hasty engagement all about?"

"It's called falling in love again," Emma answered firmly. "I know exactly what that is like." She looked her older sister firmly in the eye as she spoke. She had fallen in love with three men in succession during the course of the last war; she cherished the memories of each one of them.

"At least he doesn't *look* coloured!" Lucy declared, focusing again on the photograph of Kit and Georgina.

"Coloured?" Anna asked back flabbergasted.

"Yes! Didn't you listen to what Edwin said? His grandfather was a

277

missionary to the Zulus, of all people! And then was foolish enough to marry one of them. Obviously, he was less a man of God and more a man given to base temptation!"

"For heaven's sake, Lucy. It is far more important that Flight Lieutenant Moran holds the king's commission and was decorated for valour than who his grandmother was!" Anna retorted indignantly. She hated Lucy's bigotry.

"And I think it is more important that he *loves* Georgina," Emma added ardently.

Lucy snorted. "How would you know if he loves her or not? You haven't met him any more than I have. And in any case, that's entirely beside the point! The man is of mixed race, and if Georgina marries him he'll be part of this family. Not to mention that any children Georgina has with him will have the defect of being part-coloured too!"

"How dare you say that in this house, Lucy!" Edwin spoke from the doorway as he entered with a laden tray. He set the tray down so hard that the things on it jumped, then he addressed himself to his sister with his arms akimbo. "If I hadn't heard it with my own ears, I would not have believed it!" Anna raised her eyebrows at her brother's naivety, while Edwin continued angrily. "To make myself perfectly clear: I'd rather be related to Kit Moran, than anyone who holds such racist views — including you!"

"Edwin!" All three sisters gasped at once.

"Calm down!" Anna urged.

"Let's not quarrel!" Emma pleaded.

"If that's the way you feel, then I'll leave right now!" Lucy declared as she jumped to her feet. Edwin demonstratively stood back and indicated the way to the door. Lucy grabbed her handbag and started for the exit, only to be held back by Emma.

"Both of you," Anna asserted herself as the eldest, looking furiously from Edwin to Lucy. "Start acting like adults. Both of you sit down, and let's talk this through like rational people."

Her intervention convinced Lucy to return to her seat, but the sisters off-loaded the tray in stony silence. Edwin had brought cups, saucers, plates, and a tray of scones. The latter had obviously burned, and the charred bottoms had been scraped off with a knife. The tea itself was missing. "The kettle's on," Edwin informed his sisters as they finished setting the table. He set the empty tray beside his chair as he sat down uneasily.

Edwin's nerves were totally on edge and the last thing he needed was to hear rabid racist remarks from his own sister — although problems with Lucy were nothing new. Amanda would sing for joy, if he told her he'd thrown Lucy out of the house for good. Yet a part of him also believed a churchman ought to be patient and forgiving.

Then again, there was a time for anger, too, and a time for righteous indignation. A time to say "enough!" Hadn't Christ had been angry with the moneylenders in the temple? With this thought, Edwin turned to Lucy and asked in a voice that set the air to vibrating with righteousness, "Did it never occur to you, Miss Lucy Reddings, that one objective of this war is to stop people being persecuted for their race? The Russian reports about Auschwitz Concentration Camp have exceeded even the worst rumours — all those allegations we dismissed as 'propaganda' and 'exaggeration.' What the Nazis have been doing is nothing short of genocide. They have literally been trying to exterminate the entire Jewish population of Europe."

"Well, it doesn't surprise *me* that the Germans are capable of atrocities," Lucy replied in a know-all voice. "*I've* known what the Germans were like since the *last* war. I don't know why the rest of you are so shocked."

"There is nothing inherently 'German' about these atrocities, you fool! They are the product of an ideology, an ideology founded in hatred, racism, greed, and grievance wrapped up in nationalist colours. You can change the wrapping to match any national flag — including our own — and the results would be same!"

"I don't know what you're talking about!" Lucy protested hotly. "The Germans are the ones who have committed these crimes, no one else."

Edwin ignored her. "What Auschwitz represents is the power of modern technology to magnify the effects of hateful ideology to unprecedented dimensions. Auschwitz is nothing less than *industrialised* murder, *mass-produced* murder! The issue is that people — regardless of what nationality they happen to have — are capable of such gross inhumanity. What Auschwitz represents is the systematic murder of people simply for *being*. And before you try to change the subject," Edwin's eyes bored into his sister, "your remarks about 'coloured' people are the genesis of such policies! If you judge people simply by their race, their religion, or nationality, rather than by what they say and do as individuals, then you lay the foundations for a new, British Auschwitz!"

"How dare you!" Lucy jumped to her feet again.

Anna again tried to intercede. "Edwin! Those are very strong words,"

"Yes, and I stand by them!" Edwin answered firmly.

For several seconds no one spoke or moved, but then Emma remarked gently, "You look very tired, Edwin. Is something wrong?"

The tense tableau held its position a little longer, until Edwin admitted with a deep sigh. "I did not sleep all night." He closed his eyes and covered them with his hands.

"What is it?" Anna and Emma exchanged a look of concern. Even Lucy, while not mollified, sank back into her chair and waited.

"Not something to do with Amanda?" Anna asked.

Edwin shook his head. He sat upright again and placed his hands on his knees. With a deep breath he explained, "Just — nightmares."

The sisters exchanged glances again. They too knew about his visions.

"Not Gerald?" Emma asked in concern.

"No." For a moment the word lessened the tension in the air, but his sisters continued to stare at him expectantly. Edwin realised he couldn't just leave it at that and admitted, "It was worse than anything I've ever seen before. It wasn't one person or even an accident with several, it was thousands and thousands. All being blown up or burnt alive."

"You've taken these accounts of Auschwitz too much to heart and your over-active imagination is tormenting you," Anna diagnosed.

Edwin gazed at her sadly. "I wish that were so, but these people were being blown up by bombs and burnt in their own homes." From the kitchen came the faint yet shrill whistle of the kettle as the tea water started to come to a boil, but Edwin ignored it. "They were being killed by Allied bombers, *our* bombers. I am convinced we have committed a horrible crime. I don't know where, but I know it was utterly unnecessary." The kettle started to squeal like an air raid siren, but still Edwin ignored it to finish what he was saying. "What we have done will tarnish our just cause. It will detract from our victory and, saddest of all, besmirch the memory of those who have given so much to bring this war to a successful conclusion. We did something last night out of sheer hubris — not because it was necessary and useful but simply because we could."

"Would somebody get that flipping kettle!" Lucy demanded. Emma moved to get up, but Edwin waved her back, standing to go to the kitchen himself. He heard the words "overwrought", "over-active imagination" and "over-sensitive" whispered behind his back, but he didn't care. He took the screaming kettle off the burner and turned off the stove, but he found himself unable to pour the water over the tea leaves waiting in the pot. He was seeing the images again.

"Edwin?" The voice was gentle, and he felt a warm arm around his shoulders. It was Emma, of course. "Edwin? Are you all right?"

He drew a deep breath and shook his head. "No, I don't think I am all right. I just wish..."

Emma took the kettle from him. It was still steaming gently. She poured the water into the waiting teapot. "Come back and lets all have a cup of tea—"

Anna was in the doorway. "Edwin. There's someone on the phone for you."

"There's a telephone call?"

"Didn't you hear the telephone ringing?"

"No. No, I didn't. I don't feel up to talking to anyone. Is it something important?"

"I have no idea. I didn't recognise the voice, but it sounded like a young man."

Edwin caught his breath and then pushed past Anna as he hurried to the telephone. "Hello? Hello?"

"Reverend Reddings? It's Kit Moran, here. You asked me to ring you?"

"Kit! Thank you for getting back to me. I just wanted to check...that you're all right."

"Yes, I'm fine," Kit sounded slightly amused. "I'm about to have a cream tea at the mess after spending a pleasant morning shooting hares with some of the other chaps. Howard and Sayers asked me to go shooting with them." Edwin could tell that Kit was pleased about that. "We bagged two. I hope to see Georgina after she gets home from school this evening. Is there some reason you wanted me to ring you?"

"I — um — I was wondering. Did you fly last night?" Edwin wanted to be sure he hadn't misunderstood.

"No, they're still refitting the mid-upper turrets and replacing the armour plating after our last op."

"But there was a raid, wasn't there?"

There was a pause and then Kit admitted. "Yes, rather a large one. It will probably be on the BBC soon enough, I suppose." Edwin could hear Kit's reluctance to talk about operations.

"Do you know anything about it?" Edwin prompted. "Anything you can share?" He knew that although information about an impending raid was shrouded in the strictest secrecy, once an operation was complete details were usually released to the press and broadcast on the BBC.

Kit hesitated for a second, but then answered. "Apparently at the request of the Soviets, we and the Americans sent over three waves of bombers. Close to eight hundred RAF aircraft took part and I believe the Americans put up another five hundred. So thirteen hundred bombers altogether. I don't know anything about fighter escorts."

"But 617 squadron didn't fly on it?"

"No, none of us—"

"I'm so relieved."

"Why, sir?"

"Something terrible happened. I saw it in a dream, and it terrified me like nothing I've ever seen before. It was all so pointless and — how do I explain this? — so impossibly arrogant. Destruction just for the sake of destruction. Sheer hubris. Do you know where?"

Again, Moran hesitated, clearly uncomfortable, but the BBC would name the target soon enough. "A place I've never heard of before," he admitted. "Dresden."

"Dresden," Edwin echoed the name in a whisper, more shattered than ever. Reddings *did* know Dresden. He had been there as a student between the wars. It was a beautiful baroque town strung along the banks of the gentle Elbe. A minuet in stone, he had thought at the time of his visit.

"Pilots of 627, which did take part, report there was quite a fire storm," Moran admitted.

"What we did was wrong, Kit." Edwin had no doubt in his mind, and he spoke with the conviction of his profession. "There was no legitimate military target there — not like Hamburg. And it was full of helpless refugees with nowhere to go."

"I'll take your word for it," Kit answered respectfully. "Maybe we can discuss it when we next meet."

"Yes, we must talk about it. I want to hear what you think. For now, I'm just glad you weren't part of it. Take care. You are in my prayers daily."

"Thank you. Give my regards to Amanda."

"Gladly."

They hung up, but Edwin remained standing in the hallway, unable to face his sisters. Throughout the last five years of war, he had sustained himself with the justice of their cause. He had made excuses again and again for actions he found questionable. He had even conceded the need for 'saturation bombing' on the strength of the simple technical impossibility of precision strikes. Yet now, on the very cusp of victory, the Allies were starting to behave like their enemies — smashing things and killing people simply to demonstrate their ability to do so. They were destroying their shared European cultural heritage which they should have been striving to rebuild together.

And as if that weren't bad enough, sitting only a few feet away was an Englishwoman, his own flesh and blood, who, despite everything this appalling war should have taught, was just a bigoted as any Nazi. His own sister was ready to insult, isolate, and discriminate against people purely on the basis of their race. He was acutely aware that in less than a decade the Germans had gone from the Nuremburg Laws, that inhibited Jewish participation in the economy, to full-scale genocide. While the reports of Auschwitz underlined the need to eradicate Hitler and his ideology of hatred and racism, Edwin knew that Jews had been more integrated into German than English society. The fact that the persecution of Jews could happen in *Germany* was, therefore, particularly shocking — and telling. Far from being a specifically German problem, Auschwitz illustrated the fact that all societies and nations could commit acts of gross inhumanity when manipulated by evil leaders. Which, Edwin concluded, meant that the most dangerous 'Nazis' were those at home.

Chapter 19
Z for Zebra

RAF Woodhall Spa
15 February 1945

Fauquier stopped Moran as he left the mess after breakfast. "The ATA just delivered a couple of new Lancasters yesterday. Weather permitting, I want you to put Z-Zebra through its air-worthiness trials today. Assuming there are no fundamental faults — in which case you'll probably be dead, it will become your usual aircraft."

"Thank you, sir!" A new aircraft rather than a beat-up old one was welcome, especially after what had happened on I-Item; it was also nothing unusual. Sprog crews often got new aircraft simply because experienced crews got attached to certain aircraft and didn't like swapping them. Forrester, too, had been assigned to a new aircraft, Q-Queen, when he and his crew had gone operational.

Moran rapidly went upstairs to change into battle dress and find Peal. He told him to collect the rest of the crew and join him at Z-Zebra. The new aircraft was already the centre of a beehive of activity when Moran arrived, ahead of the others. What looked like a dozen men were clambering over, in, out and around it purposefully, all wielding different tools and instruments. A Flight Sergeant detached himself from the crowd and intercepted him. With a salute he asked, "Flying Officer Moran?"

"Yes, that's me, Chiefy."

The Flight Sergeant held out his hand, "Pete Bishop, sir. I'll be the Ground Crew Chief of Z-Zebra." Moran guessed that he was in his late twenties, maybe early thirties. His face was chiselled by wind, sun, and hard work. His brown hair was receding a bit, and he had a deep scar on his chin. Two of the fingers on his right hand were unnaturally short as well, evidently the result of an accident.

"Good to meet you, Bishop." Moran answered, removing a packet of cigarettes from his breast pocket and shaking it open in the direction of the crew chief. Bishop took a cigarette and a light from Moran with a "Thank you, sir."

"Been with 617 long?" Moran asked casually.

"Since it was formed, sir. I was just a mechanic back then."

"Must have seen a lot of aircrew come and go."

"My share, sir."

"Would you mind introducing me to the rest of the ground crew?" Moran asked. Bishop smiled and led the way.

The others had already stopped whatever they were doing and waited expectantly. The Flight Sergeant led Moran to a swarthy man with thick dark eyebrows and introduced him as "Corporal Dawson, Fitter. He's got primary responsibility for the engines, backed up by that lot over there." Bishop gestured toward five additional aircraftmen. Moran offered Dawson a cigarette before following Bishop to another Corporal, whom he introduced as "Walters, the rigger. He also does nose art, if you want something, sir?"

"Well, she's Z-Zebra," Moran remarked as he offered Walters a cigarette. The Corporal took one and lit up, while Moran continued, "so why not put a Zebra on her nose? It would make me feel more at home."

"How's that, sir?"

"Grew up in Kenya and went to school in South Africa. My father's in the Colonial Service." Such facts about the aircrew helped the erks identify with them. Moran knew this because he'd been in their shoes.

"Is that why Pilot Officer Forrester calls you 'Zulu' Moran, sir?" Walters piped up.

Moran tossed him a look of exaggerated annoyance. "Forrester likes teasing me with that epithet, yes, but I'm hardly a Zulu."

"Still, what about a scantily clad Zulu girl for the nose?" Walters offered hopefully.

Moran laughed but shook his head. "That," he pointed to the Lancaster with his thumb "carries a ruddy great bomb load and six guns. Zulu girls don't carry weapons. Let's stick with the Zebra."

"Yes, sir," Walters agreed disappointed.

They continued to the next man, "Corporal Flanagan here is the radio mechanic."

Moran shook hands and offered another cigarette as he remarked, "You'll be working closely with my wireless operator, Sergeant Tibble." He turned to see if Tibble had shown up yet. His eyes found Tibble standing shyly at the edge of the dispersal, so Moran signalled him over. "Terry, meet Corporal Flanagan, the radio mechanic."

Flight Sergeant Bishop gestured for another corporal to join them. "This is Cap'n Hook, the instrument mech," Bishop introduced a grinning erk, who seemed very young to Moran. He was also missing several front teeth, whether from a fight or an accident Moran couldn't know. Hook happily accepted the offered cigarette and the light from Moran.

"We're the core crew, sir," Bishop concluded. "The others help out under our direction — and then, as I'm sure you know, sir, there's the army of station armorers, bomb loaders, bowser operators and the like."

Moran nodded. It took nine men on the ground for each member of aircrew to keep the RAF flying. "Yes, Bishop, I know, and I appreciate them all. I was in your shoes once, you see. Started life in the RAF as an erk."

"Did you, sir?"

"Yes. Volunteered for aircrew roughly three years ago and did my first tour as a flight engineer."

The Flight Sergeant nodded. Anyone could volunteer for aircrew and Moran presumed that over the years Bishop had seen a steady trickle of men opt for the higher pay, the higher rank, the privileges like coffee and fresh eggs, and the glamour. Most would have ended up as gunners, wireless operators, or flight engineers, but a minority made it to bomb aimer, navigator or pilot. Moran was far from unique.

Turning toward the taxiway where the transport van had just dropped them, Moran gestured for MacDonald and Babcock to join him. Their aircrew badges identified their trades, but Moran made sure that Babcock knew who Hook was, while MacDonald needed no urging to become familiar with the erks. He was already shaking hands and exchanging a few words with Dawson and Walters before wandering over with them to meet the other mechanics as well.

The gunners arrived and Moran told Bishop they were going to take the aircraft up for airworthiness tests. "Did the ATA mention any quirks when they turned Z-Zebra over to us?"

"No, sir. She's straight from the factory and looks first-rate." Bishop produced the Form 700 and Moran signed it before climbing aboard after the rest of his crew.

The Lancaster still had a factory smell. The dark green surfaces glistened, and the floor was clean. Grabbing the yellow handle over the cockpit window as he swung himself over the throttles, Moran felt a thrill as he settled behind the pristine controls. He took a moment to admire the perfection of the Perspex glass surrounding him on three sides. There was not a scratch anywhere.

The petrol tanker had drawn up alongside, and to a steady chugging sound it pumped in enough fuel for a two-hour flight. Meanwhile, MacDonald and Moran went through the pre-flight drill. The battery trolley was dragged over and shortly after 10 o'clock MacDonald opened the starboard window and called out to the ground-grew. "Contact, Number Three." After a few slow turns, the Merlin coughed a couple of times before, with a belch of smoke, it caught properly and settled down. The other three engines started just as smoothly, and they were so well tuned that they rumbled rather than roared. The entire aircraft with her hundred-foot wingspan vibrated contentedly to their low, synchronised melody. Zebra was straining against the chocks without any extra throttle, and Moran felt like the driver of a chariot, the four horses prancing in eagerness and pulling at their bits. He waved the chocks away, and they taxied out to the head of the runway.

The cloud cover was breaking up to the west but over the airfield it was solid with a base at 3,000 feet. Light, dry snowflakes fell gently from the dark bellies of the clouds, dancing in the air as a very light breeze played with them. They melted the instant they hit the ground, leaving the tarmac wet and black. Only two other aircraft were in motion around the field, also for tests and maintenance, but a couple of tractors pulling four trailers loaded with bombs were crawling away from the bomb dump; others were marshalling. A detachment from the squadron would be flying tonight, and the process of getting those aircraft bombed-up was starting.

They received the green light for take-off. Moran ran up the eager engines on the brakes before easing back and letting the kite roll down the runway. With so little fuel and no bomb load, Zebra was eager to fly. MacDonald read the airspeed indicator and put his left hand on the throttles, ready to hold them there, while Moran concentrated on keeping the winged chariot straight on the runway. "One hundred and fifteen... one hundred and twenty... one hundred and twenty-five." Finally, the speed of the air rushing under the wing surface lifted them off the earth. As if they were weightless, it carried them on its back. It was a marvellous feeling.

Moran ordered the undercarriage and flaps up before reaching 300 feet. They climbed into the cloud and flew through it for another ten minutes before they broke out into brittle February sunshine.

For the next hour, working closely with MacDonald, Moran put the Lancaster through her paces. He enjoyed every minute of it. Zebra was like a docile thoroughbred: powerful, eager and yet obedient to the pressure of Moran's hands and feet. Meanwhile, the gunners tested their turrets to a stream of enthusiastic commentary. "They glide, skipper!" Osgood declared, Roper adding, "I could get seasick spinning around up here!" Babcock called up, enthusing about the view from the unscratched bubble, and Tibble reported in that his equipment worked beautifully. "The H2S is a dream to read! I didn't know it could work this well. I thought they were lying to us."

The others laughed.

Despite a few minor defects, Moran was more than satisfied with the performance of Zebra after just over an hour of normal flight. So, he flipped on the intercom. "Pilot to crew: Strap yourselves in. I'm going to do some aerobatics."

"Do you have to, sir?" MacDonald complained. "Last time you did them you said you didn't plan to do them ever again."

"Sorry, MacDonald, it's part of the airworthiness test, so, yes, I have to. In any case, would you rather find out we have problems now over England, where we can safely bail out if we have to, or when some Messerschmitt is on our tail and bailing out means captivity?"

"We'll nae ha' the chance tae bail ourselves oot anywhere, if we're doubled o'er puking us guts oot!" MacDonald grumbled, his brogue growing stronger with his distress, and the intercom erupted with a chorus of laughs.

Moran waited until MacDonald had resignedly folded down his seat and fastened his belt, and then took the Lancaster through a climbing roll. Satisfied, he gained altitude to 15,000 feet and put the kite into first a right-hand and then a left-hand stall turn. Finally, he practiced corkscrewing the bomber, until Osgood warned over the intercom, "Skipper, if you don't want this beautiful new kite of yours to stink of vomit, you're going to have to stop. No one told me we were doing airworthiness tests until *after* I'd had a full breakfast."

"Roger. We'll stop for today," Moran agreed smiling, and then asked Peal for a course back to base.

"Do you want a direct course, or one via Kirby Grange?" Adrian replied.

Kirkby Grange

The staff and pupils at Kirkby Grange School were used to the sound of aircraft engines — so used to them that they knew at once that this was different.

"That's not on approach to East Kirkby!" One of the boys announced, interrupting Mr Willoughby. "It's off course!"

Mr Willoughby spun about with a frown, but before he could utter a word, another boy spoke up excitedly. "It's flying *towards* us!"

Yet another boy joined in, declaring in excitement rather than alarm: "And it's *way* too low!" He jumped up and dashed to the windows. The other pupils rushed after him. Mr Willoughby growled, "Back to your seats!" But although he banged his cane on the floor for emphasis, they ignored him. To Georgina's amazement, the Third Form teacher shrugged and surrendered to his own curiosity, limping after the boys. Georgina and the remaining pupils followed at his heels.

The large, neo-Gothic windows offered a splendid view across the school grounds, but they could still see no aircraft despite the drone of engines getting closer and closer. What if the aircraft were out of control for some reason? What if the crew had bailed out and it was crashing? There had been a number of terrible incidents over the last year that resulted in aircraft crashing into the English countryside; most had been in bad weather, but there had also been some accidents due to technical failure. Georgina knew that crews had orders to jump if they had reason to believe they could not land safely, and while they were supposed to point the aircraft towards the sea, what if it didn't have enough fuel to reach the coast? Georgina felt a tiny tremor of fear — followed by a flash of empathy as she registered that in Germany there would be no doubt: hearing the inexorable approach of aircraft engines meant death and destruction were on the way.

The near deafening sound seemed to be directly overhead, and the whole room trembled. Pencils danced and rolled on the desktops. Something on Mr Willoughby's desk started rattling. The panes of glass in the leaded windows vibrated. Seemingly out of nowhere, a giant shadow crossed them, and a Lancaster banked hard to fly practically in front of their noses along the length of the building. One of the girls screamed and several cowered down, but the boys could hardly contain their excitement as they shouted and shoved, trying to get a better view.

The heavy bomber flew so low that the leafless rosebushes in the garden bent in the artificial gale churned up by the engines and remnants of the last snowfall were blown sideways. The boys jumped up and down, and one of the boys shouted in rapture. "It's Z for Zebra!"

"KC-Z!" Another improved on his colleague. "The Squadron letters are KC!"

Kit! It hit her like an electric shock: KC were Kit's squadron's letters. He must be the one flying the thing! What was the term? He was "beating up" Kirkby Grange!

"KC is 617 Squadron!" A third boy exclaimed excitedly.

"It's one of the Dambusters!" a fourth shouted, jumping up and down even more ecstatically than before.

"Maybe it's your fiancé, Miss Reddings?" One of the girls suggested, turning to look over her shoulder at Georgina with a sheepish smile. Several of the other pupils turned to gaze at her, awestruck with envy.

Georgina laughed, but she felt a childish pride too.

Already Zebra was gone, climbing steeply and banking back to the southwest.

Mr Willoughby looked over at Georgina with raised eyebrows. "I'm not sure that was the best means to convince Miss Townsend of the advisability of a visit by RAF aircrew."

Georgina looked back at the crowd of boys still pressing their noses to the windows or arguing excitedly about what height and speed the Lancaster had been flying along with a dozen other technical details. "Then again, Mr. Willoughby, it's considerably safer to have aircrew come and *talk* about their aircraft than decide to show it off."

Willoughby laughed. "True, but I hope your young man doesn't mind getting a ticking off when Miss Townsend complains to his CO."

RAF Woodhall Spa

"Just what *was* your altitude, Moran?" Fauquier asked blandly from behind his desk.

"One hundred fifty feet, sir, and I was over the grounds, flying parallel the whole time, never over the building itself."

"One-fifty? Not lower?"

"No, sir. They have a sixty-foot flagpole in front that I didn't want to tangle with."

"You know, if you're going to do this kind of thing you should at least try to make it a valuable exercise. Next time go down to 50 feet — and be sure to keep away from the flagpole and building."

"Yes, sir."

The following morning when Moran arrived at dispersal, Walters had already painted a Zebra on the nose. It looked more like a striped horse soaring over an invisible fence than any Zebra Kit had ever seen. On the other hand, the grace with which the "Zebra" was lifting his dainty fore hooves did suggest an eagerness to take to the air appropriate for the bomber. The more Kit considered it, the more he liked it. Smiling, he found Walters, and told him, "Good job!"

"You like it, sir?"

"It's perfect." Kit felt a bond with the aircraft already. Zebra was going to be lucky, he told himself.

Chapter 20
Earning One's Pay

RAF Woodhall Spa
17 February 1945

When the intelligence officer, the IO, pulled back the curtains over the map, a palpable wave of unease rippled across the room. Moran looked around at the other aircrew in surprise. Only eight crews had been selected for this sortie and they were being led by one of the two flight commanders rather than their squadron commander, Fauquier. Since Forrester had not been selected for this particular raid, Moran commanded the only sprog crew in the room. The other men gathered for the briefing had flown scores of sorties on 617, making it a worry that not one of them looked relaxed.

"The importance of this target," the IO opened, "lies in the fact that it's the most important transportation link between the Ruhr Valley and the Baltic ports. It is the primary route by which Sweden's iron ore — yes, they're still supplying it as long as Hitler pays for it, and he is — reaches the armaments factories in the Ruhr valley. If we stop the ore from getting to the Ruhr, we slow down panzer, artillery, flak and fighter production. In addition, prefabricated components for the U-boat construction sites on the Baltic coast travel along this canal. In short, this is a vital lifeline for Germany's war industry. If we interdict it, we shorten the war by months."

Moran nodded mentally. He could follow that logic, but a canal seemed like a singularly indestructible target to him.

"While the canal is 160 miles long, it is only vulnerable, here." The IO tapped the tip of his wooden pointer on the map. "North of Muenster. This is where it crosses the river Glane via two parallel aqueducts."

That made a bit more sense, Moran agreed mentally.

"Earth embankments lift the canal above the level of the surrounding countryside to an aqueduct over the river. They are your targets — and ideal for the Tallboys. The bombs will penetrate the earth at both ends of the aqueduct and explode *under* the surface, thus completely destabilising it."

That sounded reasonable in theory, but a look around the room told Moran that no-one else was buying the IO's story. There had to be more to this operation than met the eye.

"Naturally," the IO continued, "Jerry is aware of both the canal's importance and its vulnerability at this point. He has constructed defences accordingly. There is a heavy concentration of flak batteries and a number of night fighter squadrons are stationed in the region, so you can expect a warm reception." If that was supposed to be a joke, it fell flat. No one even smiled, let alone laughed. So much for 617's vaunted "danger is fun" attitude, Moran concluded.

The flight commander took over the briefing from the IO and explained the tactics. They would fly in two sections of four aircraft each. "A" Flight would target the east embankment and "B" Flight the west. They would fly in loose formation to the target and each section leader would make the first pass and call in the remaining three aircraft while circling the target. All aircraft would make as many runs over the target as necessary for a good drop — unless cloud cover made it impossible to see the target and the flight commander took the decision to abort.

They would cross the enemy coast at 22,000 — almost the Lancaster's maximum —but bomb from 17,000 feet. A much larger Main Force raid against Dortmund was scheduled simultaneously, and they would fly parallel to the Main Force bomber stream until the latter almost reached their target. At the designated point, 617 aircraft would turn north and attack the canal from the south. They would return individually by a route that reunited them with the Main Force bomber stream just south of Utrecht. Command believed the roughly 800 aircraft of Main Force would attract most of the night fighters.

That would be nice, but it wouldn't help with the flak, Moran noted mentally.

The flight commander continued with details such as the bomb load (one Tallboy per aircraft) and the fuel load, and then the meteorological officer took over to provide the weather forecast. Despite scattered cloud, he predicted good visibility over the target. Winds would be gusty at 15 to 20 mph out of the southwest at take-off but were expected to taper off during the course of the night. He predicted neither rain nor snow along their route. The waning moon would not rise until just after 2300, after which it would help light the target.

And the bombers, Kit thought to himself. They'd be visible to flak and night fighters — nevertheless, it was less daunting than being exposed in daylight to Me109s without a mid-upper gunner as 617 had expected on the second Tirpitz raid. This was his ticket out of humiliation, he reminded himself. It was what he'd signed on for, what they had all signed on for. It was past time that he and his crew started earning their pay and privileges.

They changed into flight kit in the crew room, leaving most of their personal items in their lockers before winding scarves around their necks and donning three layers of socks and gloves. Kit also tucked his good-luck charm into the lower right front pocket of his battle dress tunic. On learning that Kit was flying Z-Zebra, Georgina had asked her mother to send her the baby zebra from the "African menagerie" of her stuffed animal collection. Just yesterday, when Kit and she met at the *King's Head* for a quick drink, she'd given it to Kit for good luck. Absurd as it seemed, almost all aircrew had similar talismans. With his baby Zebra "Zach" in his pocket, Kit was ready to proceed.

From the edgy teasing between Roper and Osgood, Moran knew his gunners were keyed up, particularly Roper. This would be his first operational flight of any kind since he'd missed their boomerang trip. MacDonald, in contrast, looked stoically calm, but Babcock was jittery, and Peal looked pale and strained. Moran sent him a quick "thumbs up." As a group, they collected parachutes and Mae Wests. They pulled the life vests over their flight jackets and lugged the parachutes by their straps over their shoulders. Lorries waited in front of the Nissen hut, and along with other crews they climbed aboard one.

They jumped down again at the dispersal for Z-Zebra. The empty trolleys of the bomb-train bounced away as they arrived, but armorers were still passing belts of ammunition up to the turrets. From the smell in the air, the petrol tanker had only just left. Meanwhile, the ground crew was busy polishing the Perspex, removing the covers from the pitot head and tyres, and carrying out other pre-flight chores.

Flight Sergeant Bishop came over. "She's tip-top, sir. Champing at the bit."

"All four of them, I hope," Moran answered gesturing toward the engines before offering Bishop a cigarette and taking one himself. Behind him, the rest of the crew were going through their pre-flight rituals such as pissing on the tail wheel. Moran lit up for Bishop and himself and shook out the match before asking the veteran ground chief, "Any idea why everyone seems so keyed up about this particular op?"

"Oh. That." Bishop looked a bit uncomfortable, but then came out with it: "The last time the squadron tried to take out the Dortmund-Ems canal, the squadron commander was shot down by flak before reaching the target, none of the others made a direct hit, and only three of the eight aircraft returned."

Well, that explained things, Moran thought.

The crew chief hastened to add, "But they were attempting a low-level attack with traditional cookies. You're going in high with the Tallboys. Should be totally different tonight, sir."

"Should be," Kit agreed with a crooked smile, and shook hands with Bishop, glad that the rest of his crew had already boarded the aircraft.

"Good luck, sir!" Bishop called after him.

Peal dragged his heavy navigator's bag to his station behind the cockpit and settled into his seat. He carefully closed the curtain around his workstation, grateful that it protected him from prying eyes. It was standard equipment on Lancasters because the navigator needed light to do his work, yet any light that escaped into the cockpit during a night raid interfered with the pilot's night vision. It might even attract fighters. For Peal it had the added benefit of ensuring that the others couldn't see just how shaky he was.

The flight with Moran five days ago had restored his confidence — until today's briefing. As he had sat there listening to the briefers, terror returned. Memories of his flight with Forrester became so vivid that he froze. Terry had to nudge him to take notes. He managed to do that, but he left tell-tale smears of cold sweat on the chart. The moment the briefing ended he dashed to the lavatory. He needed several minutes to pull himself together and arrived in the crew room late. He hadn't been able to joke with the others. As he double checked his curtains now, however, a small measure of calm started to return.

He turned on the light directed at his table and started setting up. From his bag, he removed first his charts, on which were pencilled in the route they were to fly with the bearings of each course neatly noted above the lines. He spread the first chart out on his little table, holding the lower corners down with his slide-rule and Dalton computer. Next, he lined up his ruler, parallel ruler, dividers, pencils, pencil sharper and rubber. Beside these he placed his chocolate bar and a thermos full of sweet, hot tea.

He took a deep breath, knowing he could delay no longer. He pulled on his flying helmet and plugged into the intercom via the socket over his desk. He was connected to the others again and could hear the steady voices of Moran and MacDonald going through the cockpit check.

"Hydraulic pressure?"

"300 lbs per square inch."

"Auto pilot?"

"Control out."

"Bomb doors?"

"Closed."

"Ground/Flight switch?"

"On Flight."

"DR Compass?"

"Set to Magnetic."

Like clockwork, they went through the preparatory steps for starting engines. They did this on every flight including training and test flights, so this dull dialogue had a soothing effect on Peal's nerves. It was almost like a litany. When the engines started without mishap, he found that comforting as well. The deep rumbling would now — hopefully — accompany them unbroken until they were safely home.

The low-keyed, steady vibrations brought Zebra to life, and soon, almost imperceptibly, she rolled forward. Behind his curtain, Peal could see neither their own, halting progress nor the other aircraft moving carefully away from their dispersals, trundling onto the taxiway and lining up for take-off. He could follow their progress only by the rumble of the wheels, the squeal of the brakes, the swaying of the fuselage after each halt. Meanwhile, the laconic exchange from the cockpit continued as the final checks were carried out.

"Trim?"

"Set for take-off."

"Flaps?"

"Set for take-off."

"Propellers?"

"Full, fine."

"Fuel?"

"Tanks one and two selected. Booster pumps on."

Even blind, Peal knew when they turned onto the runway. Unconsciously he held his breath waiting for the invisible green light that would send them on their way. Finally, Zebra rolled slowly forward and gradually started to accelerate. MacDonald serenely read the speed indicator. The rumbling of the wheels picked up pace — and then abruptly stopped. The nose lifted and the whole kite swayed slightly, caught in a cross wind. The undercarriage clunked into the belly of the metal beast. Peal looked down at his chart with the course clearly pencilled in. His hand was shaking slightly, but he pressed down to stop it.

"Pilot to navigator: course?"

Peal double-checked the heading and cleared his throat once before he switched on his intercom and gave Moran the bearing. He was terrified both of what lay ahead of them and of cracking up again. If he froze or got confused, they might all die. He would deserve that fate for breaking down, but the others didn't. He mustn't let them down.

Peal forced himself to focus on the navigation. At this stage, they were still within the range of the electronic navigation aid known as Gee. He took a fix every five minutes, which he plotted on the chart, noting subliminally when Moran levelled off at cruising altitude. He also kept his eye on the repeater compass to be sure Moran was holding course — which obviously he was.

Peal drew a deep breath and reminded himself he was in good hands. Then he remembered that Moran had once been LMF too. He wondered what had happened — and how Moran had overcome his fears. Maybe Moran could have helped him tame his latent panic. He'd obviously tamed his own, as his calm voice peppered with an occasional twist of wry humour testified. Moran had no need for bravado, as Forrester did. Rather he exuded low-keyed competence. Peal would have liked to talk to Moran about what had happened when he was posted for LMF. He would have liked to ask for help. Yet that would be a betrayal of Fiona — and terribly embarrassing to boot. He couldn't seem to find the courage to raise the topic.

The abrupt crack and chatter of machine guns made Peal recoil and look up sharply. Then as the gunners reported all well, he realised this was only the routine weapons test. He checked his charts and decided to get another fix from Gee only to find it was already too late; they had crossed the invisible line that put them in range of the German jamming signals that rendered Gee useless.

Peal requested and received permission to go up to the astrodome to check their position visually. In the moonless night, they appeared suspended among the stars. Not another aircraft was visible that Peal could see. He returned to his station and plugged in just in time to hear Tibble pass on a change in wind speed and direction relayed from Group. Peal noted both down and recalculated their position based on dead reckoning. With the dividers he walked their position forward and noted it with a pencilled 'x' and the time.

Abruptly Babcock's excited voice crackled through the intercom. "Enemy coast ahead!"

The bomb aimer obviously had the wind up a bit, Peal thought with a touch of satisfaction and renewed determination not to give in to his own anxiety. Peal put his head around the instrument panel to ask Tibble if he could take a look into the H2S. This navigational device projected an image based on radar waves emitted from the aircraft and bounced back off the earth below. Tibble willingly let the navigator peer into the device, but Peal didn't trust the contraption as much as he did his own two eyes. He felt he'd be better able to pinpoint their position, if he got a good look at it. "Navigator to pilot: permission to go to the nose to look at the geography."

"Granted."

Peal switched off his light, shoved the curtain aside, and squeezed past MacDonald to step down into the nose. He lay down on the floor beside Babcock and studied the scene spread out below. In the east, a faint moon was lifting itself over the curvature of the earth and gently brightened the horizon. It cast a sheen of silver across the inland seas of the Netherlands. Peal gazed until he'd imprinted every feature he saw onto his memory, then returned to his workstation. He closed the curtain, turned on the light and searched the chart until the image before him matched that in his mind. He measured along the plot line with his dividers.

"Navigator to pilot: the wind must have shifted more westerly. We're being blown eastwards faster than anticipated. If I'm right, we're five to six minutes ahead of schedule."

"Pilot to navigator: Give me the ETA to our next turning point based on new wind."

Peal hadn't finished before Babcock called out an octave too high, "Bomb aimer to pilot: Search lights!"

"Pilot to crew: the flak will start soon."

Sure enough, within two minutes it hit them. Zebra bounced and shook, but far less violently than on the *Tirpitz* or Leipzig raids. It helped being at 22,000 feet, Peal reminded himself.

They continued inland. The blacked-out territory below them remained crushed under arrogant Nazi jackboots. The Allies might be closing in on the Reich, but the Nazis still held the western Netherlands in a death grip. Peal wondered what the Dutch people thought night after night as they heard swarms of bombers droning overhead. Were they grateful for the war being taken to their enemies? Or angry that the Allies were taking so long to break the back of the Nazi war machine? Concentrate, he reminded himself, and leaned around the partition to take another look into the H2S. He'd only just returned his attention to his charts, when Tibble's voice crackled on the intercom. "Wireless Operator to pilot and navigator: We just had a signal from Group. Zero-hour has been moved forward five minutes due to high winds."

"Thank you, wireless op. Well done, navigator. Have you got the new

ETA to the turning point?"

It was satisfying to have got that right, Peal thought; it boosted his confidence as he calculated. "Navigator to pilot: ETA to turning point: 8 minutes."

"Roger."

"What was that?" Roper's voice cracked across the intercom.

"Pilot to mid-upper gunner: make a proper report."

"Sorry, Skipper. Mid-upper gunner to crew: Did anyone else see something flare up to starboard?"

"Pilot to mid-upper gunner: night fighters have infiltrated the bomber stream. What you saw was one of our aircraft going down in flames. So, stay vigilant. There is no room for error tonight. Rear gunner, I know we've practiced a hundred times, but remember particularly to scan the space *below*." As he spoke, Moran noticeably increased the slow weaving of the bomber to help the gunners see the danger zones below and behind them better.

Yes, they'd practiced this a hundred times, Peal thought, yet nothing felt the same as "the real thing." Reality had a quality all its own. He found it hard to swallow and eyed his thermos of tea. Unfortunately, they were flying at 22,000 feet and he would have to remove his oxygen mask to drink, which might not be such a good idea. Besides, tea would fill his bladder, and he didn't want to risk another accident.

Tibble put his head into Peal's compartment. "Aren't we almost at the turning point?"

Peal shook himself from his thoughts, checked his charts and reported over the intercom: "Navigator to pilot: ninety seconds to turning point."

"Thank you, navigator."

Peal stared at the second hand of his watch until it had completed one and a half revolutions. "Navigator to pilot, turn on zero-one-zero."

"Course zero-one-zero," Moran answered. They banked onto the new course and the nose tilted down, still weaving gently.

"Wireless operator to pilot: "B" Flight Commander says to formate on him."

There was a long lull before Moran responded. "Pilot to bomb aimer: can you locate the other aircraft of our flight?"

Several more seconds of silence followed before Babcock yelped. "I see them, Skipper! Two aircraft at two o'clock low."

"Got 'em." Moran answered and pushed the nose down further.

They were losing altitude and would soon no longer be at the extreme range of the flak. The thought made Peal feel an urgent need to relieve himself. With Moran now formatting on the flight commander and soon under orders from the bomb aimer, his job was done until they had dropped their bomb and could turn for home. "Navigator to pilot: permission to go to the Elsan."

"Permission granted."

Peal turned off the light, brushed aside the curtain and squeezed past Tibble's station. He clambered over the main spar and glanced up as he passed under the mid-upper gunner. With a distinctive hydraulic hum, Frank swung the turret slowly from side to side, one foot propped on the side of the turret and the other dangling. Peal continued to the Elsan toilet. The shame of wetting himself during the *Tirpitz* raid sat deep. If his bladder was empty, he reasoned, he wouldn't wear the evidence even if he did have a moment of panic.

On his way back to his desk, he paused to step into the astrodome and look around. Behind them the sky seethed with flashes of light like a violent thunderstorm. The bright bursts rolled from left to right and then became random again, like a flickering carpet. Some explosions dazzled for a split second, while smoke dulled and partially obscured others. Below the cloud, fires smouldered and burned in an ever-widening swath. A flash erupted nearer at hand but rather than going out it grew into a large ball and then slowly started to fall from the sky. It took several seconds before Peal grasped that he just witnessed the death of an aircraft and crew. His hands shook as he left the astrodome.

He resettled himself in his tiny cabin and carefully closed the curtains again, but he could no longer concentrate on his job. Every nerve was twisted to the breaking point.

Over the radio the Flight Commander called. "Z-Zebra, Z-Zebra: your run."

Moran answered with "Roger." Then he switched from radio to internal intercom to inform Babcock. "Bomb doors open. Master switch on."

After that Babcock's boyish chirp guided them into the target. The flak jolted and shoved Zebra this way and that. At one point they sank so abruptly that Adrian's stomach jumped into this throat. Seconds later, a giant fist punched them sideways. Peal started to wonder how much more of this Zebra could take. How much longer was the bomb run?

"Adrian!" Terry hissed. Why did he keep butting in? "Have you got the course for home? We're almost on top of the target."

"I know my job, Terry!" Peal snapped back and forced himself to concentrate on the charts. The target pinpointed their position, and the next goal was Utrecht — or rather a point twenty miles south of Utrecht to avoid the flak batteries defending the city. That course, fortunately, had been given to them in the briefing and Peal had pencilled it on his chart. He checked both the chart and his notes to be doubly sure.

Babcock pleaded in an abnormally high voice, "Steady, Skipper! Steady!"

Zebra soared upwards so sharply that Peal felt compressed as Babcock sang out jubilantly, "Bomb gone!"

Before he could be asked, Peal called over the intercom, "Navigator to pilot: Steer 280."

"Well done, Navigator. Turning on 280 in fifteen seconds. Pilot to bomb aimer and rear gunner: what does the target look like?"

Babcock answered first. "Well, Skip, there's a lot of smoke obscuring it, but as far as I can see it's still intact."

"Yep, 'fraid it looks that way," Osgood seconded.

"Okay. Turning on 280."

The starboard wing lifted as Zebra banked to the left. The repeater compass swung slowly until the red mark lined up on 280 as the aircraft rolled back to the horizontal. Good. Next task, Peal told himself, was to work out the course from Utrecht to the coast. They'd been warned to fly between Haarlem and Leiden to avoid the concentrations of flak over the larger cities. He got up to check the H2S but here the landscape was flat and littered with towns, making it hard to interpret. Peal compared the H2S image to his chart several times but couldn't concentrate enough to make sense of it. Tibble was hovering again, offering to help him. It was annoying, but the wireless operator's questions helped clarify where they were. Peal started calculating based on their drift from the last fix. With his dividers, he measured their progress along the line on his chart and re-estimated their ground speed.

Every ten minutes he updated their position by dead reckoning. They crept across the face of the map at the pace of a snail. Meanwhile, outside his curtained cabin, the air was becoming rough again. Above the growl of the engines, faint rumbles reached Peal's ears. Zebra started to shake and bounce as if flying through heavy turbulence.

Abruptly something exploded directly below them. Objects thudded into their underbelly with a horrifying clang, metal ripped apart. Zebra seemed to break free of Moran's control and started plummeting to earth. Peal grabbed his desk. Any second now they were going to explode! He anticipated the roar of the tanks blowing out, the sheet of burning aviation fuel sweeping over him, the smoke choking him and the furnace-like heat that would consume them all.

Instead, the aircraft steadied and levelled.

Cool as rain, Moran's voice wafted over the intercom, "Pilot to flight engineer: go back and check for damage to the fuselage."

MacDonald pushed passed the navigator's workstation. Peal followed his progress by the changing trim of the aircraft.

Meanwhile, they were still being shaken by the flak, and Peal asked himself where they could possibly be. Had he screwed up entirely and routed them over Bocholt? Or had the wind direction changed, pushing them south? He couldn't know without some kind of a fix. If they continued to fly by dead reckoning alone, they might continue on the wrong course and fly over even more dangerous concentrations of flak.

Peal flinched as MacDonald stuck his head through the curtain to ask, "Everything all right, Adrian?"

"You're the one who just checked on the damage," Peal snapped back. He regretted the retort at once. Moran never ticked them off them for asking questions or making remarks.

MacDonald had moved on and the curtain fell back into place. Peal heard MacDonald shout over the engine noise without using his microphone. "We've got some fist-sized holes in the floor back there, but I couldn't see any damage to the control cables. Engine readings are all normal."

"Good," Moran answered.

Peal forced himself to focus again. He stared blindly at his charts, consumed by the knowledge that he must get a fix. If he didn't, they might drift completely off course and end up running out of fuel somewhere over Belgium or France. The flak seemed weaker and farther away now. Peal risked leaning around the partition to ask Tibble for another look at the H2S, but try as he might, he couldn't make sense of the images. He was going to have to take a visual fix. "Navigator to pilot: permission to go to the nose."

"Granted."

Peal went down to the nose and lay down again. The cold here seemed to penetrate to his bones. Despite his long underwear and layers of wool and leather, he might as well have been naked in an unlit refrigerator. Zebra appeared suspended in a black hole surrounded by search lights and flashes of bursting flak in all directions. Each flash of flak represented an RAF bomber struggling to get home, Peal reminded himself.

"Mid-upper gunner to pilot: Lancasters to port. We must have rejoined Main Force."

Well, that explained why there was so much flak, Peal thought, and returned to the wireless operator's desk to have another look at the H2S. He decided they were exactly where they were supposed to be, just south of Utrecht, and it was time to turn to cross the coast between Leiden and Haarlem. After that they would be able to set a course for home.

Well, for base. Home was still London, his parent's elegant house in South Kensington. It would be so good to see it again — to hear the grandfather clock strike the hours with solemn dignity, to catch a whiff of his father's cigar smoke lingering in the downstairs hall, to hear Mrs Carter calling from the kitchen, "Adrian? Is that you?"

"Fighter! Corkscrew starboard!" Osgood shouted over the intercom, making Peal recoil. He hung in the air as Zebra dropped out from under him. She twisted to starboard as she dived and started to turn on her side. Peal's thermos fell over and rolled off his desk. A second later his seat started pushing against him and the thermos hit his feet as it bounced up. All Peal could do was cling to his desk, fighting back nausea.

Moran called: "Throttling back!" Zebra hung motionless in the air as the guns erupted with furious clattering that shook her from stem to stern. Smoke and the smell of cordite enveloped Peal.

"I got him, Skipper! I got him!" Osgood yelped exuberantly.

Moran didn't answer. He simply pushed the throttles forward so hard that Peal felt as though his seat had dropped away again. Now, as he clung to his desk, his legs trembled so violently that his knees knocked. Again, he visualised that flash of light that grew before it fell away. Any second, they were going to die.

Instead, Moran reversed the corkscrew and they soared into a climbing turn. After an eternity, the aircraft levelled off again. "Pilot to flight engineer: damage?"

"Nothing that I can detect from the instruments, Skipper. I'll go for a walk in a minute or two, when I'm sure you'll nae be throwing this crate around like a wee child having a temper tantrum!"

Moran gave a short laugh. "Pilot to gunners: good shooting. The fighter dived past and kept going, but he wasn't on fire. He may simply have decided we were too much trouble. I'm content with that result, but I'm afraid it won't be good enough for a formal claim. Also, the next fighter might be more determined, so don't relax."

"Aye-aye, sir," Roper answered readily, followed by a disappointed "Understood, skipper," from Osgood.

Peal sympathised with the rear-gunner and reached down to retrieve his thermos. He didn't dare have a drink yet. He wouldn't risk that until they had crossed out of enemy airspace. Instead, he straightened his charts and found his dividers and ruler in the heap beside the partition. He started working out how long it would take to escape enemy airspace. Don't forget the headwinds, he reminded himself. As he bent over his chart, he heard Tibble look in on him. He ignored him, and the wireless operator said nothing.

"Enemy coast behind," Babcock announced triumphantly.

Moran at once warned, "Pilot to gunners: don't reduce vigilance. Enemy fighters often follow us out over the North Sea."

Still, Peal felt a weight lift from him, and MacDonald clearly felt comfortable enough to take a torch and walk down the length of the fuselage looking for damage.

"Pilot to crew: beginning descent to 8,000 ft. I'll let you know when we pass 10,000 and can go off oxygen."

They were on the home stretch. Peal risked unclipping his mask long enough for a sip of lukewarm tea, and his thoughts drifted to Fiona. He'd joined Kit last night at the *King's Head* and Fiona had been there too. She was witty and lively. Several other chaps had tried to lure her away from their table, but she'd stayed. She sincerely seemed to like him. Maybe, since he'd had no relapse of panic this sortie, he could risk taking her out for meal or to the flicks or something? She was intriguing, so different from Julia.

The thought of Julia made him squirm uncomfortably. She'd got him into a pickle. He hadn't planned to sleep with her, but it would have been so rude not to after she'd invited him up to her flat for a drink. She'd made it obvious she wanted him. It had been flattering, especially after Cynthia had left him standing. Julia was terrific in bed. Just the thought of her aroused him. Only, God knew how many other men she'd had in for a drink and, well, everything else. How could he possibly take her home to his parents and introduce her as his future wife? He didn't want to be married to her, he just wanted to sleep with her. Again. Soon. It would make him feel alive and virile. It would drive away the shame of that first op....

He was jolted from his thoughts by Tibble. "Isn't Gee working yet?"

Peal gestured irritably for Tibble to leave him alone, but reached for the Gee box, pulling it out and switching it on. It flustered him that he'd needed a prompt, and he hastened to get a fix, plot it, and pass a minor course correction to Moran. Then he watched the repeater compass as

Moran swung Zebra onto the adjusted course.

About ten minutes later, Moran called over the intercom. "We're below ten thousand. Off oxygen, everyone."

"Doesn't that make it time for coffee?" Tibble asked hopefully.

"I'm coming, I'm coming," Babcock answered sounding both annoyed and pleased with himself.

Peal switched off his desk lamp and pushed open the curtain just as Babcock scrambled up out of the nose clutching the coffee thermoses in his arms. He handed one to Moran and MacDonald, both of whom had their masks hanging beside their faces. Peal reached out for his thermos, and then retreated behind his curtains again. He turned on the light and worked on a last fix while sipping the coffee. It was stronger and hotter than his tea. "Navigator to pilot: estimate thirty minutes to landing."

In due time, Tibble reported contact with the station, and Peal's job was done for tonight. Tibble flashed "Z" to the control tower and received permission to land. Peal turned off his light and opened his curtain to watch as the heavy bomber swept around gracefully on a wide circuit to line up on the flare path. Beside Moran, MacDonald folded down his seat and strapped in before lowering first the landing gear and then the flaps. He throttled back the engines as Moran guided the aircraft to the start of the runway. The rudder clacked as Moran adjusted the yaw. Then with a squeal Zebra's tyres touched down and they hurtled along the tarmac, gradually slowing down.

Only after they'd turned off the runway and were taxiing to the dispersal did Moran press his oxygen mask back over his face to announce over the intercom. "Pilot to crew: Well done, everyone."

He got a cheer from the rest of them.

They turned in at the dispersal point and Flight Sergeant Bishop waved his hands in front of his face to indicate stop and switch off engines. One after another, the Merlins fell silent, although they continued to ring in Peal's ears.

In the tail, the gunners chatted excitedly as they opened the door and lowered the ladder. As though in a hurry, Stu left the flight deck and scrambled over the main spar to follow them out of the aircraft. In contrast, Moran and MacDonald, their oxygen masks swinging beside their faces, fretted over something. Tibble poked his head around the instrument panel to ask, "Okay, Adrian?"

Why did he ask? Did Tibble know something? Had Forrester's wireless operator been talking in the sergeant's mess about what had happened to him on the *Tirpitz* op? To disguise his discomfort, Peal shot back at Tibble,

"Wizard. What about you? It was your first op."

"Piece of cake," the wireless operator answered with a grin.

Moran and MacDonald started moving toward the exit, and Peal stuffed his things back into his bag. The last one out of the aircraft, he found the others chatting and joking over a cigarette at the foot of the stairs.

Flight Sergeant Bishop joined them. "Any damage, sir?"

"We took some shrapnel in the belly on the way back, but it didn't look too bad. Zebra flew brilliantly. Everyone else back, Chiefy?" Moran answered.

"You were the seventh, so far, sir. Just one missing, but there's still time."

They looked at their watches. A damaged Lanc on a lean fuel mixture might still manage to limp in, or it might opt to put down at another airfield. No need to write off the missing aircraft and crew just yet.

A crew bus stopped beside Zebra, and they climbed in. It dropped them beside the parachute hut, and they returned their unused parachutes and life jackets before continuing to the debriefing.

The atmosphere that greeted them was radically changed from the tense briefing earlier. Everyone seemed astonishingly wide awake for the middle of the night; voices and laughter jumbled together exuberantly. A couple of other crews conferred with intelligence officers, while palpable excitement emanated from Fauquier and the Station Commander, who stood on the far side of the room.

Moran's crew gave their name and aircraft designation to the corporal at the door one by one; he checked them off his list. They collected tea laced heavily with rum and sat at a table another crew had just vacated. The WAAF intelligence officer smiled at them and asked if they'd had a good flight.

Before Moran could answer, Fauquier called him over. As the pilots clustered together on the far side of the room, Peal heard Fauquier exclaim, "We just received confirmation! The Germans are reporting stranded barges along ten miles of the canal. You did it!" Raising his voice, he called out to the room at large, "Well done, everyone! The Dortmund-Ems Canal has been breached!"

That felt good. Peal knew he'd had some bad moments, but he'd navigated to and from the target. In doing so he'd made a tangible contribution to ending the war.

And now just 42 more to go.

Chapter 21
Intermezzo

Kirkby Grange
24 February 1945

Mr Willoughby's enthusiastic advocacy finally wore Miss Townsend's resistance down. "The fact is," he told Miss Townsend firmly, "we're surrounded by RAF stations. We hear scores of Lancasters taking off and landing day after day. We hear of their exploits on the news every night. Yet almost none of us has the slightest understanding of what they actually do — beyond bombing Germany. I think bringing a crew here and having them talk about their trades and experiences would have enormous educational benefit, quite aside from being fun and exciting for the bulk of the boys. We can make it a voluntary assembly if you like."

Miss Townsend latched on to that and insisted that the crew come on a Saturday morning and that attendance not be required. To the crew, the day of the week made no difference, as they were just as likely to fly on weekends as not. If they were stood down for a few days, on the other hand, then coming to the school in the morning was less onerous than during an afternoon.

As fate would have it, barely had Miss Townsend consented before all of 617's aircrews were stood down for three days to accommodate modifications of their aircraft after a busy week flying in the routine Pathfinder role. On these flights, over three successive nights, Adrian had performed increasingly well, building Kit's confidence in him. The prospect of him being thrown off the squadron receded, and Kit's crew were all in good spirits when, with seventy-two hours leave ahead of them, they arrived at Kirkby Grange School to give their talk.

Since the vast majority of the pupils were evacuees who could not go home at the weekend, this Saturday assembly attracted nearly one hundred percent of the children. While they gathered in the auditorium, Georgina and Mr Willoughby escorted Kit and his crew to Miss Townsend's office. Georgina could not imagine what Miss Townsend had been expecting, but apparently not the well-spoken and polite young men she met. Adrian with his Oxbridge accent completely charmed her. She seemed to purr with delight as she led him, the others in their wake, to the auditorium.

Miss Townsend took the stage and introduced the program, then the seven crew members joined her. They each gave their name, rank and trade. Kit spoke first, explaining their overall mission: destroying Germany's industrial and military capability, shattering civilian morale, and supporting Allied ground forces by preventing German reinforcements from reaching the front. He mentioned some specific targets such as the *Tirpitz*, U-boat and E-boat pens, and the V-1 and V-2 rocket launch sites.

"And dams!" Someone called from the audience, causing a minor stir as the Sixth Form Master called the boy to order.

"Dams and canals, railheads, factories — particularly synthetic oil, munitions and aircraft factories," Kit continued as if uninterrupted.

He then turned the podium over to Adrian to talk about "how we find those things and get home again." Adrian delivered his presentation with the cultivated ease of a public-school boy. His tailored uniform was a perfect fit, but he had replaced the tie with a silk cravat. He spoke with one hand stuffed in his trouser pocket and the other gesturing elegantly as appropriate. He moved casually about the stage and easily engaged his audience as if he'd done this sort of thing scores of times — as indeed he had. With his long, fine, blond hair and classic good looks, he embodied the glamorous image of RAF aircrew cultivated by the press.

Georgina glanced over at Fiona and confirmed that her friend looked completely enchanted. She smiled benignly.

"Daddy" followed Adrian, and he talked about the Lancaster. He lacked Adrian's polish and appeared less comfortable speaking to a crowd, but he had prepared well and related many interesting facts about the famous aircraft that he had meticulously jotted down. He told how the renowned bomber had evolved from the failed Manchester and provided key specifications such the power of her engines, her maximum altitude, speed and range. The girls looked bored, but the boys hung on his every word.

After Daddy finished, the gunners spoke about the Lancaster's armament. They teasingly insulted one another with half-rude expressions that delighted their juvenile audience and told stupid, often slightly off-colour jokes as adeptly as a professional comedy team. The children laughed uproariously, causing Miss Townsend to squirm and cast angry glances at Georgina and Kit. Kit tapped his watch, and the gunners took the hint, wrapping up their talk.

It would have been hard for anyone to follow this routine, but Stu fell particularly short. He seemed ill-prepared yet pompous. He rambled from one topic to another without ever really coming to a point. The laughter died away, replaced by increasing signs of boredom and lack of interest. The younger children started wriggling in their seats, whispering to one another and scuffling.

Miss Townsend abruptly stood, clapped her hands for attention, and announced that they would break up into groups by year, each regrouping in their respective classroom. The pilot and navigator would speak with the upper and lower sixth, the flight engineer with the fifth form, and so on. The assembly then dissolved.

Ten minutes later Terry shyly joined the assembled Third Form, and Georgina felt the wave of disappointment roll over her pupils. Because Miss Townsend had dispersed the assembly before he spoke, nobody knew what he did or why it was important. His bulky sergeant's uniform looked too big for him, while his slight stature, irregular face and dark-framed glasses robbed him of all glamour. Georgina overheard a boy ask whether the RAF was so 'hard up' that it had to take men who were half-blind.

Georgina glanced at Mr Willoughby. He thumped his cane vigorously and bellowed: "Silence! We have a visitor!" As a modicum of quiet spread, he turned to Georgina. "Miss Reddings? Would you like to make the introduction?"

Grateful for his intervention, Georgia hastened to the front of the classroom and turned to face the children. "Sergeant Tibble didn't get a chance to tell you about his trade in assembly, but before he does that, I want to share with you what his pilot told me: Wireless Operator Tibble saved the lives of the entire crew when the aircraft was very low on fuel after a long flight and their airfield was closed due to fog. They diverted to another station, only to find many aircraft already circling to land. Fortunately, Sergeant Tibble identified an airfield which could accommodate them and provided the weather information necessary for the pilot to fly there safely below the cloud. So never underestimate the importance of a wireless operator."

These words did the trick; interest in Terry increased — although Terry muttered as he passed Georgina on the way to the podium, "If the skipper said all that, he was lying."

In only a few humble sentences he explained his job before admitting, "And no, I can't see very well. That's why I wear these." He drew attention to his glasses. "But in my job, it's not your eyes that count — it's your ears." He pointed to his ears before adding, "And the hardest part is learning Morse Code. Do you know what Morse is?"

A general mumble suggested most of the pupils had at least heard of it. Terry turned to the blackboard and briskly wrote down the letters of the alphabet and their Morse equivalents. "Now listen!" he commanded as he drew a whistle out of his pocket. "Who can tell me what letter this is?" He blew three short and one long blasts. A dozen children raised their hands and several waved them wildly.

"Just shout out the letter to me," Terry told the children. Delighted, the children did. "That's right! It's V for Victory," Terry confirmed. Turning to Georgina, he asked "Do you want to try?" She declined. "What about you, sir?" Terry asked Mr Willoughby.

The former sergeant major took the whistle to blow S-O-S. Again, many pupils recognised it. "So," he asked, "what about this?" Excited shouts from the children correctly identified "BBC". With a stiff bow, Willoughby turned the whistle back over to Terry.

"Ready for whole words?" Terry asked, and the whole room responded in a loud, shouted affirmative. Georgina couldn't remember the children being so excited and involved in anything before.

To great and escalating enthusiasm, Terry blew: "England," followed by "Kirkby" and "Lincoln."

"Shall we do a whole phrase?" Terry asked them. Georgina and Willoughby exchanged a smile as the children shrilly demanded more.

Terry attempted "God save the King!" — but they guessed the phrase after the first two words, so Terry announced he'd do something more difficult. Before he could finish, the bell rang. Their time was up.

Some of the girls slipped out of the door at once to enjoy their usual Saturday activities, but the boys and many of the other girls crowded around Terry, jumping up and down and scuffling with one another in their eagerness to ask him questions. How many words per minute could he transmit? And receive? How long did it take to learn? Could he read Morse flashed on Aldiss lamps? Who was better at Morse, the RAF or the Navy?

Delighted by the success of the talk, Georgina watched the children clustered around Terry for several minutes before she noticed, to her astonishment, that her problem pupil Battie was at the blackboard trying to write down the Morse letters in her class notebook. She stood no more than a foot from the board, yet still she seemed to have to go on tiptoe and squint to decipher the letters at the top of the board.

As though struck by lightning, Georgina grasped that Battie was practically blind! That was the reason she took no interest in class. Almost everything was written on the blackboard, and if Battie couldn't *see* the instructions or the exercises, never mind the answers, no wonder she couldn't learn! Georgina hastened over to the girl. "Battie?"

The girl jumped away from the board and held her notebook behind her back, as if she'd done something wrong. With her eyes directed at the floor, she muttered a sullen, "Miss."

"Battie? Do you need to get this close to the blackboard to read what is written on it?" Georgina wanted to be sure she had not jumped to false conclusions.

Battie squirmed in discomfort and, as usual, said nothing. She just stared at her feet, but tears started to run down her face.

Unexpectedly, Terry appeared beside Battie and handed her his glasses. "Have a look through these, Sunshine," he offered.

Battie looked up at the wireless operator in awe. "Can I, sir?"

"You don't have to call me 'sir,' Sunshine." Terry answered with a smile. "I'm not an officer. Call me Sarge, or Terry if you like. Come on! Try me specs." He held them out to her again.

Very, very gently she took them from him, hesitantly turned them around, and solemnly placed them onto her nose. They were too big for her, so Terry adjusted them a little by bending the frames behind her ears. Finally, she looked solemnly up at the blackboard and her face lit up with a smile from ear to ear. "I can see it all! Even the top line!"

Battie started reading off the letters and the Morse equivalent, giggling with delight.

"Georgina! Aren't you ready to go yet?" Kit burst through the door.

Georgina understood Kit's impatience. His leave lasted a mere 72 hours and he'd already sacrificed a morning to be at her school. She told him to go on ahead to the car and give her just one more minute. Then she turned back to Battie with a promise that they would talk first thing on Monday morning. She nodded, her eyes still wide with wonder behind the thick lenses. Flashing a smile of pure gratitude at Tibble, Georgina hurried to fetch her things before Kit got upset.

Outside, she discovered that Adrian had also driven over in his car and was saying goodbye to Fiona — awkwardly, Georgina thought. He seemed at pains to explain why he had to go down to London and could not meet up with her. Two of the Sixth Form girls, on the other hand, were jammed in the back seat with the gunners. From what was being said, Adrian planned to drop them in Boston on his way to London. Fast work, Georgina thought, somewhat surprised that the Sixth Form Master had allowed the girls to go. Nigel and Frank were both nice young men who could be trusted not to do anything the girls didn't want, but Georgina rather suspected that the girls might well want things Miss Townsend wouldn't approve of. She reminded herself it was not her concern.

Instead, she thanked Adrian, Nigel and Frank for coming to the school. All assured her it had been fun, and then waved good-bye. Meanwhile, Daddy and Stu climbed in the back of Kit's car. Kit took her overnight case and put it in the boot, while she sat herself in front. "Where's Terry?" Kit asked impatiently. Daddy and Stu each had trains to catch from Lincoln and were in a hurry. Fortunately, Terry appeared at a run, holding his cap, and clambered in beside his crewmates. Kit turned the key in the ignition, gunned the engine, and put it into gear.

As they crunched over the gravel drive, Georgina twisted around to thank the three men in the back, and especially Terry. "I've had such a time with Battie! She never said a word about not being able to see. I feel a perfect fool for not thinking of it myself. Thank you so much for what you did! You even made her giggle. I've never seen her so happy."

"Her mum's been telling her she is worthless practically since the day she was born," Terry informed her indignantly. "The name 'Battie' comes from bat, as in 'blind as a bat.' She hates it. Her real name's Nora."

"Poor thing! I'll never to call her Battie again," Georgina promised, "And I must see about getting her eyes tested for a proper prescription, even if I have to pay for it myself!" She hoped it wouldn't be too expensive. She only earned pennies as an apprentice teacher. "I don't understand why her parents didn't get her glasses."

"Because her mother didn't want to 'waste' the money on her, that's why!" Terry explained smouldering with anger. "Dumped her on the first train out of London too, right after the start of the war. She was evacuated in September '39, and she hasn't seen anyone from her family since. Five blo — excuse me — ruddy years of war, and her Mum couldn't be bothered coming to visit her once!"

"What about her Dad?" Daddy asked scowling. He had two little girls of his own.

"POW somewhere in the Far East. Said they'd had exactly two postcards from him in the last three years."

"I don't understand why nobody said anything to me!" Georgina protested, horrified and distressed — with herself. Why hadn't she made a greater effort to find out more about Battie's — Nora's! — background and condition? When her initial efforts to get the girl to talk had failed, she'd just callously given up. She'd had so many other things to do, and other pupils to think about. She'd allowed the assessment of others to guide her. "I'm going to see she gets to an eye doctor next week. If I can't afford it, I'm sure my father will lend me the money."

"How much does an eye test cost?" Daddy asked, looking over at Terry.

"I can't remember. I haven't had to pay for one since I signed up."

"Two or three pounds, I should think," Georgina replied absently as she planned what she'd say to her father.

"Well, if we all drank one round less every night and put the savings in a piggy bank, we could collect that in a week or two," Daddy suggested.

"That's a good idea," Kit agreed. "Nigel and Frank are generous lads, and I know Adrian will agree. What about you, Stu?" The bomb aimer hesitated a second but then mumbled his consent.

"You're marvellous!" Georgina announced enthusiastically, deciding that she was in love with Kit's entire crew.

Georgina had asked for and received a day off work but finding somewhere to stay for their two days together had proved challenging. So many of the larger, more comfortable hotels had been taken over by the military or government for a variety of purposes — just like the mansion turned hotel which now served as the officers' mess at Woodhall Spa. As a result, the demand for comfortable hotels far exceeded the supply and that meant the price of most nice hotels were beyond Kit's means. Yet neither of them wanted to end up in some tawdry seaside boarding house where they would be treated like dirt, either. They could have gone down to London where affordable hotels were in greater supply, but they both wanted more peace and quiet than could be found in the capital. After considerable effort, Georgina had found a country hotel in the Lake District that had a vacancy. It was perfect, not too far away, but situated in beautiful countryside surrounded by hiking trails.

Georgina had booked one double room for two nights for Flying Officer and Mrs Moran. She put Don's engagement ring back on her finger and turned Kit's engagement ring around so only the gold band showed. Nevertheless, during the drive, they prepared for questions about their marriage.

They agreed that they had been wed on the 2 January 1945 at St. Andrews Church in Foster Clough by the Rev. Edwin Reddings. Their witnesses had been Kathleen Hart and Adrian Peal. It had been a very small wedding. Kit's family was in Africa, after all, and Georgina's brother in the Far East, so the only family present had been Georgina's parents and her three maiden aunts Anna, Emma and Lucy. "You really must meet them one of these days," Georgina commented. "Anna and Emma can be terribly amusing once you get past their forbidding exteriors."

The other guests, Georgina decided, had been a couple of her friends from the teaching college, and Kit's crew.

"And don't forget Reggie and Toby," Kit added before asking, "Did we invite Fiona?"

"No, we considered it, but decided it would be awkward. Then to our surprise, she showed up as Adrian's guest."

"Yes, he did seem rather more interested in Fiona than I had expected," Kit answered reflecting on what he had just seen at Kirkby Grange.

"I've never seen Fiona so keen on anyone before," Georgina replied. "She looked positively dejected when he said he was going to London and couldn't see her."

"If you have the chance, you should warn her that he's already engaged."

"Adrian?" Georgina gasped. Over the last fortnight, Adrian had come to Kirkby with Kit on a number of occasions and appeared to pay court to Fiona. He'd even taken her to the flicks once. Fiona had indicated she thought the relationship might "go somewhere."

"I'm not sure it's an engagement that will last," Kit conceded, "but Adrian's currently committed to a young lady named Julia. Now where were we? Tell me what you wore." He smiled over at her.

"For the wedding ceremony or the wedding night?"

Kit burst out laughing. Once he'd got a grip on himself, he asked with a sidelong grin, "I hope, Miss Vicar's Daughter, that you did not choose something too puritanical for the wedding night?"

"Well, no, not exactly puritanical, but I didn't want the tarty look either. I opted for what I call transparent elegance. Did that work for you, Flying Officer?"

"It sounds..." He glanced at her and they dissolved into giggles. Sobering but still smiling, Kit concluded, "enchanting. I do hope you are still in possession of that particular piece of attire?"

"Indeed, and it's in the boot. And you?" Georgina asked. "What did you wear?

"My bunny suit, of course."

"*Bunny* suit?" She asked puzzled. She'd expected "birthday suit."

"The long underwear we wear when flying. You know: all one piece and zips up the front. All that's missing are the long, floppy ears."

"Just what I always wanted!" Georgina exclaimed clapping her hands. "To sleep with the Easter Bunny!"

By the time they arrived at the hotel as dusk settled down upon the hills, they had invented a number of comic incidents that had enlivened their wedding. They were also a little slaphappy, and so, somewhat disappointed when they were received as Mr and Mrs Moran with warm smiles and no questions at all.

The anti-climax of not having to defend their fictional marital status was almost immediately dispelled by the magnificent room to which they were led. It was tastefully furnished in dark wood with plush carpets, solid furniture, and weighty curtains. It had an en-suite bathroom, a bay window offering views down to Derwent Water, and a large double bed under a canopy.

The door had barely clicked shut before their eyes met. Georgina couldn't contain a giggle, but then she lifted her arms and clasped her hands behind Kit's neck demanding a kiss.

"Don't you need to get changed for dinner, Mrs Moran?" he asked between kisses.

"If you'd be so kind as to help me *out* of my traveling clothes, Mr Moran...."

Kit slipped the remaining five French letters into the drawer of the bedside table. Since that first night in Stratford, he had always used them. Georgina wanted children, but neither of them wanted to risk a pregnancy before she'd completed her training and the war was over. When he'd purchased the special half-a-dozen packet, he'd thought it was rather optimistic for just two nights together. Maybe not, after all.

Georgina selected the stunning blue evening gown he had seen her wear at Ashcroft Park almost two years ago and they lingered over drinks and dinner, savouring every moment. By ten o'clock, however, bed beckoned — again — and they retreated to their room. After they'd changed out of their clothes, Kit turned off the lights and opened the black-out blinds to let the moonlight flood in. The hills and trees stood out sharply as silhouettes against a luminous sky, and the lawn lay silvery at their feet. The vista cast a spell of enchantment that intensified their feelings. Magical, too, was knowing there was no need to rush or slink away to avoid discovery. They could sleep in each other's arms the entire night.

Georgina fell asleep only partially covered by bedclothes and Kit lay on his side propped up on his elbow gazing at her. He didn't want to go to sleep. If he did seven or eight hours of his seventy-two would be eradicated in an instant. He wanted to savour every minute he had with Georgina. Yet he couldn't keep sleep at bay forever; he was simply too tired.

They hiked most of the following day. Stopping for lunch and tea but returning to the hotel for an evening meal. They drank a little too much wine with dinner and were tipsy when they went to bed. A heavy blanket of cloud hid the moon this night, and the impending return to their day-to-day lives cast its own shadow. Their lovemaking took on an almost desperate – and vaguely unsatisfying – quality.

They slept late on Monday morning, had a leisurely breakfast and checked out at 11 am. They tried to be cheerful on the drive back, but the silliness that had uplifted them on the outward journey could not be re-conjured. The closer they got to Lincoln, the quieter they became. They stopped for dinner but could not stretch their time together past 9 o'clock, when Kit dropped off Georgina at Mrs Radford's house. They said good-bye with a short kiss. By 9:30 Kit was back at the officers' mess at Woodhall Spa.

As he passed the notice board at the foot of the stairs, he saw that thirteen crews were slated to fly an op the following day. Moran's was the thirteenth name on the list.

Chapter 22
Chariots of Fire

Woodhall Spa
27 February 1945

A gentle knock announced the batman before he entered, balancing a tray with two steaming cups of tea. "Morning, sirs!" He greeted the officers lying in bed on either side of the room. "Time to get up."

Kit turned over, his pyjama top twisting on his thin frame, and sat up with a sleepy, "Morning, Blake."

"Did you have a pleasant leave, sir?"

"I did, thank you." He reached out and took one of the mugs.

"And you, sir?" Blake directed his remarks to Adrian, who lay on his belly and answered only with a groan followed by the opening of one eye. Adrian had arranged to swap places with Kit's old roommate. It made sense for officers from the same crew to room together as they flew at the same times and had the same wake-up calls.

"What time is it?" Adrian asked in a raw voice.

"Five-thirty, sir. The Ops Briefing is scheduled for 7:00 am." Leaving Adrian's tea on the bedside table, the batman withdrew to go and wake up other crews slated to fly today.

Kit looked over at Adrian. "When did you get in last night? It must have been well after midnight."

Adrian turned over and sat up with another groan. He held his head in his hands. "I was back here by eleven or so, but there was a terrific do down in the bar, so I joined in. I don't want to seem stand-offish, you know," he justified himself. "Thought it might help my reputation to be a bit more sociable."

Kit understood perfectly. Precisely because Adrian was by nature sensitive and thoughtful, he had learned early on that he could survive best by hiding in the pack. "We stacked up the furniture so Forrester could leave his footprints on the ceiling in green jelly. Then, of course, someone suggested he had to be debagged too. That led to quite a lively free-for-all during which half of us lost our trousers and a lot of glasses got broken as

317

well. How you slept through it all is beyond me."

"I did hear something but decided not to investigate. Not my kind of thing," Kit admitted, throwing the covers back and going to the wash basin to brush his teeth and shave.

"Did things go well with Georgina?" Adrian asked, yawning.

"Yes, we had a lovely time together. What about you? Are your parents well?"

"I didn't go home. I couldn't face my father. He has a sixth sense for sniffing out lies. That's what makes him such an effective barrister. If I'd told him ops were a piece of cake, he'd have cross-examined me until I broke down. I met up with Julia instead."

"Then you certainly had a good time," Kit concluded with a short laugh, scraping the razor along his chin.

"Not really," Adrian replied with a sigh. "She — I don't know — she wants me to be the glamour and excitement in her life. She's bored, she says, which I can understand. Working in the canteen of an armaments factory certainly isn't my idea of fun. Still," he sighed again, "you see, she thinks that she paid up-front, and now I *owe* her stays in fancy hotels, dinners at posh restaurants and lavish gifts... All that costs a lot of money, which I don't have. I mean, I can't ask my parents for the money, or I'd have to explain about Julia, but on Pilot Officer's pay... I'm broke, Kit. Broke and exhausted." Adrian sounded both — and depressed as well.

Kit twisted around to look at him with concern. Much as he sympathised, foremost in his mind this morning was that they were flying. He needed a navigator who was fit and focused. He refrained from comment, however, and turned back to rinse his chin clean in cold water. Drying his face with a towel, he stepped back from the basin and remarked. "Maybe Fiona would be better for you after all. She's not so demanding."

"I thought about her more than once these past three days," Adrian admitted. "I think I'll ring her next time we're stood down."

Kit took his battle dress from the wardrobe and checked the pockets to be sure there was nothing in them that might be of use to German intelligence — just in case they had to bail out. He removed some coins and a letter from his father but left the stuffed baby Zebra "Zach" in the lower right pocket. Zach had brought them luck so far; now was no time to remove him.

Just after quarter past six, they joined a stream of other aircrew making their way down to the dining room. The smell of frying bacon and roasting coffee seeped up the stairs in the opposite direction. After the hearty "ops breakfast," they climbed aboard one of the crew buses that were lined up on the gravel drive in front of the officer's mess. It dropped them at the brick building housing the operations and briefing rooms. Scores of sergeants likewise converged on the building, most riding on bicycles that they stowed in the racks standing out front. The two groups intermingled as they clomped up the stairs to the briefing room in a disorganised mob. All wore shiny whistles dangling from the collars of their battle dress tunics that swayed as they mounted the stairs. Inside, they spread out to sit at rows of wooden tables.

Although seats were not assigned, all the pilots occupied habitual spots. This being Moran's sixth operational briefing as skipper, he already had his "usual" place: the far-right end of the second table. Navigators, bomb aimers and flight engineers sat with their captains. Peal sat immediately to Moran's left, MacDonald and Babcock further along. There was a separate briefing for wireless operators and gunners.

Punctually at 0700, the adjutant called for attention, and the assembled crews got to their feet as the base, station, and squadron commanders entered. The station commander opened with a welcome and some general information. Then Fauquier took over and, after signalling that the crews could smoke, asked the adjutant to open the curtain that covered the map behind the briefing platform.

On the map a line of yarn stretched to the point where Germany, France and Switzerland met. Here the track split into two before converging and then returning to the UK on a course parallel to the outward journey. Moran leaned forward to try to see the target better. It couldn't be a rocket launch site that far away, and the nearest city was Basel in neutral Switzerland — not a likely target. It didn't make any sense. He noted the same perplexity all around him.

Fauquier let them speculate for a moment longer before opening his remarks with the astonishing announcement: "The US army is preparing to cross the Rhine. They expect to have a bridgehead on the east bank by the end of this month." His pointer tapped the map near a pin marking the position of the Ninth Army on the west bank of the Rhine. "It is imperative that their pontoon bridges not be washed away by abrupt flooding. The Germans therefore have every reason to trigger such floods, and the capability to do so by opening the Kembs Barrage located here," his pointer tapped their target. "We have been ordered to carry out a pre-emptive strike against the barrage. Thereafter, the Americans can advance without risk to their pontoons, regardless of the exact date for their crossing."

A rustle of movement greeted this announcement. Not only did this now make sense, but it was also exciting to think that the Allies were on the brink of crossing the Rhine.

"We will be using Tallboys and will attack in two groups. Seven Lancasters flown by Fawke, Philpott, Iveson, Sayers, Gingles, Watts and Castagnola will fly directly to the target, approaching from the West, and will bomb from 6,000 feet with bombs set to detonate on impact. The remaining six aircraft, Forrester, Howard, Moran, Cockshott, and Sanders led by myself, will fly the dogleg shown here," he pointed to the strings marking their planned route, "using Tallboys set with 30 minute delay fuses. We will bomb from 600 feet."

Moran's heart missed a beat. That was madness! It was sheer suicide! At six hundred feet they would be too high to slip unseen below German radar or blend in with the surrounding landscape, yet they'd be so low that the German gunners would have a hard time missing them. Jerry would have a field day.

What "genius" had come up with these orders, and why? It couldn't be Fauquier since he had to lead them in — and looked decidedly grim. So, who then? Moran glanced toward the station commander but knew that he too was just taking orders. They could only have come from Butch Harris himself. Moran's stomach started cramping up. The same Harris who had sent Don's crew and all the others to Berlin night after night regardless of the losses, regardless of the fact that they were only hardening German resolve...

Fauquier continued. "Three USAAF Mustang squadrons will fly escort." That sounded nice, but they couldn't take out the flak, Kit thought. "And, as you can see, our flight takes us over Allied-controlled territory all the way to and from the target. The only serious risk is over the target itself, which is heavily defended by flak. Note that if you overshoot the target you will end up in the balloon barrage over Basel — that's in Switzerland, for any of you who may be in doubt. Don't worry too much about flying through Swiss air space, but don't shoot anything while you're there — either aircraft or balloon. Now, please proceed to your aircraft to conduct test flights, but report back here again at 1100 for the final briefing. We will have an update on the weather at that time."

Fauquier started to walk away but stopped himself and turned back. The crews froze, arrested in motion. "I just wanted to add that we're honoured to have Mr Barnes Wallis joining us today. He'll be in the ops room while you're in the air, anxiously awaiting your reports on the success of the operation. Now, go and get those test flights out of the way."

With a scraping of chairs and the low rumble of muttering, they started to disperse. Peal rolled up the map on which he'd marked the various courses and turning points, while Babcock stuffed his notes about target indicators into his breast pocket. Neither man seemed particularly worried. Didn't they understand?

Moran looked for the other pilots assigned the low-level run. Surely, they must share his sense of doom? Or was it just him? Forrester joked loudly with his crew, apparently in good spirits, but then Moran's eyes fleetingly met those of Kit Howard. His expression was one of calm resignation. Damn! And Squadron Leader Cockshott? Their eyes also met, and the senior pilot smiled faintly — like death warmed over. No, Moran realised, he wasn't hallucinating. This was it. His stomach turned over.

Peal started to sense something was wrong and turned a questioning look toward his skipper. Moran pretended to reset his watch to the time shown on the briefing room clock. Inwardly, he struggled to suppress the cries of protest, to silence the voice that pleaded for life, for Georgina. Only when he had himself firmly under control did he met Peal's and Babcock's eyes and cheerfully suggest, "Let's go and see how Zebra's feeling this morning."

They joined up with the others in the crew room and together collected Mae Wests and parachutes. They reached the exit just as the crew bus pulled away. Annoyed, Moran looked around for another and instead caught sight of a white-haired civilian with thick glasses standing forlornly a few feet away. He recognised the famous engineer Barnes Wallis instantly. After only a moment's hesitation, he approached him. "Mr. Wallis?"

The older man spun about with an embarrassed smile. "Yes, yes. That's me." He held out his hand.

Moran took it, automatically introducing himself, "Moran. Flying Officer Kit Moran. It's an honour to meet you, sir."

"Likewise, young man. I can't tell you how much I admire what you do — all of you."

Moran shrugged and brushed off the words and what they implied. "Just doing what we've been trained to do, sir. Your bombs, on the other hand; they're amazing. I always wanted to be an engineer, but I thought in terms of ordinary things — bridges and aqueducts and whatnot."

"Oh well, we all start like that, you know." Wallis replied humbly. "I think I first wanted to become an engineer to make a better outboard motor for the family sailing boat." He laughed at the memory, and then looked seriously at Kit. "When you say you wanted to be an engineer, do you mean professionally?"

"Yes, only my parents couldn't afford university, so I started an apprenticeship at sixteen. Then the war came along."

"Nothing wrong with an apprenticeship. That's how I learnt the trade, and at the same age." Wallis assured him with an almost fatherly smile.

"You mean you haven't got a degree in engineering, sir?" Moran had always assumed that someone as successful as Wallis must have benefited from the best possible education.

"I have now, but I didn't get it until twenty years after I left school. I obtained it via an external programme with Imperial College, what's more. I won't pretend the degree wasn't useful, but those twenty years of practical experience were invaluable."

"If you don't mind my asking, sir, whatever inspired you to start developing bouncing bombs?"

"Oh, well, that's rather a long story. Let's just say the prospect of another drawn-out slaughter like the last war horrified me. I racked my poor brain for ways to shorten this war and concluded that crippling Germany's industry would be more effective than trying to crack the Wehrmacht. Yet our aircraft and bombs lacked the capacity to do much damage." He interrupted himself to ask, "Did you realise the explosive power of a bomb is proportional to the cube of the weight of the charge it carries?"

"I don't think so, no," Moran admitted, smiling faintly. He found it hard to resist Wallis' enthusiasm for the topic.

"Well, when I learnt that, I knew we had to develop bigger bombs and bigger aircraft to carry them, of course. Yet even the biggest bomb in the world still had to be dropped where it could do the most damage. I concluded that to win, we needed to focus on targets that leverage the impact of bombs. The Ruhr dams promised terrific secondary damage through the flash floods and a subsequent loss electric power across the whole region. The problem was that water protects dams from the impact of even very near misses. The odds of dropping a bomb vertically right up against the base of the dam wall, where we needed them, were miniscule. That's the reason I had to devise a means for the explosives to reach and then hug the walls before detonating *under* water—"

Abruptly, Wallis cut himself off. "There I go again. Getting all wrapped up in the science of it. I tend to do that — get so excited by the prospects of some idea that I – I lose sight of the human risks and costs. I tested the concept of the bouncing bombs on paper, in tanks, with scale models dropped from Wellingtons, and finally using prototypes dropped from Lancasters — but always here, in England and in broad daylight without anyone shooting at me."

He paused and looked hard at Moran. "Just a few days before the raid on the dams, I asked Wing Commander Gibson if he could drop the bombs at 60 feet rather than 150 — just to make them work better. He said 'yes,' but he didn't breathe a word about it being more difficult or more dangerous. He didn't say it would put him and his men at risk of flying into high tension wires. He didn't say anything except, 'yes, we can do it.'" Wallis fell silent, his eyes turned inward, and his expression clouded with sorrow.

Moran caught his breath as understanding dawned. "Do you calculate a specific altitude for each individual target?"

"Well, no, not all, but certainly for complex ones like the dams or today's target. As a rule, for targets built on bedrock — factories, marshalling yards, rocket sites, and the like — eighteen thousand feet is the optimal height for the Tallboy, but that doesn't work as well for dams. The Kembs Barrage, for example, is little more than eight massive pillars standing two stories high, with air and water flowing all around them. Air and water transfer pressure differently from rock. According to my calculations 600 feet is the optimal altitude for attacking it, and 6,000 feet is the second-best height."

"I see," Moran commented, relieved that there was a rational explanation for the seemingly mad orders. He felt better this way than believing they were being sacrificed to an arbitrary whim.

"Is something wrong?" Wallis asked anxiously.

"No," Moran lied.

Moran kept his face immobile as the older man studied him with concern. "Tell me," Wallis said finally, "Are you planning to continue your engineering career after the war?"

"Theoretically."

"Why only theoretically?" Wallis sounded baffled.

"Well, because I can't think about engineering unless I survive the war," Moran explained, trying not to sound bitter or angry.

"Oh, but I'm sure the war will be over soon. Then, if you're interested, I'd be happy to help you get back into engineering," Wallis offered with every appearance of sincerity.

Don't do this to me, Kit thought. Don't paint a picture of a future I won't live to enjoy. He forced himself to answer politely, "That's very kind, but, as I said, there's really no point talking about it just now."

Wallis understood. Nodding solemnly, he said, "Do you think you are going to see the end of the war. Is that it?"

"Let's just say the odds are against it. We aircrew tend to take life one sortie at a time. But thank you for the offer and for taking the time to chat with me." Moran held out his hand to indicate the conversation was over. Although Wallis shook it vigorously and warmly, distress, almost horror, suffused his face — as if he were shaking hands with a dead man already, Kit thought.

A hundred feet away, the crew bus stopped and the WAAF driver called her apologies out of the door. Dragging their parachutes behind them, Moran's crew stepped up into the bus one after another while Moran hastened to join them. Just before he climbed aboard, however, he paused to wave good-bye to Wallis.

At the end of the test flight, when Moran announced it was time to return to Woodhall Spa, Peal countered by asking if they shouldn't say hello to Kirkby Grange first.

Moran couldn't get a word out for the enthusiastic responses of the others. He turned on the course Peal give him, and at the sight of the school, pushed the controls forwards. He took Zebra down to 50 feet and they belted over the school grounds at 130 miles an hour. Moran imagined he could see white faces pressed to the window and excited bouncing up and down as they swept past. Georgina would think he was saying "hello" not "good-bye." Yet as he pulled the control column back to climb steeply away and banked for Woodhall Spa he wished her a last farewell.

The second briefing for pilots and navigators started at 1100. In addition to the weather, the pilots were briefed on fuel loads, take-off times, aircraft spacing and so on. The total distance was close to 1,500 miles and they would be flying for nearly eight hours. Fauquier explained that the low-level bombing would to be carried out in pairs; Fauquier would lead in with Forrester on his wing, followed by Howard and Moran, and finally Cockshott and Sanders. The latter were only to bomb if the barrage was still standing.

While the separate briefing for gunners and wireless operators took place, Moran found a notepad and a pen in the ops room. He sat down to dash off a letter to Georgina.

Dearest Georgina,

If you are reading this, it is because I failed to return from today's sortie. Words cannot express how much you mean to me or how much you have sweetened my last days on earth. Please don't grieve too long or too hard. I don't want you to be miserable, least of all on my account. Please fall in love again and make another young man as happy as you have made me. Both Don and I will rejoice in your happiness. I only ask that now and again you wear the elephant earrings in remembrance of me.

All my love, Kit

Maybe that wasn't very good, but he didn't have time to rewrite it. He should have had the foresight to write something before this. He should have taken the time to draft something beautiful and elegant, full of profound sentiments, a letter Georgina could have treasured for the rest of her life. But he'd missed the opportunity for that, and this note would have to do. Moran hurried to the squadron adjutant's office and asked for an envelope, explaining, "I want to be sure Miss Reddings gets this letter along with the telegram, if I don't return."

"Good heavens, Moran! Don't tell me you've had some sort of premonition?" The adjutant sounded concerned. Too many men who had premonitions didn't come back.

"No," Moran denied it, "but flying at 600 feet into heavy flak isn't a formula for long life."

"I'm sure the CO wouldn't have agreed to it if there was no hope."

"Of course not," Moran concurred, but still he addressed the envelope, slipped his note inside, and left it on the adjutant's desk.

The final wait before starting engines always tested a man's nerves. Security dictated that once the briefings were over, aircrew must remain on close standby and not communicate with the outside world. Dropped off at their aircraft well before the time to start engines, they could do little except smoke a last cigarette. The skipper and flight engineer might talk to the ground crew, but the others generally turned inward. No one spoke much, keeping their thoughts and fears to themselves.

Moran went through Form 700 with Pete Bishop, nodding at his comments, and then signed off, taking responsibility for the aircraft. He shook hands with Bishop and thanked him for the good work he and his crew did. The gesture made Bishop start and give Moran a second look, but the pilot had already turned away. Moran gazed up at the Lancaster looming over him, at the Zebra depicted stretching out her neck and lifting her front hooves as she leaped skywards. He wished he'd taken a photograph of the aircraft with the whole crew posing in front. That would have been a wonderful memento to leave with Georgina. She could have made a copy and given it to Kirkby Grange School as a reminder of their visit.

Moran peered under Zebra's nose toward the Lancaster at the next hardstanding. Squadron Leader Howard was gently herding his crew up the ladder into B-Baker. Moran took a last drag on his cigarette and

325

discarded the butt, grinding out the ember in the damp grass. At least the weather was good and the temperature starting to climb. Discreetly, he slipped his hand into his pocket to feel for Zach, before calling to his crew to "mount up."

Fauquier took off at 13:07, followed at two-minute intervals by the rest of the squadron. Peal recorded in the log that Z-Zebra took off at 13:13.

They picked up their American fighter escort over Manston in bright clear skies. Rather than being comforted, Moran found the presence of these single-engine fighters around them disquietingly abnormal. The Luftwaffe and RAF both painted their fighters in camouflage, but the USAAF did not, so the fighters gleamed and glinted in the early afternoon sun. That hardly seemed appropriate "attire" for a deadly attack on a bitter enemy. Likewise, flying over the continent of Europe without fear of enemy action felt eerily unreal.

Icing conditions were reported at 5,000 feet and above, so 617 flew inland at just 2,000 feet. Below them, Belgium lay flat and grey in dirty snow. Over the Ardennes, they identified the wreckage of tanks and trucks, fresh graves and large craters made by bombs and artillery. Beyond, US army convoys moved along the roads, and columns of infantry slogged along, their rifles slung over their shoulders. Farther south, the snow gave way to brown grass. Livestock grazed in paddocks. Children played in school playgrounds. Women hung out the washing on lines. Everywhere, the people on the ground looked up as the Lancasters roared overhead, wary of what these black, low-flying warplanes presaged.

Peal's navigating appeared spot on. At regular intervals, he fixed their position and informed Moran of the time and course to the next turning point. Moran acknowledged but flying in daylight made it easy to maintain his position just by slotting in beside Howard, who followed Fauquier and Forrester. Behind them Cockshott and Sanders likewise held loose formation, while the rest of the squadron aircraft streamed out behind.

Gradually, cloud started to move in, and they climbed to four thousand feet to get above it. As the face of the earth grew fainter below them, Moran nursed hopes that the operation would be scratched.

Twenty minutes before "zero hour," the formation split into two. The seven Lancasters making the high-level attack, escorted by one Mustang squadron, started rising towards their 6,000 feet bombing altitude. Meanwhile, Fauquier led the low-level group on the dogleg, accompanied by the other two Mustang squadrons. Cloud completely hid the earth below them now. If they couldn't see the target, surely they would have to scrub the raid, Moran reasoned.

Tibble reported that Fauquier had asked the Mustang leader to test the cloud base. Shortly afterward, he passed on the information that it was at 1,500 feet and the target clearly visible below. Moran's last hope that the operation would be aborted evaporated.

At Fauquier's order to descend below the cloud, Moran drew a deep breath and obeyed. As predicted, they broke into the clear at just under 1,500 feet and continued down to 600 feet. In the distance, the bellies of the barrage balloons hung below the cloud. Although invisible at this range, each one was secured to the earth by a steel cable that could shear the wing off an aircraft. Just ahead of them, the target stretched across the Rhine. It consisted of two levels, each supported by massive stone piers. Columns of dust and smoke already surrounded it, the work of the Tallboys dropped by the high-level flight.

Just when Moran was beginning to wonder if the Germans had been caught sleeping, all hell broke loose. Flak blew up across the sky ahead of him, turning it dark brown and dirty grey. Fauquier's and Forrester's aircraft visibly started bouncing and recoiling in response to the pressure waves but continued flying into the murk.

Abruptly, a sheet of flame shot up from Q-Queen's port wing, and Kit heard Roper report, "Forrester's hit."

Despite the spreading fire, Forrester kept his aircraft pointed at the target. Fauquier released his bomb and started to climb away, but by now an inferno engulfed Q-Queen's fuselage. Still the Australian pilot held course. Seconds later his bomb dropped away to fall into the Rhine in front of the barrage. Its load shed, Q-Queen rose enough to scrape over the girders of the massive dam's upper level. Forrester appeared to be trying to ditch in the river beyond, but a wingtip hit a high-tension wire. Instantly the kite went into a flat spin. It smacked down onto the bank of the Rhine. For a second nothing it lay there completely still as if time had stopped. Then it exploded with a loud boom and smoke billowed into the air.

"Curtains." Roper summarised grimly.

Moran knew that every detail of Forrester's crash was etched into his memory. He would relive these moments in the future — if he had one. Now, he could spare it only the periphery of his mind. He concentrated on flying Zebra, and it took all his strength to hold her two hundred feet behind and to the left of Howard, while they ran the gauntlet of flak toward the target. Although he managed to hold course, he could not hold Zebra steady no matter what he did. The slipstream of the others combined with the flak flung Zebra this way and that.

Babcock shouted over the intercom, "Bomb aimer to pilot: I can't fix on the target the way you're flying!" The exasperation in his voice was tangible. Moran could sympathise — he just couldn't fly any better.

Over the radio he heard faintly Howard telling Fauquier he was going around again. Clicking on his own radio, Moran called, "Hang on! We're come with you."

Howard's Lancaster banked away so hard it stood silhouetted against the white sky.

Moran kicked Zebra's rudder and tried to keep up with it. He could only hope that the sudden change of direction would surprise and confuse the flak gunners.

For an endless moment, they seemed to hang in the air, their belly exposed to the full fury of the guns. Moran awaited the crack and distinctive shudder that would indicate the flak had found them. It didn't come. Maybe the German gunners had shifted their attention to Cockshott and Sanders. The last two aircraft in the low-level attack had dropped out of the cloud and were hurtling toward the target.

Meanwhile, Moran followed Howard as they continued banking around back to the start of the bomb run. Moran kept the target in sight as they turned. Although both Cockshott and Sanders successfully released their bombs, the Tallboys fell wide. The Kembs Barrage still stood defiantly. Of course, their bombs were time-fused to go off after 30 minutes, so it might yet come down....

Howard dropped his starboard wing to fly straight and level again. Heaps of debris from the high-level attack lay in jumbled chaos at both ends of the dam. Smoke and dust smeared the air, adding to the smog created by the flak. To avoid Howard's slipstream, Moran fell farther behind him, and eased out more to the left. Although Mustangs darted around them, firing at the flak batteries in an attempt to distract the gunners, the Germans took no interest in the decoys. The flak concentrated relentlessly on the two approaching Lancasters. Moran saw no way a 37,000 lb aircraft could penetrate the wall of anti-aircraft fire ahead of them intact. He only hoped that they would die as fast or faster than Forrester had.

Ahead of him Howard's starboard fuel tanks erupted into flames, and he banked hard as cannon fire continued to hammer into his Lancaster. The fire rapidly engulfed the entire fuselage. When it reached the port fuel tanks, they burst apart scattering debris from the port wing, some of which clattered against Zebra. What remained of Howard's aircraft arched through the afternoon sky. Streaming smoke, it smashed down into the tall trees of a wood to explode with an enormous boom. The pressure waves shook Z-Zebra, and a split-second later Osgood and Roper started firing furiously and pointlessly at the flak batteries. The Lancaster shuddered as if in the grip of an earthquake, yet through it all Babcock's voice came over the intercom controlled and clear: "Steady! Skipper! Steady! We're almost there!"

A Mustang flew directly under them, making Moran flinch. He fought the urge to take evasive action. Then unbelievably, they bounced upwards as Babcock confirmed, "Bomb gone!"

Almost in the same instant, with a horrible whack, something hit Zebra's tail, knocking her upwards and sideways. Struggling to regain control, Moran stepped on the rudder pedal and his foot hit the floor without resistance or response. He had no rudder control. He throttled forward in panic, but now, unable to turn, he plunged straight into the Basel balloon barrage. The phalanx of silver monsters hung coquettishly half in and half out of the clouds, their deadly wire tethers all but invisible. Frantically, Moran rolled to slip between the balloons, sliding and skidding without rudder.

"Shall I try to shoot them out of the way?" Frank suggested over the intercom.

"No! They're Swiss!" Moran reminded him, ducking instinctively as he tried to dodge the next two by flipping vertical and slicing between them.

Moran never knew how they managed to come out the other side without being snagged and stopped. They simply burst out beyond the last balloon and found themselves belting over the red-topped roofs of Basel. Startled Swiss citizens looked up at them in amazement.

His heart still palpitating, Moran pulled the column back to start gaining altitude while banking away from Germany as hard as he dared to turn without rudder control. Gradually, Moran became aware that he was drenched in sweat and his hands were shaking, but the flak and the balloons were behind them. If he could nurse the aircraft back toward France, theoretically at least, they might make it back to England. When he thought he had sufficient control of his voice to sound normal, he clicked on the intercom. "Pilot to crew: report in. Bomb aimer?"

"I'm OK, Skip."

"Mid-upper OK," Roper reported.

"Rear gunner OK," Osgood echoed.

"Wireless Op and Navigator OK." Tibble reported for both of them. They all sounded a bit frazzled, but apparently no one had been injured.

Unclipping his intercom so that no one else could hear, Moran turned to his flight engineer. "Daddy, I'm not getting any response from the rudder pedals. Can you go back and see what the damage is?"

Daddy nodded stoically and started back down the length of the fuselage. Tibble relayed Fauquier's order for the squadron to reform on him and return to base. Moran pushed his mask to his mouth without clipping it on properly. "Pilot to navigator: do you have a course for me?"

When there was no response, Moran repeated the request with the sinking certainty that Peal had frozen.

Tibble answered. "Course three-five-five, Skipper."

Moran acknowledged, but he suspected Tibble had simply read the course pencilled in on Peal's charts at the briefing. Yet in the meantime they had veered far wide of the target in their crazy flight through the balloons, invalidating that course. Furthermore, without rudder control, he could not turn tightly and so continued to diverge from the position from which that course had been calculated. Then again, Tibble might be able to get a fix using the H2S. Ultimately, "England" was a large "target" and as long as they weren't losing fuel, they ought to be able to make a landfall somewhere. Once they were in British airspace, they could put out a 'Darky' call and get a course based on a fix from ground radar. Alternatively, they could bail out over Allied controlled territory — but only if he had enough altitude for a safe jump. Moran started gently easing Zebra upwards to gain more altitude. Their best hope, of course, was for Peal to pull himself back together — soon. Moran drew a deep breath to steady his own nerves.

The intercom clicked. "Engineer to pilot. I've found the rudder cables. They have been severed, but I think I can rig something up."

"Well done." Moran kept climbing and banking around to the course Tibble had given him. Once he had climbed above the cloud, he could see some dots far ahead of him that were presumably the other Lancasters of the squadron making for home. Unexpectedly, a Mustang swooped in over the cockpit and settled down beside him. The pilot looked over at him. He seemed to be asking if they were in trouble. Moran had no way of communicating directly, as only Fauquier knew the American frequency. He gestured toward the back of the aircraft, shook his head, and tried to indicate they were going to try to limp home. The Mustang throttled back and stayed with him. That was nice, Moran thought. If nothing else, the Mustang should know the course for England.

"Engineer to pilot: Tell me if you want right or left rudder."

"What do you mean?"

"I've rigged summat up wi' cables tied to an axe, but you'll have to gi' me instructions."

"OK," Moran agreed sceptically. "Give me left rudder." Sure enough, they turned to the left. "Right rudder." They turned to the right. That was good. "It seems to be working," Moran concluded with relief.

"For now, aye," MacDonald muttered sceptically. "But ye'll need tae get this crate home as fast as ye're able. There's a ruddy great hole in the fuselage where the Elsan used to be, and the elevator cable looks a wee bit frayed. It might snap at any moment, so go gentle on the elevators, can ye?" For the first time since Moran had known him, MacDonald sounded truly nervous.

"I'll do my best," Moran assured him. He turned his attention back to flying. With a fragile elevator cable, he didn't dare trying to climb very much. That eliminated the option of bailing out. They were going to have to try to get home at roughly their present altitude of 2500 feet. At least the engines appeared to be working smoothly but he couldn't tell if trouble was building without some instrument readings. Pressing the mask to his face again, he called over the intercom: "Pilot to bomb aimer: the engineer is occupied. I need you to come to the cockpit where you can read the fuel and temperature gauges and oil pressure for me."

"On my way."

Babcock climbed into the cockpit, and Moran told him to stand where the engineer usually stood and read off the fuel gauges, oil pressure and temperature. The primary tanks were almost empty. "Can you switch to the secondary tanks?" Moran asked Babcock.

"No problem, Skipper," Babcock replied confidently.

Abruptly Peal's voice rang over the intercom. "Navigator to skipper: correct course to three-four-oh. Repeat: steer three-four-oh."

Moran silently thanked God. Peal had evidently recovered and could be trusted to navigate them back to base. "Turning on three-four-oh. Engineer: left rudder."

Instantly, the starboard inner sputtered and fell silent, rapidly followed by the starboard outer. The Lancaster started to yaw to starboard. "More left rudder!" Moran called in alarm and then, "Babcock! What's going on?"

"I don't know, sir. I thought I'd switched over to the secondary tanks."

Celtic cursing turned the intercom blue as MacDonald barked at Roper to come down from his turret and take over the rudder controls. A moment later he crashed into the cockpit to shoulder Babcock aside. He reached down and worked the fuel switches himself. The engines roared back into life. "Dinnae touch anither thing!" MacDonald growled at Babcock and returned down the fuselage.

Moran breathed out with relief. Seeing Babcock's distressed expression, he raised his voice to be heard over the noise of the engines to tell him not to worry and suggest it was time for coffee.

Babcock agreed and dropped down into the nose, where he stowed the thermoses for everyone. It would only be lukewarm by now, but the caffeine would be good. Moran suspected the station medical officer put extra caffeine into RAF coffee.

Babcock returned, handed the first thermos to Moran, and continued aft with the others

"Pilot to navigator: Do you have an ETA for us?"

"One hour and 55 minutes."

"That's a bloody long time to hold this flaming axe in a sodding ice chamber!" came Daddy's expostulation over the intercom. "Can ye no fly any faster than that?"

Moran hesitated to increase speed as it would also increase fuel consumption and the pressure on their damaged tail. He asked back, "Could Babcock or the gunners relieve you at the rudder — at least for bit?"

"There is nae any way Osgood can leave his turret, and neither Babcock nor Roper are strong enough to hold this bloody rudder for more than a couple of sodding minutes!"

"Wilco, Engineer. Bomb aimer: keep an eye on the fuel tanks and report when we're at one quarter full."

The sun set before they reached the North Sea, and they crossed the water as the light drained out of the Western sky. Fortunately, powerful and uninterrupted Gee made navigation easy. When the English coast came into sight, the Mustang waggled its wings and turned away toward its own base, while Z-Zebra continued for Woodhall Spa. The tension on board eased noticeably. Nigel suggested to Frank over the intercom that they call over to Kirkby Grange to see if their girls could get away for a drink. Babcock said he had an extra thermos of coffee if anyone wanted it. Moran didn't have the heart to tell them that they weren't safe yet. He had to land a Lancaster without rudder control; something that was nearly impossible to do.

They found the Woodhall beacon shortly before seven pm. As Tibble flashed their ID to the control caravan, Moran swung onto the circuit like a man facing the gallows. The Lancaster's wingspan was 102 feet. The runway was fifty feet wide, and the undercarriage took up more than half of that leaving only a few yards on either side. Too much yaw in either direction could put a wheel off the tarmac. At a landing speed of 90 to

95 mph, they would be lucky to go into a flat spin careening across the grass. Alternatively, they might lose an undercarriage leg and tear along the runway on their belly throwing up sparks likely to ignite the remaining fuel. Or a wingtip could dig into the turf and fling them into a cartwheel.

They received the green light as the flare path lit up in perfect visibility, but Moran lost his nerve. He aborted, calling into Flying Control that he was going around again. He'd been so gripped with visualizing his final moments, he'd forgotten to order the crew to crash positions.

MacDonald cursed colourfully and then announced bluntly, "I cannae hold her much longer, sir! Ye've got to put her down!"

"Understood, Engineer, but I want everyone in crash positions first. Did everyone hear that? Crash positions." A scramble ensued as the others finally realised the danger they were in.

Lining up a second time, Moran called. "Pilot to engineer: we're going in."

"Just tell me what rudder ye want." The tension in MacDonald's voice was almost painful. He was, Moran judged, nearing the end of his strength.

The wheels brushed the tarmac with a small squeal, and Moran cautiously applied the brakes. They started to veer left. "Right rudder!" MacDonald over-corrected and they started to veer right. "Left rudder!" Like a drunk, they wove from side to side down the length of the runway, Moran wincing at each swerve and expecting the crash to follow. Miraculously it never came. They zig-zagged so much that as their speed fell away, Moran began imagining the commentary he would get in the mess. "Just what did you have in that thermos of yours, Moran?"

His second thought was that he had made it. He had returned alive from a sortie that he'd believed would kill him. His premonition, if it was one, had been wrong.

He slowed the aircraft to a stop before the end of the runway and used the outer engines to swing Zebra onto the taxiway. The ground crew signalled them towards a dispersal point. The Lancaster thudded over the cracks in the concrete toward the torches lighting a hardstanding. Bishop waved his arms in front of his face to indicate Moran could switch off the engines, and one after another the Merlins wound down.

Silence returned — except for the echo of the engines still ringing in his ears — until all at once his crew seemed to come back to life. A garble of excited voices filled the fuselage as they left their crash positions to return to their stations and collect their kit. Babcock's laughter sounded slightly hysterical, while the expletives peppering Roper and Osgood's dialogue revealed heightened excitement. Tibble surprisingly, joined in, laughing and chattering unnaturally, a sure indicator of the magnitude of his relief.

Moran looked down in disbelief at his hands still on the control column. He was alive. He was going to see Georgina again. Furtively, he removed one hand to give Zach a pat.

MacDonald staggered to the cockpit, sweat streaking his face. "Well done, Skipper." His hands trembled with exhaustion, and he flexed his fingers as if to ease stiffness or cramps.

Moran looked up at him and announced bluntly, "I'm putting you in for the DFM."

MacDonald looked astonished. "Ye're the one who flew the flaming thing!"

"We wouldn't be here if you hadn't jury-rigged that rudder and manhandled it for almost three hours." That said, Moran released the straps and tried to push himself up out of his seat. He couldn't. His muscles were too stiff to unfold.

Sounds of some sort of commotion filtered up from the tail. The excited voices of the gunners, exclaiming in wonder and gabbling at a hundred miles an hour, mixed with shouts of amazement from the ground crew. Peal and Tibble tumbled out of their stations to find out what the fuss was about. Torches flashed about in the tail, and with an inarticulate grumble, MacDonald turned around to go and find out what was happening. A moment later, Pete Bishop emerged out of the fuselage into the cockpit. "Do you realise you've brought our aircraft back with a man-sized hole and the entire second half perforated like a sieve? If you can't take better care of her than that, sir, we won't lend her to you ever again!"

Kit laughed appreciatively.

"Seriously, sir," Bishop stopped jesting, "I don't know how your rear gunner survived."

"Neither do I. The rudder control cables snapped, by the way."

"Only the rudder cables? You must have a flaming guardian angel!"

Kit laughed again and then asked, "Can you give me a hand?" Bishop at once reached out, bracing himself against the armour plating behind the pilot's seat to help take the strain as he pulled Moran out of his seat. "Who else made it back?" Moran asked as he painfully straightened up.

"All seven aircraft that made the high run returned safely. As you probably know, Forrester and Howard went down over the target. The CO landed with a flak shell still in one wing and one tyre shot away, but no injuries. You're the last aircraft to return."

That made two aircraft down out of thirteen, both from the six that made the low-level run. It was a casualty rate of 15%. Better than expected. Kit still felt dazed by his own survival.

Unsteadily, he made his way down the length of the fuselage, crawling more than climbing over the main spar. After a look at the damage to the tail, he stepped shakily down the ladder to the tarmac and turned to look again at the tail from the outside. Half a dozen torch beams from the ground crew slid along the surfaces of the aircraft, pausing to highlight one jagged hole after another. Nigel gazed dumbstruck at the large hole immediately behind his turret. Frank, Stu, Adrian and Daddy clustered around him pointing and exclaiming.

Kit became aware that Terry stood silently beside him. He looked over at the wireless operator and asked in a low voice. "What happened to Adrian?"

Terry shrugged. "He froze, sir. It was like he was out cold with his eyes open."

Kit nodded solemnly but postponed a confrontation with this problem. To Terry he said simply, "You did a first-rate job today. Thank you."

The WAAF driving the crew lorry beeped the hooter to draw their attention, and they turned away from the aircraft to climb up onto the benches lining the back.

Still excited, Frank exclaimed as he dropped down beside Kit, "I can't believe the way you took us through those balloons, Skip!"

"And without rudder controls!" Stu added.

"I'm glad I couldn't see what was coming!" Nigel declared, "What with the balloons popping past and the tail slewing around like a drunken skater, I thought it was all over! I bashed my head on the ceiling of the turret at least twice!" As he spoke, he reached up to feel the bumps that had formed.

"I thought we'd bought it at least ten times!" Frank admitted.

"Twenty!" Daddy corrected him.

"We were lucky," Kit told them.

"Lucky, my foot! Luck doesn't fly like that! You were amazing!" Stu insisted.

"Steady on," Kit warned.

"Ach away wi' ye," Daddy insisted, his brogue showing his strength of feeling. "I don't know many pilots who'd have managed what ye just did, especially putting her down wi'out rudder control."

After dropping off their parachutes and Mae Wests, they entered the debriefing room, helping themselves to hot tea laced with rum as they filed past. As they continued to the first vacant table, the gunners peeled off their heavy suits and Kit unzipped his flight jacket. The WAAF intelligence officer had just started to question them when Fauquier caught sight of them. He briskly crossed the room and furiously demanded. "Moran! Didn't you hear me order you and Howard to abandon your second run? I broke radio silence to give that order."

"No," Moran answered blankly. "Did you order us to abandon?"

"Yes! *Twice!*" They stared at one another. In his mind, Moran re-ran those four minutes when Howard and he had circled around to make the second approach, but he could not remember hearing anything from Fauquier. He shook his head. "I'm sorry, sir. I didn't hear you. I gather Squadron Leader Howard didn't hear you either."

Fauquier sighed, his out-of-character anger vanishing. The strain showed on his face; he seemed to have aged years during the last few hours. Moran took advantage of the moment to announce. "Flak severed my rudder cables just as I cleared the target and my flight engineer got us home by tying the cable ends to an axe and physically pulling the aircraft in one direction or the other. I want to recommend him for a DFM."

"I'll support that," Fauquier agreed without hesitation. "I'm putting you in for immediate promotion to Flight Lieutenant and a DFC — though it will easier to get both if we've been successful."

Before he could say more, Barnes Wallis arrived and interrupted with an urgent, "Moran? Is that you?" Kit still wore his flying helmet, which made him hard to recognise.

"Yes?"

"Thank God!" The engineer seized his hand and shook it heartily. "I was so worried about you!" The skin hung on the engineer's face and his eyes seemed particularly large behind his glasses. "I'm so glad you made it back after all!"

"Thank you, sir." So much attention from the famous engineer in front of his CO embarrassed Moran.

Wallis had not let go of his hand. "I understand what you said about not wanting to plan for your future, but I want to help if I can. I could put you in contact with the necessary people at Vickers, get you started on the right track. Promise me you'll get in touch after the war ends."

"All right, sir," Moran answered uncertainly. On one level he felt flattered and honoured, but he still couldn't shake off the conviction that it was bad luck to plan for after the war. He'd been very lucky today, but it didn't seem wise to press it any further. Better not to think beyond tonight, seeing Georgina again, and maybe tomorrow. Just live from one op to the next, he reminded himself. One op to the next.

"Johnny!" It was the Station Commander calling to Fauquier from the far side of the room, and excitement magnified his voice. They all looked over. "It's down! The Kembs Barrage has collapsed! Water is surging down the Rhine, flooding everything along the route."

A weight visibly fell from Fauquier's shoulders, and some of that relief transferred itself to Moran. At least the losses hadn't been for nothing. Maybe the Americans would be able to press forward faster, in greater strength and with more armour, because Forrester and Howard had added the force of their Tallboys to the sum of explosions that finally brought down the great dam. Maybe the war would end sooner because of the American offensive. In other words, maybe Forrester and Howard had not died for nothing, but to save thousands of others. Moran wanted to believe that.

Following the debrief, transport took Moran and his crew to their respective messes for a meal. As they walked through the bar, Moran glanced upwards. Forrester's footprints still marked the ceiling, and the sight of them sent a shudder down his spine. How could the self-confident Australian be gone? He'd never doubted himself. He'd never admitted that he might get the chop. Yes, he'd been an arse sometimes, particularly when drunk, but he could also been amusing, fun-loving and motivating. Their two crews had been rivals for so long that their fates had seemed entwined. Until now. In slow-motion, the image of Forrester's burning Lancaster scraping over the barrage, smacking down in a flat spin and exploding replayed in Moran's mind — for the first, he knew, of a thousand times.

Adrian followed his gaze to the green footprints. "I'm sorry he's gone," he said softly. "I hated flying with him, and I'll never forgive the way he humiliated me. Yet, in his own way, he was a good man. So high-spirited and so committed." His voice faded away, no doubt remembering the lively party of the night before.

Moran felt a stab of sorrow as he grasped that Howard, too, was dead. He had not known Howard long or well, but he'd liked him. He would never forget how he'd put Forrester in his place when he'd been harassing Peal.

Moran started forward again, but Adrian caught his arm. "I'm sorry, Kit," he murmured softly. "I — I — I had a bit of a relapse today. I know I let you down...."

Kit didn't want to be reminded of that. He didn't want to report it to Fauquier or the Navigator Leader, either. But what if next time they were

337

striking a target deep inside Germany, one where they faced flak on the return trip? "We'll talk about it later. Let's go and get something to eat."

It was almost nine when they finished their meal, but Moran wanted desperately to see Georgina. He rang through to Mrs Radford's.

Georgina answered the phone herself. "Hello?"

"Georgina—"

"Kit?" She interrupted enthusiastically, "That was an amazing fly past — or whatever you call it! Nora nearly jumped out of the window in excitement, and Miss Townsend was waving just as wildly as the rest of us."

Kit had already forgotten about beating up Kirkby Grange in what he'd then believed was a last farewell. It seemed a lifetime ago. To Georgina he said only, "I'm glad you enjoyed it. May I come over tonight? Just to talk."

"Of course! I'd love to see you!"

"I'm not very presentable, I'm afraid," Kit realised looking down. He still wore battle dress, and he'd sweated badly at some points during the flight. If he took time to bathe and change, however, he'd have no time with Georgina.

"I don't care about that. Just come."

She stood waiting at the door and ushered him into the comfortable sitting room with the words, "What can I get you? Shall I make tea, or would you rather have a hot toddy or a gin and tonic? Whisky? Whatever you want."

"I just want you to sit down beside me," he answered, sinking onto the sofa and reaching for her hand. She did not resist but cuddled close beside him. He put his arm around her shoulders, and they kissed. Then he leaned his head back on the sofa and closed his eyes without letting go of her hand.

Georgina gazed at him, noting how frail he looked. He seemed much more vulnerable in battle dress, she reflected; each glinting movement of the dangling whistle underlined the ever-present threat of ditching or crashing in fog. When she laid her head on his shoulder, she could smell cordite. It must have been a bad sortie, but she was afraid to ask anything. Then again, she felt she had to show understanding. "Did something go wrong today?"

"Forrester and Howard got the chop." He paused then continued. "I watched both Lancasters become engulfed in flames. Both times I heard a

338

choir singing in my head: *'bring me my chariot of fire.'*"

"I'm sorry, Kit. I'm so sorry." She sounded as if she'd known and liked both men. Yet Kit knew she was only empathising with his own sorrow.

Kit squeezed her hand without opening his eyes. "I didn't think we were going to make it."

Georgina leaned forward and kissed the side of his chin lightly, clinging fiercely to his hand.

"I don't know how — or why — we made it and Howard and Forrester didn't," he admitted.

Georgina supposed her father might say something about the Lord, but she couldn't bring herself to issue a sound. She just held on to Kit, breathing in the smell of cordite and sweat as if it were the most expensive perfume in the world.

"The rudder cables snapped, and I went on into a balloon barrage. It was sheer madness. I don't know how we got out of there, I honestly don't. To get us back to base, Daddy jury-rigged rudder controls by tying the cables to an axe, but landing was another ordeal. It's hard enough to keep a Lancaster straight on the runway even in normal conditions. We ended up weaving back and forth like a drunk. My crew chief thought we'd gone over the edge at least twice and told me each time he closed his eyes so he wouldn't have to watch the crash."

"But you made it," Georgina whispered, clinging to his hand as if seeking reassurance that he was not a ghost.

"Yes, and now my crew thinks I can work miracles — that I can get them through anything." Kit sounded exasperated, almost angry.

"What's the harm in that?" Georgina asked gently.

"It's not true!"

"It doesn't hurt them to think it. It takes some of their fear away."

Kit turned his head towards her without lifting it off the back of the sofa and considered what she'd said. After a moment, he seemed to decide her words were wise, "I suppose you're right." He drew a deep breath and sat up straight, but he looked down at his hands rather than at Georgina as he added, "Adrian froze again."

"Oh, no!" Georgina felt badly not just for Kit but for Adrian, as well. She liked the gentle navigator.

"Terry covered for him," Kit continued. "The others probably don't know it happened. I could — maybe I should — kick him off the crew, but I kept thinking as I drove here that I don't know who I'd get as a replacement. Some odd bod. Maybe a veteran of ninety ops, or maybe someone straight out of training. No matter who it is, he'll be an alien body in a crew that has been forged into a unit. I can't explain it exactly, but it would be disruptive. Yet, if I say nothing ... bad navigating could kill us all."

Georgina nodded, knowing that she could not give any advice on this.

After a moment, Kit roused himself. He smiled faintly at her. "I also met Barnes Wallis today. He was at the station to see how things went. He's very pleasant, humble even. He said he'd like to help me get into aeronautical engineering after the war. If I want."

"Oh, that's marvellous! How generous of him!" Georgina agreed enthusiastically, and then thought to ask. "*Is* that what you want?"

"It sounds tempting. I'm just afraid to think about it — to think about 'after the war.'"

"Then don't," Georgina advised with a smile. "Don't think about *anything* that frightens you." She leaned back on his chest again and murmured. "We don't have to think about the future or plan for it. It will come no matter what we plan."

"Thank you," he answered and then held her closer for a moment. She lifted her face for a kiss.

When they finished, Kit admitted, "I have to get back to the mess."

"I understand. I'm glad you came even if only for a few moments."

"Thank you," he repeated, feeling much better. Georgina saw him to the door. They kissed again in the hallway and then he was gone, leaving his fear behind with her.

Chapter 23
The Face of Fear

Woodhall Spa
28 February 1945

Kit woke the next morning to a sunny but empty room. The clock by his bed showed half past nine. If he didn't hurry, he'd get no breakfast. He dressed as fast as he could, didn't bother about shaving, and hastened down to the almost empty dining room. White-jacketed mess stewards were already clearing away dirty dishes and starting to sweep up. They served Kit immediately; no bacon or fresh eggs since he wasn't flying, just toast, jam and powdered scrambled eggs along with hot tea. "Has anyone seen Pilot Officer Peal this morning?" He asked the steward who brought the tea.

"Yes, sir. He only finished breakfast a few minutes ago."

Kit left the dining room and went in search of Adrian. Although several other members of 617 Squadron were in the billiards room, none of them had seen Adrian. Kit continued to the library. There Adrian sat in a leather armchair, looking relaxed, rested and content as he read the newspaper.

Adrian glanced up as Kit entered and exclaimed, smiling, "Can you believe it? The raid's all over the papers already. I don't know how they get the photos so fast."

"The Ministry must hand over the aerial reconnaissance photos taken after we withdraw."

"There's a very nice quote from General Eisenhower, too." Adrian scanned the text until he found what he was looking for while Kit gazed out of leaded windows.

"Here it is," Adrian announced cheerfully, and read aloud: "'*An outstanding piece of airmanship, demonstrating yet again the high quality of RAF fliers and the ingenuity of British engineering. The United States of America is honoured to be standing alongside such indomitable allies.*' How do busy generals find time to deliver remarks like that?"

"They don't. They have press officers who write statements up in advance — one for success and one for failure. You know: *An outstanding effort carried out with the greatest dedication. Even if the results were not what we had hoped, I have the utmost confidence that next time we will be luckier.*"

Peal chuckled appreciatively and joked, "You could go into public relations after the war."

"Not my thing. Look, Adrian, it's a nice day. Why don't we go for a stroll around the grounds? Everyone raves about the paths through the park, and we haven't had a chance to enjoy them because the weather's been so miserable ever since we got here."

Adrian stiffened. His eyes sought Kit's and then looked away. He understood what this was about. Like a condemned man, he swallowed, managed a weak smile and squeaked out, "Of course. I'll go and get my greatcoat."

They both took their greatcoats because despite the bright sunshine, the temperature hung only a few degrees above freezing. Outside, melting snow dripped from the eaves of the stately house and the surrounding elm trees. They chose one of the paths leading away from the manicured grounds and followed a wooden sign to the "Cinema in the Woods" - "Flicks in the Sticks" as the aircrew called it. Other signs pointed to the golf course, lily pond and sunken gardens. Six-foot-tall rhododendron bushes lined this particular path, and Kit promised himself to come for another walk here when they were in bloom — if he lived that long.

When they reached the sports pavilion that had been converted into a cinema theatre, Kit led the way inside. Closed throughout the winter, it exuded an air of abandonment. Dirty canvas covers protected some things at the back, the seats emitted a musty smell, the posters for last year's films rotted on the walls, while dead leaves lay about in wet heaps. Kit looked up at the ceiling beams that dripped lazily at them.

"You want me off your crew," Adrian broke the silence.

Kit turned to face him. "I don't *want* you off my crew, Adrian. I'd rather not have to do this, but I'm responsible for the Lancaster and the other five crew members. I can't have a navigator who freezes when flak goes off."

"I thought you'd be more understanding, Kit," Adrian looked at him with wounded eyes. "After all, you were LMF too."

Kit recoiled, then fired back sharply, "How do you know that?"

"Fiona told me."

"The cow!"

"That's not fair. She didn't say it to make you look bad. It slipped out by mistake. She thought I already knew and was trying to explain that it wasn't the reason she broke up with you. When she realised I hadn't known, she begged me not to say anything. And I haven't, although I've been wanting to ask you about it — about how you mastered your fears. You obviously have. Rather than discarding me, Kit, share the secret," he pleaded. "Instead of letting them humiliate and demean me, show me how it's done."

"They don't humiliate you, Adrian. The rumours are much worse than the reality. You simply leave the station discreetly, without saying farewell to anyone, and go to a diagnostic centre where a psychiatrist reviews your case. If you have a mental condition, you'll be hospitalised—"

"Is that what you think? That I have 'a mental condition'?" Adrian challenged him resentfully.

"I'm not a psychiatrist, but I can assure you that the staff at the DYDN centres are professionals. They want to help."

"Did you undergo treatment?"

"No, they decided I didn't need it."

"Meaning you *didn't* have a mental condition?"

"Correct."

"Which means you *didn't* have a medical reason not to fly either, right?"

Kit nodded warily.

"So why weren't you stripped of your rank and your DFM?"

Kit drew a deep breath. "Because I was willing to return to ops."

"But so am I, Kit! I'm *begging* you to let me stay on ops."

"Adrian, listen to me. My case was different from yours. I didn't freeze or break down while flying, I *refused* to fly."

"I don't understand." Adrian sounded and looked completely baffled.

Kit drew a deep breath. "The operation the day before had been a total cock-up; the winds much higher than predicted, the route complicated. The Germans were expecting us, and in addition to about three squadrons of wild boars over the target — Berlin — they set out diversion flares. They also used the searchlights below the cloud cover to create a luminous backdrop against which we were silhouetted like puppets — easily visible to the fighters. First shrapnel injured the bomb aimer's foot, and then a night-fighter shot up the portside of the aircraft, seriously injuring the wireless operator and the navigator while fatally wounding my pilot. He managed to fly back to Hawkinge but was declared dead on arrival. They sent the navigator, wireless op and bomb aimer off to hospital, while the gunners and I had to make our own way back to the squadron, sleeping in railway stations and standing up in trains because no-one in this bloody country cared enough about bombing Berlin to give up their seats to us!" Kit still got angry just remembering it. "I was, to be blunt, pissed off with the RAF, Butch Harris, my CO and, frankly, England generally. After just two hours sleep, they woke me up with the news that I'd been assigned as substitute Flight Engineer to a sprog crew I'd never seen before. I dragged myself to the briefing smouldering with resentment, and when I found out the target was Berlin again, I told them to go to hell and walked out of the briefing."

"You didn't!" Adrian gasped.

"I did. Fauquier called it 'bloody-mindedness,' which probably sums it up. The point is that after that public display of insubordination they didn't have any choice but to post me. I was labelled LMF and sent off to the DYDN centre as fast as they could draft orders. After I'd had time to calm down and come to terms with what had happened, however, I agreed to go back on ops. It's not that I wasn't given a choice. I could have been reassigned to ground duties. Given that I'm a trained fitter, that probably wouldn't have been so bad—"

"Kit!" Adrian gasped in shock. "It would have meant losing your commission! Demotion to aircraftsman!" Adrian sounded horrified. "Your pay would have plummeted by more than half."

"I know, but I don't have a family to maintain, and it's safe work. It's even satisfying work."

"But you didn't *take* the offer," Adrian reminded him.

"No, because the psychiatrist recommended flight training, and that attracted me much more. It represented a challenge, something to look forward to, and a means of wiping out the black mark on my record and reputation that I had so impulsively drenched over both."

"So, you admit being posted LMF *is* a humiliation."

Kit squirmed. He didn't want Adrian to see things this way because it made it harder on him. Even so, it would be absurd to pretend that being found LMF wasn't humiliating. He tried arguing, "I don't look down on erks, and I hope you don't either. So, what is so bad about being one?"

"Nothing — if that's what you've been mustered and trained for. The problem is for someone who has been aircrew — and commissioned."

"So just wounded pride, then?" Kit probed.

"No, but I'm not a trained fitter. They don't need navigators who don't fly. Nor trained architects. I have no skills of any use to them. They'll put me in some kind of 'general duties' category — a batman, or a mess orderly washing dishes from dawn to dusk. Maybe they'd even make me one of the airmen working in the mortuary, the ones they send to collect the body parts from crashes..." Adrian dropped into one of the seats of the improvised cinema and held his head in his hands.

Kit started feeling sick in his stomach. Was it truly necessary to do this? He sat down cautiously beside Adrian, but he didn't know what to say.

After several minutes of silence and immobility, Adrian stirred. He ran his hands threw his long, blond hair and then dropped them again. With his elbows still propped on his knees, he turned to look at Kit with large, miserable eyes. "You don't understand what this will do to me. Your parents are in Africa, but I'll have to face mine immediately. They've always considered me weak, even effeminate, because I like to draw and paint. My mother, because of her American background, always worried that I'd turn into a pansy. My father just thinks I'm not up to the mark at anything, that I fall short at everything I do. If — if I'm posted LMF, I'll never be able to face either of them again."

Kit could hear Colonel Selkirk shouting "lily-livered" and "yellow" at him.

"They'll throw me out of the house, Kit. Disinherit me altogether."

Damn it! From what he'd seen of Adrian's parents, he could all too readily imagine the barrister's indignation and his complete disdain for his own son.

"And it's not just my parents who will disown me. All my friends from school will too," Adrian continued. "The entire old boys' network will turn on me. I'll be ostracised and persona non grata everywhere! I'll never be admitted to any club, never invited to another wedding, never be able to get a proper job."

"I can't believe that —"

"Then you don't know England!" Adrian snapped angrily. "Old school ties and reputation are everything!" He continued in a tone of hopelessness, "When word gets out that I'm LMF, I'll be professionally and socially ruined. No decent girl will ever have anything to do with me." Adrian again dropped his head in his hands and shook it from side to side. "I'll be ruined."

Kit didn't know what to do or say. He thought back to the other men he'd encountered at the DYDN centre. Most of them had been far more terrified of operations than of being labelled LMF. Several of them had been visibly and vocally relieved to be away from it all. Others had agonised more, but with the emphasis on "bad as this is, flying is worse." Then he realised all the men he had encountered at the DYDN centre had initiated the process, as had he, by refusing to fly. They hadn't been posted LMF against their will, as he was threatening to do to Adrian.

"Adrian, I don't want to ruin your life. You must know that. But we all depend on one another up there. If you break down at a critical moment, you'll have six lives on your conscience. Do you want that?"

"Of course not!" He sat up sharply and confronted Kit. "I'm fully aware of my responsibility to all of you, but I recover rapidly, Kit — at least when I'm flying with you. Yesterday, I was only frozen for ten— maybe fifteen — minutes. After I snap out of it, I can do the navigation. How many aircraft get home with wounded or dead navigators on board? Why does a short black-out have to be treated like a capital offense?" Adrian pleaded his case.

Kit thought he'd been frozen closer to twenty minutes, but that wasn't the point. He tried to explain, "Because countless aircraft and crews have been *lost* because a navigator— for whatever reason — failed to provide the correct course at a critical moment. Do you want us to risk that every time we go up? Aren't the hazards bad enough as it is?"

"But I don't *always* freeze, Kit!" Adrian pointed out emphatically. "I didn't freeze on any of the pathfinder ops or on the Dortmund-Ems raid either. It only happens on daylight raids."

That was true, Kit registered, and it explained why Adrian had performed well on five of the seven sorties he'd flown but cracked on the other two. Yet it didn't help Kit out of his dilemma. "I can't go to the CO and tell him we're only available for night ops, Adrian. That's not the way the RAF works."

"I know," Adrian answered deflated. He sat hunched over, staring at the cracks in the concrete floor.

Kit asked himself what Don would have done and was startled to realise that Don would have sympathised with Adrian. Don's father, too, would have made his son's life hell if he 'funked,'. Don, too, understood the pressures of public schools and their networks in England. Yet none of that altered the fact that a skipper bore the responsibility for the lives of the entire crew.

Kit knew that some of the other skippers consciously avoided befriending their crews to prevent themselves from being swayed by sentiment when they had to make hard choices. One of the veterans of some sixty ops had told him outright, "You may have to sacrifice a crewman's life to the target, pressing ahead even while a man bleeds to death. It's easier to do that if you don't care too much about anyone."

By the time he heard these words of wisdom — if that was what they were — it had been too late. Kit had already worked hard to make his crew a surrogate family for all of them. He did not believe he could sacrifice one of his men to the target. There had to be another way.

Adrian looked up at him, his hair falling in his eyes, and his lips starting to tremble. "Please, Kit. Don't do this to me. Let me stay on your crew. I can beat this. We can beat it together. We're a team. Never in my whole life have I felt so strongly that I belong somewhere the way I feel I belong with Zebra and her crew. And, up to now, you've been the best friend I've ever had. Please don't discard me, Kit. Please."

Kit drew a deep breath, hesitated momentarily, and then nodded. His crew was a unit. It couldn't be broken up and remain strong. If Adrian was weak, then he as skipper— and the others — were simply going to have to take up more of the burden. They would all be weaker, not stronger, if he tossed Adrian aside. "You're right, Adrian. You're one of us. We'll see this through together." He held out his hand to help Adrian to his feet.

Adrian broke into a tentative smile, "You mean it?"

"Yes, I mean it. If one day you decide you can't face another sortie, let me know, but as long as you *want* to fly with us, you stay on the crew. However, there are two things I want you to promise me."

"Anything!" Adrian responded exuberantly.

Kit gestured for him to calm down. "First, I want you to close your curtain during daylight ops as well as night ops. Just close yourself into your workstation and try not to go or look out unless it's absolutely necessary. Bring an empty milk bottle along, the way we pilots do, so you don't have to go to the Elsan to relieve yourself. Try to focus on your charts and instruments rather than on what is going on around us."

Adrian nodded. "You're right, Kit. If I hadn't seen Forrester..."

"Exactly. The other thing I want you to do is to show Terry as much about navigation as you can—"

"Yes, of course!" Adrian agreed jumping to his feet, his smile widening. "I'm happy to do that. I promise you won't regret standing by me!"

"No, of course not," Kit assured him. "Let's walk around the grounds some more. I'm chilled through."

Chapter 24
April Fools

Kirkby Grange
23 March 1945

Spring term was over. Exams had been marked and the results announced. Georgina felt proud that the students she had helped showed measurable improvement. Even Mr Willoughby noticed that all but one of her pupils had performed significantly better than in the autumn term and congratulated her. "I didn't expect it of you," he admitted, "but the proof of your success is here in black and white."

As usual, there was a little ceremony where the pupils who finished top of their class in each subject were honoured. After all the others had received their certificate from Mr Willoughby, he turned and nodded to Georgina. She stood to announce that "Starting this term, we will also honour the pupil who has shown the most improvement." She paused to let the tension rise as the pupils — particularly those who had not done so well! — looked hopefully at her. "This past term, no one has shown more improvement than Nora Shields." Georgina started clapping vigorously and the children joined in. Nora slouched down in her chair with her head bowed, but Georgina knew the gesture sprang from embarrassment, not indifference. Behind Nora's curtain of unruly hair, she was smiling.

Luckily, Georgina and Fiona were not among the staff required to remain with the children over the Easter holidays. Instead, they planned to spend the two weeks together at Foster Clough. Fiona had visited Georgina's family home twice before, but she had never acted so excited about it before. Nor had her suitcase ever bulged quite so much. Georgina smiled knowingly; Kit and Adrian hoped to join them for a portion of the holidays.

The train trip was unpleasant as always, yet the long waits for connections and even the crowding seemed more bearable in company. Georgina and Fiona talked about Kirkby Grange, the other teachers, and their pupils. "I'm surprised how much I enjoyed it," Fiona admitted. "It's a refreshing challenge to teach boys. I'm no longer sure I want to take a permanent position at a girls' school."

Georgina wasn't surprised.

Fiona knew all about Nora, of course, and she took the opportunity to admit, "I have to hand it to you for getting her to *wear* glasses. When you first told me what you were planning to do, I thought it was a waste of time and money. Most girls hate wearing glasses! Yet Nora seems to love hers so much, she probably wears them to bed!"

Georgina laughed. "You're right. She does. She told me she likes reading in bed to put herself to sleep. Which reminds me, I must bring back some more books for her. Her reading ability is not up to her age level yet and I have to feed her things she *can* read and that are *fun* to read, with plenty of pictures. Mummy will have fun helping me find four or five books to bring from home."

"Why didn't she tell anyone that she was half-blind?" Fiona wondered out loud.

"I've asked myself that many times and I think it's because she didn't care about school. Why should she? She didn't think she could ever be good at it, so rather than try and then fail, she simply switched off altogether. While she physically sat in class, her mind wandered off somewhere else. Then Terry walked in, admitted he couldn't see well, yet was obviously doing an important, exiting, even glamorous job. That interested her enough to jerk her out of her cocoon of indifference. Terry made her care about learning and reading. I shouldn't be taking credit for Nora's improvement at school; Terry should."

Fiona was nodding seriously, then suddenly she frowned slightly and asked, "Are you saying she's keen on him? She's only 13!"

"You don't have to be grown up to fall in love," Georgina countered.

As they settled on the bus from Mytholmroyd station, the last leg of their journey, Georgina, as casually as possible, ventured to ask Fiona, "Did you ever get a chance to ask Adrian about his fiancé?"

"Yes, I did." Fiona answered, straightening her skirt and setting her handbag beside her. "He's not formally engaged at all. There's just this girl who *assumes* they're going to get married. Adrian admits he hasn't told her flat out it won't happen, but he isn't committed." An outsider might have induced from Fiona's tone of voice that she was confident, but Georgina knew better. Fiona was fussing nervously with her things.

She was also doing something Georgina had never known her to do before: she was chasing after a man. Georgina couldn't help wondering why. Fiona could have had Kit, but she claimed never to have wanted him. Adrian on the other hand had attracted her from that very first night.

"What is it you like so much about Adrian?" she risked asking.

"He's a gentleman."

"Oh, and Kit and Don weren't?" Georgina shot back with a raised eyebrow.

"Don't be ridiculous. Of course, Don was a gentleman — and Kit too," she added almost as a second thought, making Georgina bristle inwardly. "But Adrian isn't just well-bred and well-mannered, he is genuinely *gentle*," Fiona explained, adding enthusiastically, "Did you know Adrian is a talented artist? He sketches beautifully and he does divine watercolours. He's just so shy about showing them to anyone. I've asked him to bring his sketchbook when he comes to Foster Clough so I can see more of his work. I thought we might go sketching together."

"Why not? — if it doesn't rain the whole time," Georgina agreed, concluding that it was just Fiona's fascination with artists that made her prefer the dreamier Adrian to the practical Kit.

Fiona and Georgina went for a long ride the day after their arrival, and on Palm Sunday, they helped Amanda serve tea and buns after the service. Many of the parishioners came to congratulate Georgina on her engagement, admire her ring, and ask, "Have you set a date for the wedding?"

Georgina gave a standard answer: "When the war is over."

Dinner that night was vegetarian, as Mrs Reddings was saving their meat coupons for Easter. She did, however, splurge with the cheese ration to make potatoes au gratin, and the use of spices made the vegetable stew tasty. Edwin brought a bottle of French red up from his wine cellar, lamenting, "It's almost empty down there. We must pray that the war is over before the year is out, or we'll be reduced to drinking less biblical spirits!"

After dinner they put a record on the gramophone and talked about a thousand things: the war, fashion, books, horses, Georgina's aunts and Fiona's family.

The telephone rang.

"I'll get it!" Georgina offered and jumped up to go into the hall. She didn't bother switching the light on, as she knew her way in the dark. Well-trained since childhood, she answered with: "Reverend Reddings' residence. This is his daughter Georgina. How may I help you?"

"Well, I can think of *several* things, but I'd prefer not to mention them over a public telephone with half my fellow officers listening in," Kit answered.

"Kit!" Georgina exclaimed delighted.

"Georgina, I hate to say this but—"

"You can't come," she guessed instantly, and her joy drained away.

"I wouldn't go that far, but something is brewing. If leave is suddenly cancelled, I won't be able to ring, so I thought I better warn you."

"I understand."

"Adrian and I will come as soon as we can, just don't plan on us for any specific event, or meal or even day. We will eventually get away, it's only a matter of when."

"That's all right, Kit. I understand."

"How was the end of term?"

"Almost all the students I helped did better, and Nora showed the most improvement of anyone. Mr Willoughby told me he was glad I'd been assigned to his class, and Miss Townsend seemed pleased in her way. Can you believe it?"

"Of course! I've always believed you could do it! It's just a shame you're on term break, because it's no fun beating up Kirkby Grange when no one is there."

"Nora's there. And Miss Townsend, of course."

"Yes, but if we beat the Grange up when *you're* not there, Miss Townsend might cotton on to the fact that Adrian fancies her."

Georgina laughed.

"I'd better go," Kit told her reluctantly. "A queue is forming."

"Okay. We'll have plenty of time to talk when you get here."

"Yes, of course. Goodbye for now."

"Goodbye, Kit darling. And good luck!"

"I love you, Georgina." He hung up.

Georgina replaced the receiver and stood in the dark. He had never said that over the phone before. She couldn't move.

Edwin found her there several moments later. "Georgina? Is something wrong?"

She shook her head, then changed her mind and nodded.

He moved closer, a concerned look on his worn face. "What is it?"

"I'm afraid I may have heard Kit's voice for the last time."

"Ah." He put his arm around her shoulders and his chin on her head before gently reminding her, "A coward dies a thousand times before his death; a hero never tastes of death but once."

"No, it's not that, Daddy. It's that if I remind myself each day that it may be his last, I cherish every moment and every word more consciously. Because I didn't do that with Don, I don't remember what his last words to me were — or mine to him. My last words to Kit just now were 'Good luck,' and Kit answered with 'I love you, Georgina.'" She paused, reflected, and then asked rhetorically, "That's lovely, isn't it?"

Edwin held his daughter closer for a moment and nodded. "Yes, that's lovely."

Woodhall Spa
27 March 1945

Security had never been so tight before any other operation in Kit's career. The public phones were cordoned off. The guards at the gates stopped anyone trying to leave. An unfortunate corporal who tried to slip under the perimeter fence — as almost all the erks did from time to time — found himself demoted to aircraftsman. Meanwhile, at a feverish pace, the bomb-bay doors, mid-upper turrets, forward turrets and guns, along with two guns from the rear turret, were removed from most of the squadron's aircraft. On these modified aircraft, even the wireless operator's station and all his equipment were stripped out to lighten the aircraft and make room for a monstrous bomb. At 26 feet long, it was almost twice the size of the Tallboy, weighed 22,000 lb and was known as the "Grand Slam" or Earthquake bomb. It was the latest invention of Barnes Wallis.

The first prototype had been used less than two weeks earlier against the Bielefeld viaduct, which collapsed under the impact. Its second outing had been against the Arbergen railway bridge, a few miles south of Bremen, only six days ago. Both operations had been carried out by 617 squadron, but on the first occasion with only one aircraft, and on the second two, modified to deliver Grand Slams. Now it was to be fourteen.

Moran was glad that Zebra was not among those subjected to these — to his mind — disfiguring modifications. Although Peal had performed well on the last four ops, including the daylight op to Bielefeld, Moran did not want to lose the back-up offered by Tibble. Nor did he like the look of the

Lancasters carrying the Grand Slam. When laden and in flight, the fuselage sagged between wings that visibly curved upwards, and the slightest turbulence caused the wings to flex dangerously. It took every ounce of power from the four Merlins to drag the laden aircraft off the runway, and when the Grand Slam dropped, the aircraft sprang up 500 feet or more. Squadron Leader Jock Calder's bomb aimer, who had dropped the very first of these bombs, said that after the release he'd been pressed to the floor of the Lancaster only to then be flung up again so hard that he was winded when he smacked down again. Meanwhile, Moran flying behind in Z-Zebra with a Tallboy, had been hit by the pressure wave following the detonation of the Grand Slam; Z-Zebra had been flung across the sky. Moran happily left the glory of delivering Grand Slams to others.

Although the briefing took place in broad daylight, the blackout blinds and curtains remained closed, and a tangible sense of nervousness agitated the briefers. This edginess spread rapidly to the assembled crews. Cigarettes glowed across the room and swirling smoke accumulated under the low ceiling long before they came to attention at the arrival of the senior officers.

The intelligence officer opened with: "Gentleman, at great risk to their own lives, a number of intelligence operatives have smuggled information out of Germany about a new kind of U-boat, designated Type XXI. These U-boats, being primarily battery driven, can operate for *days* underwater. They make less noise when underwater than conventional U-boats, rendering them almost undetectable to sonar. Furthermore, they have a submerged speed of 17 knots." A ripple of astonishment swept the room. Many merchantmen couldn't travel at that speed even on the surface. "They dive faster than conventional U-boats, recharge at periscope depth, and have no fewer than six forward torpedo tubes. They put to sea with a total of 23 torpedoes."

There was an uneasy stirring among the aircrews.

"Needless to say, U-boats of this type would wreak havoc with our merchantmen and with the sea lines of communication to our ground forces on the Continent. It would be too much to say that they can save Germany from defeat, but if they are deployed in the numbers planned, they could prolong the war by months — not to mention send hundreds of Allied ships with their cargoes and crews to the bottom."

We get the drift, Moran thought to himself, lighting another cigarette. Get to the point.

"Tens of thousands of slave-labourers, working under appalling conditions, have built a factory capable of mass-producing these Type XXI U-boats. It is 90% complete and the machinery installed. Our intelligence suggests that within a week it will begin production and start turning out three of these superior U-boats every week." He paused again and looked toward the Station Commander.

The latter stepped onto the stage and announced: "Gentlemen, His Majesty's government expects you to ensure that does not happen."

Moran raised his eyebrows and glanced over at Squadron Leader Martin, who was sitting beside him. They exchanged a look of mild irritation.

The Group Captain gestured for the curtains covering the target map to be opened. On the revealed map, a line of yarn led to a suburb of Bremen on the Weser River, and the whole room groaned. Bremen possessed some of the heaviest flak and best fighter protection in Germany. Tapping with his pointer, the Station Commander continued. "Here you see the large concentration camp housing the slave labourers. Here you see the flak fortresses." His pointer tapped on the map at least a half-dozen times. "What you *can't* see is that the factory," as he spoke, he traced the outline of a large rectangular area with the tip of his pointer, "is protected by a concrete ceiling 14-feet thick at the western end and 23-feet thick at the eastern end."

The crews shook their heads and the cigarette smoke fogged the air more and more.

"You'll be going in at 18,000 feet, which will allow the Grand Slams to reach supersonic speed. This should enable the bombs to pierce the concrete and explode inside this massive structure, where the machinery for producing the submarines has already been installed. The fuses will be set to detonate with a ten-minute delay. When the bombs go off, the factory's protection will be transformed into the cause of its destruction. The massive walls will contain the blast and wreak more destruction than if the building were blown open. This means, of course, that you may not *see* much damage, certainly not from 18,000 feet. However, we have operatives among the workforce and the local community who will report back on the effect of our assault.

"Meanwhile, those of you carrying Tallboys are to concentrate on the surrounding structures that house the guards, the staff, and the railway sidings used for the delivery of raw materials, component parts, and so on." The Station Commander tapped targets with his pointer as he identified them.

"What about the slave labourers? Will they be inside at the time of our strike?" The question popped out, and only after he'd voiced it did Moran wonder if he'd spoken out-of-turn.

The Station Commander looked annoyed, but Fauquier stood and turned to face him. "The Nazis have slaves working around the clock to get this finished, Moran. There is no time when it is not full of labourers. This is one op, I'm afraid, when we cannot take any measures to minimise the civilian casualties. We must press ahead."

Moran nodded. His question, however, had loosened tongues.

"Will we have an escort?"

"You will. One squadron of USAAF Mustangs and one of our own Spitfire squadrons."

"How many German fighter squadrons are stationed in the area."

"Five."

"Will there be a diversionary attack?"

"Yes, ninety-five Lancasters from 5 Group Squadrons will carry out a simultaneous raid on a nearby oil storage depot." Fauquier paused. "Any other questions?"

There were none, and the briefing continued with the details of fuel loads, routes, marking and timing.

The fourteen aircraft with the Grand Slams took off first, while Moran in Z-Zebra awaited his turn on the taxiway. He found it painful to watch them struggle to get off the ground and gain altitude. Shortly after take-off, two aircraft turned back due to engine difficulties, which Moran assumed had been triggered by the strain of taking-off with a weight far beyond design specifications. The remaining eighteen aircraft of the squadron, including Zebra, picked up their fighter escort over the North Sea. Their briefed route kept them over water as long as possible, before turning southeast in a direct approach to the target.

617 Squadron flew in a loose formation, unlike the regimented and tight "boxes" Americans favoured. With 18 aircraft, however, it was easy to fly in vics of three, loosely grouped in three flights of two vics each. Moran tucked his starboard wing behind and to port of Squadron Leader Cockshott, who was leading the flight of six Lancasters with Tallboys. In the distance through broken cloud, they could see the stream of "decoy" Lancasters from Main Force on a parallel course.

As this was a daylight raid, only their second since the attack on the Kembs Barrage, Peal kept his curtain closed around his workstation. He seemed to be working with his usual night-time efficiency and called out the course change to turn toward Bremen a moment before Cockshott lifted his port wing to bank southwards. Shortly afterwards, Babcock announced, "Enemy coast ahead."

Bursts of flak started to smudge the landscape before and below them. They had barely begun passing over the landmass of Europe when Roper sang out over the intercom, "Fighter! Ten o'clock high!"

A second later something seemed to flash down from their left at a speed Moran couldn't grasp. Zebra leapt in his hands, Roper screamed, and MacDonald called out "Port inner on fire!"

Moran looked around for the fighter, unsure if he needed to take evasive action or not. The gunners should have been giving him instructions to corkscrew left or right. "Pilot to gunners: can you see the fighter?"

"Nothing. I didn't see a flamming thing!" Osgood sounded furious.

A Spitfire wheeled by, apparently chasing after the German, but there was no sign of the fighter that had hit them. Moran spared a glance toward his damaged engine. "Flight engineer: have you engaged the extinguisher?"

"Of course!" MacDonald snapped in evident irritation. "Prop feathered as well."

Moran looked again. The engine seemed to be smoking, but he could see no flames. Zebra appeared to be flying normally. Moran switched on the intercom: "Roper? Are you all right?"

"No!" Roper responded in a terrified voice. "There's blood everywhere! I think — think — I'm bleeding — to death — Skipper."

This is Reggie all over again, Moran thought, remembering Don's mid-upper gunner getting injured during his first tour of operations. "Pilot to Wireless Operator: Go and assist the mid-upper gunner!"

"Navigator to pilot: Terry's already gone aft. I'll see if I can help."

Moran wanted to stop Peal. He didn't want him leaving his curtained space and seeing the sky full of flak, but it was too late. Peal tore open his curtain, and with an oxygen bottle in hand started squeezing his way down the fuselage. When Reggie had been injured there had been no decision for Don to make; they had already dropped their bombs and were heading for home.

Moran turned his attention back to the engine. "Engineer, what's the damage?"

"Fire's oot. Engine's feathered. No apparent damage tae the fuel tank."

"Tibble, Peal: how's Roper?"

Peal answered, sounding a little out of breath but remarkably collected and calm given the circumstances. "He's lost a lot of blood and he's in shock. We're moving him forward to the rest bed and will apply first aid."

Meanwhile, the flak was getting closer and more intense. They were being shaken continuously. Moran eased away from Cockshott but increased the revs on his remaining three engines to be able to keep up. As he did so, MacDonald gaped at him as though he were mad.

"Pilot to bomb aimer: Can you see the target yet?"

"Not yet, Skip."

"Keep your eye on Cockshott. Peal and Tibble are dealing with Roper."

"Understood, Skipper."

"Are ye no turning back?" MacDonald asked in disbelief.

"I don't know yet. She's flying well, and we're no more than five minutes from the target." Even as he answered, Moran remembered thinking not more than a month ago that he would never put the target ahead of the welfare of his crew. Yet this wasn't just any target. On the other hand, there were seventeen other aircraft, and he wasn't carrying a Grand Slam. His contribution would be at best auxiliary. "Peal: can you give me an update on Roper's condition?"

"He's on the rest bed now. He's shivering badly from the shock, so I'm wrapping him up in all the blankets we have."

"Is the bleeding under control?"

"For the moment."

Moran nodded to MacDonald. "We're going in."

"On three engines, wi' no mid upper gunner?"

"Yes."

The leading flight of six Lancasters carrying Grand Slams appeared to have levelled off at the bombing altitude already, and Cockshott was sinking down towards the same 18,000 feet.

"Target in sight, Skipper!" Babcock reported.

Over the radio rather than the intercom a voice broke in. "Z-Zebra. Z-Zebra. Go in first then turn for home. We'll follow."

"Roger. Thank you!" Moran reached down and pulled the lever beside his seat opening the bomb bay doors then flipped on his intercom. "Babcock: Bomb Bay doors open. Master switch on. Talk me in."

"Aye, aye, Skipper."

Flak burst all around them, turning the air dirty with smoke and debris — dirtier than Moran had ever seen it. Or, he wondered, had Main Force squadrons hit the fuel depot causing smoke from burning oil tanks to soil the sky? Moran risked a glance farther afield and decided this was indeed caused by billowing smoke from the tank farm carried on the wind.

"Steady! Steady!" Babcock admonished him.

"Port outer overheating!" MacDonald called out in alarm.

"Steady!" Babcock answered.

"Spitfire going down in flames!" Osgood reported.

"Bomb gone!" Babcock announced — unnecessarily as the Lancaster bounced upwards and they were all pressed down into their seats.

Moran held Zebra steady for another fifteen seconds.

Babcock broke in over the intercom so excited he was nearly shouting: "We got the railway siding, Skipper! Smack on! An ammo or torpedo train must have been waiting there! Things are blowing up all over the place."

Osgood joined in as Moran started to swing away and pull up. "You should see this, Skip! Our bomb set off a bloody beautiful chain reaction!"

"Explosions are going off, one after another all along the railway." Babcock enthused.

"We've wreaked havoc over two miles of track or more!" Osgood confirmed.

"Well done!" Moran answered as he eased back on the throttles to take some of the strain off the port outer. "Pilot to Navigator: I need a course for base. The fastest way home."

"Wireless Operator to pilot: give me thirty-seconds and I'll give you the briefed course from target."

Moran didn't like the sound of that. Did it mean Peal wasn't able to give him a course? "Where's the navigator?"

"Navigator to pilot: I've got a compress on Frank's injury. It's the second one because the wound started bleeding again. If I let go, it might start bleeding a third time. Terry's getting the course now."

"Steer 360 for about five minutes." Tibble's voice was tight with tension. "When you're out of enemy air space we'll give you a new course."

Moran drew a deep breath. "Steering 360." Once he steadied on course, however, his attention turned back to his engines. He wanted them out of enemy airspace as fast as possible and that meant increasing speed. "How's the port outer engine, engineer?"

"It seems to have stabilised now we're rid of the bomb, but it's still too hot."

"Pilot to Navigator: how is Roper doing?"

"The bleeding has definitely slowed. He's stopped shaking too. I've given him morphine. I'll be back at my station in two minutes, take a fix, and give you a course."

Peal sounded remarkably calm. Moran at last remembered to ask, "Adrian, where was Frank hit?"

"It's a neck wound, Skipper, just below the ear. He's lost a lot of blood."

Damn, Moran thought. That sounded more serious than he'd assumed. Automatically, he'd pictured the same kind of injury as Reggie had had. How foolish of him. Then again, this probably meant Frank would either recover fully or die. For Moran, either of those options was preferable to being left a cripple the rest of his life, as Reggie had been. Turning to MacDonald, Moran announced, "I'm going to risk increasing the RPMs to 2850."

"I dinnae think that's a good idea," MacDonald told him bluntly. "If we lose the port outer, it'll slow us down more than if ye keep all three at 2600."

"2700," Moran compromised. "Keep a close watch on the dials."

MacDonald drew a deep breath and turned to stare stubbornly at the instrument panel.

"Pilot to rear gunner: can you see anything?"

"I've seen two Lancasters from Main Force go down, Skipper, and at least three fighters as well. There aren't that many Jerries that I can see, but the one that hit us must be one of the new ones they warned us about in the gunners' briefing, the jet-powered Me 262."

Moran had feared that too. They could only pray that none of the bastards caught sight of them limping home on three engines with a smashed mid-upper turret, or they'd come in to finish the job.

Slowly the flak receded. The sky cleared. Below them the North Sea glistened in the afternoon sun.

"Navigator to pilot: Steer 255."

"Turning onto 255, navigator."

Aside from the two aircraft that had aborted, they were the first to return. As they came onto the circuit, they fired a flare for "wounded on board" and Moran saw the ambulance jolt into motion. The fire engine swung onto the taxiway too, probably because the port outer engine had started to smoke, but Moran wasn't worried about it. With a screech, Zebra's tyres touched the tarmac and they rumbled down the runway to turn off at the far end with a squeal from the brakes. Moran made a mental note to mention that squeal to Bishop; he'd been meaning to do so for at least a week, but he kept forgetting.

As soon as he was clear of the runway, Moran stopped without shutting down his engines. The ambulance came alongside, and Osgood and Tibble lowered the ladder so the medical staff could clamber aboard. Efficiently, the 'body snatchers' transferred Roper from the rest bed to a stretcher and took him out to the ambulance. Only after the 'blood wagon' wailed away toward sick quarters did Moran continue taxiing to their dispersal. As he switched off the engines, he noted mentally that he had just completed his tenth sortie with 617 squadron. Added to the thirty-six he had flown before, he had completed the equivalent of two full operational tours plus one.

Other crews started to arrive in the debriefing room as Moran's crew stood to leave. They were in good spirits.

Cockshott came over to ask if everything was all right.

Moran nodded. "My mid-upper was wounded in the neck. I'm on my way over to sick quarters to see what the MO has to say now. How did the rest of you do?"

"We're all back and it looks like two of the Grand Slams penetrated the roof of the target. If so, there's a good chance that we achieved the objective, but the CO says we won't know for sure until we get intelligence back from our agents on the ground."

Moran nodded. "Thanks for letting me go first."

"No question about it once I saw you were down to three engines. Hope your gunner pulls through."

Outside, Moran talked one of the WAAF drivers into taking them over to the sick quarters, and the receptionist there told them to wait while she enquired about Roper. Shortly afterwards, a doctor with the rank of Squadron Leader emerged and they got to their feet. He held out his hand and introduced himself, "Quail." He shook hands with each of them and then turned to Moran. "Are you Sergeant Roper's skipper?"

"Yes, sir."

"I've got good news for you. Although the injury bled profusely — as head wounds do — the harm was minor. It appears that a small piece of shrapnel, probably no bigger than my thumbnail, tore off his lower ear and grazed the side of his neck. He's lost his earlobe and a lot of blood, but I've given him a transfusion. I expect he'll have a scar on his neck for the rest of his life, but he should be back on his feet in a day or two."

"Frank is never going to live this down!" Nigel declared, only half in jest, as he took a swig from his pint of frothing beer. "He's grazed by a piece of shrapnel no bigger than a thumbnail and he's screaming 'I'm bleeding to death! I'm bleeding to death!'" Nigel's high-pitched imitation of panic triggered laughter among the others.

"Well, there *was* a lot of blood," Terry pointed out as they quieted down. "I nearly fainted when I came into the fuselage and saw blood dripping out of the turret! I looked up and a drop fell in my eye. Thank God Adrian arrived at that point and took over. He got Frank down and together we heaved him onto the rest bed, then Adrian got a compress on and wrapped him in blankets to stop him from shaking. He even gave him the shot of morphine! He was amazing!" Turning to Adrian he asked, "Have you ever thought of going into medicine after the war?"

"No," Adrian retorted firmly. "I actually don't like dealing with things like that, but —" He shrugged. "It had to be done and done fast." His eyes met Kit's, who nodded in understanding. He'd been in Adrian's shoes when Reggie was hit. He also understood that Adrian's focus on saving Frank had prevented him from noticing the flak around them. To the others Adrian declared emphatically, "I hope I never see anything like that ever again."

Terry nodded vigorously in agreement, but Nigel leaned forward and remarked pensively. "I don't know. After the war, I think I'd like to learn more about first aid. It can save lives, and that would be a nice change."

"You know what I want most when this war is over?" Stu spoke up. "I want *never* to get up in the middle of the night or have breakfast in the dark again!"

They laughed.

"When the war's over, I want to go to places like the British Museum and the National Gallery and be able to *see* things!" Terry confided. "You lent me that book, Skipper, remember? But when I tried to go and look at some of the things in it, I was told that everything had been moved into a cave somewhere in Wales 'for the duration.'"

"Sorry, about that."

"When this ruddy war is over, I'm nae getting in an aircraft again as long as I live," Daddy growled downing his beer in a long, sustained series of gulps. The others gazed at him astonished. He thumped the glass back on the table and pugnaciously returned their stares. "*Anyone* who willingly entrusts his life tae a fragile contraption made frae bits o' aluminium and steel riveted together is insane!"

"Are you saying you're afraid of *flying*?" Stu asked in disbelief.

"Damned right!" Daddy confirmed meeting his eye squarely.

"Every time we fly?" Kit couldn't grasp it.

"From the minute we get a green until I hear the squeal of the tyres on tarmac on landing."

"But why did you volunteer for aircrew?" Nigel asked for all of them.

"Because I was nine tenths of the way through flight engineer training before I had my first ride in an aeroplane and found oot what madness it was! By then it was too ruddy late! If I'd said I didnae want to fly, they'd have posted me LMF. Thank you very much! How am I supposed to feed the missus on erk pay? But the day Germany surrenders, I swear to God, I'm nae leaving the ground ever again."

"On that note, let's get another round," Nigel suggested. "What are you drinking, Skipper?"

"I'll have another whisky-tonic but excuse me a minute while I make a phone call." Kit made his way to the phone booth and put a call through to Foster Clough. All he got was an engaged signal, so he returned to the table.

The others were discussing their plans for leave, but as Kit joined them Adrian could sense Kit's unease. "Is something wrong?" he asked.

"I can't get through to Georgina."

"Probably the trunk lines."

"Yes, maybe. I'll try again in a little while."

Kit rang twice more before the evening was over, but both times all he got was the same engaged signal. It unsettled him. What if there had been an accident at Foster Clough? He'd seen how difficult a horse Teros could be, and the worst riding accidents happened to experienced riders — like Georgina.

Foster Clough, Yorkshire
28 March 1945

Edwin hunched over his desk staring at the pad of paper and nibbling on the end of his pen. Good Friday was only two days away and he did not have a sermon. That is, he'd written one, but he'd discarded it. Yesterday, Mrs Witherspoon had learned that her twin sons had gone down with their ship after it was torpedoed off the coast of Norway whilst carrying ammunition for the Soviets. The brothers had joined the Merchant Navy together and always signed aboard the same ship, inseparable in life and now in death.

Mrs Witherspoon had been a pillar of the parish longer than Edwin himself. A widow since the last war, she had been at the heart of almost every activity from collecting books for the troops and overseeing the "Spitfire Fund" to the choir and the decoration committee. She was large, loud, fond of broad-brimmed hats with silk flowers on them, and she was broken. Edwin did not know how she could possibly withstand this double blow. He did not know why she should have to. He certainly did not know what he could say to console her.

Yet the entire parish expected him to stand in the pulpit on Good Friday and deliver a sermon that would ease her suffering. Edwin didn't have any words of comfort, and it didn't help that they'd had no word from Kit since last Sunday. Georgina pretended not to be on edge, but she tensed every time the phone rang — and it had not ceased to ring for almost twenty-four hours as word spread through the parish of the fate of the Witherspoon twins.

Edwin drew a deep breath. Random thoughts floated through his consciousness. Sacrifice. Greater love hath no man. The Lamb of God slaughtered. For the Lord he slays the first born that the people may go free. But why the *second* son as well? Why both together? For whom? For what? A war already won and nearly over?

Everything had been said already. Every phrase was hackneyed. He had no new message. He had no succour to give. He was empty. Maybe he should admit that. Just get up in the pulpit on Good Friday and announce: "Dearly Beloved, I am no wiser than any of you. I do not know why this tragedy happened. I don't think it was fair. And if it was the Will of God, then I hate God for his cruelty."

That was not likely to make anyone feel any better.

He had to offer something more uplifting than that, even if his heart was not in it.

There was a gentle knock on the door. Irritated, Edwin frowned and swivelled around in his desk chair. Amanda usually had the sense not to interrupt him when he was working, but when she did, she burst straight in. The door, however, did not open. He called out in an uninviting tone, "Yes?"

The door clicked open, and Kit Moran peered around the edge tentatively.

Edwin joyously sprang to his feet and went to shake his hand. "Kit! Thank God! You made it! We were worried about you!"

"I tried to ring last night—"

"Oh, it was impossible. There's been a local tragedy. Everyone wanted to tell me about it. When did you get here?"

"Half an hour ago. Amanda tells me Georgina and Fiona are out somewhere, and so we sorted out the accommodation first. Adrian's upstairs settling in now."

"Sit down, sit down!" Edwin indicated an armed chair. "You look tired." Edwin could see marks where the oxygen mask had chafed around his nose. "Were you over again last night?"

"No, during the day. It should be in the papers soon."

"Another important raid then?"

"It looks like we destroyed an important U-boat factory. I don't think I'm allowed to tell you more than that."

"Did you all get back safe?"

"Yes, although one of my gunners was wounded, but not badly. You look tired too," Kit added with a faint smile.

Edwin sighed in exasperation and removed his glasses, pinched the bridge of his nose, and then replaced them. "Nothing important. I'm just having a crisis of faith."

Kit chuckled, then seemed to realise Edwin wasn't joking. He stopped laughing and looked at Edwin concerned. "Are you serious?"

"Well, let's just say I've run out of words of comfort. I don't know how to explain or justify the losses any more. I don't understand how a benevolent God could allow human slaughterhouses or fire-bombing either. I know, I know: God isn't to blame. We humans are to blame, but … what can I possibly say to make it all sound meaningful? In two days' time, on Good Friday, they'll all be looking to me for wisdom and faith, and I haven't a clue what to say."

Kit thought about that, and then remembered something his mother had said. "Good Friday is a day of grief. When Christ died, it seemed to all those left behind that He had failed. It looked as though he wasn't the Son of God. He was human, vulnerable, and helpless. He had been betrayed by one of his closest friends, and He thought he had been betrayed by God as well. He was feeling just as you feel now — forsaken, confused, and without faith. My mother always said that on Good Friday we should feel as He did. The *meaning* doesn't come until Easter."

Edwin gazed at Kit in astonishment and murmured a heartfelt, "I really *must* meet your mother one day." Then he frowned slightly and added in a voice that was both amused and annoyed. "Your suggestion, however, does nothing but put the burden of writing a triumphant sermon off for another two days! I *will* have to deliver something cheering on Easter day."

Kit smiled. "Well, maybe God will inspire you before then."

Foster Clough, Yorkshire
Easter Sunday
1 April 1945

Kit was woken by songbirds calling at the break of day. A pale pink sky peeked through the window next to his bed, although darkness shrouded the rest of the unfamiliar room. For several seconds he had no idea where he was, nor did he know the season of the year, never mind the day. His dreams had taken him back to Africa, but it was too cold for Africa. He sat up and looked about, slowly regaining his orientation.

With Fiona occupying the only camp bed and Adrian in Gerald's room, Kit had been given the choice of sleeping on the sofa in the sitting room or occupying the vacant servant's quarters off the kitchen. Amanda had seemed disturbed by the idea of him out in the servant's quarters, but Kit preferred the privacy offered by the Spartan accommodation with its separate little toilet and sit-down bathtub.

Kit pushed aside the starched but well-worn sheets and rough, heavy blankets and pulled on his battle dress. Using the door that led directly into the courtyard, he stepped into the chilly morning, marvelling at the stillness. No Merlin clattered and barked as it sprang to life. No transport engine growled. No tyres rumbled on concrete. No bicycle squeaked and no batman whistled. There was no clanging of pots from the kitchen nor car doors closing nor footsteps crunching on the gravel drive. Only the birds and the rustling of the trees. It was as if the war had never been.

Kit supposed it was because he'd lived in so many different places in his short life — Pretoria, Nairobi, Moyale, Kisumu, Cape Town, Calabar, Bristol and a dozen different RAF stations since — that he found it easy to settle in almost anywhere. Whatever the reason, he already felt at home here in Foster Clough.

He crossed to the stables and slipped inside. The horses stirred in the box stalls and nickered in greeting. Teros kicked at the door impatiently. He checked his watch: it was seven minutes past six. Usually, the horses weren't fed until half-past seven, but Georgina had warned him that today would be hectic and busy. It was the most important church festival of the year, and in this rural community her father was at the heart of it. Kit decided he could help by getting this one chore out of the way.

He measured out and distributed the sweet feed to all three horses — careful to close Hannibal's padlock before he climbed to the loft for the hay. He'd just started refilling the water buckets when Georgina slipped in. She was dressed for work in the stables in old slacks, a worn jumper and scuffed-up wellingtons. "Kit, what are you doing here?"

"I just finished the feeding."

"You're an angel!"

"No, I just wanted to help. Is everyone awake now?"

"Fiona's making herself beautiful and my mother's starting breakfast. Daddy's fussing with his sermon again — he's always nervous and irritable on Easter morning — and I don't have a clue where Adrian is."

"Tell me again about the programme for today?"

"We have to get to church by nine o'clock. I help set up the tea for afterwards, while Mummy helps the other ladies with the flowers. The choir and organist will arrive at about ten o'clock and the congregation usually starts to drift in shortly after that. Easter service starts at half past ten and lasts about an hour, followed by tea and buns in the church hall. Then there is a children's Easter egg hunt in the early afternoon, and a church bazaar to raise money for the repairs to the belfry. Daddy will read Vespers at seven o'clock before returning home for dinner. You don't have to spend the whole day at church, Kit. Fiona and Adrian are going off immediately after the service to attend a concert in York Minster. Fiona says they'll stay there for dinner and won't be back until late."

"What do you want to do?"

"Be with you."

He took her into his arms and kissed her. "We'll be together whatever." He paused. "What do your parents expect?"

"Well, usually I help Mummy with the tea and buns, the Easter egg hunt and the bazaar, but then we come home and make dinner while Daddy reads Vespers. After dinner, we all gather around the fireplace for a nightcap or three and talk over the day. Eventually, we go to bed very late and a little tipsy."

That sounded tame, trite, and timeless — as if it had always been and always would be the same. Which made it irresistibly appealing to Kit. "We'll do that then — although it would be nice if we could have just one hour to ourselves, alone...."

Georgina went on tiptoe to give him a quick kiss and then declared, "I'll offer to make dinner so that Mummy can attend Vespers with Daddy. He'll like that; he insists on offering the service, but almost nobody comes. That way we'll have an excuse to leave the bazaar no later than four o'clock and won't see Mummy or Daddy until after eight. That should be enough time for — whatever we might want to do." She smiled up at him.

He bent and kissed her. "Thank you."

There wasn't a cloud in the sky when the Easter service started in a church adorned with daffodils and lilies and full almost to the last seat. The sunlight shone through the stained glass and the organ music swelled to the rafters. As they sang the familiar Easter hymns, Kit was transported back to his childhood, singing together with his mother around the piano, teaching the hymns to the village children and then singing them in round and back and forth. They developed a different, African rhythm in the dusty heat, but they never lost their magic. Yet when he looked sidelong at Georgina in her pale blue gloves and hat, it was as though he'd always been here. He could picture his mother standing on Georgina's other side, his father beside her, and two children, a boy and a girl — rather like the ones giggling in the pew opposite.

When the time came for the sermon, everyone sat and waited attentively with an air of eager anticipation. The Reverend Reddings' parishioners evidently expected good sermons. With good reason. Just two days ago on Good Friday, Redding's skill had impressed Kit when he had made — and let — the congregation weep. They had grieved together, and it had cleared the air. Today Reddings spoke of resurrection, renaissance, life and rebirth. He talked of rebuilding upon the ruins of an ethically eviscerated world. He talked of "eradicating the vestiges of the dark, satanic world of fascism" and "restoring the moral fibre" of society, but also of putting an end to the "the tyranny of class and racial privilege." He spoke of the need to liberate the underprivileged from "economic oppression and religious bigotry." Finally, he echoed the words of the Easter hymn, saying that "the strife is o'er, the battle won, the song of triumph has begun." He concluded with: "That triumphal song must not be one of gloating and complacency, but rather a song to inspire us to new accomplishments." To the strains of the named hymn, they filed out of the church into a bright English spring day.

Adrian and Fiona slipped out through the side exit to go to York, but Kit, Georgina and her mother shuffled out of the main door after the rest of the congregation. Since most people at once started drifting towards the hall for tea and buns, Amanda and Georgina felt obliged to go and help serve. Kit was left alone with Edwin.

"Did you like the sermon?" Edwin asked eagerly, hungry for a little well-earned praise.

"It was brilliant," Kit assured him, harvesting a look of glowing pride from Edwin, before adding with a laugh, "I just hope it wasn't a jinx."

"A jinx? Whatever do you mean by that?" Edwin asked baffled.

Kit shrugged and tried to sound light-hearted. "Oh, you know, an April Fool's joke or the like. Or maybe it's just bomber crew superstitiousness, but it seems as though it might be a bit premature to start the song of triumph before Germany has surrendered. The strife isn't over quite yet. At least, not for Adrian and me. We have to report back for duty next Wednesday."

Edwin suddenly felt sick in his stomach.

Chapter 25
Second Sight

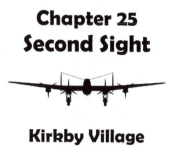

Kirkby Village
8 April 1945

Georgina and Fiona lingered over breakfast still wearing their dressing gowns. They'd spent the entire previous day getting back from Foster Clough, and tomorrow they had to report back to Kirkby Grange for the last term of their apprenticeship. They made a point of sleeping in late one last time before the new term started. Georgina checked her watch. Before leaving Foster Clough, Kit had promised to take her to lunch unless he left his regrets with Mrs Radford. Since he had not, Georgina expected him at around noon, but as it had just gone ten, she still had plenty of time to get dressed. So, while Fiona read a novel in her dressing gown, Georgina perused the Sunday papers with a cup of tea beside her.

The front page was filled with reports about a new Allied offensive in northern Italy, but Georgina wasn't terribly interested in the Italian front. She scanned down the page until she caught sight of a small article about the Me262. Kit had told her he thought it was one of these aircraft that had damaged Zebra almost two weeks ago, so she looked more closely. According to the article this "jet" fighter, as they were calling it, was capable of speeds of 550 mph and could outperform all Allied fighters. Fortunately, it was being deployed only in small numbers, the article said, largely due to effective bombing of the Messerschmitt factories by Bomber Command. Nevertheless, it had already accounted for "large numbers" of Allied aircraft casualties. Georgina regretted reading the article.

She shifted her attention to an editorial by the Dutch Ambassador pleading for Allied action to prevent the starvation of some 3.5 million Dutch people still living under Nazi occupation. The Allied armies had swept forward, thrusting towards the Rhineland, Ruhr and ultimately Berlin, but in doing so, they had severed the rail, canal and coastal traffic to much of north-western Holland, which remained under Nazi control. The Germans kept nearly all the available food for themselves, and three and half million people were starving after the long, hard winter. As many as 1,000 people were dying every day, the editorial claimed.

"*The Dutch people,*" the Ambassador wrote, "*have aided countless Allied airmen. They have given them shelter, medical assistance, food, clothing and help in evading capture. For the people of occupied Holland, each RAF and USAAF aircraft passing in the sky overhead was and is a symbol of hope and a promise of liberation. As long as they were there, taking the war to Germany, we knew that one day Hitler would be defeated. Now, when we are so close to victory —*"

The doorbell rang.

Georgina looked at her watch to be sure she hadn't lost track of time. No, it was only 10:25. Much too early for Kit.

"I'll get it," Fiona offered. She had already closed her novel and put her teacup in the sink, preparing to go upstairs and dress for the day.

"Thanks," Georgina said absently as she turned back to the newspaper. She had lost her place and started scanning down the paper again looking for where she had left off. From the door came the sound of a male voice murmuring in a low, solicitous tone. Georgina froze and the hair stood up on the back of her neck. Every fibre in her body listened. She heard her name. No!

The paper slid unseen to the floor as she turned to face the door. Fiona was back. She stopped in the doorway with tears streaming down her face. She couldn't bring out a sound. She just held out the telegram.

Georgina understood. Woodenly, she crossed the room to take the official notification from Fiona's hand. She opened it:

DEEPLY REGRET TO INFORM YOU THAT FL/LT C MORAN DFC, DFM AND CREW ARE MISSING AS RESULT OF OPERATION 7 APRIL 1945. LETTER FOLLOWS. PLEASE ACCEPT MY PROFOUND SYMPATHY. OC 617 SQUADRON

"I'm so sorry," Fiona gasped out. "I thought he was going to make it."

Georgina nodded. She had started to believe it too. She sank back down into her chair, too weak to stand.

From what seemed like a great distance Georgina heard Fiona ask. "Are — are they *all* gone? Adrian too?"

"It says 'and crew' and it says 'missing' which implies the aircraft did not return," Georgina answered with surreal calm. "All or some of them might have bailed out. There might be survivors. We'll have to wait and see what Group Captain Fauquier's letter says." She was answering on "auto pilot" with prepared phrases she had drummed into her head long ago.

Then a car door crunched shut outside the house and footsteps approached the front door. Georgina wanted to bolt upstairs. She couldn't deal with anyone now! Go away, she screamed silently. The doorbell rang again, and Fiona, wiping tears away with her hands, once more answered it.

Georgina waited to hear her turn whoever it was away. Instead, she heard Fiona gasp out, "Reverend Reddings! I'm so glad you're here! You're just the person Georgina needs. We only just received a telegram...."

Her father? Here? Now? It didn't make sense. She'd only left home yesterday morning. He hadn't said anything about travelling. Had a telegram been delivered there as well? But there wasn't time for him to have driven — then she understood. Sometimes he didn't need a telegram to know about accidents and death.

Georgina sprang up and rushed into the hall still hoping it wasn't true. She met her father's eyes and the hope died. When she spoke, it was not a question, just a dull statement of fact. "You had a vision." Only then did she start to crack. Kit was dead.

Edwin pulled his daughter into his arms. "His last thoughts were of you, Georgina. He was trapped in the cockpit, another man was trying to help him, trying to pull him free, but he couldn't. Kit was crying and kept saying 'I'm sorry, Georgina. I'm sorry.' And then there was a terrible explosion, and everything went black."

Georgina clung to her father as the whole world seemed to spin around her.

Edwin Reddings took Georgina home with him leaving Fiona to cope on her own. She had no one to turn to and no one with whom to share her grief. She went for a long walk, crying most of way. She grieved for Kit, but mostly she mourned for Adrian. Their days together at Foster Clough had been the most beautiful of her whole life. Exquisitely patient, sensitive and understanding, he had not been like most men. He'd been interested in what she did, what she thought and what she wanted out of life. They'd gone sketching together, and he'd been so encouraging about her efforts. Oh, she couldn't explain it! Of course, Kit had been nice too, but things were just different with Adrian. He was shy and humble, sweet and tender, and a good listener. For the first time in her life, she'd *wanted* to give up some of her own plans in order to be with him. And he, too, was probably dead.

The following day, Fiona got up early and cycled to Kirkby Grange where she waited outside Miss Townsend's office for nearly an hour before the headmistress arrived.

"Miss Barker!" Miss Townsend greeted her in surprise, but quickly discern her mood. "Is something wrong?"

"Yes, I'm afraid so." She drew a deep breath. "Miss Reddings received word yesterday morning that Flight Lieutenant Moran and his entire crew failed to return from an operation over Germany on Saturday."

"The entire crew?" Miss Townsend asked shocked.

"Yes, Ma'am."

"All those wonderful young men that came here just six weeks ago?"

"Yes, Ma'am. I think you can understand that Georgina —"

"Of course. She needs time to herself. Tell her to take a week off."

"Yes, Ma'am." Fiona noted it was a good thing Miss Townsend had reacted like this, since Georgina was already in Yorkshire.

Meanwhile, Miss Townsend's eyes gazed at nothing, and she seemed lost in thought or memories. Eventually, she shook her head. "So sad. And so close to the end. I'm sure Germany is going to surrender in the next few months. I'm lost for words, Miss Barker." Still shaking her head, she entered her office, and the door clunked shut behind her.

Fiona put a call through to the vicarage at Foster Clough and reached Amanda with the news that Georgina did not need to return to the school until the following Monday. Then she went in search of the Sixth Form Master and received permission to pass the word to the two girls who had been seeing Nigel and Frank. They responded as one would expect of sixteen-year-olds, with considerable melodrama. One kept gasping, "No, no! Not Frank!" The other burst into tears and fled to the lavatory.

Finally, Fiona sought out Nora. Fiona told Mr Willoughby what had happened, and he summoned Nora to his office so Fiona could deliver the news to her in private.

Nora came timidly into the room, her eyes behind the lenses of her glasses wide with apprehension. Mr. Willoughby greeted her with the warning, "Miss Shields, Miss Barker has some sad news for you."

"Did something happen to Miss Reddings?" Nora asked, looking at Fiona with frightened eyes.

"In a way, yes," Fiona agreed. "She has been given a week's leave to recover from the tragic loss of her fiancé, Flight Lieutenant Moran."

"He's dead?" Nora asked in horror, her eyes wide. "Terry's skipper?"

"We don't know for sure whether he is dead," Fiona modified, "but he failed to return from a sortie over Germany on Saturday."

"What about the others?" Nora asked urgently.

"They too are missing," Fiona told her softly but firmly.

"No!" Nora protested, shaking her head. "No! I don't believe you! That can't be true! Terry can't be dead. No."

Fiona shook her head. "I'm sorry, Nora. There's nothing we can do about it. We'll have to wait and hear if there is more news from the Red Cross."

Suddenly, Nora became obstinate. Her face became hard, rigid. She shook her head sharply and turned on Fiona furiously, as if she were the enemy. "No, Miss Barker. I know better! I *know* Terry isn't dead. If he were dead, I would feel it!"

Chapter 26
Carousel

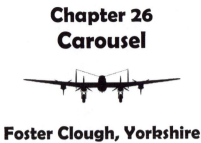

Foster Clough, Yorkshire
April 1945

For the first few days at home, Georgina was only vaguely aware of her surroundings. She did not cry or sob hysterically as she had after Don's death. She appeared calm, but only because her numbed psyche was incapable of expression. Her parents' efforts to comfort her penetrated only at a superficial level of consciousness, making her thankful for their consideration and kind words without listening to what they said. She spent hours out in the barn grooming Teros and Hester and cleaning out the stalls, benumbed. She went on long rides with her mother and for long walks with her father. They spoke very little.

Once, Edwin broke through the fog around her by saying, "For what it is worth, Georgina, I think Kit accomplished what he intended when he returned to ops."

"Dying?" She challenged him unbelieving and outraged.

"Yes. I think he felt he should have died instead of Don and went back on ops to pay the price. I have to confess that, when he became engaged to you, a part of me hoped he had found a way to evade that fatalistic sense of duty. Yet it wasn't in his character to shirk responsibility. In the end that overrode even his love for you."

Georgina stared at her father, angry at him for suggesting this, and angry at Kit too. How dare he make her love him if he *intended* to die? And how could his dying ever make up for Don's loss? Dying certainly didn't bring Don back. It amounted to punishing her twice for the same crime, the crime of loving. But she could not entirely dismiss her father's thesis either. Kit had too often hinted that he believed death stalked him. Then again, that was only rational; anyone who knew the statistics had to consider the probability.

On another walk, Georgina reminded her father of his own words about marriage in the early Middle Ages being an act of consent only. "I was betrothed to Don, but in the eyes of God I was married to Kit," she told him firmly.

Edwin absorbed that statement calmly before asking, "Are you trying to tell me you are carrying Kit's baby?"

"No, unfortunately. He was too careful. He didn't want me to be the object of any scandal."

Edwin considered this information carefully before remarking softly. "I'm sorry. I would have enjoyed being a grandfather to Kit's child."

"Oh, Daddy!" Georgina flung her arms around her father in gratitude for his understanding. After crying for a short time, they carried on with their walk, and said nothing to Amanda.

On the third day, the letter Kit had left with the adjutant arrived. It made Georgina cry so violently that she started vomiting. Her mother gave her a sedative and put her to bed. She fell asleep clutching the stuffed mother zebra, whose "baby" Zach she had sent to Kit as his good luck charm.

By the next morning she appeared calmer. When she dressed, she put on Kit's earrings. She presumed that the day would come when she would not, when she would want to wear something different, something that better matched her outfit, or the earrings of a new beau. But today they comforted her. Whenever she turned her head sharply and felt an earring lightly brush her neck, it was like a kiss from Kit.

She consoled herself with the knowledge that she had given Kit as much of her love, her time and herself as she possibly could. She had made him as happy as it was in her power to do. Furthermore, she had *chosen* to love him, knowing what the consequences might be. She did not have to go through life with the regrets Philippa had about Yves. Maybe she could have reduced her pain by giving Kit less love, yet she had rejected that course. Instead, she had consciously risked taking the cross of pain upon her shoulders, so that their time together would be as bright and beautiful as it could possibly be. In time, she told herself, she would be able to savour those memories and find in them again that joy and beauty.

Georgina took all the newspaper clippings she had collected since Kit joined 617 squadron and carefully glued them into a scrapbook. She worked meticulously, ensuring that they were in chronological order. Between the clippings, she pasted other mementos – the theatre ticket stubs from the Royal Shakespeare Company festival, the brochure from their hotel in the Lake District, snapshots of Kit and of the two of them together — hiking, dancing, dining. The final photo was of Z-Zebra with the entire crew lined up in front. It had been taken only last week, with Frank wearing a bright, white bandage under his service cap. The adjutant had included it with

Kit's letter. Georgina knew that many crews considered it bad luck to take a crew portrait before the end of a tour, but Kit had regretted not having one of Don's crew. He'd argued that not taking the picture had not saved them.

The letter from Fauquier arrived on her fifth day at home. The Group Captain explained that Kit had flown one of sixteen Lancasters that took part in a daylight attack on the submarine pens in Hamburg. Objectively, Georgina understood that this target had been worth the loss of seven men. After all, the submarine war was still raging unabated and unaffected by the Allied advances on the Continent. Fanatical U-boat captains sought with renewed frenzy to strike back at the advancing Allies by targeting merchant ships, like the one Mrs Witherspoon's sons had served aboard. Scores of lives were lost every day at sea. Logically, Georgina recognised the legitimacy of the target, yet in her heart she resented the sacrifice of a Lancaster and its crew to destroy submarine pens when the imminent end of the war would put an end to their ravages anyway.

Fauquier's letter continued with the news that the raid had been extremely successful, but the squadron had encountered Me 262s over the target. Most of these were engaged by the fighter escort, which lost two fighters. His letter continued: *"Unfortunately, in the debrief several crews reported seeing one of the German jets make a pass at Moran's aircraft. No one reported seeing either an explosion or an aircraft out of control. Thus, while we can be certain that Moran's Lancaster received damage which prevented its return to base, there is every reason to hope that Flight Lieutenant Moran and his crew were able to abandon the aircraft successfully before it crashed. In these circumstances, I would encourage you not to despair. Try to remain patient until we receive word from the Red Cross. I shall, of course, be in touch as soon as I have any further information on the fate of Flight Lieutenant Moran or any member of his crew. Please accept my deepest sympathy in these uncertain and trying times. Sincerely, J. Fauquier, CO 617 Squadron."*

A shock went through Georgina. Maybe Kit *wasn't* dead. It was true her father's visions had never been wrong before. Yet his vision only clearly indicated that Kit had been injured, in trouble and in pain, but maybe not *dead*. The explosion and the blackout might simply have been loss of consciousness. She sought her father out and showed him the letter. He read it attentively and then handed it back to her. Their eyes met.

"He might have survived the crash, Daddy," Georgina pointed out hopefully.

Edwin looked very old when he answered her, "Yes, he might have, but it would have to have been a miracle." He closed his eyes as he spoke, clearly replaying the vision again in his mind.

"Don't you believe in miracles any longer, Daddy? You used to tell Gerald and I that we should never stop believing in them."

He drew a deep breath and met her eyes. A chill went through her. There was not a trace of benevolent indulgence, not a hint of joyous faith. "Believing in miracles is pious, expecting them is presumptuous."

Georgina turned away and went out to the stables. She went into Hester's stall, put her arms around the mare's neck and cried. She sank down in the clean sawdust and curled up in a ball to weep. Hester nuzzled her with her soft muzzle and blew in her face. In her grief, Georgina imagined Hester was a zebra, a mother zebra separated from her foal, and abruptly she knew that it didn't matter what her father said, she *wanted* to hope a little longer.

When Don had been killed, she had not been given a chance to hope. His corpse was in an RAF mortuary by the time she was informed. She had seen the body before it was put in the ground. Don had been dead. But she told herself, maybe Kit wasn't.

She decided to contact Kathleen Hart. Kathleen's husband, Ken, had been Don's navigator, and Georgina had known her almost as long as she'd known Kit. After Don was killed, his crew broke apart going different ways, and Kathleen's husband, assigned to a new crew under a different pilot, had been lost on a sortie to Berlin. That had been just over a year ago now, and she had since joined the WAAF.

Kathleen was naturally distressed to hear that Kit was missing, but as Georgina had hoped, she encouraged her not to despair. "When Ken went down last March, several members of his squadron saw his aircraft catch fire and spin out of control; there were no 'chutes, so I had no cause for hope. However, when he was in the Merchant Navy before joining the RAF, his ship was sunk by a U-boat at night and not even the escort commander could give me specific information about what had happened to the crew. No-one knew if or how many lifeboats got away. It would have been easy to assume he was dead, to grieve and give up all hope. In fact, one of his shipmates came home to find his wife had already held a memorial service and cleaned his things out of their house! I'm so glad I didn't do that! Because, you see, three weeks later, I got a cable from Halifax. The lifeboat with Ken aboard had been picked up by a westbound vessel, and he was safe and sound.

"In your case, Georgina, it doesn't make sense to assume the worst. After all, Kit went down over the Continent. It's not like being lost at sea. The fact that you haven't heard anything from the Red Cross yet means absolutely nothing. With our troops advancing so rapidly, there are thousands of refugees, freed POWs and slave labourers streaming westwards. The relief services are completely overwhelmed. Eventually the Red Cross will provide details, but until Kit is confirmed killed, for God's sake, hope! That's why Ken and I named our daughter Hope, you know? Because hope is a wonderful gift that can help us weather many storms."

Fortified by these thoughts, Georgina announced that after her week's leave she would return to Kirkby Grange. Amanda protested, suggesting she might not be able to take the strain. "No, Mummy. Sitting here and wondering what has happened to Kit won't change anything. If Kit really is dead, then teaching will be more important to me than ever, and if he's not, he'll be happy to hear that I didn't go to pieces again. I think, dead or alive, Kit would rather see me doing my duty just as he did his. And I *do* have a duty to the children, Mummy. The improvement they made last term proves that I am helping them. If just one of these poor boys gets a better job in the future because I helped him to do sums faster or write a better letter of application, then that's a hundred times more important than sitting here feeling sorry for myself."

Amanda had never been so proud of her daughter.

Kirkby Grange
17 April 1945

Georgina was surprised to find that she could function quite normally at school. She did not let herself go as she had when Don was killed. It wasn't just that she had decided to keep hoping, it was also that when Don died, she'd lost not only the man she loved but her whole world and future. In contrast, because Kit had been afraid to think about 'after the war,' they had deliberately made no plans for a future together. As a result, no fantasy world went up in smoke with him — even if Kit *was* dead.

Strangely, it helped her to cope when she discovered that Fiona was having a terrible time confronting the loss of Adrian. Fiona had allowed herself to hope that she would have a relationship with Adrian, and those dreams had gone up in flames with his disappearance. In a reversal of roles,

Georgina found herself comforting a crying Fiona. As her father had long ago taught her, helping others was often a wonderful way to strengthen oneself.

So, unlike after Don's death, Georgina continued to look after herself. She ate regular meals and forced herself to go to bed and get up on schedule. She wore make up and lipstick, washed and did up her hair, dressed professionally — especially in clothes Kit had liked — and she wore Kit's elephant earrings every day.

It helped, too, that everyone, from Miss Townsend down, sympathised with her. Since the pupils not only knew what had happened but could remember Kit from his visit to the school — not to mention his flypasts — they showed rare consideration. Several of the boys even offered their condolences, for which Georgina was sincerely thankful.

She did worry about Nora, however, who stubbornly insisted that Terry would return. Georgina chose not to contradict her, not least because the experience of her own father's visions had made her hesitant to dismiss such things. Only time would tell if Nora's feelings were correct. Georgina hoped Nora would be able to cope if Terry was dead, but for now she had as much right to hope as Georgina did herself.

What would help them both, Georgina decided, was giving extra tutoring to Nora to keep them both focused on something else. She was still at the school on Wednesday evening when one of the boys burst in on her half-covered in mud.

"The gunners are back!" He shouted breathlessly. "The gunners are back!"

Georgina did not immediately grasp what he meant, and started to ask, "What —"

"Sergeants Roper and Osgood!" The boy interrupted her. "They're back."

Georgina jumped to her feet and followed the messenger in a state of excited confusion. If they were back and Kit wasn't, did that mean he was dead? No, she told herself, if they were back, then the chances of Kit's survival were greater.

All the boys who had been down at the playing fields crowded around the RAF sergeants and the commotion drew other pupils like a magnet. Frank already had his arm around his girl. Nigel caught sight of Georgina first and broke away from the throng to come towards her. He offered his hand, but she embraced him instead, putting her cheek to his. "I'm so glad to see you, Nigel." Frank joined them, and Georgina repeated the gesture, saying "I'm glad you made it, too, Frank. Is your wound all right?"

Frank grinned and put his hand to his ear and neck, both of which were still swollen and covered with a scab but no longer bandaged. "No worries, Miss!" he assured her

"We don't know what happened to the skipper," Nigel answered her unspoken question. "He ordered us to bail out and we went out the door in the tail of the fuselage, but the rest of the crew was still forward. Still, we thought you'd want us to tell you as much as we know."

"Of course!" Georgina looked around at the horde of children and realised that Nora had followed her out. Pulling Nora into the circle of her arm, she insisted, "But first, what about Terry? Do you know what happened to him?"

The two gunners shook their heads. "As I said, Mess, we got out from the tail, but there's an escape hatch on the floor of the bomb-aimer's compartment that the bomb-aimer, pilot and flight engineer use to bail out. The navigator and wireless op can use either exit, but Terry went forward." Nigel explained.

Mr Willoughby and Mr Baines, the sports instructor, at last caught up with the gaggle of excited boys. With a nod to the RAF, they shooed their charges back towards the sports field so that Georgina could talk to the gunners without spectators. Georgina, with Nora still enclosed in her arm, led the gunners towards the unused tennis courts. Here she stopped and faced Frank and Nigel. "Now. Please. Tell us everything you know."

"Well, trouble started when the oxygen on Z-Zebra wouldn't work properly during the test flight. Bishop thought he might have it repaired in time for the sortie, but the skipper didn't want to take any chances, so Fauquier assigned us to M-Mickey Mouse, instead." Nigel explained.

Frank jumped in, "Everyone knew Mickey Mouse was jinxed. It always had problems. But, just our luck, nothing went wrong with it on the outward leg, so we had no excuse to turn back. Instead, we reached Hamburg dead on time. As we started the bomb run, we saw the escorts dogfighting. Someone called over the radio that there were Me262s in the dust up, but, of course, that didn't bother the skipper. He did the run anyway."

Nigel continued, "We'd turned back for England, when one of the bastards fell on us out of the sky."

"We returned fire with everything we had, Miss Reddings, but just like last time," Frank unconsciously fingered his ear and neck scar, "it just flashed past us."

"There wasn't even time to corkscrew," Nigel emphasised. "I think I shouted at the skipper to corkscrew port, but it was too late."

Frank took over the narrative again. "The Lanc bucked and shuddered violently, so we knew we'd been hit. A moment later I noticed fire almost immediately below me. I dropped down and started fighting it with the blankets from the rest bed — which didn't do a lot of good. Luckily, Daddy and Terry arrived with two fire extinguishers, and somehow the three of us managed to put the fire out. It was quite frightening, but at least Jerry hadn't hit the engines or the fuel tanks. If he'd done that, it would have been curtains. As it was, despite the damage, we thought we could still get home."

"Only we were leaking hydraulic fuel," Nigel explained, "and the oxygen feed to my turret was broken. I managed to gasp out that I couldn't breathe just before I blacked out."

"The skipper dived to below ten thousand feet as fast as he could," Frank assured an alarmed Georgina, "while Daddy and I went back to try to drag Nigel out of his turret. Together we pulled him inside and hooked him up to oxygen in Terry's workstation, but then the starboard inner sputtered and went dead. The skipper called for Daddy to come forward to help him restart it, and a few minutes later he asked Adrian for the shortest course to take us over Allied lines."

"That was when we realized that he didn't think we could get home," Nigel put in.

Frank nodded. "I think we lost a second engine. We couldn't see from where we were, and things started happening rather fast after that. At least it seemed like it. Adrian gave the skipper a course, but then he changed it, I think."

Nigel's face was taut with remembered tension now. "The skipper told us to prepare to bail out, so we clipped on our parachutes, and Frank and I went back to the tail. We waited for what seemed like a long time, but we thought it was just to be sure we bailed out over Allied-controlled territory."

"We didn't want to fall into German hands because they've been shooting Allied airmen lately," Frank explained. "Finally, the order came to 'abandon ship'. We might have been losing altitude, but the skipper was still flying smooth as silk — except for some intermittent vibrations. We had little difficulty jettisoning the door or getting out. Nigel went out first. I followed and kept my eye on him as I went down. As soon as I landed, I buried my 'chute and started in the direction I'd last seen him."

Nigel flashed a quick grin at his crewmate, "I'd watched Frank come down and started walking in his direction, so within an hour we found one another. We'd already cut off the tops of our flying boots and we had our silk maps. The problem was we didn't know which way we'd been flying when we'd jumped, so we didn't have a clue which way to walk."

"But what about the aircraft?" Georgina interrupted. "Did you see the others jump? Or did Kit try to crash land?"

The two gunners looked at one another and shook their heads. Nigel, looking a little shamefaced, admitted, "We didn't see or hear the aircraft go in, Miss."

"Or see any other parachutes either," Frank added. "There was a forest very nearby that blocked our view."

"And I suppose we were a bit over-excited and confused by then. We just started walking until we came to a road and turned onto it."

"After a while, I needed to step into the bushes," Frank blushed a little at mentioning something so indelicate to a lady, and hastened to clarify why he mentioned it, "and that was what saved us. While we were in there, a bunch of Wehrmacht soldiers trudged past on the road."

"That was when we realised that we were still in German-held territory, after all." Nigel's face had grown harder. He was only a few years older than the boys playing sports nearby, Georgina reflected, but a world of experience apart. "We started to be careful after that. We hid out in the underbrush until dark and then, using the North Star as our compass, we started walking west. We did that for two days."

"Yeah. There was plenty of rainwater to drink, but we were getting seriously hungry when we came to this village and noticed that white sheets were hanging out of all the upstairs windows. We crept up and waited, hiding behind a barn for a while, and sure enough, a Comet tank rolled up the main street followed by half a dozen others flanked by columns of Canadian infantry."

Nigel shrugged. "So, we came out of hiding, walked over to the first officer we spotted, and identified ourselves as Allied airmen."

Frank smiled at the memory. "The Canadians were jolly nice to us. Fed us a great meal with bags of chocolate, and after about six hours they put us in a jeep going back to their support troops. We eventually made it to a collection centre for released prisoners of war, and in due time we were processed and flown back to the UK. After some more bumpf, we were finally sent on to re-join our squadron."

"But when we reached Woodhall Spa," Nigel spoke up in obvious agitation, "we found out they hadn't even been informed that we'd been found! They told us they had no news of the others, either. That's when we thought we'd better come over to see you and tell you as much as we knew."

Georgina sensed the gunners' distress. Despite their excitement over their lucky escape, they feared for their crewmates. They wanted to be optimistic and to help her, but they could tell her no more than they already had. Georgina thanked them for coming to Kirkby Grange and begged them to stay in touch.

Later in the day, a call from 617's adjutant provided a dry summary of the information Nigel and Frank had already delivered in person.

Kirkby Village,
19 April 1945

After a night mulling it over, Georgina decided that Nigel and Frank's story was full of hopeful signs. Apparently, the aircraft had neither exploded nor caught fire, as the gunners had not seen or heard a crash after they landed. Kit had been flying straight and level, an indication that he was not injured and the controls were undamaged. Besides, she was beginning to feel like Nora. If Kit were truly dead, surely, she would know it in her heart?

She decided to send Mr and Mrs Moran a short cable. She knew they would have received an identical one to the one she'd been sent eleven days earlier, but this was new information. She wrote:

TWO MEMBERS OF C. MORAN'S CREW BAILED OUT SAFELY. REPORT NO FIRE OR EXPLOSION. AIRCRAFT OVER ENEMY LINES. WILL SHARE ANY ADDITIONAL INFORMATION. YOUR (ALMOST) DAUGHTER-IN-LAW G. REDDINGS

Two days later she had the reply:
DEAREST DAUGHTER GEORGINA, THANK YOU. WE PRAY DAY AND NIGHT. LOVE DOROTHY AND HENRY MORAN

Meanwhile, Bergen-Belsen Concentration Camp had been liberated by British troops and the descriptions of the horrors discovered were beyond imagining. Georgina could not understand how people could lose all empathy for their fellow humans. She did not understand how a state could become an instrument of systematic murder. She rang her father to talk to him about it, but he too was struggling to grasp these revelations and come to terms with their implications. They agreed that the news undermined their fundamental faith in mankind — if not the Almighty.

Her father, however, also made a point of reminding her that evil multiplied and grew greater unless it was opposed. "You cannot stop an aggressor by giving in to him as the democracies did in Munich in 1938. People intent on mass murder respect neither law nor religion; they can only be constrained by force. These revelations of the magnitude of Nazi depravation make the sacrifices of all our young men more meaningful and necessary." He did not mention Don or Kit specifically, but Georgina knew they were who he was thinking of.

It ought to comfort her, Georgina told herself, that if Kit truly had died, it had been in a good cause. Yet, no matter how *necessary* his death might have been, it still denied her the joy she'd felt in his presence. If he truly were dead, then his smile and his laugh were lost forever. She would never again see that sidelong glance he gave her before he said something particularly provocative — or erotic. She would never again feel the touch of his hand or his lips, nor laugh at his silly, spontaneous, African dance-steps when he was particularly happy.

She pulled herself together. There was still hope he would return. She reminded herself that it was less than two weeks since he'd gone missing. It was too soon to grieve. She refused to grieve! So, each morning she put on his earrings and went defiantly to school.

Kirkby Village, 23 April 1945

Four days later, Georgina had just settled down in the attic to correct some maths papers, when the doorbell rang. Fiona had stayed late at Kirkby Grange with her drama group and Mrs Radford was operating on a cat, so Georgina and Mrs Kennedy were alone in the house. Georgina lifted her head and waited tensely. Since Mrs Radford's customers usually rang on the telephone, the bell might indicate another telegram, perhaps with news from the Red Cross — or simply a neighbour come to borrow a little extra sugar or milk. She held her breath, listening as Mrs Kennedy answered the door.

A moment later the housekeeper called up the stairs. "Miss Reddings? There's an RAF sergeant here to see you."

Georgina jumped to her feet, and from halfway down the stairs recognized Terry. She ran the rest of the way and greeted the shy wireless operator with an exuberant hug and the words, "Oh, Terry! Thank God, you made it! We've all been so worried about you, although Nora insisted you couldn't be dead. She'll be over the moon."

Terry nodded absently, and his discomfort warned Georgina that he brought bad news. She sought to delay the blow. "Wait!' she stopped Terry from speaking. "Don't say anything yet. Let's sit down, and I'll get you a cup of tea. Or would you like something stronger?"

"Tea would be lovely, Miss Reddings."

"Shall we sit in the kitchen?" Instinctively, she knew that Mrs Radford's sitting room would seem formal and intimidating to him. The kitchen would put him more at ease. She led the way, indicated a chair, and put the kettle on. Then she sat down opposite him and smiled sadly. "You've got bad news for me, haven't you?"

He shook his head helplessly. "Miss Reddings, I came to tell you everything I know, but..." He stopped, his courage failing him.

"Thank you, Terry. I'm so grateful you came. Let me just get the milk and sugar." She stood again, took the cups, saucers, milk jug and sugar bowl out of the cupboard. With her back to him, she brushed away the tears forming in her eyes and took a deep breath. She laid the tea things out before Terry, put tea in the teapot and poured the boiling water over the leaves as soon as the kettle started to whistle. The activity gave her time to pull herself together. She was determined not to break down and cry. She would be brave. It was what Kit would have wanted of her.

As she sat down opposite Terry, she told him, "Nigel and Frank came to the school to tell me all they could."

"So, you know we were in Mickey Mouse rather than Zebra and that an Me262 struck after the bomb run?"

"Yes," Georgina confirmed.

"What you probably don't know is that Adrian went to pieces again. Not over the target — he was fine through the bomb run — but after the fighter struck, he froze. He didn't help put out the fire, and when the skipper needed a course to take us not home but south so we could bail out over Allied-held territory, he didn't respond. I sent out an SOS, but we had no Gee reception because we'd lost the radio antenna in the fire. I did my best with H2S and the charts to work out a course, but when Adrian came to, he was indignant to find me at his station and ordered me out of his way. A moment later he called a course correction to the skipper, but he hadn't heard that we were no longer trying to return to England but rather to get over Allied-held Germany. The skipper challenged him and told him what we were trying to do. He apologised and gave another course, but while that was going on we had lost two engines and were sinking fast.

"I think we were below five thousand feet when the skipper told us to prepare to abandon ship. By then the kite had developed a strange vibration. I got my parachute on and helped Adrian into his as well. He was shaking so badly that he needed help, but I got him to the nose. As soon as the order came to bail out, Stu jumped, but Adrian balked. Daddy and I had to force him out, prying his hands away from the rim of the hatch as he tried to hang on. It was terrible." Terry shook his head and ran his hand through his hair, the scene replaying before his eyes.

Finally, he resumed his account. "All the time we were losing altitude, and the vibrations were becoming steadily worse. When Adrian was finally out, we were at no more than two thousand feet. We were still flying straight and level, but the crate seemed to be shaking itself to pieces. We had to get out in a hurry, yet that was when I realised the skipper wasn't in the nose. I turned around and asked Daddy, 'Where's the skipper? He's got to get out too!' Daddy answered: 'I'll go and get him' — and shoved me out of the forward hatch before I knew what was happening."

Terry pleaded with Georgina. "Please believe me, Miss! I wouldn't have left him there! I wouldn't have! Daddy pushed me. I wasn't ready for that. He pushed so hard that I knocked my head going out." He indicated a large scab over his eye socket that covered what must have been a bad gash.

"It's all right, Terry. I understand," Georgina assured him, though she was fighting back tears.

"I didn't want to leave him, Miss, but the next thing I knew I was spinning round and round and falling. I didn't know which end was up. I fumbled for the parachute handle and yanked it with all my strength. The silk opened with a violent jerk that twisted me around so sharply I almost threw up. I must have been upside down when I pulled the cord. The ground was coming up fast. I landed badly, fell over, and was dragged a long way before I came to rest. I staggered up just as the aircraft hit the ground — belly first — maybe a mile away. It was in open countryside. The skipper must still have been at the controls because it didn't go in nose first. He had the nose up and put it down on the main spar. The tail broke off at once and was left behind as the aircraft bounced up once. A second later, it crashed down again, breaking into two. The cockpit was flung through the air spinning like a ball, and the fuselage just disintegrated into a ball of flame.

"I started running towards the wreck, but suddenly there were Wehrmacht soldiers in front of me. I don't know where they came from, but they were between me and the burning wreck. I shouted at the Germans that there were still people inside. I remember screaming, 'My skipper's in there!' and pointing. But an officer, who didn't look any older than me, lifted his pistol and aimed it straight at me."

Terry paused, shaking his head. "You aren't going to believe this, Miss, but just when he was about to shoot, he fell flat on his face. For a second, I thought he'd been hit from behind by the ammo from Frank's gun that was exploding as the fire reached the ammo belts, but then I realised he'd been shot by one of his own men, a sergeant. When he lowered his rifle, he gestured for me to lie down on my face. He and the other soldiers came over and crouched down beside me, but with a gun to my head. All the while the aircraft was burning. The smoke was nearly choking us, and ammo kept going off, and then there was a second explosion when the fire reached the port fuel tanks." He held up his hands helplessly. "There was nothing I could do to help, Miss. Nothing."

Georgina put a hand on Terry's. "It's all right, Terry. I understand."

Everything in her father had seen fell into place now. Kit had been injured and trapped in the cockpit after it broke away from the rest of the aircraft. Daddy MacDonald had been there with him, trying to help him escape when the fuel tank exploded behind them. Terry, on the other hand, was already safely out of the aircraft when the explosion came. Both her father's vision and Nora's feeling, contradictory though they had seemed, had been correct.

After a long pause, Georgina drew a breath and asked. "How did you escape the Germans?"

"I didn't have to. Remember, the men who captured me had just killed their own officer! They wanted out of the war sooner rather than later. The problem was that there were masses of other Wehrmacht troops all over the place. They'd apparently converged on the crash too. This band of eight men used the distraction of the crash to creep away, taking me with them. They were led by led by a sergeant wearing an Iron Cross, and one of the men spoke broken English and he kept saying, 'We surrender! You translate!'

"Because they wanted to avoid being seen by their comrades, they crawled more than walked away from the tail of the wreck. After we'd been going almost an hour, we heard voices shouting in English. It was Adrian and Stu. Adrian had broken his leg on landing and screamed to attract help. Stu heard him and followed his shouts to join up with him. On seeing Adrian's leg, Stu realised he couldn't help, so he started shouting too.

"The Germans who took me prisoner must have been seasoned veterans. They applied first aid like medics and improvised a stretcher from branches. They ordered Stu and me to carry Adrian on it. As it got dark, they made a camp and shared their rations with us. I tried to ask why we didn't go to one of the villages, seeing as we were in Germany. When they understood my question, they shook their heads vigorously. The sergeant said: 'SS!' and made the gesture of having his throat cut. He also said: 'Nazis kill *Terrorflieger*,' and jabbed his finger at the three of us. When I told this to our intelligence during the debriefing, they said that as far as we know only German civilian authorities or vigilantes have murdered Allied aircrew, whereas the Wehrmacht continues to honour the Geneva Conventions.

"Anyway, we spent the night out in the open, but next day we reached the front. The Germans sent Stu and me out with a white flag in the direction of the Allied lines, ordering us to negotiate their surrender. They reminded us that they had Adrian, and if the Allies came for them shooting, he'd be the first to die. It was quite frightening, but luckily no one fired at us. We were taken to a Canadian major and explained the situation. He sent his men over to capture the Germans and bring Adrian out. The Canadians took Adrian to a field hospital and arranged for Stu and me to go to a collection point for freed POWs. I came here as soon as I got back to England, Miss. I knew you had to know what had happened." Terry fell silent and started nervously licking his lips.

This report crushed Georgina's hopes. She realised she ought to say something to Terry, but her mind was blank. What could she say? Kit was dead. Again. All over again. She'd been through this with Don, and now with Kit. She ought to be getting good at it. But she wasn't.

"I'm sorry, Miss. I'll go now," Terry said getting to his feet.

That got through to her. "I'm sorry, Terry. I can't—"

"It's all right, Miss. I'll go."

"You have to see Nora. I know she's just a kid to you, but you're her hero."

"Yes, Miss. I'll go and see her."

"Please spend a little time with her," Georgina heard her own voice from a great distance.

Although she never heard from Stu Babcock, three days later a letter came from Adrian. He was at home in London. His broken leg was still in a cast and he was on crutches, making it impossible to come in person, he explained. Georgina found his letter disjointed. He wrote about the Me262, the lost engines, the vibrations and Kit ordering them out. He explained in detail how he'd broken his leg on landing and been unconscious for several minutes. He wrote that he could provide no information whatsoever on what had happened to Kit. He said he would write separately to Fiona and ended the letter with: "I'm so unspeakably sorry. Kit was my best friend. I shall never forgive myself."

For what? Georgina asked herself. For breaking down? Or was this just a repeat of Kit feeling guilty about Don dying, when he had managed to survive? She hoped that Fiona could comfort Adrian in his grief because she did not have any strength to spare for him. Her heart was on the brink of collapse.

Chapter 28
The Greatest Test

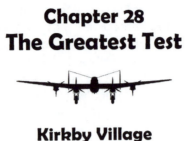

Kirkby Village
29 April 1945

Somehow, Georgina got through another week, but her emotional state had become noticeably more fragile. Now when Kit's earrings brushed her neck, they chilled her; rather than his kiss, she felt the breath of death. She hovered on the edge of a complete break-down, but tried to hold herself together, not wanting to go to pieces as she had after Don's death. While she kept tears at bay, her energy levels sank desperately low. She struggled to get up, get dressed and go to school. At the weekend, she did not bother to wash her hair or make herself look nice. Listlessness set in. She wondered vaguely what was the point of anything?

It didn't help that the Ministry of Health, which had responsibility for school evacuations, announced the "imminent" return of all evacuees to their homes. The city schools relocated to rural "refuge" areas to escape the ravages of German bombings no longer had anything to fear. The Ministry ordered them to return to their own premises — assuming they were still standing. The impending exodus of Old Palace School pupils and staff to London rang the final death knell for Kirkby Grange School. The government subsidies per evacuated child that had kept Kirkby Grange solvent throughout the war disappeared with the evacuees and their teachers. With the fee-paying student roll depleted both by the war and the horror of having to share the school with deprived children, there was only one decision left to take. Miss Townsend announced the closure of Kirkby Grange School with fortitude, but Georgina saw through her stoic demeanour; behind her brave façade, the headmistress had been broken.

That was the way Georgina felt, too, as she sat in her faded dressing gown leafing through the Sunday morning papers apathetically. They described a devastating air assault on Hitler's prized retreat, his "Eagle's Nest," at Berchtesgaden in the Bavarian alps. 617 Squadron had led the attack, dropping Tallboys and Grand Slams to mark the target for some 400 additional aircraft of Main Force. Even to Georgina that sounded like excessive force just to obliterate the dictator's home. She turned away from the article without the faintest interest in clipping and saving it. Kit hadn't been flying.

Her attention turned instead to accounts and photos of a massive humanitarian effort to end the famine in the western Netherlands. Hundreds of British and American bombers were dropping grain, powdered milk, powdered eggs, and other vital foodstuffs at specified points. "Flying in at only a few hundred feet to prevent the sacks from bursting and the food from pulverising on landing, RAF and USAAF aircraft have already delivered tens of thousands of tons of vitally needed supplies to the starving Dutch population," the journalist wrote. A few hundred feet? Georgina scoffed mentally. Kit would have delivered the packages at fifty feet. Then again, at least the story spoke of human kindness rather than the reverse. Several aerial photos showed signs made out of bedsheets that spelt out "Thank You".

The telephone rang. Georgina looked over indifferently. It couldn't be Kit, so why should she bother answering? Then she remembered that Mrs Radford was treating a dog with a broken leg, and Fiona was out somewhere. She was alone in the house. It was probably one of Mrs Radford's customers and might be an emergency. She must at least take a message. She dragged herself to the telephone and answered in a dull voice. "Radford residence."

"I'm trying to reach Miss Georgina Reddings," an unfamiliar male voice declared.

"Speaking." Georgina's voice sharpened and her body went rigid with dread. It was almost certainly the Red Cross with confirmation of Kit's death.

"This is the adjutant of 617 squadron. British army units have overrun a Wehrmacht hospital and found Flight Lieutenant Moran."

"Alive?" Georgina gasped out. "Kit's alive?" On one level she couldn't believe it, and on another she was already starting to feel giddy with joy.

"I must warn you, Miss Reddings, that Flight Lieutenant Moran was severely injured in the crash. Until RAF medical personnel have had a chance to examine him, I can't give you any prognosis regarding his chances of full recovery. The station medical officer has agreed to fly across in one of our aircraft this afternoon. We'll bring him back and see that he gets to an RAF hospital at the earliest possible opportunity. If you wish, I can arrange for you to be granted access to the station to meet the aircraft when it touches down here this afternoon. Although you'll have only a moment or two, you would be able to see Flight Lieutenant Moran during the transfer."

"What time should I be there?" Georgina answered, her head filled with images of Kit burned beyond recognition, or with a broken back or missing limbs. She remembered with horror how he'd always said he would prefer to die than to live as a cripple. She had argued the opposite. The time had come to prove *her* moral fibre. This would be the greatest test of her love.

Germany
April 1945

The pain and thirst obliterated all else. Reason fled; every thought aborted before it could fully form. Kit remembered the aircraft shuddering uncontrollably — so badly he could not trust the autopilot. He remembered Daddy returning. He remembered the cockpit catapulting through the air, spinning and whipping him about, leaving him dizzy. From the instant they smashed into the earth, pain engulfed him as completely as the flames that erupted from the Lancaster and the blood that filled his eyes.

Hands dragging at him, trying to pull him free and incomprehensible shouting penetrated the pain only imperfectly. The attempts to save him increased his agony, and in the midst of it was a sense of overwhelming guilt. He was going to die, and Georgina was going to suffer all over again. He should never have sought her love, nor accepted it. He should not have been so selfish. God would never forgive him.

Kit briefly lost consciousness, but the pain dragged him back from oblivion. It consumed his entire left side, starting with his left foot, which felt as if it had been crushed into a thousand pieces. Rough handling jostled and flung him this way and that, triggering new waves of pain so intense that he screamed and struggled to escape. Sweat and blood drenched him, and he writhed in growing terror as his brain frantically requested information from eyes that refused to give it any. Around him he felt flames, smelt smoke, and heard guns going off as men shouted in gibberish.

He woke up in a bed with rough sheets but could not open his eyes. Blood-caked bandages glued them shut. Thirst spread down his parched throat from a dry mouth. He cried out for water, and eventually a woman answered angrily in garbled Afrikaans. She shoved a glass into his hands, but with his eyes bandaged shut he couldn't guide it. He poured half the water over his face and down the side of his neck, provoking curses and insults from her. Later someone came to wash the blood and grime from his face and change the bandages. He tried to open his eyes when the bandages came off, but the swelling overpowered his strength. He caught only a hint of light, but it suggested he might not be totally blind.

The urgent realisation that MacDonald had returned to the cockpit to help him and had been beside him when the Lancaster crashed woke Kit. He started shouting, "Daddy!" Then thinking that might be too generic, he revised it to "MacDonald! MacDonald!" This elicited angry shouts, apparently for him to shut up, but he heard no response from MacDonald. He'd killed him.

Repeatedly the pain returned, associated with motion — being put on a stretcher and carried somewhere. When he was lifted, the agony was so great that Kit screamed or simply broke down into helpless sobs, begging them to stop. The periods when he wept helplessly because the pain wouldn't go away and no-one seemed willing or able to help lasted even longer. The inability to open his eyes preyed on his psyche and nerves. What if he was blind? He couldn't be an engineer, if he were blind, no matter how much Barnes Wallis wanted to help. If he couldn't see, he couldn't study anything. He wouldn't be able work to work at all. He'd be a useless cripple for the rest of his life. Utterly exhausted and helpless, his thoughts increasingly transformed themselves into fervent wishes for the agony end. Just let me die, he begged mentally.

Instead, a tremendous flap erupted. Someone bumped into his bed and jolted him from his sleep, causing his left side to explode with pain. Kit's ears strained to interpret what was happening around him. Explosions grew louder, closer, more frequent and more threatening. Footsteps hastened this way and that. Clatters and crashes betrayed panic as angry voices boomed out orders in the incomprehensible Afrikaans that Kit knew was actually German, yet still thought of as Afrikaans. Boots pounded, heels clacked, bed wheels squealed, and doors slammed. Motor engines gunned and faded into the distance.

An eerie calm descended. Nervous muttering from the beds around him slowly waxed. Kit could smell the panic rising. More vehicles. Doors slamming shut, doors opening. Boots on tiles. Silence. Then someone started calling out from the bed next to him. "Here! Here! RAF. RAF." They repeated it several times, until booted footsteps approached Kit's bed.

A clipped English voice asked, "Are you RAF?"

Kit was lucid enough to suspect this might be a Gestapo trick, so he gave his name, rank and service number. The man answered by putting a hand on his shoulder. "Flight Lieutenant Moran, you don't have to worry any more. We're British."

Moran didn't believe him. "Who are you and where did you come from?"

"I'm Major Dr Benjamin Howe of the Royal Medical Corps, serving with the XII Corps, Second Army. We have just taken control of this hospital from the Wehrmacht."

Could any German have managed such a perfect English accent? "You're a medical officer?"

"Yes, do you need anything?"

"There was another member of my crew in the cockpit with me when we crashed. Flight Sergeant MacDonald, Gordon MacDonald. Have you found him?"

"Not yet, but we'll keep an eye out for him. He'll be in the sergeants' ward."

Of course, Kit registered. Why hadn't he thought of that? The Wehrmacht like the RAF separated patients by rank.

"Is there anything else I can do for you?"

Should he risk asking the English medical professional about the extent of his injuries? No, the doctor hadn't had a chance to examine him yet. He chose instead to ask, "Can you give me something for the pain?"

"Yes, of course. Nurse, bring some morphine over here, please," Howe called out. That was what finally convinced Kit that this man was not a Gestapo agent in disguise. Howe's voice was near his head again, "If you provide me with your unit details, it will make it easier to get word back to your family."

"MacDonald and I are on No 617 Squadron."

"Well done! Even I've heard of them!" Kit could hear a smile in the doctor's voice. Then the nurse arrived with the morphine.

For the first time since the crash, Kit was able to sleep properly. It was a profound, healing sleep, interrupted only occasionally by hallucinations.

He was back in Africa, on safari with his father. He was with Georgina in the Lake District. He was a child, playing the piano with his mother. He was standing behind Don as Don flew a Lancaster through a brilliant, golden sky.

Once a soft, East African voice woke him. "Sir?" the voice asked. "Sir? I'm going to cut away the bandages over your eyes so we can see how they are doing."

Tensely, Kit waited while hands as gentle as his mother's slipped cold scissors under the bandages, and with an incredibly loud crunching sound severed the bands blinding him. Kit held his breath, but very soon he started to see light seeping under the edge of the cut bandages. Then they were gone, and he was blinded by the light rather than by darkness. He screwed up his eyes in a desperate effort to try to see something.

"Just relax and let your eyes adjust," the voice of Dr. Howe suggested. Kit forced himself to do as he was told. Gradually, quite naturally, his eyes started to open. They were still badly swollen, at least his left eye was, but he *could* see — with both of them. He smiled at the doctor.

"That's better," the doctor declared. Holding up his finger he asked, "Can you follow this?"

Kit's right eye could follow the movements easily; his left could not, giving him severe double vision.

"Not to worry," the doctor told him. "The muscles and nerves were badly damaged, but they should heal."

Kit next tried to lever himself upright so he could look at his other injuries, but Dr. Howe held him down firmly. "I don't want you sitting up just yet. Be patient."

"I have terrible pain in my left foot," Kit told him, to explain why he wanted to sit up.

"That's quite normal. I'll see that you get more morphine."

"Did you find Flight Sergeant MacDonald?"

"Yes, we did. He's alive, but in fairly bad shape. We've laid on transport for both of you to get back to England together, but I want you in as stable and comfortable a state as possible for that trip. Rehabilitation won't start until you're in the hands of the RAF medical establishment. Now relax and let Corporal Solomon give you a little clean up." Howe moved briskly away.

"Would you like a sponge bath and a shave?" Corporal Solomon asked gently, drawing Kit's attention away from the doctor.

"Are you from Kenya?" Kit asked the smiling orderly hopefully.

"No, Rhodesia, sir. So would you like that bath and shave?"

"Yes, very much, thank you." Kit closed his eyes again, filled with a sense of childlike trust induced by the gentleness in the orderly's hands.

Not long afterwards, he was woken from his sleep to see Z-Zebra's nose above him. He seemed to be on the tarmac below the Lancaster looking up at the jumping zebra and the two neat rows of bombs cataloguing her sorties. He thought he was hallucinating again until someone jostled his stretcher. He winced automatically and gripped the frame in anticipation of pain that did not come. The stretcher tilted and a Geordie-accented voice called, "Hold tight, sir." Doing as he was told, he felt himself being swung nearly upright and then lowered before being lugged and hauled to the sound of thumps, bumps and suppressed curses. They deposited him onto a flat surface, and from just beyond the metal skin wall around him he heard a Merlin engine cough before starting up. Soon the world was vibrating to the deafening, oppressive, reassuring roar of the engines. Embraced by this familiar cocoon, he fell back into sleep.

The distinctive, short squeal of the tyres touching the tarmac woke him. His eyes flew open, and he knew he *was* in a Lancaster, on the rest bed. The aircraft rattled and fishtailed as the pilot put on the brakes. He lifted his head and saw a bundle of his belongings beside him. He put his hand inside and groped until he found the lower right pocket of his tunic; Zach was still with him. They reached the end of the runway and with that distinctive squeak from the brakes, Zebra came to a halt. They swung off the runway onto the taxiway. The tyres thumped rhythmically over the cracks in the concrete until the aircraft turned again and with an almost human sigh stopped. The engines wound down, and Kit heard someone opening the door and getting the ladder out. A man emerged and hovered over him. "Moran?"

"Yes?" He looked up. The man looked vaguely familiar, but he couldn't place him. It was not Major Howe.

"We've made it."

"Where?"

"You're back at Woodhall Spa. Don't you remember me? I'm Squadron Leader Quail, the Station MO. An ambulance is waiting outside to transfer you and MacDonald to the RAF hospital at Ely. They're just removing MacDonald now."

"How badly is he injured?"

"His spine was fractured in multiple places. It will take some time to get him up and about again, but we'll do our best. Just as we will with you. You were lucky that none of your broken ribs punctured a lung or any other vital organ, and although your left eye-socket was crushed there was no damage to your eye. FYI, I understand from the chief British medical officer at the hospital, Major Howe, that the Wehrmacht was extremely short of anaesthetics and used them only sparingly. Although used for surgery, they apparently didn't spare any to control post-operative pain. I'm acutely aware of how terrible that must have been for you — a medical professional's nightmare. I can understand that you may feel you've been poorly treated."

Kit did not respond. It had been hell, but they had also saved his life. They could have left him in the cockpit to burn. They could have shot him. Now that he was back in England and in the hands of the RAF, he preferred to pull a blanket of oblivion over the worst of it.

Quail drew a deep breath and continued, "Moran, I don't want you to go through life thinking that if only you'd managed to fly another fifty miles or so, your condition would have been substantially different. Based on available information, Major Howe and I believe the Wehrmacht doctor who operated on you must have been a superb orthopaedic surgeon. He did a first-rate job setting your ribs and hip and reconstructing your eye-socket — although we'll want an optometrist to examine that eye ASAP. They also probably saved as much of your leg as they could." Then with an efficient: "Here, I'll carry your kit," the MO reached for the bundle of clothing beside Kit and started toward the exit. A moment later the medical orderlies arrived.

It wasn't until that moment, when the 'body snatchers' threw back the blanket to lift Kit from the rest bed onto the stretcher, that he realised his left foot and most of his lower left leg was gone. He had not had time to adjust to the shock when Georgina's face appeared beside the stretcher. She reached out her hand. Kit grasped it and gasped in surprise, "Georgina!" His next thought, however, was that she didn't yet know he was a cripple. When she found out, she might abandon him. The thought terrified him, and he clung to her hand. "Please don't leave me! I know it's not fair to ask you to be married to a cripple, but—"

"Kit darling! I don't care about a *foot*! Not when I have the rest of you! It's all right, Kit! I'll be with you! I love you!" She brushed the tears away from his still bruised and badly swollen cheeks with her free hand, and then bent and touched her lips to his. It wasn't a kiss so much as a promise of future kisses. Then she drew back to allow the orderlies to push the stretcher into the waiting ambulance. The doors clanged shut, and the engine started, shaking the entire vehicle.

Georgina stood beside Dr Quail as the ambulance swung onto the taxiway. She was crying now too, and the MO handed her his handkerchief.

Then lighting up a cigarette for himself, he remarked, "Thank you. You just did more for that young man's recovery than anything I, or any medical professional, could have done."

"I wasn't lying," Georgina insisted defiantly. "I don't care about one foot. I came so close to losing all of him."

"Quite right. That's the spirit. But I warn you, it isn't going to be easy."

Epilogue
Those Whom He Loves Less

Liverpool
5 October 1945

Henry Moran sensed his wife's growing nervousness as the battered old passenger liner, still in her wartime camouflage, manoeuvred towards the P&O quay. Mrs Moran wore her best British clothes: a tailored tweed suit over a white blouse with lace-trimmed collar and cuffs, a small, tan hat and brown leather gloves. Not a flash of African colour, not even in the form of a scarf, enlivened her austere attire. Henry put his arm around her waist and brushed the side of her face with his lips. "Everything's going to be all right, Dorothy. This isn't South Africa. This is England."

Dorothy clutched his hand, unable to speak. Over the last days of the voyage, fears of snubs and racial slurs and damaging Kit's career prospects had plagued her. Kit looked so white that no-one without knowledge of his background viewed him as coloured, but Dorothy knew her African blood showed in her round face, dark eyes, and dark skin. Once people associated him with her, might they not look on him differently? Would it have been better for her to stay away, hidden from sight, a secret to the British who would decide his future?

She feared the answer to those questions was 'yes,' yet she wanted to see — to hold — the son she had come so close to losing. She also wanted to meet his bride, the girl who had not only captured his heart, but stood by him despite his handicap and was now prepared to be the breadwinner so that he could realise his dream of obtaining an engineering degree.

The knowledge that she would see Kit's beloved Georgina in a matter of hours, however, set off another attack of nerves. Since the receipt of Georgina's first letter almost a year ago, Dorothy had believed that Georgina and she were kindred spirits. In the tense weeks after Kit went missing, that feeling had grown even stronger. Georgina, she felt, was her daughter— whether Kit lived to marry her or not. That feeling had only been reinforced by Georgina's twice-weekly updates on Kit's treatment and recovery ever since his miraculous survival — and by her continued commitment to teaching.

Yet, as the distance separating them dwindled to just a dozen frothing feet of dirty water alongside the quay, Dorothy suddenly feared she had been deluding herself. What could a dumpy, half-black woman raised in the African bush possibly have in common with the daughter of an Anglican clergyman? Hadn't her advice to the younger woman about teaching and children been impertinent? Wouldn't the English woman, now secure in Kit's heart, resent his negro mother for 'presuming' so in her letters? Her fears induced near paralysis.

"That's Kit there!" Henry called out, too excited and relieved to keep his voice down. Kit wore his best blues, the trouser creases sharp, and his decorations on full display, yet he had one hand in his trouser pocket and there was an informality about his stance that conveyed complete ease with his situation. That, more than anything, enabled Henry to relax at last. "He looks wonderful!" He declared with so much relief that anyone hearing him immediately sensed the mental agony he had endured ever since learning of the amputation of his son's left foot. Henry removed his white, Panama hat and waved it to attract Kit's attention.

Kit spotted his parents, and his face lit up as he waved back. He pointed his parents out to the slender girl beside him, and Dorothy realised that she had formed a mental picture of Georgina based on an Englishwoman she'd known in South Africa. She had always pictured Georgina as a tall, stunning, blond woman with sharp, aristocratic features and a svelte but sensual figure. The girl beside Kit, on the other hand, was of only medium height, with light brown hair and a fragile rather than film-star figure. Altogether, she looked rather ordinary — until her face lit up with a smile that transformed her whole being. She was waving at them with a bright yellow-orange scarf. Dorothy's eyes filled with tears of gratitude.

Before they could meet, however, the formalities of customs, immigration and disembarkation demanded tribute. Despite traveling with little luggage, it took almost an hour before the bureaucratic gods released the Morans. They emerged from the customs hall, Henry carrying a large wicker suitcase, and Dorothy clutching her handbag as if it were a lifebuoy thrown to a drowning sailor. By then, the crowds in the waiting room had thinned. Kit started forward with an awkward, unnatural yet determined gait. Georgina glanced up and said something before rushing ahead to take hold of Dorothy by both her hands. "Welcome to England, Mrs Moran!" It sounded formal, but Georgina accompanied her words with the most un-English gesture of delivering kisses on both cheeks. Then she slipped an arm around Mrs Moran's waist and started guiding her to Kit.

Dorothy gazed at the slender, younger woman and felt a different sense of wonder. Georgina wasn't a glamorous beauty, yet to the missionary's daughter from South Africa something about her was like light from heaven. Meanwhile, Georgina put into words what her arm had already said. "It's so wonderful to meet face-to-face at last, Mrs Moran! Yet, at the same time, I feel like I've known you almost as long as I've known Kit. You are so much a part of him. Kit and I are very grateful that you and Mr Moran have made this long trip to be with us for the wedding, and I can't wait to introduce you to my parents. We want to show you a little of our world, but I hope one day to visit yours. Kit has painted Africa so brilliantly that I can't wait to see it for myself." Little zebras grazed on the yellow and orange scarf Georgina wore, while ebony elephants danced below her ears. Dorothy beamed.

Georgina continued, "My parents have planned a whole programme of sight-seeing for you. I hope you don't mind?"

"There is nothing in the world I want more than to spend time with them, you and Kit."

Then Kit was there. Having embraced his father in the meantime, he took his mother in his arms and she clung to him, unable to say anything but "Kit, Kit, my little boy. I'd thought I'd lost you!"

Eventually, Kit led them to the car, where the luggage had already been loaded. Georgina insisted that Dorothy sit beside Kit in the front, so she could see more, while she settled in the back with Henry. Georgina had the maps, however, and for much of the next hour they focused entirely on finding their way out of Liverpool. Such conversation as there was slipped into easy, British superficialities about the weather and the voyage.

Once they found the route, they tried to put some of the trip behind them, not stopping until nearly five. While waiting to be served cups of tea at a dreary roadside restaurant, Kit turned to his mother and announced. "At last, I have someone I can complain to about Georgina."

Dorothy caught her breath and glanced towards Kit's bride. She glimpsed a fleeting smile as Georgina looked down and instantly understood this exchange was staged. Kit meanwhile jestingly insisted, "Georgina has been terrible to me, mother. She doesn't understand how devastating it is for a young man to lose his foot. Even when I pointed out I wouldn't be able to dance well ever again, she told me I had always been terrible at it and that at least I now had an excuse. When I said I would never be able ride again, thinking that would upset the ardent horsewoman, she promptly set me astride the most intelligent mare I've ever met. Hester has more sense than Georgina and me put together, and we ride more than ever before. There is nothing that Georgina allows me *not* to do, mother.

She's an absolute tyrant!"

Dorothy leaned over and kissed Georgina on the cheek. "Bless you child. Bless you!"

But as the long journey continued and rain set in, driving became difficult. It soon became clear that increasing discomfort — if not pain — bothered Kit, but he irritably rebuffed offers from both Georgina and his father to take over the driving. His mother realised that Kit's handicap represented more than a minor inconvenience; it brought problems and tensions with it. The last forty minutes in fading light and pouring rain tested the nerves of them all. Georgina became increasingly sharp-tongued about Kit's stubbornness, while Kit grimly ignored her remarks and refused to surrender the wheel. Dorothy concluded that strong as their love was, they were nevertheless under exceptional strain and would require much grace in the days and years ahead.

They arrived half an hour late at the vicarage, only to find that Reverend Reddings had been called to deal with a drunken parishioner whom the police did not want to arrest again. Mrs Reddings seemed lovely and welcoming but her son, Gerald, with his Oxford accent and Royal Navy airs, unwittingly intimidated Dorothy. Kit precipitously decided he should take his parents on to the farmhouse inn where he and they were staying until the wedding. As Kit hustled his parents back to the car, Dorothy noticed tears in Georgina's eyes. Dorothy wanted to go to her, but Kit had his mother by the elbow and was firmly pushing her into the car. All she could do was call out, "We'll have time together later!"

At least Henry was able to put his foot down and insist on driving, so they arrived safely at the inn. By then, however, the promising start to the day had been eclipsed, and the Morans retired to bed vaguely dissatisfied.

Yorkshire
6-7 October 1945

Returning from the lavatory in the pre-dawn grey the following morning, Henry Moran heard a clatter, thump and then violent cursing as he passed his son's room. He paused and listened. No additional noise escaped, which increased his concern. Approaching the door, he knocked softly, and called in a low voice, "Kit? Can I help in any way?"

There was no answer. Alarmed, Henry tried the handle and to his surprise the door opened. At once, he realised what had happened. Kit had evidently wanted to go to the lavatory himself and taken his crutch rather than putting on his artificial foot. He'd unlocked the door from the inside only to drop the crutch, lose his balance and fall. He lay with his head against the side of the bed and his one and a half legs stretched out before him, tears streaming down his face.

"Kit! Are you hurt?" His father went on his knee beside him

Kit silently shook his head. Henry laid a hand on his shoulder and waited. Eventually, Kit croaked out, "Do you honestly think I should go through with this?"

"With what?"

"With the wedding? With binding Georgina to a cripple for the rest of her life? She only just turned twenty-one."

Henry settled himself on the floor beside his son, sitting so their shoulders touched. When he spoke, his words were unhurried and pensive. "In the last war, the thing I feared most was becoming an invalid. The thought of losing a limb or my sight terrified me. I believed I would rather die." Henry paused to let this sink in. His son opened one eye and fixed it on him. Only then did he continue. "Yet when you went missing, I did not think to myself: 'Well, that's better than him coming home a cripple!' When I learned you were alive but had lost a limb, I did not curse God or feel distress, anger or sadness. No, I rejoiced with all my heart, and I thanked God a thousand times that you had survived despite the loss of your foot. I suppose that sounds hypocritical, but it should tell you something."

"Such as?"

"How those who love you feel about your condition."

Kit considered him without lifting his head. "I understand that you and mother would rather have part of me than nothing at all. But I'm not asking you to be my nurse for the rest of my life. Even if I were, it would be different; you have had half a lifetime without the burden of a caring for an invalid, and you have each other. Georgina is barely starting her adult life, and she will be alone. She has no one to help her look after me — not to mention that she's continuing her career as a teacher in order to put me through university."

"Before we talk about Georgina, will you first answer one question?" Henry eyed Kit, who just waited. "Do *you* regret surviving?"

"Good God, no! Georgina has given me so many happy moments since the crash —they alone have made survival worthwhile. I'm looking forward to showing you and mother England. I'm excited about going to university at last, studying engineering properly, understanding how things work, and learning how to create useful things. When I'm finished, I'll be able to find interesting and rewarding work. I'll be able to provide for a family. I am not condemned to uselessness. I know that..."

"Good. And from what you just said, your doubts about this wedding do not spring from any doubts about your feelings for Georgina either."

"Yes and no. In the initial shock of discovering I'd lost a foot, I begged her not to leave me. I was frightened and still in shock and on painkillers. But under the circumstances — with the MO and Adjutant of the squadron looking on, not to mention me on a stretcher with a bruised and swollen face — what choice did she have but to say she would stand by me? Don't you see? It was wrong for me to ask her in those circumstances. I was thinking only of myself, wasn't I? If I *really* love her, I should put her best interests ahead of my own, shouldn't I? How can I ask her to spend the rest of her life with a cripple, with half a man?"

"Calling yourself 'half a man' is utter nonsense! And calling yourself a 'cripple' is nearly as ridiculous! That is nothing but false pride!" Henry spoke bluntly and emphatically. He continued, "Oh, I understand that you'd rather be perfect for Georgina, and I know you'd rather be able to do everything yourself. You've always been so damned independent that you could never accept help from anyone. But while you may not be perfect anymore and you may need some modest assistance from time to time, you're not bedridden and you are not helpless. Your so-called *handicap* is not a terrible burden at all. The real burden is putting up with you when you're in one of your stubborn moods!"

Kit laughed. His father did not. "I'm quite serious," Henry told his son. "Your attitude is far more burdensome than your injury. Yet even in that regard, no one is forcing Georgina to take up this burden. You *asked* her if she was willing to marry you – just as you are, stubborn, bloody-minded and handicapped. Georgina agreed — and not just at that moment after you were repatriated. She's had nearly six months since then to back out of this marriage if that were what she wanted. It's not, or there would be no wedding tomorrow. Tomorrow's ceremony is nothing more than a public expression of a private decision taken months ago. Georgina is an adult with a very good brain and a strong will of her own. You have no right to insult her by refusing to respect her decision."

Kit met his father's eyes, considered his words for a moment and then grinned. "You're right. Thank you for that piece of your mind. Now, help me back on my feet physically as well as emotionally." As he spoke, he started getting his right leg under him. With a smile, Henry retrieved his son's crutch and handed it to him. "You can manage just fine on your own."

On the evening before the wedding, Kit joined his friends for what passed as his "stag party" at the Wuthering Heights Hotel, where most of them were staying. His entire crew assembled along with Teddy Hamad and Reggie, from Don's crew. None regretted that the war was over, or that they would never again climb aboard a Lancaster with a belly full of high explosives bound for hostile airspace. Yet as the war receded into the past, they remembered more vividly the good moments they had shared. Excited and delighted to be together again, volleys of laughter accompanied the first several rounds, and a raucous and exuberant mood mushroomed.

And yet... Much as they wanted to, they couldn't quite recapture the atmosphere of their former RAF drinking bouts. For a start, except for Kit and Daddy, they were all "de-mobbed" and in civvies. More importantly, however, the sense of triumph and accomplishment that had buoyed them up on VE Day had long since worn off. In its wake lingered a vague feeling of dissatisfaction. In its place, like the heavy overcast skies that all too often had kept them grounded, uncertainty and unease hung over them.

The future looked murky and far from inviting.

Rationing and shortages continued. Bankruptcy threatened factories, shops and the nation. The wartime coalition had disintegrated, and politics divided the country again —right down the centre of the table at the Wuthering Heights Hotel. Adrian, Stu, Reggie and Daddy remained staunchly loyal to the Conservatives and expressed outrage at the ungratefulness of Terry, Teddy, Nigel and Frank for voting Labour and thus throwing Churchill out. To stop the argument from getting out of hand, Kit deflected the discussion to their personal plans for the future.

Of those assembled, Stu appeared to have landed most securely on his feet. He had joined his father's firm. Unlike many other small businesses unable to adjust to the post-war world and forced to close, Stu's family print shop and photographer's studio was prospering. Being a partner with his father and uncle, however, meant that Stu also saw the books. To his surprise, he'd discovered that with paper supplies severely controlled they had to scramble, flatter and cajole the right people week after week just to stay open. He'd learned that keeping costs down, retaining reliable workers and attracting customers required skill and effort. "I never knew how hard business was!" He complained. "I thought the money just flowed in steadily like a river running by."

Adrian hadn't been so naïve about business, yet he, too, was struggling as a novice architect. He admitted to bidding unsuccessfully on one project after another. He explained to the others how much time and effort he expended making design proposals that customers then decided against, often without explaining why. "I'd be happy to revise things for them," he stressed in a plea for understanding, "but the clients don't give me a chance. They just disappear with a 'we'll give you a ring' — which they never do."

Kit suspected that some of Adrian's evident unhappiness stemmed less from his business failures than from living at home with his domineering and critical father. Nor did it help that he'd broken up with both Julia and Fiona over the summer, and was solo again.

Terry, Nigel, Frank and Teddy Hamad from Don's crew were all justly furious with the RAF for demoting them from sergeant to aircraftmen as soon as they went off ops. The humiliation of being chased about by corporals with no operational experience had precipitated hasty departures into a civilian world for which they were not prepared. In consequence, none had yet found employment, although Terry hoped to get a position with the Post Office any day. His plan was to work sorting mail at night, while studying for his school leaving certificate during the day. The other three youths didn't know what sort of jobs they wanted. Their fathers had gone to sea and that seemed the obvious option since Britain had such a desperate appetite for imports of all kinds. Yet Frank summed up their feelings in a single question: "Is that all there is? After all we've been through, are we going to end up no better off than our dads?" Somehow it didn't seem fair.

Everyone wanted to know what Kit planned, and he surprised them by announcing he had turned down an apprenticeship with Vickers organised by Barnes Wallis in order to study. Except for Terry, they seemed to think he was mad, chasing an indistinct dream rather than grasping a concrete opportunity. Kit knew they might be right, but something held him back from committing to any job. He feared that taking a paid position would put him on a career path before he had a chance to explore his capabilities and interests.

"Did you get a scholarship?" Adrian asked, remembering that Kit had always claimed he didn't have the money for university.

"No, but I will get a small disability allowance from the RAF. Georgina has secured a teaching position, and both my father and Reverend Reddings have agreed to help out. We'll be living on a shoestring for a few years, but we should be able to manage," Kit explained.

It had barely struck midnight, when Kit declared he was turning in while urging the others to carry on drinking. He'd taken a room at the hotel so he wouldn't have to drive after the anticipated — but unrealised — excessive consumption of alcohol.

Adrian jumped up and offered to see him up the stairs. Kit accepted the offer because he could sense that Adrian wanted time alone with him. At the door to the room, Adrian asked if he needed help undressing, and Kit said 'no.'

"Kit," Adrian started.

"Yes?"

"There's something I need to know."

Kit just waited.

"Do you — do you blame me for not getting us back over Allied lines? For not giving you the right course?"

Kit thought about that carefully. Terry had mentioned it to him on one of his visits to the RAF rehabilitation centre, and Georgina too had speculated. Kit, however, shook his head. "Adrian, we weren't going to make Allied lines no matter what course we flew. Besides, as you know, I could have thrown you off my crew any time I wanted. I didn't. So even if you put up a black on that last flight, I'm the one holding the can."

Adrian searched his face, and Kit looked steadily back at him.

"Thanks, Kit. That is a huge relief." Adrian smiled and they said good night.

As Kit watched him walk back down the hall, however, he knew that Adrian would never forgive himself, and his guilt would always stand between them.

The wedding day broke clear and sunny and promised to be warm for October. Much still needed doing before the service at six o'clock. Georgina had an appointment at the hairdresser's and then planned to meet Kathleen Hart's train from London and bring her back to the vicarage. Amanda wanted to pick up the flowers and deliver them to the church. Aunt Emma needed to make final adjustments to the wedding gown, and Aunt Anna was busy getting Georgina's bedroom ready for the Morans, who would be staying at the vicarage after the wedding. Edwin fussed with his sermon, Gerald worried about ensuring sufficient alcohol for the reception, and, of course, the horses couldn't be neglected just because two people had decided to get married.

Thus, the grandfather clock struck one before Edwin managed to draw his daughter aside and insist on a word with her. He pulled her into his study and shut the door behind her. "Sit down," he ordered.

Bemused, Georgina obeyed.

"I know you'll think this isn't the right time, but I don't know when there will *be* a right time, so I must say a few things to you now," Edwin declared earnestly.

"I do already know about the birds and the bees, Daddy," Georgina teased him.

"Ah, yes. I'd gathered that." He tried to look sternly at her, but they both ended up laughing instead. Then he became serious again. "No, what I have to say is much more serious than that. First, I feel I must apologise to you for telling you about my vision of Kit dying. It caused you much needless pain and anguish."

"Daddy, you never intended to hurt me. I know that."

"That's not the point. The point is I presumed to know some greater truth — and I was wrong."

"Not really. What you saw was correct — simply incomplete."

"Exactly! Like all human understanding of things divine. It is hubris to think we understand God's will and His plan for us. I'm humbled. Deeply humbled."

Georgina could tell her father was more than humbled, he was disturbed. She reached out to him. "What is it, Daddy? What is upsetting you? Surely, you have no reservations about my marriage to Kit?"

"Good heavens, no! Not for a second! On the contrary, it is a ray of sunshine in the gloom that seems to grow by the day. Do you know the Nazis murdered the German theologian Dietrich Bonhoeffer?" His tone of voice reflected both his shock and his sadness.

"Yes, you mentioned it earlier," Georgina tried to sound sympathetic, although to her Bonhoeffer was only a name.

"On April 9th, just two days after Kit was shot down, they killed Bonhoeffer, knowing that they had lost the war and that he could do them no harm. It was an act of vengeance and hatred — a dark desire to destroy as much light and goodness as possible. And yet, two days earlier, Wehrmacht soldiers risked their lives to drag Kit and MacDonald out of the cockpit of their Lancaster as ammunition went off all around them. Kit and MacDonald are alive today because Germans not only rescued them but also provided the necessary medical treatment to keep them both alive. I find that baffling."

"The Germans who killed Bonhoeffer were different Germans from the ones who saved Kit and MacDonald," Georgina replied reasonably.

"Yes, of course, but..."

"But what?"

"I no longer understand this world. It was so much simpler during the war. We were fighting evil, and the Nazis' atrocities justified almost anything. But now I wonder. Did they excuse *individual* acts of injustice? Or cruelty? Was the atomic bomb truly necessary? Was it justified? It certainly wasn't targeted or precision bombing. Those two bombs destroyed two entire cities — every single living thing, man, woman, child, cat, and dog. Vaporised! And what about the Soviets? Are they any better than the Nazis? Haven't we in fact made a pact with the Devil? Haven't we created a new threat to humanity and decency by bringing Stalin's troops into the heart of Europe? How do we prevent a new tide of evil, one armed with atomic power, from sweeping over us? How do we root out the causes of these orgies of mass violence — the selfishness and hatred, the jealousy and the greed? How do we emasculate the godless and destructive ideologies they breed?"

Georgina knew his questions were rhetorical, but she could also see that he was digging himself ever deeper into a hole of despair. She reached over to touch his hand gently. "Daddy, Rome wasn't built in a day — nor Jerusalem either. It is going to take a concerted effort by legions of people working together over a long period of time to build Jerusalem in England's green and pleasant land." Her father nodded, but he did not seem comforted, so Georgina continued. "I think that one stone in the new Jerusalem must be a memorial to the past. We must not let people forget the cost of institutionalised hatred and greed. We must teach our children that the aggressor, no matter how victorious in the short term, will ultimately be annihilated."

"Oh, child! You are wiser than your old father! Why am I even talking about these grim things on your wedding day?! Today is a day for rejoicing, not for thinking about the sad state of the world. Forgive me!" He stood and flung open his arms.

Georgina willingly went to them, saying, "Daddy, you wouldn't be you, if you didn't worry about the state of the world. So don't apologise. I don't want you to stop being who you are."

"But what am I to do for your wedding sermon? I can't find the right message — or even the right tone. I've tried at least a dozen themes already. Everything sounds trite or downright insipid!"

"Then just talk to us. Tell us what is in your heart."

"All these doubts and questions?"

"Kit and I don't need verbal hearts and flowers — or platitudes, either. We know we aren't going to just 'live happily ever after.' But we also know that there can be no Easter without Good Friday. No resurrection without death. Share with us your doubts and questions. Inspire us to go on living for the sake of *finding* the answers that none of us yet have. Now, it is high time for me to go and get dressed and for you to go to the church." She kissed his cheek softly and left him still lost in thought his study.

The church was beautifully decorated with asters and chrysanthemums and bright light steamed through the tall Gothic windows, chasing away the reminders of the failed dreams of past generations. The parishioners turned out in force to see their vicar's daughter wed, making the invited guests the minority. No one cared; the church was full.

Georgina wore a gown designed by her Aunt Emma. It had been made from a silk sari brought back from India by her Aunt Anna long before the war. Simple in style without any obvious fitting, it evoked the gowns of ancient Greece as the silk cascaded in abundance from her neckline to the floor and fluttered and swayed as she moved.

Because her father was officiating at the altar, Georgina's brother Gerald escorted her up the aisle in full-dress naval uniform, after her bridesmaids, Kathleen and Fiona. MacDonald "stood up" with Kit at the altar, performing his duties as best man from a wheelchair, while his wife watched on beside Kit's parents.

The formalities were rapidly concluded. Georgina's hand was transferred, vows were exchanged, and the wedding ring slipped over her left ring finger to join the engagement ring. Kit and Georgina were pronounced man and wife and knelt to receive communion.

Kit stumbled as he tried to get up, but Georgina deftly caught his hand and steadied him. Surprisingly, Kit accepted the gesture without apparent irritation. He even smiled his thanks at her. A step in the right direction, Edwin thought as he climbed to the pulpit for the sermon.

But as he looked out across the expectant congregation of wedding guests and neighbours, a cloud extinguished the sunlight. A gust of wind rattled the ancient windowpanes. The naked twigs of the apple tree tapped insistently against the stained-glass like a ghost demanding admission. Melancholy slipped into the church, to lurk in the shadows and lounge against the gravestones lining the walls. It settled on his daughter's beloved but no-longer carefree face. Fear and sorrow had chiselled their marks upon her brow and cheeks, the scars from grieving for Don and fearing for Kit. Georgina's advice now seemed doubly wise.

Edwin had discarded his earlier, unsatisfactory attempts at a sermon to write something more forthright. He had only loose notes before him now and felt even more nervous than usual. Clearing his throat, he declared, "Today represents a small miracle. A miracle of survival that many of us doubted. Indeed, whilst all of us gathered here today enjoy the boon of extended life, I dare say all of us also mourn the loss of someone dear."

Edwin saw Georgina grasp Kit's hand and saw him squeeze it.

"Thus, we cannot help but ask ourselves: Why? Why have we survived and not the others?" Edwin paused to let the congregation reflect on the question before continuing.

"I have often wondered whether an immortal God who has granted us eternal life, considers a marginally longer human existence inconsequential." He paused. "After all, how important can a handful of years be to the Almighty? He has dwelt with us since before the flood. He comforted us with His son almost two thousand years ago. He will still be here two thousand years from now? So, what do a handful of earthly years, a few more or less, mean to Him?

"If we believe in the Gospel of the Holy Spirit, our souls are immortal, and we do not die. All those whom we so sorely miss have not been obliterated. They are not gone. They are merely invisible to us. Perhaps they are the lucky ones." Again, he paused to let this thought sink in.

"They have gone on to greener pastures, while we are left the poorer for their absence. We must come to terms with the fact that tens of thousands of young people who would normally be making their contribution to our society have instead been swept away into a vast Unknown, leaving us behind — like the debris deposited by the outgoing tide.

"We must also come to terms with a world in which millions — a number so vast that our little brains can hardly grasp it — *millions* of helpless and innocent people were slaughtered in the worst known case of systematic genocide in recorded history. We must face the sobering fact that while Hitler and his political regime have been destroyed, racial hatred lives on. Not only that, it lives on in a world where new forms of mass destruction have been unleashed. We must face the fact that the next Hitler may control atomic weapons.

"And make no mistake. There will be another Hitler because the evil that spawned him still skulks in the dark, awaiting the chance to re-emerge wearing new, alluring trappings," Edwin turned his eyes on his sister Lucy, who pretended not to understand him. "It lurks among *us* — in the hearts and minds of far too many who pretend to be on the side of righteousness. The war with Hitler is over — but not the greater war against the evil that he momentarily embodied. Our victory over Hitler was significant, but not final.

"Yet his defeat was essential, nevertheless, and the sacrifices made by Kit's colleagues, by our sailors and soldiers over the past six years, were all necessary. By making that sacrifice, they not only brought an end to this murderous and depraved regime but also accelerated the passage of their souls into paradise. They have earnt their rest and a place in heaven." He paused to let this thought sink in, and saw several of his parishioners, including Mrs Witherspoon nod, apparently comforted.

Then he resumed his sermon. "But what does this mean for us who remain?" An uneasy stirring rippled through the church.

"Yes, we have a debt we'll forever owe, but isn't the issue greater than that?

"We all know the phrase: 'The Lord takes those whom He loves best.' Does that imply that we, the survivors, are those whom He loves *less*?" Edwin paused once more and again a restless squirming gripped the congregation. It sprang not from boredom but from discomfort.

"Are we the souls God loves *less*?" He continued, "Or, are we the souls of whom He expects *more*?

"Perhaps He granted us longer life for a purpose. Perhaps rather than forgotten, we were *chosen*. Might He have given us a second chance to demonstrate our moral fibre? Might His gift come with the obligation to counter lies, prejudice, hatred and arrogance with truth, tolerance, justice and righteousness? Might the price of our extended survival be the duty to strive at making this brutal and imperfect world a better place for those who follow us?

"Let us pray that He who has chosen us for this task will stand beside us as we try to fulfil His purpose for us. And let us not cease our mental fight 'til we have built Jerusalem in England's green and pleasant land."

The organist, recognising the text, immediately took up the introductory chords to "Jerusalem." As one, the congregation surged to their feet to sing.

Although Georgina had warned him the sermon might be "unusual," Kit was momentarily stunned by her father's ability to speak so directly to his heart. For the first time since Don had given his life, Kit felt at peace with that sacrifice — and with his own survival. He could let go of his guilt and accept that maybe benevolent design lay concealed in the darkness after all. As the congregation called for chariots of fire, Kit looked up at the ceiling of the Church. He thought he heard a Lancaster flying low overhead.

"It must be Don come to wish us well," Georgina whispered beside him, and for once her eyes did not fill with tears at the mention of her former fiancé. She was smiling.

Kit thanked God that both he and Georgina had been given a second — or was it a third? — chance for a full life, one that they could live together.

Historical Note

- Throughout the Second World War, RAF aircrew were volunteers. Conscription was, of course, introduced for the other services, other trades, and eventually for industry, but not for aircrew.

- Air Marshal Arthur Harris, the C-in-C of Bomber Command, was popularly known as "Bomber Harris" in the press, but within Bomber Command he was often referred to him as "Butch" (for "Butcher") Harris. He was regarded with respect and even awe, yet widely believed to be cold-blooded, heartless and indifferent to casualties as well.

- The process of "crewing up" was haphazard, and almost all aircrew describe it as chaotic and unnerving given its importance. Aircrew newly arrived at training centres were simply told to "sort themselves out" and basically went around talking to one another until they had the requisite number of individuals with the necessary trades to form a complete crew. However, the exact timing at which this process occurred does not appear to have been consistent. Some aircrew describe it happening immediately after arrival at an OTU, others after a fortnight or more. On the assumption that the process varied either over time or from Station to Station and from Commander to Commander, I have chosen to have it occur after a fortnight in accordance with one of the most detailed accounts of the process provided by Sidney George "Stevie" Stevens in *Tomorrow May Never Come*.

- When drafting this novel, I relied upon the descriptions of training I had read in a variety of memoirs and personal histories. These, while vividly describing incidents, individual characters and feelings, are often vague on the time span involved. To further complicate matters, throughout the course of the war the RAF altered the length of training courses in response to operational needs. Other factors also impacted the length of training for any individual pilot, for instance, waiting times until mustering, travel times to distant training locations such as the U.S., Canada and South Africa, and the time of year when critical phases of training took place. Training in England during the winter months could be seriously inhibited by bad weather that precluded flying and extended the time needed for a pilot to obtain the necessary flying hours requisite for passing on to the next stage of training or assignment. The fourteen months the novel gives Moran from "ab initio" to operational status is on the short side, but given that he was not a new recruit but rather re-mustering in a new trade not impossible.

- Learning to fly to the RAF's operational standards was extremely hazardous. Roughly seven thousand aircrew were killed in flying accidents during training. Pilot error (simple mistakes can be fatal in an aircraft!), technical failures and above all the English weather contributed to the high casualty rates.

- Bad weather also seriously impacted operations and accounted for appalling numbers of aircraft and aircrew losses. After returning from operations over the Continent, RAF aircraft — many of which were damaged and/or extremely low on fuel — all too often confronted fog and rain that closed multiple airfields across a wide swath of the country. On the night of 16/17 December 1943, for example, forty-five aircraft crash landed, were abandoned, or collided in fog over England. A total of 150 airmen were killed in these weather-related accidents. This was far from an isolated incident and inspired my chapter "Fog."

- During the Second World War, Great Britain was not a producer of crude oil and had only limited capacity for oil refining. Most aviation fuel for the European Theatre of Operations had to be brought by ship across the Atlantic or around Africa from the Middle East. German U-boats which patrolled the sea lanes prioritised tankers. Petrol was severely rationed and aviation fuel allocated first and foremost to operational, not training, airfields.

- The tactic of pausing in the midst of the corkscrew to allow the gunner to get in a good shot was developed and practiced by Flight Sergeant Tom MacLean, a gunner on 617 Squadron. Using this technique, he shot down four German fighters during a 30-minute running battle on a single night. He was awarded the DFM and promoted to Warrant Officer. He also served as an instructor in Training Command, albeit a station training pilots of Coastal Command, and was the inspiration for Nigel's instructor.

- While "sprog" crews were recruited directly from training to 617 Squadron in 1944 and 1945, they trained for months, not weeks, before being allowed on "ops." I have compressed the time in training to enable Moran to take part in key raids.

- As described in this novel, the Officers' Mess at Woodhall Spa was located in a former mansion, which had been turned into a hotel before the war. The Petwood Hotel as it was called had been built in a pseudo-

Tudor style and provided comparatively luxurious accommodations. The "cinema in the woods," golf course, and other features mentioned are historical fact.

- The second and third attempts by 617 Squadron to sink the *Tirpitz* took place September 11 and 28 October 1944 respectively, rather than in February 1945. Otherwise, the course flown, the defences and results are historical. The then squadron commander Wg/Cdr Tait flew alongside the aircraft with the hung-up bomb four times to divert some of the flak. I have only substituted Fauquier for Tait to conform to the timeline of the novel. The other crews mentioned, both the aircraft that crash landed in Sweden (F/O Bill Carey) and the aircraft with difficulties releasing the bomb (Malcolm Hamilton) were real crews.

- The "adventures" attributed to I-Item are based on what happened to the Hubert "Nicky" Knilans during 617's first attack on the *Tirpitz*. Knilans was an Irish-American pilot who flew 30 ops with 617 squadron. His aircraft suffered the damage described, flew on the first raid against the *Tirpitz,* and returned safely to Woodhall Spa. In fact, however, his aircraft was scrapped immediately afterwards and not flown on the second attempt on the *Tirpitz* a few days later.

- Barnes Wallis sat in the operations room during some key operations, including the initial raid on the dams. On one occasion, a rear gunner let him fire off some rounds from his Lancaster.

- The attack on the Kembs Barrage was historically flown on Oct. 7, 1944. The then squadron commander Tait led the low-level raid, and I substituted Fauquier for him. All the other crews who participated in that assault are named and their fate corresponds to the historical record with the exception of Squadron Leader Drew Wyness — for whom I substituted Forrester, and Flight Lieutenant Philip Martin, for whom I substituted Moran. The fate of Wyness and his crew have been given to Forrester, and the events described as happening to Moran's crew are largely based on those experienced by Flight Lieutenant Philip Martin. Namely, Martin's aircraft was hit by flak that severed the rudder cables, he flew in that condition through Basel balloon barrage, and his flight engineer tied the severed rudder cables to an axe, by which he controlled the rudder throughout the return flight. As described in the novel, Kit Howard and his crew were killed on the raid.

- 617 Squadron flew the raid against the "super submarine" factory near Bremen on 27 March and attacked the submarine pens at Hamburg on 7 April as in this novel. Historically, all of 617's aircraft returned from the operation to Hamburg.

- Surprising as it may seem, Nazi Germany largely adhered to the Geneva Conventions with respect to prisoners of war from the Western Allies. (The Nazi regime justified its horrendous treatment of Soviet prisoners on the grounds that the Soviet Union was not a signatory to the Geneva Conventions.) This included providing medical assistance and care to Western Allied POWs. Thus, just as Luftwaffe pilots downed over England were given medical care as needed by the British, so RAF and USAAF airmen shot down over German occupied territories generally received medical assistance and care.

- Where violation of the Conventions occurred, German civilians and Nazi civil officials rather than members of the German armed forces were more commonly responsible. The Luftwaffe had a comparatively good record of treating their prisoners correctly. There would, therefore, have been nothing unusual about a downed pilot and flight engineer receiving surgery in a German military hospital. Germany medical knowledge and facilities were world class at this time.

Note on the RAF Term "Lack of Moral Fibre"

The term "Lack of Moral Fibre" (LMF) was introduced into RAF vocabulary in April 1940 to characterise aircrew who refused to fly without a medical reason. The RAF needed a means to deal with this unexpected problem because flying was voluntary, hence refusal to fly was not technically a breach of the military code. After investing as much as two years in training aircrew, the RAF could not afford to let refusal to fly become widespread.

Men designated "LMF" (Lacking in Moral Fibre) faced swift disciplinary action. For the airmen who continued flying operations, the fate of those 'expeditiously' posted away from their squadrons for LMF was shrouded in mystery. Rumours spread and legends still abound. The threat of being designated "LMF" acted as a powerful deterrent to wilful or casual malingering. Tragically, the threat of humiliation may also have pushed some men to keep flying when they had already passed their breaking point, leading to errors, accidents, and loss of life.

In the post-war era, popular perceptions conflated LMF with "shell shock" in the First World War and with the more modern concept/ diagnosis of Post Traumatic Shock Syndrome (PTSS). In literature — from Len Deighton's *Bomber* to Joseph Heller's *Catch 22* — aircrew were increasingly depicted as victims of a cruel war machine making excessive and senseless demands upon helpless airmen. Doubts about the overall efficacy of strategic bombing, horror stories depicting the effects of terror bombing on civilians, and general pacifism in the post-war era have all contributed to these clichés.

In reality, LMF was a more complex and nuanced issue. Historical analysis of the records show that over the course of the war, less than one percent of aircrew were posted for LMF. Furthermore, while nowadays LMF is most commonly associated with bomber crews, the statistics show that only one third of LMF cases came from Bomber Command. Surprisingly, fully another third came from Training Command, while Fighter Command and Coastal Command had their share of cases as well. Significantly, only a tiny fraction of those initially posted away from operational squadrons for presumed LMF were ultimately designated LMF or the equivalent. (The term used for describing aircrew deemed cowardly varied over time, including the terms "waverer" and "lack of confidence.") Last but not least, the process for determining whether aircrew were LMF or not was far more humane than the myths of immediate and public humiliation suggest.

While the decision to remove a member of aircrew from an operational unit was an executive decision, applied when a member of aircrew had "lost the confidence of his commanding officer," the subsequent treatment was largely medical/psychiatric. Thus, while a squadron leader or station commander was authorised — indeed expected — to remove any officer or airman who endangered the lives or undermined the morale of others by his attitude or behaviour, the man found LMF at squadron level was not automatically treated as such by the RAF medical establishment.

The medical and psychiatric officers at the NYDN (Not Yet Diagnosed Nervous) Centres (of which there were no less than 12) were at pains to understand the causes of any breakdown. They did not assume the men sent to them were inherently malingerers or cowards. On the contrary, as a result of their work they made a major contribution to understanding — and helping the RAF leadership to understand — the causes for aircrew behaviour. These included not only inadequate periods of rest, but irresponsible leadership, lack of confidence in aircraft, and issues of group cohesion and integration. As a result of their interviews with air crew, the medical professionals were able to convince the RAF leadership to reduce the number of missions per tour in Bomber Command and to exempt aircrew on second tours from LMF procedures altogether.

The psychiatric professionals increasingly came to recognise that "courage was akin to a bank account. Each action reduced a man's reserves and because rest periods never fully replenished all that was spent, eventually all would run into deficit. To punish or shame an individual who had exhausted his courage over an extended period of combat was increasingly regarded as unethical and detrimental to the general military culture." [Edgar Jones, "LMF: The Use of Psychiatric Stigma in the Royal Air Force during the Second World War," The Journal of Military History 70 (April 2006). 456]

Meanwhile, roughly one third of the aircrew referred to NYDNs returned to full operational flying (35% in 1942 and 32% in 1943-1945), another 5-7% returned to limited flying duties, and between 55% and 60% were assigned to ground duties. Less than 2% were completely discharged.

RAF Rank Table

RAF	USAAF
Marshal of the Airforce	Five Star General
Air Chief Marshal	General (4 Star)
Air Marshal	Lt. General (3 Star)
Air Vice Marshal	Major General (2 Star)
Air Commodore	Brigadier General (1 Star)
Group Captain	Colonel
Wing Commander	Lt. Colonel
Squadron Leader	Major
Flight Lieutenant	Captain
Flying Officer	First Lieutenant
Pilot Officer	Second Lieutenant

Because the USAAF had ten non-commissioned ranks to the RAF's seven, it is not possible to provide exact equivalents, however, the lowest rank in the RAF was "Aircraftman." This is the term from which term "erk" derives in RAF jargon.

The RAF non-commissioned ranks from highest to lowest were:

- Warrant Officer
- Flight Sergeant
- Sergeant
- Corporal
- Leading Aircraftman — or LAC
- Aircraftman (1)
- Aircraftman (2)

Glossary
of RAF WWII Terminology

A/C: Aircraft.

Ace: A fighter pilot who has an extraordinary number of victories; in WWI this as "over five" but in WWII the number was not really defined.

Ack-Ack: Friendly anti-aircraft guns (as opposed to Flak — enemy anti-aircraft guns).

Adj.: Short for adjutant, the administrative assistant to the commanding officer of a squadron.

A/G: Air gunner.

Airscrew: Complete assembly of three or four propellers, hub and spinner.

Aircrew: Men who served in aircraft, regardless of their specific trade (i.e. pilots, observers, navigators, bomb-aimers, wireless operators and air gunners).

Angels: A term used in airborne radio communications to designate altitude. One angel equaled 1,000 feet, e.g. angles twenty was 20,000 feet.

AOC: Air Officer Commanding a Group.

AOC-in-C: Commander of a Command (e.g. Bomber Command, Fighter Command, etc.).

Armourer: Ground crew responsible for bombs, defensive ammunition, flares etc.

Arse-end Charlie: In Fighter Command an aircraft that flew behind a section, flight or squadron weaving back and forth to see the enemy better; in Bomber Command the rear gunner.

Availability, Squadron or Flight: The status of a squadron or flight requiring pilots to remain on the station but not at the dispersal hut or in flying kit yet ready to take off in roughly 30 minutes.

Bacon, to save one's: To save one's life.

Bag: To collect or secure, including illegally.

Bags of: A large quantitity, as in "bags of fun" or "bags of flak".

Bale or bail out: To abandon an aircraft using one's parachute.

Bang on: Right on.

Battle dress: Woolen working uniform.

Bandit: Enemy aircraft.

Beat up: To fly very low.

Belt: Travel at high speed.

Best blues: Dress or parade uniform.

Binder: One who nags or bores.

Binding: whining or complaining.

Bits and pieces: a crashed aircraft.

Black, a: as in "put up a black", doing a bad job of something.

Black out: To lose consciousness due to the force of gravity or "g".

Blitz time: Time for aircraft to be over the target.

Blood wagon: Ambulance.

Bloody: At this time a fairly heavy-duty profanity.

Blotto: Drunk.

Bods: Short for "bodies" and used to refer to personnel.

Body-snatcher: Stretcher bearer, medical orderly.

Boffins: Scientists.

Bog: A latrine.

Bogey: Unidentified aircraft.

Boomerang: Return to base due to technical difficulties before reaching the target.

Boost: The amount of supercharging given to an engine to increase power.

Bounce: A surprise attack, usually from above, and/or out of the sun.

Bowser: Tanker used to refuel aircraft.

Brass: Senior officers.

Brassed off: Extremely annoyed or unhappy.

Brevet: Cloth insignia worn over the left breast pocket of the uniform (battle dress and dress blues) to indicate status as aircrew and trade. Pilot's brevets had two wings. All other aircrew had one wing attached to a circle with a letter designating their trade, e.g. "N" for Navigator, "AG" for Air gunner, "E" for Engineer etc.

Brew up: To prepare a pot of tea.

Browned off: Same as brassed off.

Brown jobs: Army personnel.

Bull: The formalities of the service, e.g. parades, salutes, etc.

Bumpf: Useless paperwork.

Burton: (As in "gone for a Burton") killed in action.

Bus: Aircraft.

Buster: Use maximum boost/speed.

Buy it: Killed in action — past tense is "bought it".

Cart, in the: To be in trouble.

Chain gang: Aircraftmen, general duties.

Chairborne division: RAF personnel working in offices (also wingless wonders and Penguins)

Cheesed off: Fed up, bored, had enough.

Chiefy: Flight Sergeant.

Chop: (As in "get the chop") to be killed in action.

Circuits and bumps: In training, the act of landing and immediately taking off again to practice landings and take-offs.

Civvy street: Civilian life, before and/or after RAF service.

Clapped out: An aircraft or person nearing the end of its useful life.

Clock: Airspeed indicator.

Clot: Idiot

Cloud x/10: Cloud cover described as a percentage of the sky covered, e.g. 10/10 complete cloud cover, 5/10 50% cloud cover etc.

CO: Commanding Officer.

Cockup: A disorganized mess.

Cookie: A 4,000 lb bomb creating a surface blast.

Coned: Multiple searchlights fixing on a single aircraft.

Corker: A woman.

Corkscrew: Evasive maneuver to disrupt the aim of flak, searchlights and night fighters.

Crabbing: Side-slipping usually on landing or approach.

Crate: An aircraft.

Crumpet: A woman.

Curtains: Killed.

Cushy: Something comfortable.

Dalton Computer: Early mechanical handheld computer used in air navigation.

Darky: Call sign of an emergency channel to help aircraft find nearby airfields or get navigational assistance.

Debagging: To forcibly remove someone else's trousers, a rowdy form of entertainment popular in the RAF at this time.

Deck: The ground

DFC: Distinguished Flying Cross for officers only in WWII.

DFM: Distinguished Flying Medal for NCOs and other ranks.

Dicey-do: A particularly dangerous operation, comes from "dicing with death."

Dim view: (As in "take a dim view") to view with skepticism or disapproval.

Dispersal: Area on an airfield to which aircraft are dispersed to protect against enemy attack.

Dispersal hut: A small building close to dispersed aircraft with lockers for clothing, tables, chairs, camp beds, and a phone connection to the control room. In Fighter Command pilots on readiness waited in or around the dispersal hut waiting for a "scramble."

Ditch: To crash-land on a body of water in an emergency.

Dicky or 2nd Dicky: Co-pilot, second pilot. Since the RAF discontinued the practice of assigning two pilots to an aircraft early in the war, pilots only flew "2nd Dicky" for specific reasons. Most common was for a pilot arriving at his first operational squadron to fly 2nd Dicky with an experienced pilot on one operational flight before flying his first operation with his own crew.

Dicky Flight: A training flight for inexperienced pilots.

Dicky seat: The fold-down seat used by the second pilot

Do: An event, action in the air, an operation.

Drink: A body of water

Drome: Aerodrome, airfield

Driver, airframe: Derogative term for the pilot used by other aircrew.

Duff: Bad or not accurate.

Dust up: Heated action, aerial combat.

Elsan: Chemical toilet carried on aircraft

Erk: General term for ground crew from the Cockney pronunciation of "aircraftman."

ETA: Estimated time of arrival

Fishheads: The navy

Fitter: Ground crew responsible for engines — more qualified than a "mechanic"

Flak: German anti-aircraft guns (derived from Flug Abwehr Kanonen).

Flame float: Small incendiary device that could be dropped from the flare chute to measure wind speed and direction.

Flamer: An aircraft shot down in flames.

Flaming: Mild, all-purpose expletive.

Flannel: To bluff, to deceive.

Flap: Unnecessary excitement or panic.

Flare path: A row of lights marking the boundary of the runway for take-off and landing.

Flat out: As fast as possible.

Flat spit: To be bewildered, confused, at a loss.

Flight: Subdivision of a squadron. In Fighter Command, each squadron had two flights of six aircraft designated "A" and "B" and usually commanded by a Flight Lieutenant; in Bomber Command each squadron had two flights of six to eight aircraft, also designated "A" and "B," ususally commanded by a Squadron Leader.

Flying Brevet: See Brevet.

Fruit salad: A large number of ribbons denoting decorations (worn under the flying brevet).

Gee: An early form of radar-based navigational aids.

George: The automatic pilot.

Gen: Information (from intelligence).

Get cracking: Get moving.

Get one's finger out: To hurry up or pay attention.

Get some in: Get some experience.

Get the drift: To understand.

Gone for six: Dead.

Gong: A medal, decoration.

Green: Untried, inexperienced.

Gremlin: A mythical creature that lived on certain aircraft and caused malfunctions at inconvenient times.

Green, in the: All engine control gauges reading normal. (A needle in the "red" indicated a malfunction).

Green, get the: To receive permission. Originated from permission to take off as indicated by a green light flashed from the caravan beside the runway by airfield control officer.

Grief, come to: Get in trouble or crash.

H2S: early airborne navigation system using radio waves to create an image of the landscape below the aircraft. Used in conjunction with charts and maps. Although a navigational aid, H2S sets were located in the wireless operator's station due to space constraints at the navigator's station.

Hack: An aircraft used for general duties.

Half-pint hero: Boaster, braggart.

Hare after: To pursue.

HCU: Heavy Conversion Unit, a training unit dedicated to training aircrew on the heavy (four-engine) bombers.

Hedge-hopping: Flying so low an aircraft looks like it has to hop over hedges.

Hit the silk: To bail out, parachute.

Hold the can: To be responsible.

Hoof it: To walk.

Humid: Without personality.

Hun: A German.

Illuminator: An aircraft tasked with dropping flares to illuminate a target. Load ca. 54 flares.

Jankers: Punishment, extra duty.

Jerry: The Germans.

Jink: To take evasive action.

Kill: A victory, a downed enemy as in "a fighter pilot needed five kills to become an ace"

Kip: Sleep.

Kite: An aircraft.

Laid on: Supplied, as in "extra beer was laid on."

Let down: To descend.

Line abreast: To fly wingtip-to-wingtip, on a broad front.

Line astern: To fly nose-to-tail in single file, one aircraft after another.

Line shoot or shooting a line: Exaggerating, bragging, fabricating.

LMF: Lack of moral fibre.

Look See, A: Reconnaissance.

Lose your wool: Lose composure.

Lowdown: Inside information.

Mae West: Inflatable life vest worn over flying kit.

Maggie: A Miles Magister training and communications aircraft

Meat discs: Metal ID worn by all aircrew, "dog-tags" in USAAF.

Mess: Dining room, bars, and quarters for personnel, separated by rank: officers' mess, sergeants' mess and other ranks mess.

Met: Meteorology Officer.

MIA: Missing in Action.

MO: Medical Officer.

Mob: The Royal Air Force.

MT: Motorized Transport.

MU: Maintenance Unit, where aircraft that could not be repaired at squadron/station level were sent for more extensive maintenance and repairs.

NAAFI: Navy, Army, Air Force Institute, an organization which attempted to bring comforts to crews to raise morale. Mobile canteens provided tea, buns, cigarettes and the like.

Natter: Chatter, talk.

NCO: Non-Commissioned Officer, in the RAF, Sergeant or Flight Sergeant

Odd bod: Any spare personnel, particularly crew member left over after the rest of the crew had been killed or finished their tour.

Old Man: The squadron commander

Op: Operational flight

Ops Room: Place where information was collected, tabulated, and operations planned and controlled.

Orbit: To fly in circles, usually over an airfield or a marker.

OTU: Operational Training Unit, a training unit where aspiring pilots few operational aircraft/service aircraft for the first time, having previously learned to fly on training aircraft.

Pack up: To break down.

Packet, to catch a: To receive something unpleasant such as flak or a reprimand.

Pan out: To happen

Panic: Intense flap.

Panic bowler: Steel helmet worn during air raids.

Pancake: To land.

Pansy: Effeminate.

Party: A sexual experience, or an air battle or any difficult experience.

Pasting: Punishment.

Peel Off: To turn away from a formation.

Penguin: Derogatory term for non-flying personnel.

Perspex: Comparatively shatter-proof, transparent material used for windscreens, cockpit hoods and gun turrets.

Pickled: Drunk.

Piece of cake: Easy.

Piece of nice: Anything very pleasant or attractive.

Pie-eyed: Drunk.

Plaster: To bomb heavily and accurately.

Popsie: A girl, girlfriend.

Prang: An accident.

PSP: Perforated or pierced steel planking, steel mats used for runways, hardstandings and taxiways instead of concrete.

Pull one's finger out: Same as Get one's finger out

Quack: Derogatory term for the Medical Officer.

Racket: Swindle, scam.

Readiness, Squadron or Flight: The status of a squadron, flight or section requiring pilots to remain at the dispersal hut in flying kit ready to take off in a short period of time, usually 10 to 15 minutes.

Recce: Reconnaissance flight.

Rick view: To view with pleasure.

Rigger: Ground crew responsible for airframe.

Ropey: Bad, no good, duff, decrepit, doubtful.

Saturated: Without personality, even worse than wet or humid.

Scram: To leave in a hurry.

Scramble: Get airborne as quickly as possible.

Scrambled eggs: Braid on a senior officer's hat.

Scrap: To fight, aerial combat.

Screw: Propellor.

Scrub: Cancel.

Shakey-do: see "dicey do" — a particularly dangerous operation.

Shot down in flames: (In addition to the literal meaning) to be reprimanded.

Skipper: Pilot/captain of an aircraft and crew leader.

Sky Pilot: A chaplain, priest.

Smashed: Drunk

Smashing: Marvelous, super.

Snappers: Enemy fighters.

Snogging: Kissing.

Soaking glass of wet: A gin.

Soggy: Description of when an aircraft that does not respond properly to the controls.

Sortie: One aircraft doing one trip, e.g. if eight aircraft take-off on an operation, that is eight sorties, if twelve aircraft scramble to intercept a raid that is twelve sorties.

Sozzled: Drunk.

Spill the beans: To disclose information.

Spoof: A diversion.

Spot on: Same as "bang on", precise.

Sprog: Someone fresh from training without experience. Also used in "sprog crew" to mean an inexperienced crew.

Squirt: A quick burst of gunfire.

Stand-by, Squadron or Flight: the status of a squadron or flight requiring pilots to be in their cockpits with engines ticking over ready for immediate take-off.

Strip, to tear off: To be severely reprimanded by a superior. Refers to having one's rank insignia stripped off to denote a demotion.

Stooge: To idle around, an uneventful sortie.

Streamlined piece: A slim, lovely woman.

Take the day off: Never mind, something's not important.

Tallboy: Bombs developed by the British engineer Barnes Wallis, which penetrated below the earth and exploded after a timed delay causing an earthquake effect. The bombs weighed 12,000 tons and were custom made. A Lancaster bomber could carry only one at a time.

Tally ho!: Enemy in sight

Through the gate: Flying at maximum power.

T.I.: Target Indicator, colored flares dropped by the Pathfinders to identify targets, used after April 1944.

Ticket: Pilot's certificate.

Ticking over: An engine running slowly and using little power.

Tick off: To reprimand or criticize.

Tracer: A type of machine gun round that glowed showing the direction ammunition was going and allowing a gunner to adjust his shooting. Usually, every fourth round was tracer.

Twirp: Same as clot and twit, idiot.

Twit: Same as clot and twirp, idiot.

Upstairs: In the air.

U/S: Unserviceable.

UXB: Unexploded bomb.

Vic: Flying formation of three aircraft, with the middle aircraft forward of the flanking aircraft.

Waffle: An aircraft out of control, losing height or not on a steady course, or a person not giving a straight answer to a question.

Washed out: To fail, particularly in training when qualifying for a trade.

Wet: Without personality, boring.

Whack: An attempt

Whiff: To take a breath of oxygen.

Window: Strips of metal dropped from bombers to confuse German radar.

WingCo: Wing Commander.

Wizard: Excellent.

Biography
Helena P. Schrader

Helena P. Schrader is an established aviation author and expert on the Second World War. She earned a PhD in History (cum Laude) from the University of Hamburg with a ground-breaking dissertation on a leading member of the German Resistance to Hitler. Her non-fiction publications include *Sisters in Arms: The Women who Flew in WWII*, *The Blockade Breakers: The Berlin Airlift*, and *Codename Valkyrie: General Friederich Olbricht and the Plot against Hitler*. In addition, Helena has published nineteen historical novels and won numerous literary awards. Her novel on the Battle of Britain, *Where Eagles Never Flew*, won the Hemingway Award for 20th Century Wartime Fiction and a Maincrest Media Award for Historical Fiction. RAF Battle of Britain ace Bob Doe called it the "best book" he had ever seen about the battle.

With the *Grounded Eagles Trilogy*, she explores the fate of two secondary characters from *Where Eagles Never Flew* in greater detail and in the third tale introduces a new character, who will be the central figure in her next book, *Lancaster Skipper*.

Over Aviation Books
by Helena P. Schrader

Where Eagles Never Flew: A Battle of Britain Novel

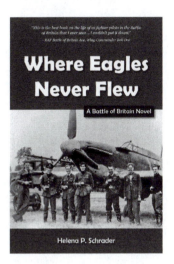

Winner of a the Hemingway Award for Twentieth Century Military Fiction, a Media Crest Award for Military Fiction and Finalist for the Book Excellence Award.

This superb novel about the Battle of Britain, based on actual events and eye-witness accounts, shows this pivotal battle from both sides of the channel through the eyes of pilots, ground crews, staff — and the women they loved.

Summer 1940: The Battle of France is over; the Battle of Britain is about to begin. If the swastika is not to fly over Buckingham Palace, the RAF must prevent the Luftwaffe from gaining air superiority over Great Britain. Standing on the front line is No. 606 (Hurricane) Squadron. As the casualties mount, new pilots find a cold reception from the clique of experienced pilots, who resent them taking the place of their dead friends. Meanwhile, despite credible service in France, former RAF aerobatics pilot Robin Priestman finds himself stuck in Training Command -- and falling for a girl from the Salvation Army. On the other side of the Channel, the Luftwaffe is recruiting women as communications specialists -- and naïve Klaudia is about to grow up.

Grounded Eagles:
Three Tales of the RAF in WWII

Disfiguring injuries, class prejudice and PTSD are the focus of three heart wrenching tales set in WWII by award-winning novelist Helena P. Schrader.

A Stranger in the Mirror: David Goldman is shot down in flames in September 1940. Not only is his face burned beyond recognition, he is told he will never fly again. While the plastic surgeon recreates his face one painful operation at a time, the 22-year-old pilot must discover who he really is.

Lack of Moral Fibre: In late November 1943, Flight Engineer Kit Moran refuses to participate in a raid on Berlin, his 37th 'op.' He is posted off his squadron for "Lacking Moral Fibre" and sent to a mysterious DYDN center. Here, psychiatrist Dr Grace must determine if he needs psychiatric treatment -- or disciplinary action for cowardice.

A Rose in November: Rhys Jenkins, a widower with two teenage children, has finally obtained his dream: "Chiefy" of a Spitfire squadron. But an unexpected attraction for an upperclass woman threatens to upend his life.